Morris Automated Information Network
0 1029 0407923

P9-CFG-759

PARSIPPANY-TROY HILLS
PUBLIC LIBRARY SYSTEM

TWO WOMEN

Recent Titles by Brian Freemantle from Severn House

AT ANY PRICE
BETRAYALS
DIRTY WHITE
GOLD
HELL'S PARADISE
ICE AGE
THE IRON CAGE
THE KREMLIN CONSPIRACY
THE MARY CELESTE
O'FARRELL'S LAW
TARGET

Charlie Muffin

DEAD MEN LIVING
KINGS OF MANY CASTLES

TWO WOMEN

Brian Freemantle

This first world edition published in Great Britain 2003 by
SEVERN HOUSE PUBLISHERS LTD of
9–15 High Street, Sutton, Surrey SM1 1DF.
This first world edition published in the USA 2003 by
SEVERN HOUSE PUBLISHERS INC of
595 Madison Avenue, New York, N.Y. 10022.

British Library Cataloguing in Publication Data

Freemantle, Brian, 1936-
Two women
1. Mafia - Fiction
2. Money laundering investigation - Fiction
3. Suspense fiction
I. Title
823.9'14 [F]

ISBN 0-7278-5973-0

Typeset by Palimpsest Book Production Ltd.,
Polmont, Stirlingshire, Scotland.
Printed and bound in Great Britain by
MPG Books Ltd., Bodmin, Cornwall.

To Charlotte, who said it was her turn.
With love.

We will use the full weight of the law to expose and root out corruption . . . When abuses like this begin to surface in the corporate world, it is time to reaffirm the basic values that make capitalism work. There can be no capitalism without conscience, no wealth without character.

US President George W. Bush, demanding 'new ethics of personal responsibility' from American business leaders after a series of Wall Street scandals. 10 July, 2002

One

Alice said: 'It's all right.'

'It's not. I love you.'

'We don't have to *make* love every time to prove we're *in* love. That just makes it screwing. Ugly.'

John Carver turned away, his back to her.

She said: 'It's not just this, is it?'

'This didn't help.'

'Do you want to talk about it?'

'It's business. Boring.'

'Business's never boring.' Alice Belling had graduated from Harvard Business School with a letter of introduction to a Boston stockbroking firm and the overly confident and quirky idea of turning her degree thesis on corporate avarice eroding American entrepreneurialism into an Op-Ed commentary for the *Wall Street Journal*. Unable to decide which to try first she wrote off to both at the same time. The Op-Ed piece, which prompted two more articles and two days of top-of-the-page correspondence, was published three days before Alice got an invitation to join the stockbrokers. Her choice was a freelance media career, specializing in analyses and commentary on global finance and corporate stock market movements and trends. In the past year she'd exposed insider dealing and profit inflation in two multinationals just prior to new bond issues.

'Business and family,' further qualified Carver.

'Involving Jane?'

'It's complicated.'

'Turn around and talk to me properly,' insisted Alice. 'And hold me. I like it when you hold me.'

He turned back, reaching out for her, and she came easily, comfortably, into his arms. She said: 'You're wonderful.'

'So are you.'

'You know what I'd like?'

'What?'

'To go up to the cabin again soon.'

'I've got the annual conference.'

'I didn't mean *now*. Just soon. It's been more than two months.' They'd taken a long time finding the perfect wood-built cabin in the Bearfort Mountains, alongside a small river feeding into one of the West Milford lakes. On the bedroom bureau Alice had a time-release photograph of herself and Carver there – she with her hand in front of her face because she hadn't been ready when the shutter clicked – and another in the living room. Carver was by himself in that shot, wearing a lumberjack shirt and hiking boots and proudly displaying the fish he'd caught, his first ever, on their initial visit.

'Let's get the conference out of the way. One or two other things. We'll make a long weekend out of it. And you can take the toy.' One of the rituals involved in the visits to the Catskills was their going in Alice's carefully preserved Volkswagen, her proudest souvenir of her college days.

'Thank you. And you can fish again.'

'I'm sorry that today . . .'

'Stop it!'

'You know what I wish?'

'I don't want to go that route, either,' refused Alice. 'You can't, we both know it and I accept it. I'm happy the way things are with us. It's enough.' She clamped his leg between both of hers, bringing them tightly together, she slightly on top of him. 'How was George's birthday this weekend?'

George W. Northcote was Carver's father-in-law and founder of the Wall Street accountancy firm that bore his name and represented a forty-year symbol of propriety and rectitude. Carver said: 'He came over for dinner. Jane gave him some golf clubs which he looked at as if they'd come out of an Egyptian tomb.'

'How is he?' The affair between Carver and Alice had developed from their meeting when she had come to Wall Street to interview Northcote for a profile for *Forbes* magazine. Northcote had a copy framed.

'Not so good. He even sometimes forgets the end of his sentences and gets mad when anyone tries to help.'

'He told me he was frightened of retiring. Of atrophying with nothing to do,' Alice remembered, from their interview.

'The problem is his still trying to do too much: he's refusing to let go of a few clients to give himself the reason to come into the city at least two days a week.'

'His firm, his name?' she anticipated.

'No one can ever be as good as he is, in George W. Northcote's opinion,' Carver agreed. Holding her like he was, naked, was enough for him today, too.

'What are the other partners saying?'

'So far there haven't been any major mistakes for them to discover but I am going to have to keep a check on what he does to make sure it stays that way: he hasn't yet realized I'm doing it but I feel like a goddamned spy going behind his back, conspiring against him.'

'You're talking the firm: *his* firm, with his name on it.'

'That's exactly what I'm talking about,' agreed Carver again. 'A firm he might be endangering!'

'You're just putting off confronting him: postponing it.' They never discussed it, secure as they were with each other, but Alice knew that despite self-confidence verging on arrogance Carver would always be intimidated by the overwhelming personality of George Northcote – the sheer physical presence, even, of someone 6′5″ tall and weighing almost 200lbs.

'You imagine I haven't worked that out!'

They'd never before seriously argued – fallen out – and Alice, who had never felt intimidated by anyone, was unsettled by the unexpected vehemence in his voice. 'So when's it going to happen?'

'Maybe even today. He's in town. And there are things he needs to explain.'

'Then demand an explanation.'

'I will.'

'You talked to Jane about it?'

'Not like this.'

Alice felt a brief warmth of intimacy. 'Shouldn't you? She's his daughter.'

'She's been proposed for the charity secretaryship at the country club. He's agreed to help her with the accounts. That's what the golf clubs were for, to try to get him to spend more time at the club.'

'It'll get in the way of his other hobby.' One of the accompanying photographs in Alice's *Forbes* profile had portrayed Northcote in bib-and-brace overalls astride a tractor mower on which he frequently relaxed, supervising the gardeners at his weekend estate in upstate New York. The caption had given his Wall Street nickname of 'Farmer George.'

'Jane's not happy at his doing that any more, either. Thinks it's dangerous at his age.'

'You don't think golf's going to be the alternative?'

'He hasn't played regularly for years.' He hesitated. 'Charity secretary will mean Jane staying up in the country more.'

Alice didn't say anything.

'I could stay over sometimes.'

'I'd like that.'

'Would you?'

'You know I would. When will she know?'

'Soon. Certainly by the fifteenth.'

'Let's hope she gets it.'

'It's pretty guaranteed.'

'Can you make Friday?'

He shook his head. 'All the overseas executives are starting to arrive from Wednesday onwards for the conference.'

'I've got another *Forbes* commission I can work on.'

'You're soon going to need your own accountant!'

'I thought I had one.'

'You have.'

'Call me. Let me know what we can fix.'

'Of course. And it's a promise about the cabin.'

She shifted slightly, looking beyond him to the bedside table. 'It's gone three already.'

'These business lunches get longer and longer.'

'You should be going. And I should be working.'

'I'm sorry . . . I . . .'

'Stop it!'

'I've got a feeling that there's a serious problem,' he suddenly blurted.

Alice pulled away from him. 'What?'

'I want to be sure first.'

'You're not making sense.'

'That's the problem: it doesn't make sense.'

She separated from him entirely, going up on one elbow. The sheet fell away from her but she didn't try to cover herself. 'Has George made a bad mistake?' She'd eulogized him in the profile, put her own judgement on the line.

'He could have done.'

'Then you've *got* to talk to him today.'

'I know.'

He had chosen to talk it through with her, decided Alice, feeling a warm intimacy again. 'Can you put it right?'

'I don't know, not yet.'

'It might help if you told me about it and we tried to think of a way together.'

'I can't involve you.'

'Darling! What *is* it?'

He shook his head, not speaking.

'So it's bad?'

'It could be.'

'Could you be in serious trouble?'

'It depends what I do.'

'You know the answer to that – you've got to do the right thing. That's all you can do.'

'It might not be that simple.'

'Please let me help!'

'I won't involve you any more than I already have,' he refused again. He twisted abruptly out of the bed but stayed sitting on its edge, his back towards her again. 'I shouldn't have said anything.'

'But you did. Now it's stupid to stop.'

'I've got to speak to George.'

'Then will you speak to me?'

'I don't know. It depends.'

'On what?'

'Too many things that even I don't know about, not yet.'

'You've frightened me.' That wasn't true. She was irritated at his refusal.

'I'm sorry. I didn't mean . . . oh shit!'

'We are going to talk about it,' Alice insisted. 'If not now then soon. Talk about it and fix it.'

'I'd like to think we could: that I could.'

'We can.'

'I have to go.'

'Talk to him this afternoon.'

'Yes.'

'Call me later, if you can?'

'If I can.'

Alice remained in bed, watching him dress, loving him. As he moved to leave she said: 'Whatever it is, it can't be the end of the world.'

Carver kissed her, holding her tightly against him for several moments, but left without replying.

With the concentration upon the annual conference it was easier than usual for Carver to plan his days to include Alice, leaving himself with only two, easily satisfied clients and the morning's dictated letters to sign.

When he called his father-in-law, George Northcote said: 'You just caught me. Got a meeting here in town tonight: staying over.'

'We need to talk, George.'

'Tomorrow. My meeting's at six, so we'll talk tomorrow. Lunch maybe?'

'Now, George!' insisted Carver. 'It's important.'

'What the hell are you talking about?'

'You. Me. The firm. Everything. That's what I think I'm talking about. Everything.'

Two

'There'd better be a hell of a good reason for this!' greeted Northcote. The voice was big, like everything about the man. He remained seated at the antique desk, hunched over it, bull-shouldered beneath a mane of white hair. It was a familiar, confrontational pose Carver had seen the other man adopt dozens of times with IRS inspectors and company tax lawyers and opposition, challenging accountants.

'I think there is,' said Carver. Or was he over-interpreting, imagining an aggressive defensiveness about the older man? Maybe. Or maybe not. There was enough for him to question this man who had always been unquestionable. Again the qualification came. The problem was that there wasn't enough. There was a huge, gaping black hole that had to be filled with something he could understand.

'What?'

Carver lowered himself into a facing, button-backed chair. 'I happened upon some current working figures for three of our oldest clients . . . your oldest clients . . . Companies that for years have made up the bedrock of our business . . .' He hesitated at the moment of commitment. 'Mulder Incorporated . . . Encomp . . . Innsflow International . . .'

A flush began to suffuse Northcote's face, accentuated by the pure whiteness of his hair, but when he spoke the loudness had gone from his voice. 'None of your business . . . How . . . ?'

'In the vaults. Your safe was open. And it is my business,

because I'm taking *over* this business, which I intend to do as a memorial to you.'

'Spy!' accused the other man.

'I went to close it properly. Which you hadn't done.'

'My personal clients . . .' The unaccustomedly subdued voice trailed away.

'Yes, George,' picked up Carver. 'Always your personal clients. And still your personal clients, whom no one else had anything to do with.'

'Retained with the full agreement of the partners. Yourself, my successor as senior partner, included. In signed minutes.'

Why, wondered Carver, had Northcote felt it necessary to remind him of his succession to the chairmanship upon his father-in-law's semi-retirement? Or of the minutes acknowledging Northcote's continued handling of the three accounts being officially signed and recorded? 'They never went through general audit: haven't done for years. Always your personal audit and you always personally signed them off.'

'There is no regulation – Security Exchange Commission or otherwise – requiring that they should go through general audit. Everything was perfectly legal.'

Carver decided that Northcote wasn't sufficiently outraged – offended – at his having gone into a safe to which he officially had no right: wasn't even asking the proper questions. 'All three are offshore.'

'Which is declared. There is no contravention of any regulation.'

'They've all grown, since their formation all those years ago.'

'Well-run – well-audited and well-accounted companies – all grow and return profits.'

'Mulder Inc. has a seven hundred and fifty million dollar entertainment investment, worldwide. Encomp has five hundred and fifty million dollars of utilities supply portfolios, again worldwide. Innsflow International is diversified into publishing, hotels and entertainment in Europe, the Far East and even Russia.'

'You've spent a lot of time checking on me.' There was still no outrage.

'I did check, George. In-house. Called them up, on the computer. They're on the client list. But that's all, just listed as names and holdings. There aren't any details, apart from that.'

'They're offshore. There don't need to be computer records – any records – on file for offshore countries.'

Carver sighed heavily, feeling like an irritating fly bouncing from impenetrable window to impenetrable window. 'You're a legend on Wall Street, George. I want it to stay that way. You *deserve* for it to stay that way.'

'I'm still waiting for you to make your point.'

'The figures don't add up, not the ones you left in your open safe. They *do*, on what's been submitted by their accountants for independent audit by you. And which you've signed off. But they don't if they're audited properly. You've legally attested their accuracy. And by doing so exposed this firm, *your* firm, to criminal investigation! You've sanctioned a massive profit-inflating operation. On a scale that I haven't been able yet to calculate: am frightened to calculate. They're being floated, right? Blown up to suck in the punters: open at ten, finish the week at two hundred, insider traders getting out with enough to buy the villa in the Caribbean or South of France before the bubble pops.'

Northcote snorted a laugh. 'You want my advice, on that assessment don't try to calculate anything.'

'It's not advice I want. It's explanation. I told you we were talking about you, me and the firm. About everything. And that's precisely it. If this ever became public: if . . .' Carver actually just stopped himself from saying that if it ever became an innuendo in the sort of financial commentary Alice Belling was so adept at compiling. 'The house – this house, all our houses – would come tumbling down.'

'You think . . .' started Northcote, lost his way and then managed: '. . . believe I haven't worked all that out!'

'I'd like to know exactly – very exactly – what you have worked out. And where you – where we all – are going from here?'

'Nowhere,' declared Northcote. 'That's precisely and exactly where we're going. Nowhere. At the annual meeting I am going to announce the reluctant severing with this firm of Mulder Incorporated, Encomp and Innsflow International. Their choosing alternative, independent auditing accountants will be based upon their long-standing personal relationship with me, which the partners already know about and recognize. And which is being brought to an end by my finally – and fully – retiring . . .' Northcote smiled at last. 'Which is what I am going to do. Live in the country, cut my grass, help Jane with her charity fundraising and start playing with my new golf clubs.'

'Just like that!' said Carver, snapping his fingers.

'Just like that,' echoed Northcote, mocking the finger snap with one of his own.

'What's it all about, George?'

'You don't need to know that.'

'I do, if I am going to protect this firm: keep it safe.'

'I'm protecting the firm.'

'Who are they?'

'You don't need to know that, either.'

'They know what you're going to do?'

'That's why I stayed on, for the extra year. To tidy things up and to bring it all to an end. You think I . . .' There was another familiar hesitation. 'It's all going to be resolved.'

'*Going* to be,' seized Carver, at once. 'Hasn't it been, yet?'

'It's my problem. I'm sorting it out.'

Carver gazed around Northcote's mahogany-panelled,

leather-Chesterfielded office with its corner-window glimpse of Battery Park City and the intervening pillared monuments to wealth and power and corporate cunning, for once – for the first time – not feeling the comfort, and the pride, of being part of it. He said: 'I'm aware of a possible criminal activity. There are regulations governing that. Quite a lot, in fact.'

Northcote looked blankly at him. Then indignantly – close to being big-voiced again – he said: 'Don't be *ridiculous*!'

'I'm being professional. In everything you've said – every inference you've made – you've assumed I'll go along with what you've got in mind: everything you've got in mind but won't tell me.'

Northcote held up a hand. 'A long time ago, when I was first starting out and needed every break I could get . . .' The block came but he made jerky gestures with the still raised hand against Carver intruding. 'I got caught up in a situation which developed as it did . . . innocently caught up, with no idea what was happening until I *was* involved. Couldn't get out. I've lived with it, all these years. Now it's over: I'm promising you that it's over. I'm leaving you with one of the foremost accountancy firms in the financial world. You're already a rich man and you're going to become richer. You've got it all and not just because I'm handing it over to you: because you're *good* – the successor I hoped you would be – and because you deserve it . . . I . . . you . . .' he stumbled once more to a halt. 'You earned it. You trying to tell me you're now going to tear it all down – pull all the houses down, to use your words – by going to the SEC or whoever to put the gun into your own mouth and pull the trigger?'

At that moment Carver wasn't sure what he was telling anyone and certainly not what he was being told. 'We're involved with organized crime! The Mafia!'

Northcote took a long time to reply. Finally he said: 'I'm handling it.'

'You going to be able to give me an unbreakable assurance

that by Friday it'll all be over?' What was he saying? Why was he accepting it?

'Dead and buried,' insisted Northcote, at once. 'Who I'm seeing tonight is their representative . . .' He looked at his watch. 'And I'm already late.' There was another brief smile. 'I telephoned, to warn him. He'll be waiting.'

'I want to come with you,' announced Carver.

Northcote snorted yet another dismissive laugh. 'It began and it ends with me. Only me. The protection for this firm – and for you – is your knowing nothing, your meeting no one.'

'I do know!'

'You're staying away. Out of it.'

'You said you were staying over tonight?'

'Yes?'

'We have to talk tomorrow. I need a lot more guarantees.'

'You've got them.'

'Tomorrow,' insisted Carver. 'Tomorrow we talk specifics.'

'Lunch,' agreed Northcote. 'It'll be our own farewell celebration.'

Nothing had emerged the way it should have done. The way he'd wanted. What he'd wanted – fervently hoped for – was booming-voiced offence and a provable, point-by-point, figure-by-figure denunciation of his every suspicion. What he'd got instead amounted to a confirmation – a near-immediate admission – of fraud and false accounting and involvement in organized crime – which meant Mafia – and criminal conspiracy and criminal complicity and probably a lot more indictments he couldn't, and most certainly didn't want, to think of. It was all too much, too overwhelming, to contemplate. What did he want to think of? The best answer. Or was it the right answer? And was the best and right answer the easiest way out? Or the most difficult? He'd examined George Northcote's argument from every which way and from every which way what the older man had said about bringing the house down around him – throwing his own words back at him – made the only logical sense. Of course he would prove his professional integrity and rectitude by disclosing the indications of crime to the SEC – to every governing authority – but in so doing he'd bring about the collapse of one of Wall Street's most prestigious and internationally trusted financial names. Every sort of criminal and governing-body investigation would take months, during which they would most likely be suspended and during which any proper work would in any case be impossible. And there would also be the personal fallout. No matter how right and correct his actions, he would publicly be seen – and despised – as a man totally destroying his own father-in-law by exposing the man at the age of sixty-seven to inevitable imprisonment and an inevitable multi-million-dollar fine. And even if George Northcote accepted every responsibility, in Wall Street – in the global financial village – the mud would stick and those clients who didn't despise him personally would rush to wash their hands of all and every association. George W. Northcote International would be relegated as another greed-driven, illegally operating financial pariah.

'Hello. My name's Jane and I'm your wife.'

So engrossed was he that Carver physically started at his wife's voice, smiling apologetically across the dinner table. 'Sorry. I was thinking.'

'Darling, you were so deep in thought you were out of sight! You haven't said a word for at least the last thirty minutes. Or eaten a thing!'

Carver sipped his wine, setting his knife and fork aside. 'I ate a big lunch,' he lied. How would their marriage withstand his blowing the whistle on her father? Her mother had died when Jane was fourteen and practically from the time she was sixteen until their marriage – and even after – Jane had been at her father's side at all the charity events he'd sponsored and hosted, which were literally beyond count. The feeling – the bond – between father and daughter was umbilical. Jane, whom Carver sometimes thought to be even stronger than her father, would be the person to despise him the most.

'I don't ever remember you like this!'

'Trying to sort out one or two things in my mind. Making choices.'

'Involving me?' she asked, with coquettish confidence.

'You know the answer to that.' He smiled back, trying to match her lightness. There was no feeling of hypocrisy or guilt, both of which he'd long ago rationalized, as he had all the uncertainties about morality.

John Carver was not a promiscuous man: indeed, he'd sometimes considered himself undersexed. His affair with Alice was his first and he was sure it would be his last. And hopefully lasting. He'd never consciously set out to seduce Alice Belling, nor she him. George Northcote had introduced them when Alice had come for the first interview session and he'd asked Carver to handle any subsequent questions, which he did on three occasions, twice over lunch. The fourth occasion, at her apartment on the West Side, had been to read the finished article, which was immaculately factual and in his opinion brilliantly written, which he told her, and her intended joking kiss of gratitude had become something more when he'd inadvertently turned towards her. She'd said, 'Why did you do that?' and he'd said, 'Why did you do that?' and they'd kissed again, intentionally this time, and after they'd made love they'd solemnly agreed it was one of those unexpected, accidental things that had been wonderful and should be immediately forgotten. He'd telephoned the following day and they'd lunched together and gone to bed together and the excitement – the flattery – of his first sexual dalliance had become a deeply loving affair.

Which was what it was. Quite simply he loved two women, neither of whom were endangered by the other. Carver would never leave Jane. Nor did he want – nor intend – ever to leave

Alice. If their relationship ended it would be Alice's decision – which she insisted she'd never make – and if she did he knew he would consider it an unsought and very much unwanted divorce. The word – divorce – lodged in his mind, refocusing it. Carver was sure Jane loved him as much as she was able: as she ever would. Maybe, even, that there would be love – bruised, wounded, but still some love – if Jane ever learned about him and Alice. But he was equally sure – surer even – she wouldn't be able to love him, stay married to him, if he were responsible for publicly ruining and humiliating a father she adored. At once the conviction that Jane would reject him overwhelmed his fear of what effect any disclosure would have upon the firm and even more upon him, personally.

'It must be important, for you to be like this?'

'I'm sorry,' he repeated, not knowing what else to say.

'You want to tell me about it?'

'I've gotten things out of proportion,' he said, shaking his head. 'That's what I meant about making choices, which wasn't it at all. I'm trying to balance things.' He never compared Jane with Alice or Alice with Jane, because they were incomparable, but physically they were remarkably similar, except for the most obvious difference of Jane being naturally deep brunette against Alice's blondness, again natural. There was nothing to choose – a wrong word because he would never choose – between them in height nor in their small-busted slimness.

The difference was in their personalities: their imbued motivations. Jane had always been cared for: cosseted, accustomed from childhood to the best, although she had by no judgement or criticism – certainly not by him – grown from a spoiled child into a spoiled woman. Jane was someone grateful of her privileged upbringing, recognizing her advantages and working always to give back. Which she did sometimes with an almost relentless determination better fitted to a business environment than a charity organizer: indeed, Carver had occasionally wondered why Northcote had not groomed Jane to take over the firm upon his retirement. Carver's reflection stopped at the thought. Knowing what little he did now about George Northcote's criminal involvement was the most likely answer to that uncertainty.

Alice's character had come from a similar but cracked mould. As far as Carver understood, although it was not a biography he'd deeply explored, her parents had at one time – briefly – been even richer and she more indulgently cared for than Jane. But her father had been a bull-and-bear-market gambler whose fortunes appropriately rose and fell upon his prediction of which way the market would go. His disastrously misplaced switch, between bull and bear when the markets were going in the opposite direction – and not reversing, when he'd further invested in the expectation that they would – financially ruined Alice's family. Alice was left with a suicide note of apology, a final year at Harvard Business School, a roller coaster personal awareness that money was a buy-or-sell marketable commodity, not the green stuff in her purse, and a street savvy to invest her way extremely comfortably to her graduation ceremony. Unrecorded upon that graduation certificate – although an indication, perhaps, of how successfully she would later pursue her chosen heads-or-tails career – was that Alice Belling was not just a woman totally emancipated in mind, body and attitude but more inherently streetwise than her finally unable-to-cope father.

'Hello, again!'

Shit, thought Carver. 'It's not my best night, is it?'

'Is it a big problem, whatever it is?'

'I don't bring work home, remember?' That wasn't even true.

'You just did.'

'Let's forget it, Jane.'

She looked surprised at the tone in his voice. 'It's nothing to do with us, is it?'

'Absolutely not.'

'Promise?'

'I promise.' He should have handled everything better than this!

'Did you see Dad today?'

'Briefly.'

'He's going back up to Litchfield tomorrow.'

'I know.' It had been Jane's urging that they buy a weekend house less than five miles from her father in Litchfield County, both close to Woodridge Lake.

'I thought I might drive up with him, for company.'

'Why don't you do that?'

Manuel came enquiringly into the dining room and Jane said to Carver: 'Do you want anything else? Dessert?'

He shook his head. 'I'm full.'

'That's a lie, but OK.' To the butler she said: 'After you've cleared away we shan't need you any more tonight. Thank you. Tell Luisa it was a wonderful meal, as usual. But we weren't hungry.' Neither Manuel nor his wife, who cooked, lived in.

'Den or where?' she asked Carver.

'Den,' he decided, following her along the linking corridor. The eight-room duplex on East 62nd Street had been her father's wedding present.

'You want a brandy?'

'No thanks.'

'I'm worried about Dad,' she announced.

'Worried how?'

'So often losing the thread of what he's saying. That's why I want to go up with him tomorrow: persuade him to see Dr Jamieson.'

'It'll take some persuading.'

'I want you to help me.'

'How?'

'I want him to stop work. Completely. That'll be twice as

difficult as getting him to see a doctor. But I'm asking you to try.'

'I'll do my best,' said Carver. 'I really will.'

Stanley Burcher was unique and knew it and was not concerned that no one else ever would, because fame – or rather notoriety – held no interest for him. The total opposite, in fact. Stanley Burcher prided himself upon being the person no one ever saw or noticed. He was a totally asexual bachelor whose only sensuality came from his association with the people for whom he practised and the knowledge of their criminality. Total evilness – and the people he acted for in such an unusual way were totally evil – fascinated him, as anthropologists are fascinated by unknown species. Which Burcher recognized himself to be too, because he was not revulsed by anything they did. Burcher maintained a small house on the unfashionable north side of Grand Cayman, in the Caribbean, and a box-numbered office in the capital, Georgetown, because Grand Cayman was the tax-avoidance haven in which the people he represented hid their vast fortunes. However, he lived for the majority of the time in distinguished but discreet hotels throughout the world, ensuring that the affairs of his exclusive clients never attracted public attention, most particularly from any law-enforcement authority.

The Harvard Club, in which he waited that night, just off New York's Fifth Avenue, represented an unaccustomed luxury, as did most of his regular meeting places with George Northcote. Burcher liked the meetings and he liked Northcote. Northcote was a man who, like himself, had been presented long ago with an opportunity, taken it and prospered. He was surprised at Northcote's lateness: Northcote had never before delayed an appointment and was now running later than the rescheduled time. But at that moment he appeared at the maître d's station.

'Sorry I'm so damned late,' apologized Northcote, approaching with his hand outstretched in greeting.

'Not a problem,' insisted the quietly spoken Burcher, who represented – through their combined *consigliori* – the five Mafia Families of New York.

Three

George Northcote was a meticulous dawn starter ('I originated the early-worm philosophy') but when Carver made his first attempt at nine thirty he was told Northcote hadn't arrived: there'd been no warning of a delay, either. Carver was told the same when he called fifteen minutes later and again at ten. Carver telephoned Northcote's apartment on West 66th Street to be told by Jack Jennings, the butler, that he'd missed Northcote by minutes but that he was on his way.

Northcote came on to Carver's inter-office phone at ten thirty. 'Sorry I'm late.'

'What's the problem?'

'There isn't one.'

'George! You know damned well there is a problem, a big one! Why are you signing off double-accounted figures if the companies aren't going public?'

'It's totally the opposite to what you think: what you imagine you've worked out. Which isn't important. I've said I'm resolving it.'

'I'm looking forward to hearing how it went.'

There was a pause in the still subdued, no-longer hectoring voice. 'I think it would be a good idea to postpone lunch.'

'I don't. Nothing's being postponed, George. I've made the reservation and we're going to keep it. And you're going to tell me what the hell's going on.'

'You think *you* can talk to *me* like this!'

'In these circumstances, yes.'

'You feel good?'

The rumble-voiced belligerence, too long in coming, momentarily silenced Carver before giving him his platform. 'No, George. I don't feel good about any of this. You know how I feel? I feel so sick so deep in my stomach that any moment I might physically throw up.'

'You watch – and listen – to too much television.'

'Stop it, George! We're not talking television. We're talking one great heap of shit you've gotten this firm, yourself – us all – into . . .' Carver stopped as the thought came to him. 'And gotten Jane into, as well. The booking's for one o'clock, at the club.'

'I've things to do. I'll see you there.'

Carver gave way to his anger. 'Don't be late, George. I don't want anything to be too late.'

Northcote wasn't late. The meticulous timekeeper was actually early but Carver was intentionally ahead of him by more than thirty minutes, ensuring their table was beyond overhearing, nursing his mineral water until his father-in-law arrived, trying to rehearse himself for a scene for which there was no script. Too late acknowledging the emptiness of the gesture to be just that, empty, he matched Northcote's previous day's refusal to stand. Northcote compounded Carver's belated embarrassment by pointedly standing beside their table, refusing the chair withheld as an invitation to sit from the frowning maître d'.

As he finally sat Northcote said to the man: 'I'll have Macallan. Large. With a water back.'

Carver said: 'Gin Martini. Large. Straight up with a twist.'

Father-in-law and son-in-law remained looking at each other, unspeaking, for several minutes before Carver said: 'So tell me.'

'There's a few things that still need sorting out. Not a problem.'

'I'm getting a little tired of being told there isn't a problem.'

'And I'm getting tired of telling you there isn't one.'

'What are the few things still needing to be sorted out?'

'Understandings.'

They pulled back for their drinks to be served.

Carver said: 'What's understandings mean?'

'Agreements.'

'With whom? About what?'

'The dissolution.'

'For fuck's sake, George: talk in words that make sense! Are you – the firm – out?'

'There are still some things that need to be agreed.'

There was another long silence.

Carver said: 'They don't let you go, these people, do they?'

'They're going to.'

'I don't believe you. You don't believe yourself!'

Without knowing what it was, they both disinterestedly ordered that day's special when the head waiter returned and at the same time nodded to the house claret.

'They don't have a choice.'

'George! I've got to know!'

Northcote shook his head, gesturing for another whisky. There was a tremble in his hand of which Carver hadn't been aware before. Don't over-interpret, Carver told himself. 'George?'

'They know it's all over,' insisted Northcote. 'They want all the files and records . . .' The block came. 'The . . . the . . .'

'Evidence,' finished Carver. He nodded again in acceptance of the wine, without tasting it.

'It solves the problem. That's how it was always going to be. Separating the firm. No evidence, either way.'

For a moment Carver could not respond, silenced by the other man's seemingly easy acceptance of what he considered a disaster threatening – even impending.

'So you give them all our records dating back . . .' Carver

paused, stopped by an abrupt question. 'Dating back how long, George? When did it all start . . . ?'

'A long time ago,' said Northcote. 'And it took a lot more years to build up to what it became. There aren't many records with us any longer. But enough.'

'Where?' demanded Carver, remembering his fruitless computer search.

'Safe.'

What was missing from the older man's voice, Carver asked himself. Guilt? Remorse? Embarrassment? Acknowledgement of wrongdoing? All of them, Carver decided. If there was an intonation, it was of pride, in whatever it was he had created. He'd always accepted that his father-in-law was self-confident to the point of overwhelming arrogance, which Alice had more than once accused him of being as well, but this went beyond that. But then, Carver further asked himself, how could Northcote be otherwise, after the unstoppable international success he'd achieved, now with offices in every one of the world's financial capitals? But this . . . Carver was stopped again by another numbing, unthinkable uncertainty. 'You told me you were trapped into it . . . that you didn't realize it was criminal?'

'That's what it was . . . how it happened.'

'When – remember we're talking precisely, exactly – did you realize what you were into?'

'It wasn't like that.'

'George! For fuck's . . .' Carver abruptly stopped with the arrival of their food, which they discovered to be rack of lamb. As soon as the waiter was out of earshot Carver said: 'George. Tell me true. Don't tell me things weren't like I imagine them to be or that I'm misunderstanding or that I shouldn't be as pig-sick worried as I'm worried at this moment. How long ago?'

'Maybe twenty years.'

'How long ago?' persisted Carver. 'Precisely. Exactly.'

'Twenty-two. But it was a longer evolving process, to get everything set up.' The attitude reflected in the voice now was truculence.

Carver recognized it was a different story from that Northcote had first offered, of a struggling accountant, just starting out. 'How'd they keep you in line? They blackmail you: tell you how you'd be debarred if you didn't go along with everything?'

Northcote moved his meat around his plate, eating none of it. Saying nothing.

Carver completed his own non-eating carousel, despising himself for matching the earlier verbal mockery. Then he said: 'They've had you, George, haven't they? For most of your career they've had you, just like this . . . ?' Carver closed his hand, as if crushing something.

'I could handle it then: can still handle it now,' insisted the other man, pushing his plate aside.

Carver said: 'How's about this? How's about a stomach-against-his-spine hungry guy who got initially caught, but who then went with the flow? Paddled the boat, even? You had the choice, all those years ago, of blowing the whistle. But you stayed with the system: their system, your system. Same system. Everyone gets rich. And you, additionally, got protected. Wasn't that how it ran, George: you their willing guy, all the way along the line?'

Northcote's face flushed redder than the previous night. 'I didn't have a choice!' The voice – the anger – was cracked.

Carver waved for their untouched meal to be taken away, waiting until it was. 'You did a Faust on everyone, George. You sold out to the Devil . . .' He sniggered a laugh. 'How about that! You sold out to the underworld! Isn't that how it was . . . how it is . . . you got the joys of this life, leaving those who inherit to pay your dues . . . ?'

Northcote shook his head against the new approach from the waiter. To Carver he said: 'What the fuck would you have done, dirt poor, knowing you could climb the mountain, but not knowing *how*: which way to go? Not knowing, then, even which way you were going? You want to tell me that?'

'No, I can't tell you that,' admitted Carver, totally honest. 'I'd have certainly been frightened. Tempted, too . . . maybe even have been eager. But mostly tempted, I guess. I don't know.'

'So that's how it is,' said Northcote.

'No,' refused Carver. 'That's how it *was*. Now is how it *is*. Tell me about last night.'

'I told you about last night.'

'George!'

'I won't let them win . . . beat me . . .'

They'd won. Made this man their own mob-backed Wall Street colossus, Carver accepted, his numbness growing into a tingling feeling of total unreality. 'They've owned you, George. Owned the firm – owned all of us – from the word go!' How could he be talking like this, in an ordinary manner – conversationally – like everyone else around him in this safe, protected, uninvadible bastion of total, privileged security!

'There's a way,' declared Northcote.

'What way? Which way?'

'I kept some records . . . the records you – no one – was ever supposed to find . . . I . . . they . . .'

Carver seized the stumble. 'Janice! What does Janice know?' Janice Snow was Northcote's black, permanently weight-watching but constantly failing personal assistant who averaged 190lbs when she followed the regime and ballooned way above when she didn't, which was most of the time. She'd been with Northcote before Carver had entered the firm. It had been Janice who'd earlier insisted Northcote hadn't arrived in the office, when he clearly had.

'Absolutely nothing: only that they're my personal accounts.'

'How many are "they"?' demanded Carver, determined to

discover as much as he could from a man who was clearly as determined not to volunteer anything. 'How many more companies are there than Mulder, Encomp and Innsflow?'

'None.'

'I have your word on that?' What the fuck use was the word of a man who'd been a Mafia puppet . . . Yet again, Carver's mind stopped at a conclusion he didn't want to reach but had to, because it was the only one possible. They *were* talking – conversationally, quiet-voiced, how-was-the-weekend? where's-this-year's-vacation? – about the *Mafia*!

'You have my word,' recited Northcote, in immediate reply.

He despised this man, Carver abruptly decided. It was as much a shock as all the other revelations of the last thirty-six hours. Maybe even greater. Until now he had been in awe – in trepidation – of this lion of a man with a lion's mane (but a bull's shoulders) who had dominated his life and Jane's life and so many other lives but whom he was now coming to regard as nothing more than a clay effigy – a hollow clay effigy at that – of the supposed Colossus who could not have stood guard, legs astride, over any empire. Most certainly – and provably – not over his own, which wasn't his at all but which had been allowed and granted him, in return for his usefulness.

'You're going to give them all the records?' Itself a criminal – certainly a professional – offence but that no longer seemed a consideration.

'Yes.'

'But you're making copies?'

'Yes.'

'Over so long you're talking in tons!'

'Things went back, after the statutory limitation. It's just what's in my personal section of the vault.'

'Where are the copies?' Carver repeated.

'Safe,' insisted Northcote.

'Where are the copies?' persisted Carver.

'Not all together yet. You'll know, when they are. And where they are.'

'Don't you think they'll expect – suspect at least – you'll do this?'

'There's no reason why they should. Everything's amicable.'

Both men shook their heads to the offered humidor but both ordered brandy, Carver deciding he genuinely needed it. He said: 'Only for as long as they choose to let it be amicable.'

'I told you, you watch too much television.'

Carver had to push the calmness into his voice. 'George. Don't you have any idea how serious . . . dangerously serious . . . all this is!'

'This is not Chicago in the twenties, Al Capone and machine guns. I know these people. Have done, over a lot of years.'

He was wasting his time, Carver realized, incredulously. 'I'll need more than the location.'

'What?'

'Names.'

'It'll involve you.'

'I *am* involved, for Christ's sake!' said Carver, in continued exasperation.

'Let me think on it.' Northcote smiled abruptly over his brandy snifter. 'I'm driving up with Jane this afternoon.'

'I know. What about Friday?'

'It'll all be settled by then. You got everything in hand?'

Carver didn't answer, looking across the table at his father-in-law, who stared back. Finally Northcote said: 'I'll make the formal retirement announcement in the keynote speech. Everything will be confirmed by Friday.'

Carver acknowledged that he'd condoned a crime: crime after crime after crime, more crimes than could be counted. Which had – astonishingly – been easy. All so logical. All so acceptable. All – all and every aspect of it – so illegal. Was he prepared to go with that? Was he ready, prepared, to be Superman in the red shorts? Or Eliot Ness? Or John Carver, trying to preserve an empire from crumbling? He said: 'You were my icon. You were Jane's icon. Everyone's icon. God.'

'Grow up, John.'

'I just have,' said Carver. 'I didn't enjoy it.'

Alice was already at their table, at their place – the place in the Village he couldn't remember choosing for those early lunches but which had become *their* place since. Everyone called everyone by their first names, the moment they were regulars. A very different club from the Harvard: a preferred club even. In which he felt comfortable. Easy. Here – despite the suit in which he definitely felt *un*comfortable – he was John: anonymous John, no one John. In the Harvard Club he was Mr Carver. Or more often, sir. Rich son-in-law of richer father-in-law, both of whom could order, as they had carelessly ordered, $250 lunches and not eat anything, nor drink more than a token sip of their matchingly expensive wine. Alice was drinking beer.

He said: 'Sorry I'm late.'

She shrugged. 'Not a problem.'

How many more times was that phrase going to jar through his mind. 'Beer?'

'I was thirsty, OK?'

'OK. You look fantastic.' She did, wearing blue jeans, a white shirt and with a blue sweater as a wrap around her shoulders.

'You don't. You look like shit on a stick. What's up . . . ?'

The waiter, who'd had a walk-on part in a movie that no one could remember but who called himself an actor said: 'Hi John. You wanna cocktail?'

'Straight up gin Martini. A twist.'

'Please,' added Alice, before the man left. To Carver she said: 'There's bad days and there's bad days. This was a *very* bad day, right?'

'The baddest day in the history of bad days.' That sounded flip, like a joke, and the last thing in which he imagined himself was a flip, one-liner joke scenario.

'So, yet again, do you want to talk about it?'

He did, decided Carver. He couldn't, to Jane, because he would be talking about her father. And he shouldn't, to Alice, who was a financial – even an investigative – journalist. But he needed – had – to talk to someone. And he trusted Alice as much as he trusted Jane: just as he trusted Jane as much as he trusted Alice. It would not occur to Alice to use anything he told her professionally: doing so would risk exposing their relationship. His Martini arrived and he said: 'Thanks. And sorry, about before,' and the waiter smiled and shook his head. To Alice, Carver said: 'I'm going to tell you something you won't believe. That I don't want to believe. But which has happened . . . I . . .' He shook his head, a lost man not knowing his direction. 'Just listen.'

Which Alice Belling did, through two nodded-for replacement drinks and head-shaking against menu offers and when Carver finished, Alice, who'd held back her impatience, said: 'This is absolutely fucking unbelievable!'

'I thought I'd said that already. More than once.'

'It needed saying again.'

Carver said: 'You're the guy on the white horse, wielding the sword of truth. What would you have done?'

'I'm not going to become your conscience, darling. Or your reassurance. You're old enough to go to the bathroom by yourself. You decide which way to piss.'

'I've decided.' It hadn't ever seemed like a decision. Nothing more than a natural progression. He raised and dropped his arms, the stupidity of the gesture heightening his embarrassment. 'It was like . . . like . . . the obvious thing to do.'

'You know you've compromised me!'

'Yes.'

'Bastard!'

Their passing waiter said: 'Nothing's terminal, guys.'

Picking up the remark, Alice said: 'This could be.'

'It was the only way I could go. *Is* the only way I *can* go.'

Briefly they enclosed themselves in their own silence.

Alice said: 'Thank you.'

'For what?'

'Trusting me, so completely.'

'Didn't you think I did?'

'Not this much.'

'I do.'

'I'm sorry, about that compromise shit. I'm not compromised.'

'You are. But thank you.'

'You told me everything?'

'Everything that I so far know. I still don't understand what the scam is: just that there is one, very, very big-time indeed. Or why are the figures being massaged like they are if the companies aren't being floated!'

'I want to know whether George W. Northcote was an entrapped innocent, like he says. Or is long-established Mafia big-time.'

'I can't decide that, either,' said Carver. He would though. He'd understand it all and resolve it all and keep the firm he was destined to inherit safe from whatever Northcote had involved it in.

In New York the Mafia, despite some investigative setbacks, remains a pyramid structure, the five predominant Families of Bonanno, Luchese, Gambino, Genovese and Colombo at the pinnacle with minor although named Families permitted to exist and operate beneath them, sometimes paying tributes and sometimes providing services. The Delioci clan were the most entrepreneurial and successful of those minor groups, largely because it was Emilio Delioci who had all those years ago enmeshed George Northcote and originally sold his money-laundering services to all of the five. Although, because of the accountant's importance to the five, Northcote's individual control had passed to Burcher, Mafia protocol decreed that any working difficulty had first to be raised with the Delioci Family before any reference to New York's ruling Mafia Commission and that was why Burcher that day drove over the East River to Queens to meet the elderly, white-haired Emilio Delioci.

Burcher didn't like operating with minor groups. They were unpredictable, nearly always imagining they were more important than they were, and there had been no attempt to hide the Delioci resentment when, at the superior Families' insistence, he became liaison between them and Northcote. Nor was there now when he was ushered into the inevitable back room of the Delioci headquarters in the inevitable restaurant on Thomson Avenue.

'To what do we owe this rare honour,' wheezed the asthmatic don.

'A problem that at first has to be discussed with you,' said Burcher. He was glad he had advised the *consiglieri* of all five New York Families of the visit and was able to indicate at once that the resolve could easily be taken away from the Deliocis.

Four

John Carver had cleared his diary to give himself a final review before the scheduled arrival of their overseas chief executives. The head of the Tokyo office was arriving that night, all the others some time during the following day. Carver strictly, determinedly, maintained his already planned agenda, obviously unable to forget his one overpowering concern but managing – mostly – to relegate it sufficiently to concentrate upon the annual international conference.

With the financial director he went through the country-by-country performance of each of their overseas divisions before analysing their own twelve-month growth and underscoring New York's 15 per cent increase over the previous year – 5 per cent higher than any of the subsidiaries – for particular mention in his speech, which was to be the expanded global overview immediately following George Northcote's now limited farewell keynote address. Carver physically shifted in flushed discomfort at the director's urging him to include instructions to all their overseas divisions to take particular care – essentially with new clients – against inadvertently becoming caught up, even by accident or inference, in the sort of financial manipulation that had so disastrously tainted Wall Street, hurriedly insisting it was already his intention, which it hadn't been until that moment, to close the discussion with that imperative warning.

Carver personally checked the boardroom seating arrangements – which put Northcote for the last time in the ultimate position of authority – and had the technician test the projection equipment for the visual presentation to accompany what he had to say, which he still only had in draft form but which was already fairly well established in his mind. Corporate and accountancy fraud warning was the only addition and he made a mental note to alert Northcote in advance, to avoid any wrong interpretation – but more importantly wrong reaction – from the other man.

His personal assistant, a grey-haired spinster named Hilda Bennett whose English accent had survived thirty years in Manhattan, as had her demeanour of a public-school matron, met him there, clipboard and itineraries in hand. All the hotel suite reservations had already been doubly checked and confirmed: the floral displays were predominantly roses. She had already established there were no cultural difficulties in the choice of flowers for the Tokyo manager's Japanese wife, for whom floral tributes might have had unintended connotations: roses were good flowers. Also doubly checked were the already approved seating plans – as well as the special dietary requests – for Thursday's welcoming dinner and Friday's formal gala. The gold gift pins for the wives and cufflinks for the men – the cufflinks in the shape of the Northcote logo – were being delivered from Tiffany's that afternoon. She'd personally gone through every detail of the Sunday brunch party at Mr Northcote's Litchfield estate with Janice Snow. Helicopters had been laid on from the East 34th Street helipad. Every guest had guaranteed they had no difficulty with helicopter travel. Both she and Janice would be on hand throughout to handle any unexpected problems. She had made up a personalized dossier, with details of every arrangement, for Mrs Carver when she got back from the country the following day to host the arrival cocktail party. Seven limousines were on permanent standby to chauffeur wives on shopping expeditions while their husbands were in conference.

It took Carver an hour to dictate the speech he'd imagined he had fixed in his mind and less than fifteen minutes to realize, when it was typed, that it wasn't fixed at all. His difficulty, unsurprisingly, was the corporate scandal warning, which didn't seem to fit logically wherever he tried to introduce it. After once removing it altogether he reinserted it where he'd slotted it in the first place.

Jane came on to his private, direct line just after lunch – which he hadn't bothered to eat – to say she'd just heard she'd been unanimously elected the charity-fund organizer.

Carver said: 'Congratulations.'

'That was hardly effusive!'

'It was pretty much a shoo-in, wasn't it?'

'I've just told Dad. He said it's going to be great, our working together. He seemed very excited coming up yesterday: said you and he had talked and he was definitely going to quit. So thank you, darling. I didn't think persuading him was going to be that easy.'

'What about getting him to see Dr Jamieson?'

'Another surprise. He went, this morning. Said he had a lot of tests and there should be some results next week.'

'That's good.'

'What did you do last night?'

'Worked on my speech, for Friday,' lied Carver. That was certainly what he would have to do tonight. What he had at the moment wasn't an address from the head of an international accountancy conglomerate. His first Harvard attempt at Keynesian philosophy – which had been rejected with the demand to try again – had been better than this. And this wasn't Keynesian philosophy.

'I'm coming down with Dad, obviously.'

'Hilda's got you a bunch of stuff.'

'I could be in Manhattan by lunch time.'

'Call me from the car. We could eat.'

'Maybe I should look over what Hilda's done first.'

'I'll leave it up to you.'

'I love you.'

'I love you too.'

Carver tried to rework his speech but wasn't any better satisfied and decided he really would have to work on it that night, at home. There were enough excuses to call his father-in-law but Carver held back from telephoning, confronting another doubt. The conference organizing was his responsibility so there was absolutely no reason why Northcote shouldn't have gone up to Litchfield. But Carver couldn't remember the man ever doing so before with everyone arriving from all over the world. Which surely wasn't the main consideration, in the circumstances. The people from whom Northcote was supposedly extricating himself – extricating himself and the firm and everyone else – were presumably *here*, in New York: this is where they'd met earlier in the week. So how could Northcote be so sure that by Friday it would all be over? Was he lying, avoiding, as he'd lied and avoided for so long: long enough to have become a world expert? Carver remained staring at the telephone but still made no effort to pick it up. If that's what Northcote were doing there was absolutely nothing he could do about it. Apart from one thing, the one thing he'd already decided against doing. Couldn't do. Carver felt a wash of impotence, which was the word that came into his mind and he wished it hadn't because of its reminder of his difficulty with Alice. Last night he hadn't suggested going back to her apartment. Neither had she. Instead of calling Northcote he dialled Alice's number but got the answering machine. He left a message that he'd call later, from home. As he went uptown he decided to see Alice, after polishing the Friday speech. They'd eat in the Village again if he reached her early enough, so he told Manuel he didn't want dinner and that he and Luisa could leave early. Carver got Alice's answering machine on his next two attempts, in between which he worked on the speech and decided it was getting better.

He knew it wasn't Alice when the telephone rang, because she never called the apartment, so he was half expecting Jane's voice but not the hysteria. 'What is it?' he said, trying to talk over her. 'Jane! I can't understand what you're saying. Slower! Speak slower.'

'Dad!' she sobbed. 'There's been an accident . . .' She choked to a stop. And then she wailed. 'Dad's dead.'

Murdered, thought Carver, at once: George W. Northcote had been murdered. Killed, for transgressing whatever code these bastards – these sons of bitches – obeyed. A code he didn't know. Which clearly George Northcote hadn't known or understood, either. Carver felt physically paralysed, his arms and legs incapable of movement. But they had to move: everything had to work. He had to . . . Had to what? He didn't know, Carver accepted. He felt the acid of vomit – and fear – rise in his throat. And thought, please help me God, and hoped God was listening.

He brought forward one of the already chartered helicopters, which was waiting for him by the time he reached 34th Street. It was normally a familiar way of his getting up to Litchfield, so familiar that the procedure was virtually automatic. But this early evening it wasn't normal. He read the cab driver's displayed ID, trying to remember the number – actually comparing the photograph – and questioned the traffic-jam detour for what was a direct downtown drive and, while they were blocked, tried – and failed – to reach Jane from his cellphone. He tried Alice, too, and once more got the answering machine. He said George Northcote was dead and he'd call as soon as he could and wished that instead of a recording he could have heard Alice's voice, from her own mouth.

And all the time couldn't stop – couldn't co-ordinate – the turmoil in his mind.

Carver had always had a problem with coincidence, which made it seem impossible George Northcote's death could be anything but murder. There had to have been a reason (what the fuck reason!) for Northcote going up to Litchfield – risking Jane, for Christ's sake! – but he didn't know, would now never know, what it was. One of the eight trillion things he had to work out. The handing over of the incriminating documentation. That surely could be the only purpose. Or was it? Why? Why Litchfield? Why do it in the boondocks instead of in Manhattan, where this week's meeting had been between Northcote and . . . ? And who? Where – oh dear God where! – were the supposedly protective copies of all the incriminating evidence: very much supposedly, because they hadn't protected Northcote. Had to have existed somewhere, he tried to reassure himself. But where? Northcote's personal safe within the firm's vault had to be the place. The place that had remained closed since that one time, which Carver knew because he'd gone into the vaults to check and if Northcote's personal safe had been open, he would have gone far more intently through whatever was there than he had on the first discovery. He most definitely had to get back in. Go through everything that was there. Janice Snow would have access. And now he had the authority – the unarguable right – to insist she open it for him. That was the obvious place for it to be. The *only* place for it to be. What was he going to do with it, when he got it? He didn't know, not yet. But from whatever there was, he'd be finally able to get names! What the fuck protection was that! It was an objective question but he didn't have an objective answer, any more than he had to all – or any – of the rest. Why did you do it, George? Why did you leave me – so many others – exposed like this? You bastard! You absolute, pig-fucking bastard. *Why?* It would, Carver accepted, always remain the biggest question of all, which would never be resolved.

The flight only took half an hour and there was still sufficient light when they reached the lake-shore estate for Carver to look down upon the scene, which was additionally illuminated by emergency lighting rigged to a generator van.

It was nearer the lake than the main, rambling house complex. A limp-rotored medivac helicopter was already on the ground, although at a distance from everything else. There were an ambulance and two police cars, their coloured bar lights still revolving and reflecting off other vehicles, which prompted Carver's illogical – immediately embarrassed – impression of a funfair attraction: roll up, roll up and see what happens to someone who thinks he can stiff-middle-finger the Mafia. There were two other cars and a 4 × 4, completing the semicircle around a piece of equipment Carver couldn't at first identify. But then he realized it was a small crane, its hawsers strained around what became visible as they descended further, Northcote's familiar tractor mower. Carver didn't bother to count the figures concentrated around it. There were certainly a lot but then George W. Northcote had been the leading figure – and a generous benefactor – in the community. Which deserved an unnecessary medivac helicopter, an ambulance, two police cars and a crane that appeared to have been designed like a crab with its legs splayed.

Carver's helicopter put down some way away, to avoid downdraught, and Carver was out in a crouched run before the rotors stopped. When he straightened he saw people already coming towards him and recognized Al Hibbert, the sheriff, in the lead with his hand already outstretched.

'Bad business, John,' greeted the bulge-bellied, balding man. 'Damned bad business.' He wore a holstered pistol and his badge of office on the shirt of his official uniform.

'Where's Jane?'

'Up in the house. Dr Jamieson is looking after her.' Hibbert turned to the second man. 'You know Pete Simpson?'

'What happened?' demanded Carver, shaking the medical

examiner's hand as he walked towards the brightly lighted scene.

'Still piecing it together with Jack here,' said Hibbert, as they got to the vehicles.

Jack Jennings had been George Northcote's major-domo for fifteen years, controlling a staff of eight between the Litchfield estate and the Manhattan apartment. He was a tall white-haired black man whom Carver couldn't ever remember seeing in anything but striped trousers, black jacket and white shirt. It was the uniform he was wearing now. The man said: 'So sorry, Mr Carver. So very, very sorry.' His voice was thick.

'Let's start again, shall we, Jack?' said the sheriff.

Jennings coughed. 'After lunch Mr Northcote said he was going to drive the mower a little . . .' He smiled at Carver. 'You know how he used to like to do that. Haul the cutters around the lower paddocks: said it relaxed him and that he needed to relax with what was coming up this week.'

'What's that mean?' broke in the sheriff.

'We've got the annual conference: people flying in from all over,' supplied Carver. *Which is what I am going to do. Live in the country, cut my grass . . .* He remembered Northcote's statement, as clearly as he remembered the photograph that accompanied Alice's profile.

'That's what he said,' agreed Jennings, his voice still thick despite the constant coughing. 'He was in the study all morning, working on his speech.'

He had to see that speech, as soon as possible, Carver decided. And go through the study with a toothcomb. There'd be a safe. Would Jennings know the combination? Or where the key was kept?

'Go on,' urged Hibbert.

'It wasn't unusual for him to stay out all afternoon,' picked up the man. 'I looked out for him around five: that's about the time he likes a Macallan when he's up here in the country.

When he wasn't back by five thirty I came out looking, in the golf buggy. Here's where I found him . . .' The man choked to a halt. 'God, it was awful.'

'What?' persisted Carver.

'See that dip there?' Hibbert took over, moving closer to the rim of the depression and the crane with its legs spidered to support the dangling tractor mower.

Carver did see it. And saw for the first time, too, that hanging down from the tractor itself was the separate multi-bladed attachment that cut a swathe at least six feet wide on each traverse.

'The way it looks, he took the tractor too close to the edge, so it tilted. That threw him backwards, into the blade, and then the whole rig turned over, on top of him . . .' Hibbert nodded to a photographer of whom Carver had until that moment been unaware, taking shots of the suspended machine. 'We got pictures . . '

'He was trapped underneath the tractor itself,' said Jennings. 'Crushed. I tried to get to him but I thought it all might topple further, on to me. I called out but he didn't say anything. I couldn't hear him breathing. I went back to the house and called emergency. Then I called Mrs Carver.'

'The injuries are bad,' threw in the medical examiner. 'I won't know until I complete the autopsy whether he died from blood loss, from going into those sharp-as-hell blades. Or from being crushed by the tractor. His chest is virtually gone.'

'It took a time to get the lifting gear here, to get it off him,' said Hibbert, as if in apology.

'Where's the body now?' asked Carver.

'On the way to the morgue,' said Hibbert. 'Jane wanted to see him but I said no. I didn't know how long it was going to take you to get here . . . didn't think of the helo . . . so I decided it was better to get the body away.'

'Thank you,' said Carver.

'There's supposed to be an official identification, but I know . . .' began Hibbert but Carver talked over him.

'I'll do it. Tomorrow OK?'

'Just give me a call,' said Hibbert. He shook his head. 'One hell of an accident.'

'One hell of an accident,' echoed Carver. If only you knew, he thought. If only you knew that George Northcote had been murdered by people who wouldn't let him go.

But what people? And what were they going to do next? John Carver supposed what he was feeling was fear: total, numbing, skin-tingling, stomach-emptying fear.

Five

Jane was cried out of tears but dry sobs still shuddered through her and the first time it happened Carver was frightened she wouldn't catch her breath and would choke. Which wasn't his only fear. She sat stiffly upright on the very edge of the lounge chair, her eyes blinking but unfocused, seemingly unaware of anything or anyone around her. Charles Jamieson, the Litchfield family doctor, called it deep shock and asked where they would be staying that night and before Carver could reply Jane said, so loudly and unexpectedly that both men jumped: 'Here, with Dad.'

'Then we'll put you to bed,' announced the doctor, recovering before Carver.

Jane let herself be led upstairs to the room she and Carver always occupied when they stayed over, which they often did. Carver and the doctor undressed her between them and obediently she took the sedatives Jamieson gave her but remained staring up at the ceiling, still occasionally racked by a breath-snatching sob. Carver felt the doctor's pressure on his arm and followed the man from the bedroom.

In the downstairs lounge Jamieson, a fat, haphazardly dressed man, said: 'It's not going to be easy for her. They were very close. It's most likely she won't accept it at first: talk as if he's still alive.'

'What should I do?'

'Let it go, for a little while. You going to stay up here?'

Carver hesitated. 'I can't. I have to go back to the city.'

There were a lot of calls he had to make, so much he had to do: so much, somehow, somewhere, he had to find or discover. What Northcote had promised to give him had to be here somewhere because the intention had been for the man to come direct from here for their meeting. But what? Where?

'You got staff in Manhattan?'

'Yes.'

'Live in?'

'No,' frowned Carver. 'What the hell does that mean?'

'It means you should take her with you but that for a few days I don't think she should be left by herself.'

'You mean she might harm herself?'

'No,' said Jamieson, impatiently. 'Just that she shouldn't be alone.'

'I'll get nurses in.'

'That would be good. Manhattan would be good. It'll get her away from here. What time are you leaving tomorrow?'

He had to make the formal identification of the body, remembered Carver. 'Late morning. We'll fly.' He should have arranged it before dismissing the helicopter. He was going to have to speak to Hilda shortly. It could be added to the list of all the other things that had to be done.

'I'll call by around nine: see how she is.'

'Jane told me you'd examined George.'

The doctor nodded. 'He told me he was giving up entirely and I told him it was a damned good idea. His blood pressure was sky high. I put him on immediate medication. It could even have been a stroke that made him fall off the tractor . . .' He was slowed by a thought. 'Maybe I should mention it to Pete Simpson.'

'Maybe you should,' agreed Carver. He had to end this conversation and this encounter: get on with all the other things. But at the same time, irrationally, he didn't want the doctor to go. Although it was a tragedy – a tragic accident in everyone's opinion except his – there was a normality about talking with the other man. But when Jamieson went it wouldn't be normal any more. What he had to do – the calls he had to make, the arranging and rearranging that had to be done – would be normal in the circumstances of a tragedy but in this case he would be involved – *was* involved – in murder. Mob murder; organized crime murder; once-you're-in-you're-never-out murder. Or was he? Could, despite everything he knew – or thought he knew – George Northcote have genuinely suffered a stroke because of sky-high blood pressure and toppled backwards into the multiple spinning blades of a mowing machine? Could a stroke be, even, why Northcote went too close to the depression in the ground he would have known all too well to be there, and to be dangerous, because he was unconscious in those last few, badly steered seconds? Only George Northcote had known that he knew the firm's – Northcote's – link with organized crime. And George Northcote was dead and that knowledge would have died with him. He knew the names of the companies that had to be divested and that could be – would be – easily achieved by the excuse of Northcote's death. The words and the phrases began to move through Carver's mind. Retrenchment, necessary reorganization after the death of such a dominant, leading corporate figure, no one any longer available to provide the personalized service that George W. Northcote provided, with obvious regret . . . It fitted. Fitted perfectly. They'd all be out. Out, home free: no connection, no association, no danger. If . . .

'I'll just look in now, before I go,' said Jamieson and so lost was he in thought that Carver was actually startled although he didn't think it showed.

'Let's both look in,' he said.

Jane was lying as they'd left her, on her back, but was deeply asleep, snuffling soft occasional snores, although once another sob shuddered through her. At Jamieson's gesture they backed out of the bedroom, without speaking until they got outside in the hallway. Jamieson said: 'That's good. I didn't want to have to give her anything stronger.'

Carver met Jennings as he turned from seeing Jamieson out, anticipating the man before he spoke. 'I don't want anything to eat. There's too much to do. I'll be in the study.'

'Everyone's together in the kitchen, if you want anything.'

'I'll let you know,' said Carver, already walking towards what he considered the most obvious place to find what it was essential he locate.

Carver pressed the door closed behind him but remained against it, confronting his first awareness, which was not within the room at all. The windows looked directly out in the direction of the depression in which the tractor and mower had overturned. It was dark now but beyond the slope there was still a glow from the generator lights illuminating the lifting of the unseen machinery on to an equally unseen removal truck and the word *unseen* fixed itself in Carver's mind. Where Northcote had died couldn't be seen from the house: couldn't be seen from anywhere. Making it the perfect place for murder.

Carver brought himself back inside the room, as heavily mahogany-panelled as the Manhattan office, unsure where – how – to start. Where? Where would Northcote have kept hidden sufficient secrets to protect the firm? The computer, blank-eyed on its own workstation beside the desk – antique again like its twin in Manhattan – was obvious, but Northcote had a late-starter's problems with electronic technology. And they dealt in printed, written words and figures: that's what it had been in Northcote's safe; written, printed incrimination. So the computer – the computer he'd already accessed and found nothing but titles on the client list, with no cross-referenced file records – was not at all the logical initial search. The desk itself then. But not at once, frustrating though it was to delay. Calls – arrangements – had the priority. Or did they?

Carver saw the neatly stacked paper as he approached and realized as he lowered himself into the padded leather chair that it was Northcote's intended valedictory speech. For a moment Carver hesitated, as he'd hesitated going into Northcote's personal safe in the firm's basement vault, but then, abruptly, he snatched it up. It was comparatively short and easily legible in Northcote's neat, round handwriting. It really was a genuine farewell address.

He was a proud man, Northcote had written. He was finally, irrevocably, leaving the firm at the peak of its international success and prestige. It was due to the financial business ability and acumen of their overseas divisions as much as to that of the Wall Street head office – 'command centre', Northcote had written with a question mark beside it – that they had survived the market upheavals that had affected, in some instances destroyed, other firms of less able people. In entrusting the future ultimate control to John Carver – 'my worthy and deserving successor' – and the New York partners – 'an unrivalled team, on any continent' – he was assuring the continued success of George Northcote International. He wished them well and goodbye.

Carver laid the three sheets directly in front of two silver-framed photographs of Northcote with Muriel, his wife who had died eighteen years earlier, and two others of Northcote with Jane, one in her graduation robes. He'd take the speech back to Manhattan, Carver decided: have it duplicated to be shown to everyone gathering for the conference. Less than a week ago he would have been moved by the words, applauded with the rest of the people for whom they were intended and shaken Northcote's hand and maybe even needed to clear his throat before he could respond. Now he felt nothing. Not contempt nor sadness and certainly not admiration. It was as if George Northcote had been a total stranger and then, surprised, Carver belatedly acknowledged that was exactly what George Northcote *had* been, someone with whom he had been in daily contact and whose daughter he'd married but whom he had known not at all, a man playing – performing – a part.

Hilda Bennett answered his call on the second ring and said, 'Oh my God,' when Carver told her, hesitating fractionally when he used the word accident. He wanted all the overseas executives advised the moment they arrived – she was to call the Tokyo manager as soon as their conversation ended – and a full meeting convened for the following afternoon. The cocktail party that Jane had been scheduled to host was cancelled, as well as Friday's gala banquet and the planned reception at Litchfield. The welcoming dinner would, however, still take place. He expected all the incoming delegates to attend the funeral, so hotel reservations had to be extended. She was to advise the funeral directors that Northcote would be buried in the same vault as his wife: there were still legalities to be completed – he had the following morning formally to identify the body – so it was not yet possible to suggest a specific date for the interment. He would speak separately with the firm's lawyer, with whom she should liaise the following morning about death notices and obituaries. He would also speak separately to his own staff at the East 62nd Street apartment, to move them in permanently, but wanted her additionally to arrange a twenty-four-hour nursing staff there to care for Jane. He'd talk personally with their Manhattan doctor and put the man in contact with Dr Jamieson, up here in Litchfield. He wanted the helicopter to collect them at noon, from the Northcote estate. He couldn't think of anything else that had immediately to be initiated but if he did he'd call back, providing it wasn't too late. Hilda said it didn't matter how late: she probably wouldn't sleep anyway. Should she tell Janice Snow?

Carver told her to wait fifteen minutes, for him to break the news to Northcote's personal assistant.

Janice Snow broke down at once and kept asking what she should do and Carver started to suggest she work with Hilda on the arrangements he'd already asked Hilda to make, but suddenly stopped, realizing his oversight. He allowed himself a rehearsing pause before asking if Janice had personally programmed Northcote's computer, his irritation at himself transferring itself to Janice's reply that it was one of her daily functions. Mr Northcote hadn't liked or understood computers: scarcely known properly how to operate one. Just as promptly, without the need for any reference, she gave him what she insisted were all George Northcote's entry codes and passwords.

Carver remained undecided for a few moments, before saying: 'This may seem a strange question in the circumstances. But it's extremely important. Is there a special code or password that George used for extremely sensitive stuff . . . secret stuff, in fact?'

Now the hesitation came from the woman. 'You've got them all. They all duplicate with Manhattan, of course.'

'In which file or folder, of those you've given me, would George's personal accounts have been kept?'

The curiosity was discernible in Janice Snow's voice. 'I already told you, Mr Carver. He didn't work like that.'

'You telling me there isn't one?'

'That's very much what I'm telling you. That there isn't a specific one.'

Could Janice Snow be part of it, whatever *it* was? She'd have to be if she was the person who'd entered all Northcote's computer information. Would Northcote have told Janice what he knew? He'd be exposing himself, disclosing names to her. But only if she *were* part of it: was complicit. If she wasn't, it would be an enquiry that only had relevance to him.

He said: 'I've some names I want to put to you. Do you know where the files are on a company named Mulder Inc.?'

Janice gave time for her answer. 'No.'

'Have you ever handled accounts on behalf of George for Mulder Inc.?'

'I've typed completion letters to them, in the Caymans, after an audit.'

'To go with the returns?'

There was another hesitation. 'They were sent separately.'

'So how were the returns made?'

'I don't know.'

'You don't know!'

'Mr Northcote had a special way of working, with some clients. Mulder was one of them. There were a lot of personal meetings.'

'You know the names of some Mulder executives: their in-house accountants?'

'No.'

She had to be part of it, thought Carver. 'Did George ever have you computerize any details of Mulder?'

'No.'

'What about anyone else on his personal staff? Other girls?'

'I did all that.'

'What about a company named Encomp?'

There was a further pause. 'I've typed some sign-off letters, to Grand Cayman again.'

'But no returns?'

'No.'

'What about Innsflow?'

'The same.'

There was no purpose in continuing this long-distance conversation. With the passwords he could make a computer check of his own, despite what Janice had told him. 'I want you to help Hilda, like I said. We'll talk some more about George's personal files when I get back.'

'OK.'

If the woman were involved his asking about them would give her all the time in the world to hide or destroy everything.

'Is there something wrong?' demanded Janice, openly.

'Nothing wrong at all,' said Carver. 'With everyone here in

New York – with meetings and discussions to be held – I'm trying to bring myself as fully up to date as possible, as quickly as possible.'

'I'll have it done by the time you get here tomorrow,' promised the woman.

Now with increasing impatience Carver endured fifteen minutes going through what the firm's lawyer thought important to emphasize in the death notices and obituaries, which mostly concerned the assurance that Carver's already agreed succession would ensure the uninterrupted business continuity of George W. Northcote International. Manuel said he and his wife would return to East 62nd Street that night, to ensure that everything would be ready before anyone arrived. He was very sorry about Mr George. It was terrible.

Alice started lightly: 'I thought you'd forgotten me . . .' But at once became subdued when he talked over her to tell her what had happened. She said: 'Shit,' and then: 'An accident?'

'That's what it's going to be described as.'

'Do you really think he was killed?'

'The doctor says he could have suffered a stroke, from high blood pressure: that it could have been the cause of his falling into the blades.'

'I asked what you thought,' persisted Alice.

'I don't want to, but I think he was killed,' said Carver, hearing the casual, conversational tone of his own voice. He was talking of murder as if it was a normal topic, like the weather or some commuter gridlock and wasn't Manhattan a shitty place to try to get around in.

'This doesn't seem real: sound real,' said Alice, matching his thinking, which she often did.

'No.'

'What are you going to do?'

'I can't think of anything to do.'

'He didn't give you what you asked for?'

'No. But it should be here somewhere.' Carver was impatient to get off the line.

'How's Jane?'

'Sedated.'

'It won't be easy for us to meet?'

Now it was Alice who sounded remarkably sanguine: unmoved. But then although she'd been impressed by the man – wrongly as it transpired – she'd only met George Northcote two or three times. 'Not over the next few days,' he agreed.

'Call me, when you can.'

'When I can.'

'And be careful, darling.'

'I will,' said Carver, wishing he knew how to be.

Carver pushed the chair slightly back with the same motion of replacing the telephone, momentarily looking between the desk and the workstation before deciding he couldn't wait for Janice's search the following morning: that he had to look – try to look – for himself. The moment he booted up he recognized the duplication with the Manhattan office, curious that Northcote had required the copies here in the country in view of his operating difficulties. Carver scrolled his way through every one of Northcote's personal files and accessed every password and entry code, each time carefully entering the names of the three hovering, criminal and incriminating companies. None registered.

He turned, hurriedly, to the desk. The top left-hand drawer contained receipted bills, each annotated with the number and date of the cheque that had settled it, the one below that cheque books with the stubs meticulously completed and co-ordinated with the invoices above. The bottom drawer held only stationery. The diary, a duplicate of the appointments book from which they all worked in Wall Street, was in the top right-hand drawer. Carver momentarily hesitated before picking it up, aware as he did so of the shake in his hand, reminding himself how important it was going to be when he reached the office the following day to retrieve Northcote's office copy.

Carver initially held it up by its spine, hopefully shaking it, but it concealed nothing loose. After that he turned at once to the day Northcote had been in New York for the supposedly severing encounter with his mob controllers. The entry read: 'S–B. Dinner. Harvard.' There was a dash between the two letters and against the name of the club there was an asterisk. There was also an asterisk against today's entry, which simply read: 'J. 2.30.' When, according to Jennings, Northcote was on his tractor, hauling across a field completely hidden from anyone's view the cutting machine beneath which he'd fallen.

It took Carver more than an hour painstakingly to go through every entry, which Northcote appeared always to do by initials, never recording a name. Those of S–B appeared a total of six times, always marked by asterisks, and by carefully going back through the marked pages Carver calculated the meetings were regularly once a month, nearly always the last Tuesday. They were always for lunch and never at the same restaurant. This week had been the first time the Harvard club was mentioned. Where would Northcote's diaries for the previous years be? Carver wondered. The man's personal safe in the vault? Another check, for the following day.

In another right-hand drawer Carver found a cuttings book of newspaper and magazine articles on Northcote. The long, admiring feature by Alice was quite near the top. Even more recent was a *Wall Street Journal* interview in which Northcote had urged tighter financial supervision by the SEC and all the other authorities governing accountancy, both locally in New York as well as federally.

Neatly arranged in a multi-sectioned tray in the bottom right-hand drawer was a selection of keys, some – the country-club locker and spare sets for the cars, for instance – clearly labelled, others not. The age and model – and insecurity – of the safe surprised Carver when he found it. It was floor-mounted inside one of the cupboards beneath the bookcase and was key, not combination, locked. It took Carver less than fifteen minutes to find the key that fitted from among those unmarked in the bottom drawer.

The safe was only about a quarter full, all of it easily carried in a single trip back to the desk. Carver began to go through the contents in the order in which they had been stored, which was with the money on top of the pile. He didn't bother to count but guessed there were several thousand dollars in newly issued, uncreased one-hundred-dollar bills. There were three personal insurance policies, in total with a face sum of $3,000,000 but in the one he glanced through there was an endorsement increasing the value in the event of accidental death. There was a stock portfolio of perhaps twenty certificates, which Carver scanned through not even registering their valuations, interested only in any possible mention of the three companies. Once more there was none. George Northcote's will was unexpectedly brief. Apart from bequests to the staff – $50,000 for Jack Jennings – the bulk of Northcote's entire estate went to Jane, passing to Carver if she predeceased him in Northcote's lifetime. The only exception was a single legacy of $100,000 to Carver if she did inherit. In the event of their both predeceasing Northcote, the estate was to be divided equally between any surviving children. The will had been made soon after their marriage, Carver saw from its date, long before the difficulty of Jane conceiving had been realized. There was a codicil, attested just one week after the partners' meeting at which Carver had been proposed by Northcote and unanimously approved by the partners as Northcote's successor, appointing Carver the sole and absolute executor of the will.

The only things remaining in front of Carver when he put the portfolio aside were a small selection of photographs, the first easily identifiable as Northcote with Jane, when she was a child, and with his wife – one showing Muriel actually on their wedding day, in her wedding dress – which had to have been taken at least thirty if not more years ago.

Carver didn't recognize the woman in the last four photographs, although it was very clearly not Muriel Northcote. Each was inscribed on the back with a date – a two-week period in 1983 when Carver knew Northcote to have been married and Muriel to be still alive – and locations, Capri and Madrid. There was also a name, Anna. One showed she and Northcote openly embracing, two more with their arms entwined, the fourth holding hands.

Each was a picture of two very happy people, very much in love.

George Northcote's bedroom was once again heavily furnished, the bed and dressing-room wardrobes thick, dark wood, although Carver didn't think it was mahogany. He imagined he could detect the smell of the man, a musky cologne mixed vaguely with cigars, but decided in the pristine surroundings that was what it had to be, imagination. He supposed the neatness was not Northcote's but one of the staff, maybe even Jennings. There was what was clearly pocket contents in a segregated tray on the nightstand, house keys, a cigar cutter and lighter, a wad of money, hundred-dollar notes on the outside, in a silver clip and a snakeskin wallet. One half of the wallet was a personalized, week-by-week diary. The entries for that week were identical to those in the larger version downstairs, even to the entry for this day simply reading '2.30'. There was a selection of credit and business cards in their separate pockets at the top of the opposing side, with a slim jotting pad at its bottom. It was blank.

Carver felt a quick flare of hope when he opened the nightstand door and saw the bundle of fine-lined accountancy sheets, lifting them all out and laying them on the bed to hurry through. His first awareness was that they were old files, all dated five years earlier. His second was that none contained any references to Mulder, Encomp or Innsflow. They were the accounts of two companies – BHYF and NOXT – neither of which Carver could remember discussing personally with Northcote, nor more generally at partners' meetings. And he was sure they hadn't shown on the computer search he'd attempted downstairs of Northcote's personally handled accounts. More mob companies? His unavoidable question. Which prompted another. Why left like this, not in the downstairs safe? Because, incredibly, unbelievably, Northcote had believed *he* was safe: that there was no need *for* security. Could they be, even, part – maybe even all – of what Northcote had planned to give him, the insurance against the firm's destruction? Carver wanted to believe it: wanted to believe it more than anything he'd wanted to believe in his life. Whatever, they were potentially the most important discovery he'd made that night. There was a bedside table on the opposite side from the nightstand, free of anything except a biography of Maynard Keynes, and Carver carefully stacked the sheets there to go downstairs with everything else he'd already set aside to take back to Manhattan.

Carver went painstakingly through all the drawers in Northcote's dressing room, discovering nothing more in any of them but the expected underwear, linen and shirts. He actually explored every pocket of every one of the twelve suits that hung from the dressing-room rails, as well as the two topcoats. Carver had half hoped for another, better-hidden safe but he didn't find one, despite looking behind every picture for something wall-mounted, checking every cupboard and recess for an upright model to match that downstairs, and finally scuffing his feet across the carpet, as he had in the study, searching for a security vault sunk into the floor. There was no tell-tale unevenness wherever he looked or felt.

Enough, Carver decided. He ached with tiredness: ached so much he couldn't think straight, could hardly see straight. It had to be BHYF and NOXT. He didn't know how or where to take it forward from here, but there had to be some significance. Would Janice Snow know? Or rather, would Janice Snow show him a way forward? At that moment he thought of one himself, feeling another spurt of self-criticism that it hadn't occurred to him before. Northcote's bank. That had to be a source, whatever the importance of BHYF and NOXT. It was unimaginable – like so much else was unimaginable – that Northcote didn't have a safe-deposit facility: several safe-deposit facilities, in Manhattan banks. What better place – what more obvious place – to hide secrets but in a bank safe-deposit box?

Carver was so tired he had literally to force himself to move, simply to walk back into the dressing room, where he found by feel more than sight the valise, in which he packed the five-year-old files from the nightstand and stumbled back downstairs into the study to add the will, diary and the four photographs of the laughing, dark-haired girl named Anna.

Jane still lay on her back but there weren't any more sobs. He let his clothes lie where they fell and eased as carefully as he could into bed beside her, anxious to avoid movement or contact that might awaken her. There was no instinctive, automatic shift at his presence.

Who, wondered Carver, was Anna?

'So what the hell happened!' demanded Burcher, the soft voice unaccustomedly loud.

'He wasn't up to it. He croaked,' said a crinkle-haired, heavily built man.

'Who are you?' said Burcher.

'Who wants to know?'

'I want to know because the Families want to know. Because they're not happy.' Burcher thought again how wise he'd been letting the people he represented know that he was strictly adhering to the pyramid procedure. There were far more people in the restaurant back room than when he'd last been there. The attitudes and atmosphere were bravado.

'He's my *caporegime*, Paulo Brescia,' wheezed Emilio Delioci.

'Were you there?' Burcher asked the man and knew at once from the discomfited shift that he hadn't been.

'I sent people.'

Burcher let the silence build and when he spoke he was quiet-voiced again but sounded every word, as if he were tasting it as he wanted them to taste it. 'Aren't you aware of how important George Northcote was to the Families?'

'He was ours,' said Emilio Delioci.

Burcher shook his head. 'You were allowed to believe that as a mark of respect. Northcote created a system that benefited not just New York but every other Family in this country and so every other Family in this country is going to be as sore as they are in New York and that's as sore as hell. You're close to being put out of business.'

'You can't threaten us like that, asshole!' said Brescia.

'You want to put that to the test, asshole?' challenged Burcher. 'Let's all of us get something very straight and very clearly understood. What I say is what New York say: you insult me like some bit player in *The Godfather*, you insult New York and if they feel like it – if they feel you are not doing what you've been asked to do, then . . .' Burcher extended his hand towards Brescia and snapped his fingers dismissively, '. . . you're gone. History that no one remembers. Have I made that very straight and very clear to everyone here?'

'I don't want any misunderstandings,' said Delioci.

'Neither do I,' said Burcher. 'So I'll ask again. What happened?'

'My people told Northcote they wanted what he'd held

back,' said Brescia, all the truculence gone. 'He said he'd given you the message: that that was how it was going to be. They tried to persuade him. He suddenly went stiff and died on them. They made it look like an accident: that's how the local radio and newspapers are reporting it.'

'So somewhere there's a load of stuff that could cause us a lot of harm?'

The *capo* smirked and Burcher realized the man was playing to the rest of the audience in the room. Brescia said: 'He was being persuaded. There's a guy taking over the firm, married to Northcote's daughter. Carver. He knows all about it. And a woman, Janice Snow, did the computer entries.'

It could all be turned into a coup, Burcher decided. And if it could be, it would be his coup, not that of these half-assed small-timers. 'What about the material Northcote was holding back?'

'I told you, he passed out before they could get that out of him.'

'What about in the house?'

'There's staff. We couldn't get near it.'

'Here's what you're going to do,' said Burcher. 'You're going to send people back to Litchfield, to find some way in. You're going to find out everything I need to know about this Carver guy. Use a legitimate private detective agency in the city. And you're going to find out how much the woman, Janice Snow, knows. All that very straight and very clear?'

'I don't enjoy disrespect, Mr Burcher,' said Delioci.

'I mean no disrespect to you,' said the lawyer. 'I was told very specifically to pass on the feelings of those to whom we are all answerable and most specifically of all to ensure that everybody understood there are to be no more mistakes.'

'I think you have done that,' said the old man.

'Then it's been a good meeting,' said Burcher. How much more, to his personal benefit, could he manipulate it? He wondered.

Six

John Carver thought he'd prepared himself for what he had to do but he hadn't. He gasped, aloud, and felt his legs begin to go at the sight of George Northcote's body on the gurney. He instinctively snatched out for the table upon which the body actually lay, pulling further aside even more of the covering sheet and seeing more awfulness and when he tried to speak he couldn't. What he tried to say came out as an unintelligible hiss. He finally managed: 'Oh dear God,' his voice still a dry whisper.

He felt Al Hibbert's supportive hand at his elbow. The sheriff said: 'Easy, John. Take it easy.'

'I'm OK,' croaked Carver, his voice better but only just. Stronger still he said: 'What the hell happened to him? It's like . . . it's like he's been flayed . . .'

Northcote's face was practically non-existent and there was virtually no skin and most of the lion's mane had been torn off, scalping the man. There seemed to be no skin either on much of Northcote's chest, from which Carver had tugged the sheet. It was flat, not a body shape at all, and there was a lot of bone and grey, slimed viscera.

'The mower got him first, then the tractor,' said Hibbert.

'No,' refused Carver. 'It isn't possible. I saw the rig. The mower blades were covered, shielded against just such an accident. If he fell backwards he wouldn't have been cut . . . skinned like that. He'd have maybe broken an arm or a leg on the protective covering but that's all. And going backwards would have taken him *away* from the tractor, when it tipped over, not underneath it . . .'

'That's what Pete and I thought at first,' said Hibbert, nodding to Simpson on the other side of the slab. 'We stayed up there past midnight last night: got engineers in. Here's how we worked it out. George goes too close to the dip, throwing the tractor sideways. The force of it going tips the mowing rig, which runs on its own motor. When George hits it, it's upside down, the blades going full belt. Does that to him. The mower is wider than the tractor that's pulling it. For a moment or two – God knows how long – it prevents the tractor going right over but swings it back towards where George has been tossed . . .'

'He would have most likely been dead by then . . . unconscious, certainly,' broke in Simpson. Belatedly the medical examiner put the sheet back over the corpse. 'This is an odd one, sure. But I get a dozen accidents like this every year, guys driving – operating – machinery they're not used to . . . something goes wrong . . . bang, they're dead . . .'

'The tractor is heavier than the rig, finally makes it give way . . . we've got photographs of how it bent, when it finally wasn't able to stop it going right over,' picked up Hibbert. 'And when it goes, there's George right under the whole fucking thing.'

The perfect murder, thought Carver: the absolute, totally unprovable, perfect murder. Once you're in, there's only one way out. Out like George, in front of him although covered again by an inadequate sheet. Skinned alive. Not actually alive. Skinned by being thrust in and out of the mower blades to an agonizingly slow death. Would he have told them: given them what they wanted? He would have screamed. Been demented. Carver went to Simpson. 'Charlie Jamieson examined him, day before yesterday. Says his blood pressure was so high he could have had a heart attack.'

'Charlie called me, at breakfast,' said Simpson. 'George's readings were at record-book levels.'

Carver was sure he was snatching at straws but would have been glad of one no matter how slender. 'Could he have had a stroke, because of it? Could that have been the reason he went too close to the dip and turned over?'

Both men – the sheriff and the examiner – looked emptily back at Carver. Hibbert said: 'I'm sorry, John. I just can't quite get your point . . .'

It was a point he couldn't make, Carver realized. He felt physically encased, as if his ribcage was being crushed by his impotence like that of the man lying, flat-chested, on the metal table in front of him. 'George knew his land: knew where he couldn't take his rig. Knew how to handle it, too. There must have been a reason for his going too close this time.' Why was he saying this? In front of a law officer! What self-justification was he trying to make, to absolve himself from the self-recrimination of not having tried to have George Northcote's death properly investigated? Which he well knew couldn't be properly investigated.

'It happened *because* he knew his land so well,' said Hibbert. 'He wasn't thinking, wasn't taking enough care *because* he'd done it a hundred times before. All it needed was inches to make the mistake he made. The engineers we had up there last night are professionals. I'll show you the photographs: the way they're sure it happened.'

The way it had been intended to be worked out, thought Carver. 'There going to be an inquest?'

'Into what, John?' demanded Hibbert. 'There's nothing officially to inquire into.'

Carver felt the impotent straight-jacketed constriction again. 'I can go ahead with the funeral arrangements then?'

'As and when you wish,' assured Hibbert, as if he were giving away a raffle prize. 'It's gotta be a shock, John. Hang in there.'

Carver's feeling now was of burning irritation at the filed-away clichés. 'That's what I'll do, Al: hang in there.' Hang in where, with whom?

Hibbert said: 'I'm sorry but I officially need to hear the words. Is the body you've just seen that of George Northcote?'

Of course it was! But then again it wasn't: wasn't the bull-shouldered – most certainly not the bull-chested – lion's-maned founder of the best known, most prestigious accountancy firm on Wall Street. 'That's the body of George Northcote.'

Hibbert said: 'I hate this. Of all the things I have officially to do, I hate this the most.'

'Me too,' said Simpson.

'I'm sorry to have put you through it,' apologized Hibbert. 'I tried to indicate last night . . .'

'I know,' stopped Carver. 'It's OK.'

'We lost a good man here,' said Simpson. 'The best.'

'That's what he was,' Hibbert hurried on. 'The best. We're sure as hell glad you and Jane are still here in the community, to carry on.'

Carry on what? wondered Carver. Near to cliché himself, he said: 'We're still here.'

'How is Jane?' asked Simpson. 'Charlie told me there was pretty heavy shock.'

'She was still sedated when I left,' said Carver. 'Charlie's with her but I need to get back. Is there anything else?'

'We're through,' declared Hibbert.

Simpson said: 'I'll tell my guys to expect a call from your funeral directors.'

'It'll come sometime today,' promised Carver. An even-voiced, calm, conversational exchange, he thought. We're talking about a murder, you fucking idiots! A murder committed by people professional enough to be able to skin a man alive but make it appear to these boondock boneheads a typical country mishap. *I get a dozen accidents like this every year*. Just another one of those accident stories, to go into the Litchfield folklore.

'Anything I can do to help, John, you just call. That's all it needs, a call.'

'I appreciate that.'

'I mean it.'

'I know you do.'

The sheriff and the medical examiner both solicitously escorted Carver from the building and stood together as he drove away. Simpson said: 'That guy's suffering shock, just like his wife. Worse, maybe. His is delayed. It'll properly hit him in a couple of days.'

'I must admit I've never seen anyone quite so badly hurt as George from falling into mower blades,' said Hibbert.

Simpson shook his head, a patronizing you-don't-know gesture. 'Happens all the time.'

Carver drove home by the longer, round-about route that took him by the bottom of the lake, a way they rarely used, intent upon landmarks when he approached Northcote's estate and grunting with empty satisfaction when he identified what he was looking for. The hollow into which George Northcote had been tipped was invisible from the house but it was very much in view from this rarely used back road. In view and easily reached through the simple pale fencing. And from where he was standing the mow-line was distinctly marked, going from this boundary up the incline but stopping at the hollow into which it had tipped. Carver remembered quite clearly that when he'd been there the previous evening all the talk – all the indications – had been that the rig had come in the opposite direction, down the incline.

From the moment of entering financial journalism through a fluke of shall-I-shan't-I timing, Alice Belling had recognized that the World Wide Web was the trampoline upon which to bounce anywhere she chose through cyberspace.

And had become a far more expert and adept surfer than any on Wakiki beach. There were few firewalls she could not electronically scale or burrow beneath or systems she couldn't hack into. She justified the intrusion to her own satisfaction by only ever using what she discovered to expose financial wrongdoings, never valid business manoeuvrings. It was an operating integrity with which she had no difficulty and would have been uninterested in that of others had others known, which none did, not even John Carver, from whom she had no other secrets.

Normally she roamed the world and its Web from the comfort and convenience of her SoHo apartment on Princes Street. Today, persuaded by what Carver told her, she decided against working from home, even though she always avoided the possibility of inadvertently leaving her own electronic fingerprint on any detection equipment or device with which she was unfamiliar by never going direct into a target system but always hacking first into an unsuspecting intermediary business or organization to make her penetration via their site.

Alice set out early and was at the door of the Space for Space cybercafe on Canal and West Broadway when it opened, to ensure she didn't have to queue for a station. She surfed and at random chose the European headquarters booking system of an international hotel chain based in the southern-English town of Basingstoke to be her cut-out host, isolating their password after just five attempted hits and within minutes established her Trojan Horse, her personal password-accessed site undetectable within the chain's mainframe into which she could come and go without their having the slightest knowledge of her presence.

The obvious search was for the three names Carver had given her. Alice selected Mulder first, in a global sweep, and was startled by the number of immediate hits, just as quickly recognizing the names to be the parent company registration in Grand Cayman. She began the familiar password hunt and after thirty minutes became irritated, as well as impatient, at the repeated rejections from Grand Cayman. Frustrated, she scrolled through the other listings, which curiously covered a large number of the American states, with the addition of overseas subsidiaries in a matching number of European and Asian countries. Obeying the hackers' lore when confronted with initial refusal, she closed down on Mulder, moving at once to Encomp, and got what appeared to be a virtually identical number of hits, with the same American state and worldwide spread. Innsflow International matched the preceding two. She spent more than an hour trying to get into Encomp and Innsflow in Grand Cayman and was consistently rejected.

'Mystery upon mystery,' she said, at once embarrassed at having spoken aloud, although she often did when upon such expeditions from her Princes Street apartment. She answered the manager's enquiring look with a half wave and a gesture towards her empty coffee cup, genuinely needing a refill after being so effectively and irritatingly defeated.

Knowing the frequency with which initial registrations were often used as cut-outs in much the same way as she was using the hotel chain's computer set-up, she surfed all the Caribbean offshore islands for minimal variations on the three parent companies she was trying to penetrate but found nothing she considered a possibility. Alice spread the search further afield, to Switzerland and Israel, but found nothing. She entered the market registrations in London, Frankfurt, Tokyo, Singapore and on Wall Street – even though any listing should have shown with her first search entry of the names – with the same lack of success. Which was the same when she hacked into the newspaper reference archives of the *Wall Street Journal*, the *New York Times* and *The Times* in London, the *Washington Post*, London's *Financial Times*, *Fortune* and *Forbes*.

Alice recognized that the surfeit of subsidiary but linked

names risked overwhelming her, certainly in such public surroundings. She needed the quiet, reflective security of Princes Street. And to try to evolve a way to get past the Grand Cayman hacking shield. As she, with forced patience, printed out the state-by-state and international listings, Alice conceded to herself that it was not the first time she'd drawn such a total blank. But she couldn't remember it happening more than twice before. And both of those had eventually emerged under police investigation to be criminal enterprises, which objectively she further acknowledged had no real bearing on this attempt but which nevertheless inclined her to regard it in that light. It took her a further thirty minutes to print out.

As Alice paid for her time the manager said: 'You've been working hard.'

'Not sure what I've got,' complained Alice.

'There's good days and bad days.'

'Today's a confused day.'

'Come back again: better luck next time.'

'I think I'm going to have to come back a lot,' said Alice. After all, she had a new Trojan Horse password in an unsuspecting host system and John might come up with something that would give her a short cut. How long would it be before she and John could get together again? Not long, she hoped.

Jack Jennings was in the hallway, waiting for him, when Carver got back, and he said at once: 'Mrs Carver's just woken up. The doctor's with her. And Manhattan called. The helicopter will be here by eleven thirty.'

Carver held back from going directly upstairs, instead gesturing the other man towards the study and going immediately to the desk holding the unidentified keys, which he laid out close to the wedding photograph of Muriel Northcote. 'I need your help with these, Jack. You know what the unidentified ones fit?'

Jennings stared down for several moments, separating some from others with a finger before isolating a second country-club locker, the pool house and several garden-equipment outhouses. One had housed the fatal tractor. Three were left unnamed and Carver thought one, oddly coloured red, could have been a safe deposit or left-luggage locker.

Carver said: 'You don't know these three?'

Jennings shook his head. 'Don't mean anything at all.'

'Something else,' encouraged Carver. 'Where did Mr Northcote keep things: things that needed to be carefully looked after?'

Jennings indicated the bookcase cupboard. 'The safe, I guess.'

'Nowhere else? No special place?'

There was another head shake. 'No, sir. Nothing like that.'

'What about yesterday?' persisted Carver, sure he was right about how Northcote had been tortured. 'It's a long way from the house, I know. But I think you might have heard if Mr Northcote yelled out, when he fell?'

'If he had and I'd heard it – if anyone had heard it – I'd have gone looking. I didn't hear any cry for help. Nor, obviously, did anyone else in the house.'

'Anyone visit Mr Northcote yesterday? A stranger, maybe? Someone you didn't know?'

'No, sir. No one came all day.'

'So there was nothing.'

The other man considered the question. 'There was a phone call.'

'What phone call?'

'Just after lunch. It was a man who said he wanted to talk to Mr Northcote. I asked for a name but he said it didn't matter: that Mr Northcote was expecting the call. Which seemed to be right. Mr Northcote heard the phone and came out into the hall behind me. Would have got it first if I hadn't already been there.'

'Did you hear the conversation?'

The butler's face stiffened. 'I don't listen to other people's telephone conversations, Mr Carver. Anyway, Mr Northcote took it in here, in the study.'

'Had he told you before then that he was going to take the mower out?'

Jennings frowned, in recollection. 'No, not before then.'

'So he wasn't dressed for it: wasn't in his usual work overalls?'

'No.'

'How'd he seem, after the call?'

Jennings shrugged. 'Just like always.'

'Were you with him when he left the house? See him?'

Jennings looked curiously at Carver. 'I wasn't with him. I saw him through the kitchen going towards the tractor lock-up.'

'Was he carrying anything . . . anything like an envelope?'

The man paused. 'Has something come up with the sheriff, Mr Carver?'

'No,' said Carver. 'Just one or two things I need to get sorted out in my mind.' When Jennings didn't speak Carver said: 'So, was he carrying anything like an envelope in his hand?'

'No, sir,' said the other man. 'He was just setting out to drive his tractor!'

Jane was still in bed, propped up against the backboard, when Carver got to the room. Jamieson was in a chair alongside.

She smiled up wanly and said: 'Hello.'

'Hello.'

'You OK?'

'Yeah.'

'It all go OK?'

'I guess.'

She nodded towards Jamieson and said: 'There's a helicopter coming?'

'Everyone's coming in for the conference.'

'Sure.'

'I don't want to leave you here by yourself.'

'I don't want to stay here by myself.'

'Take your time.' There was at least an hour, Carver knew, without needing to consult his watch.

'How was it?'

Carver instinctively looked to the doctor for guidance. Jamieson remained turned too far away for any facial hint. 'I had to say it was George, that's all. A formality.'

'Would it have been bad?' There were no tears and her voice was quite even. It almost sounded like a casual enquiry.

'Pete Simpson was positive about that . . .' Carver nodded to the half-turned figure of the local doctor. 'Charlie thinks it's possible your father had a stroke: that that's how the accident happened. If it wasn't that way, he would have been knocked out, hitting the cover guard of the mower. Either way he wouldn't have felt a thing.'

'It was blood pressure,' came in Jamieson, supportive at last. 'It was bad.'

'I'm glad he wouldn't have felt any pain.' Jane straightened, against the headboard. 'If I've got to get dressed I need space.'

Outside in the corridor, where they'd been the previous night, Carver said: 'She seems OK. Looks OK.'

'Remember what I said about denial.'

'This it?'

'I'd have liked her to be more obviously grieving.'

'Maybe she's more resilient than you guessed. Than any of us guessed.'

'Maybe,' said the doctor, doubtfully.

'You examined her?'

'Physically she's fine.'

Jane came downstairs with the arrival of the helicopter. As

they walked out towards it she said: 'We've got a lot to talk about.'

With the exception of one subject, thought Carver.

Stanley Burcher had a trained lawyer's objectivity and from every angle from which he examined the idea that had immediately come to him in the Queens restaurant the more he became convinced that it was perfect. He had actually raised with the *consiglieri* of the New York Families the problem of Northcote's age and impending retirement. Now there was no longer a problem. Northcote's informed and therefore complicit successor could simply continue to act as Northcote had acted for so long in the past. The man more than likely knew where Northcote had kept the withheld documentation, too.

It was tempting to tell the *consiglieri* how perfect his resolution was but Burcher decided to wait until he'd confronted Carver. He wondered if he would enjoy his association with the man as much as he had in the past with Northcote, until that very last meeting. Northcote had been stupid, imagining he could behave as he had.

Seven

It was not until Jack Jennings asked if he and the housekeeper were to fly back to Manhattan with him that Carver remembered that despite his earlier dismissal of there being any further possible hiding places apart from banks, George Northcote had another home in which the protective secrets could be concealed. That realization triggered more, the most pertinent a correction to another earlier misbelief. As George Northcote's already acknowledged successor, he *did* have the right of access to each and any safe-deposit vaults in all – if any – company vaults or additional banks. In which – although he had not yet properly looked – it was inconceivable that Northcote would have deposited any incriminating material, aware it would be too easily discovered. But knowing, as Carver did know from the will he was taking with him back to the city, that Jane was the controlling beneficiary, Carver accepted that he had no legal right to access any private security facility in any personal bank account George Northcote held. The only person who held that right under the terms of the will was Jane. How much more convoluted, spinning in upon itself, could this become?

Carver told the man that of course they should come and thanked him for suggesting something that had not occurred to him. Accustomed to commuting back and forth between the city and the country, both Jennings and the housekeeper had clothes permanently in each so there were only a few things necessary for them to pack. While they did so, Carver assembled what he had put aside from his search of the Litchfield house.

As they walked out to the helicopter, Jane nodded to the valise into which Carver had packed his previous night's discoveries and said: 'What's in there?'

'Stuff I think I might need.'

'Anything I should look at?'

'Nothing at all,' insisted Carver. She obviously knew of her inheritance. But not, he guessed, anything about the laughing, so-much-in-love photographs of her father and Anna which were in the case.

Inside the aircraft Jennings and the housekeeper determinedly placed themselves at a distance on the opposite side of the passenger cabin, an unnecessary but thoughtful courtesy. Directly after lift-off Jane said: 'Tell me what I need to know: everything that's happening.' They were practically over the city before Carver finished his strictly edited account.

Calmly, with no catch in her voice, Jane said: 'You haven't spoken to the funeral director yourself?'

'Hilda's setting everything up for me.'

'I'll take over the funeral arrangements. All of it,' announced Jane.

'Are you sure . . . ?' started Carver, but Jane stopped him.

'I'll do it.' Her voice was still calm, without a hint of hysteria, but at the same time positive, allowing no argument.

'OK.'

'What about Burt Elliott?'

'He's on my list for today.' Elliott was the family lawyer. Another likely secrets repository, Carver thought. But one to which Jane again had access over him.

'I'll do that, too,' declared Jane, in the same, no-argument tone.

Let it go, Carver decided, nodding in agreement. Better for Jane to occupy herself with as much activity as possible than to retreat within herself. Amateur psychology, he recognized.

But it seemed to fit: to serve a purpose. 'I've got Manuel and Luisa staying permanently at the apartment for a while,' Carver said.

'That'll probably be useful, with everyone in town,' accepted Jane.

'And some nurses,' he added, not looking directly at her.

'Some *what*!' Jane demanded, her voice rising for the first time.

'Charlie Jamieson thought it would be a good idea.'

'I don't. Cancel it.'

'It's fixed now. Let's see how it goes.'

'I don't want to see how anything goes. I'm OK. Really OK.'

'I want them around,' insisted Carver.

Jane turned more fully in her seat, to look at him. 'Is it important to you?'

'It's important to me.'

'It isn't to me, because I don't need nursing. I'll give them their minimum week and that'll be the end of it. I'll take care of that, too.'

'That's good.' If there was going to be a mood swing – a switch in her reaction – it would surely be during the next nerve-stretched week. Reminded, Carver said: 'Jamieson's also going to talk to Dr Newton.' Paul Newton was their Manhattan physician.

'I don't need a doctor and I don't need nurses!'

'You don't know that.'

'I *do* know that.'

'Charlie's only going to tell Paul what happened, so he's in the picture.'

'We all know what happened. Dad had an accident and got killed under an over-turned tractor.'

'It's right that Paul should know, one doctor to another.'

'I don't want to see him. I don't need *anyone*!'

On the other side of the cabin Jennings shifted uncomfortably.

'He needed to be told.'

'And I told you I'm quite all right!'

'I'm not,' honestly admitted Carver, deflating her vehemence.

At the 34th Street helipad the reception committee was made up of the company lawyer, the two most senior partners below Carver, Hilda Bennett and Janice Snow and, unexpectedly, a media contingent, photographers and two journalists, whose questions – the sound of words, not their content – were the first things of which Carver became aware when they cleared the noise of the helicopter. He moved to shield Jane but she shrugged him aside, stopping both for questions and pictures. A Wall Street legend had been taken from them, she said. They were all devastated. It was a mark of her father's professionalism that the future of the firm that bore his name had been guaranteed before his death by his personal choice of successor, her husband. The firm of George W. Northcote would be the memorial to the man who founded it.

Carver and Jane went into the lead car of their cross-town cavalcade, with the lawyer beside Carver and the two personal assistants facing them from the jump seats. As they began to move Carver said: 'How the hell was that allowed to happen!'

The lawyer, Geoffrey Davis, said: 'It's not something we anticipated. Or could have prevented.'

'It's all right,' said Jane, from the other side of the car.

Across Carver, the lawyer said: 'If you'll allow me, Mrs Carver, you did very well. Thank you.'

Belatedly Carver realized that from his unspeaking part in the impromptu press conference he would appear very much the puppet. 'There been a lot of media coverage?'

'Just the formal announcement, so far,' said Davis. 'It was late . . .'

Janice Snow said: 'I've got a list of interview requests.'

Carver at once wondered if Alice's was one of them and even more quickly was angry at the stupidity of the thought. He'd have to try to call her. 'I'm not sure if there'll be time today.'

'I'll do them,' declared Jane, beside him. 'It's got to be done today.'

'We'll do it together,' Carver recovered. To Hilda he said: 'What's the schedule?'

The matronly woman said: 'Partners at three, overseas people at four thirty. Drinks in the boardroom at five thirty.'

Carver said: 'Set up a press conference for me at six fifteen . . .'

'For both of us,' broke in Jane, addressing Hilda. 'I'm staying at the office . . .' She nodded to the cellphone on its central pod. 'Perhaps you'd call the funeral director now: fix a meeting there for me at four . . .' She paused. 'I'll use father's rooms.'

'Is that . . . ?' Carver started but stopped.

Jane said, heavy in rebuke: 'Thank you!'

There was a stir throughout the car, with Hilda looking imperceptibly at Carver, who hoped she noticed his equally imperceptible nod to indicate that Jane had to be humoured, in everything. He wouldn't be able to continue his intended search with Jane occupying her father's office! To his personal assistant he said: 'Perhaps, Hilda, you'd help Mrs Carver. You can be with me today, Janice.'

Both women nodded, Hilda at the same time reaching out for the console-mounted telephone.

Janice said: 'Everything you asked for last night has been fixed.'

As vital as it was he wouldn't anyway have had time today to go through Northcote's office and personal vault safe, Carver acknowledged. But Jane wouldn't be in the office tomorrow. Nor would it have been possible for him to have got to Northcote's apartment, where he'd told Jennings to disturb nothing, just tidy whatever needed tidying. Would there be a safe or a hidden place there that would open to one of the unidentified Litchfield keys at the bottom of the valise securely clamped between his legs? Deciding that it was a question that wouldn't upset Jane he said: 'What's the reaction been?'

There was a hesitancy between the lawyer and the two women. Finally Davis said: 'Overwhelming. We've got two girls listing the calls. I guess there'll be as many letters in tomorrow's mail.'

To Hilda, who was replacing the car phone, Jane said: 'I'll personally sign the reply to each one.'

Hilda looked to Carver for another nod of agreement. To Jane she said: 'Four's fine for the funeral people. And I'll keep a note of the letters and messages.'

Jane separated with Hilda the moment they reached the executive floor. Walking with Carver to his office suite, the lawyer said: 'Jane's standing up remarkably well.'

'Remarkably well,' agreed Carver. For how much longer, he wondered.

Within fifteen minutes of settling behind his own desk Carver fully realized just how impractical his idea of searching Northcote's office had been, even if he'd known exactly what he was looking *for*. He handed his diary over to Janice to rearrange his appointments over the next week, together with Northcote's valedictory address to be copied in time for the partners' meeting, which she managed, along with more than sufficient duplicates for the following overseas assembly. The partners' meeting inevitably began with the ritual of condolences, with which Carver supposed he and Jane would become all too familiar over the coming days. At the company secretary's insistence the partners took a formal vote of acceptance of Northcote's posthumous speech, which was repeated later at the gathering of the overseas chief executives, also attended by the American partners. At the combined meeting there was the additional formality, again insisted upon by the company secretary although this time endorsed by the lawyer, of another vote unanimously accepting Carver's succession. Carver hadn't anticipated the need to make this speech and in effect didn't. He thanked them for their support and confidence and in a jumble of clichés pleaded his inadequacy to fill Northcote's place but pledged to do his utmost to try, which would need the help and assistance of them all. There were grunts and mumbles of assurance when he said he hoped he would get that help and assistance.

Jane was waiting in his office and announced at once that the funeral would be in three days. She'd agreed the flowers and the limousines and booked the wake at the Plaza Hotel. There was to be a memorial service at Litchfield at the end of the month and, as he had already instructed, her father was to be interred alongside his late wife. The will was going to be read in Burt Elliott's office, which the household staff needed to attend to hear about their inheritances. She'd already told Jennings here in Manhattan to arrange that. The remaining staff at Litchfield were coming down in the morning. She'd called Al Hibbert to warn him there would be no one at the estate.

There was no hesitation – or question – in her accompanying Carver to the boardroom drinks gathering, where she spoke individually to practically everyone and called for silence to thank them for their condolences and to announce that the cocktail party at East 62nd Street, which had been cancelled, was going to be held after all and she looked forward to meeting the wives there.

'It's what my father would have expected of me,' she concluded.

Jane was totally composed at the press conference and although she deferred to Carver for most of it she was always ready when a question was directed personally at her. On their way uptown afterwards Carver said: 'I didn't think you'd want the cocktail party.'

'Like I said, it's what he would have expected. I've organized caterers and warned Manuel to expect their call. We're having steak tonight, incidentally. It was the easiest thing I could think of, with the uncertainty of our not knowing what time we'd be back. We're actually much earlier than I expected.'

'You've pretty much filled your day,' said Carver. In terms of actual achievement she'd accomplished far more than he had.

'How are you feeling?'

'*Me?*' said Carver, surprised.

'You're the *numero uno* now.'

He refused to recognize the real meaning of her question. 'I've been practising for over a year.'

'Frightened?' she demanded, openly.

'Of course I'm not,' Carver lied, although still not in direct answer to her intended question. 'Why should I be?'

'It's a responsibility. You've got an empire to protect and people will expect you to build another, to prove yourself.'

If only she knew what he had to protect! 'Like I said, I've had time to prepare.'

'I'm going to be right behind you, all of the way.'

At the apartment Jane thanked the senior nurse for their attendance but announced at once that they had been engaged prematurely and wouldn't be required beyond the contractually agreed first week. She didn't need painkillers for a headache or any other discomfort, nor would she require sedatives later.

As they ate, Jane said: 'She patronized me. Expects me to collapse. By the way, I spoke to Paul Newton. Told him I was all right and that it wasn't necessary for him to come over.'

She *would* collapse, Carver guessed. Not immediately. For

the moment – for the coming days – she was going to be wired by all the things that she'd determined personally to do. The breakdown would come when it all quietened: after the memorial service perhaps. He'd speak to Newton tomorrow. And quietly to the nurses, too.

Carver reached out consolingly to her when they got into bed that night and didn't anticipate her immediate expectation that they would make love and was even more astonished that he was able to and that it was as good as it was.

Afterwards she said: 'Dad had a saying, that there's always a birth to make up for a death.'

Carver shifted, unsure what to say. 'I never heard it.'

'We should have a baby, John.'

'We've talked about it,' reminded Carver. But not recently, he reminded himself. He'd actually put the thought out of his mind and didn't, in the present circumstances, welcome its return.

'Not properly. Like we haven't tried properly. I want to undergo IVF treatment.' If she could become pregnant she would be continuing her father's bloodline. She wanted very much to do that.

'We'll talk about it later,' said Carver.

'You're patronizing me, like the nurse. This isn't hysteria. I've been thinking about it for a long time. Now's the *right* time.'

It wasn't, thought Carver. Now wasn't the right time for anything.

People who deal in them – accountants, financiers, bankers, mathematicians – can see a beauty in figures and the patterns that their controlling logic dictates. But it was not actually a pattern of figures that Alice Belling believed she saw when she began going through the printouts of all the worldwide subsidiaries of Mulder Inc., Encomp and Innsflow International. To confirm it she hauled a world atlas on to her desk and was sure she was right as far as the United States was concerned – which if she *were* right made them very united indeed – and the templates first of Europe and then of Asia were sufficient further to convince her. The temptation to start at once from her terminal in Princes Street was very strong but prudence won over impatience. Using the cyber-cafe gave her a second cut-out and considering the organization she believed she had discovered, Alice acknowledged that she needed to continue as carefully and as protectively as possible. Which meant waiting until tomorrow. Even though the cafe didn't open until ten she was still up by seven, determined not to forget anything because today was going to be a long one.

John Carver was up by seven, too, so he was fully awake when Al Hibbert telephoned from Litchfield. Hibbert said: 'Everything's wrecked, John. I've never seen a place stripped like it. It's terrible. Bastards!'

Stanley Burcher was irritated at the need constantly to cross the river to meet the Deliocis but acknowledged that he had to show the respect of going to them, on their territory. He also acknowledged that he'd gone too far, confronting the old man as he had, at the last encounter. He knew the New York Families would back him, if Emilio Delioci protested. But they'd be unsettled by the way he'd spoken to a Don, even a minor one. It was essential that he recover by replacing Northcote with Carver to keep the system working smoothly.

The Thomson Avenue restaurant wasn't open but they were waiting for him in the back room, the old man, the elder son and Family heir, Enrico Delioci, and Paolo Brescia. Burcher wondered idly if they had cots in a closet somewhere, so that they were able to sleep in the damned place. He said: 'So what did you find?'

'Nothing.' It was Enrico who replied, to spare his father the embarrassment.

'Nothing!' echoed Burcher, disbelieving. 'There must have been something.' It would be he who switched the operation to John Carver, so there wouldn't be any need in the future to deal with this amateur crew who believed muscle was the answer to everything: in future it would just be he and Carver and all the power-by-association that the arrangement would give him.

'I was there,' said Brescia. 'We took the place apart, everything. Kept the cash and valuables, to make it look like a burglary. But there was none of the documentation or the names you gave us.'

'Then who's got it?' demanded Burcher.

'Maybe it wasn't there,' wheezed Emilio Delioci.

Burcher looked at the son. 'You made the call, telling him you were sending collectors, right?'

'Right,' agreed the darkly saturnine man.

'What did he say . . . the exact words?'

'That he'd talked it all out with you. That there wasn't any point in our coming because there was nothing to collect.'

'What about when your people were trying to persuade him?'

Brescia said: 'He died without saying anything about documents. But Carver knows. That's what Northcote said – Carver knows.'

'Let's not forget the woman, the personal assistant,' said Enrico. 'You want we should ask her?'

A trick, Burcher instantly realized. They were putting the responsibility on to him, covering themselves if anything went wrong as it had up in Litchfield. 'Not like you asked Northcote. Looks like you got away with it but I don't want to stretch coincidence unless we have to.'

'What then?' demanded the old man.

Another trick, thought Burcher. It really hadn't been a mistake insisting his word was the word of the Families.

Burcher said: 'I guess I – and the people I speak for – have to get personally involved.' As much as he wanted to do that and pick up the recognition, Burcher felt a stir of uncertainty as he spoke.

Eight

Jack Jennings flew with them and as they began to descend over the Litchfield estate Carver gazed down at the assembled police vehicles with a feeling of déjà vu. The impression was heightened by it being the same pilot in the same helicopter and of their landing almost in the same place as before, to avoid those on the ground being disturbed by the down draught. And as before Al Hibbert was already on his way towards them when they hurried from the machine.

The sheriff said: 'This sure as hell isn't what you needed, on top of everything else.' When he saw Jane he said: 'Sorry, Mrs Carver. Didn't realize it was you.'

Jane shook her head impatiently and said: 'How bad is it?'

'As bad as I've ever seen around these parts. Worse,' said Hibbert. 'The place – the house as well as the outhouses, the pool house and all the staff quarters – hasn't just been turned over, to get anything and everything that's valuable. It's been totally trashed.'

It had.

Very little furniture in any of the rooms remained intact. Seats and cushions were slashed apart and the frames and coverings of couches and formal and easy chairs dismembered. Every drawer of every desk and cabinet had been taken out, upended and then broken into pieces: Northcote's antique study desk had been crowbarred apart into something close to matchwood and the heavy, button-backed desk chair disembowelled. Every book on the shelves had been taken down and its leaves torn out and strewn across the floor. The doors of the cupboards below had been wrenched off their hinges. The safe gaped open, empty. The drapes hung in shreds. Carver was glad he'd salvaged Northcote's family photographs: every one that remained had been smashed. The devastation, through which protectively white-overalled forensic specialists were working, was repeated throughout the ground floor. It was only when they reached the sprawling, split-level drawing room that Carver realized through the mess that no antique ornament or any of the silver that Northcote had collected remained. Nor did any of the paintings, prints or original nineteenth-century photographs of early American settlers and native American tribes, a collection in itself unique if not antique.

The kitchen and staff accommodation had been overturned, in some instances literally. Three huge, free-standing fridge freezers had been thrown forward off their feet but only after the doors had been opened, for their contents to smash and now seep over the floor. The same destruction had been carried out on two separate, smaller refrigerators. Every single thing in every storage cupboard had been heaped, smashed, on the floor, to mix with the seepage from the freezers. What wine and spirits had not been taken from the cellar were smashed and soaked the floor.

Every room in the staff wing was demolished, apart from the shell itself, even to every article of clothing being slashed beyond repair and every personal item – photographs, ornaments, momentoes – smashed.

Because there was so much soft furnishing and bedding the havoc appeared worse upstairs because every piece – bed coverings, duvets, pillows, mattresses, couches and easy chairs – had been eviscerated. The carpet had even been lifted in Northcote's bedroom and adjoining dressing room, where all his suits hung in tatters from their rails and in the middle of which were piled slashed shirts and sweaters.

Hibbert said: 'It's the same in the outhouses. Everything – cars, equipment – totally wrecked.'

Carver saw that Jennings was standing with a handkerchief to his face, silently crying. Jane was gazing around, face unmoving, quite emotionless. His voice muffled, the butler said: 'Everything's gone . . . there's nothing left.'

'This wasn't local,' insisted Hibbert, defensively. 'I know the people around here, particularly the bad ones. They burglarize, sure. But not much. And when they do they don't do this. Here's how I see it. There's a lot of publicity, in the city. It's a professional gang. And got to be a heavy gang of four, five, maybe more, guys to do all this. Overturn things like the freezers downstairs and tear off doors as they did. They decide on a big hit. They drive up – it would need a truck, obviously – and see the staff go: it's in the papers that everyone's going to Manhattan for the funeral. With the staff gone, they've got the whole place to themselves, to do with what they want.'

Would they have found what he hadn't? wondered Carver, impatiently uninterested in the country sheriff's failed theorizing. It would have been impossible for anything anywhere here to have remained undiscovered. Stirring himself, if only for another token protest, he said: 'Why trash it? Why not do what you think your locals would have done, simply steal what's valuable?'

'Looking for something that wasn't so obviously sitting around to be snatched,' said Hibbert, with unwitting perceptiveness.

'What about the burglar alarm?' demanded Jane, speaking at last.

'Proof that they're professionals, like their being able to open the safe,' said the sheriff, at once. 'Place as remote from any utilities as this has to be an individual electricity supply, a pole-mounted cable coming off the main supply, way down in the lane by the lake. And then carried here through two other pole mountings, with transformer boosting. Forensics have already found the gizmo. A bypass clamp between the input cable and the transformer on the last pole. The cable's cut in between, immobilizing the system, but the alarm that should go off precisely *when* the cable is cut doesn't operate because it's still got a local battery supply.'

'A system like that has to be at least thirty years old!' exclaimed Jane. 'Maybe more.'

'At least,' agreed Hibbert, shaking his head. 'Litchfield's a peaceful place, most times. Folks around here don't think much of updating their equipment, once it's in.'

Northcote hadn't bothered to hide the still unstudied BHYF and NOXT documents that had been in the night-stand, remembered Carver. Carelessness, like not bothering about an out-of-date alarm system? Or complacency, Northcote's belief after so many unthreatened, unendangered years that he had mob protection far more effective than anything electrical. Carver said: 'Perhaps now they will.'

'Forensics are going through the place as minutely as the burglars did,' promised the sheriff. 'They couldn't have done all this without leaving something behind. We'll find it.'

'That kitchen floor's a mess,' reminded Carver. 'Difficult not to have left a footprint, I would have thought?' Why was he bothering, he asked himself again.

'Now maybe,' agreed Hibbert. 'It would have taken time for it all to leak out like it has. By then they would have moved on. I already thought about it.'

He deserved that put-down for attempting to play Sherlock Holmes, Carver accepted. 'If there was no burglar alarm, how come you discovered the break-in?'

The big-bellied man nodded towards Jane. 'Mrs Carver's call, yesterday. Telling me that the staff were all going early into the city. Told one of my car patrols to drive by every so often. When one did, first time this morning, the front door was wide open. He didn't need to go in and see the state of the place to work out what had happened.'

'There's nothing left to steal,' declared Jane, decisively. 'We'll go back to New York, do what we have to do there. I'll tell the insurance people and perhaps you'll come back directly after the funeral, to be here, Jack . . . ?' She paused, looking around the destroyed bedroom. 'When you come back you'll need to bring a sleeping bag.'

'You got any idea what might be missing, Mrs Carver?' asked Hibbert. 'It's important for the crime report.'

'Absolutely none at all,' said Jane, uncaringly. 'It could be listed on the insurance details. I'll get the underwriters to contact you.'

'I'd appreciate it.'

In the helicopter on the way back yet again to the city, Carver said: 'Hibbert was right. We didn't need that.' So much was crowding in on him that Carver found it difficult to get his thoughts in sequence: in any order at all. He needed space, an uninterrupted hour, to think.

'It's a decision reached for us,' announced Jane, conclusively. 'The house would have been sold anyway: I certainly wouldn't have wanted to keep it, after what happened. Now we just throw everything out for garbage and call in the realtor.'

'If that's what you want,' said Carver.

Jane said: 'I wonder what they were looking for?'

As he unlocked the door the cybercafe manager said: 'Here again, bright and early,' and Alice remembered that during her interview with George Northcote he'd told her his work adage had always been that the early bird caught the fattest worms and hoped he was right in her case. She said: 'I told you yesterday I've got a lot to do.'

She set out to work alphabetically, state by state, through her American subsidiary company listings for Mulder Inc., Encomp and Innsflow International, which started her in Alabama, where Mulder Supplies Inc. was headquartered in Birmingham, with ten outlets throughout the state. She spent a firewall-blocked hour password-probing, which by hacking standards was hardly any time at all, but which Alice calculated against the number of sites she wanted to penetrate would take her two months, working eight hours a day, seven days a week and then only if she allowed herself two hours successfully to get into each one. It was far easier – taking just ten minutes – getting into Alabama's state tax records. There were filed-ahead-of-time returns for Mulder Supplies Inc. for the past five years, each showing a rising, after-tax profit. The first had been $250,000, the last $1,800,000. It took Alice less time – just five minutes – to find the password into the local Companies Register to confirm the trading designation for Mulder Supplies Inc. was as a blank video tape provider to Mulder's entertainment division, the history of which was in the so far impenetrable Grand Cayman parent company files. She tried again – and failed – to get into Mulder Supplies headquarters before, strictly according to her alphabetical schedule, moving as far north as it was possible to get, to Anchorage, Alaska. She gave herself another hour to get undetected into Mulder Marine and was again defeated, but got into the state tax files just as easily as she had in Alabama, and they were again immaculate. Once more – although this time for only three of the last trading years – they showed an ever-increasing after-tax profit, that of the last year $2,750,000. The Companies Register listed the business, with five separately managed companies, listed as seafood providers to Mulder's restaurant and hotel division, once more disappearing into the Cayman parent company.

Alice had drunk her way through five cups of coffee by midday and was hot with the frustration of not being able to get where – and what – she wanted. What she *did* have were the immaculately kept financial records of a pyramid of seemingly superbly managed companies which never suffered financial setback and whose profits climbed each year to new heights. It was far too soon to reach even ballpark conclusions but calculated against the minimum after-tax returns she'd so far accessed, Alice estimated that if every subsidiary of Mulder Inc. showed annually cleared profits of $2,000,000, the yearly income into the tax exempt Grand Cayman was in excess of a billion dollars. And conceivably could – if she worked her way through all the subsidiaries and their associated companies – be double, even treble, that.

All legal. Except that it wasn't legal. If what she believed she was seeing had been true for God knows how many years, millions – trillions – had been laundered sparkling white. But there was no proof: no evidence. Why, for fuck's sake, hadn't John Carver demanded Northcote's personal files straight away? But John always expected rectitude, or something close. She, always, expected the wrong, the sly, the manipulative and the questionable. The dichotomy hadn't arisen between them before. But now John, financially brilliant but . . . Alice hesitated at continuing the judgement but then did, because it needed to be continued . . . naive in the back alleys of the professional money netherworld, was potentially being sucked down into a blackness he'd never known. And one from which he was going to need help to find his way out. Her help.

What – in which direction – was her way, the way she needed to go to find the all-important, so-far missing conduit? Which there had to be, a pathway along those black alleys through which those millions were carried to be untraceably lost in the sunshine of the Caribbean.

England. It was a logical choice, because Alice didn't speak any of the languages of the other European or Asian countries, although she was more than able to interpret their figures and hopefully the patterns they made.

In England Mulder Inc. was registered, ironically, in Cheapside, London, and predictably she was defeated attempting to break into their Caribbean system using their local password. She found English subsidiaries for Mulder, Encomp and Innsflow spread throughout the country, from Brighton and Bristol in the south to Manchester, Liverpool and Newcastle in the north. It was in Liverpool that she penetrated the local tax office and pulled up the returns for the previous seven years, which – predictably again – showed a rising after-tax profit. In the last full financial year, it had been £2,700,000. But, at last, there was more. The Liverpool company, Mulder Enterprises, was listed as a video and CD supply company, owned again by the Cayman parent company, but also recorded on the tax return was importation from the Alabama supply company through an import-export company named as BHYF International. The Companies Register recorded a branch office in London, with headquarters in Toronto, Canada. There were subsidiaries in Paris, Berlin, Rome and Tokyo. It took Alice four further hours to penetrate every relevant British tax office and in every case their overseas trade was conducted through BHYF International.

Alice hadn't realized it was dark until the cafe manager, who'd provided her with coffee and offered sandwiches – which she'd declined – appeared at her elbow and said: 'We're closing in an hour. You seemed kind of engrossed. It happens, once you get caught up in the Web.'

It was a line he'd used before, she guessed. She said: 'Thanks. I guess I'll need the hour. Maybe a lot more.'

Which she almost at once realized she would. For that last hour she computed every password she could think of for Encomp and was consistently rejected, which by now was not an unfamiliar experience. As she paid the manager said: 'I've seen some concentration: you're way up at the top.'

Alice said: 'I don't like being at the bottom.'

The man, whom she guessed to be around thirty, said: 'That's not my speed either: hurts too much. But maybe you'd get the cramp out if I bought you a drink?'

That most definitely was a line he'd used before, she decided, at the same time as accepting that she was cramped, over her back and shoulders. 'Thanks, but no. It's been a long day that a drink won't fix.'

'Another time maybe?'

'Maybe.'

'Am I going to see you tomorrow?'

'Don't be late opening up.'

'I'm Bill, by the way,' he said, invitingly.

'Alice.'

'Look forward to seeing you tomorrow, Alice.'

Jane was the superlative hostess at the welcoming cocktail party. People arrived protectively en masse, with obvious pre-planning, and in the first minutes remained respectfully subdued. Jane quickly put people at their ease, circulating among the couples as easily as she had earlier moved among the overseas executives, chatting – laughing occasionally – and towards the end making the briefest of announcements that she would regard the following night's dinner as a tribute to her father, not his wake.

Carver was anxious for the reception to end and the moment it did announced there were things he had to do and locked himself into his study, hesitating before picking up the telephone to call Alice, never before having called her from the apartment while Jane was there. Alice picked up the telephone on its second ring and the moment she recognized his voice she said: 'Where are you?'

'At the apartment.'

'Where's Jane?'

'Here.'

'It isn't a good idea.'

'Just listen,' he insisted, which she did without interruption as he told her about the ransacking of Northcote's Litchfield house.

Her reaction was not what he expected. Instead of expressing surprise she said, quiet-voiced: 'We need to meet.' It would mean finally disclosing her hacking but things were happening too fast – too dangerously – for that any longer to be a consideration.

'You know I can't!'

'Now you listen. I think I've got something.'

'What!'

'About those companies.'

'I told you not to do anything.' Why had he been stupid enough to tell her in the first place!

'It's quite safe.'

'You know damned well it's not.'

'You'll understand when I explain.'

'Stop it, whatever it is you're doing.'

'I think I know how it's done. Maybe even how George set it up. It's brilliant.'

'Alice, darling! Please don't do anything else – anything more – until we meet.'

'When?'

'Not until after the funeral.'

It gave her a lot of time, Alice calculated.

Although he was the liaison between all five New York Families, Stanley Burcher reported directly to the *consigliere* of the Genovese organization. Charlie Petrie was a non-Italian, like Burcher, and like Burcher a qualified lawyer. There was no regular pattern of contact between them but Petrie always knew when Burcher was in Manhattan and where to find him if there was a need. Burcher liked the Algonquin, both for its history and for its discretion. Burcher's automatic thought, when Petrie's call came, was that there had been a complaint against him from the Delioci people and he was early for their appointment in the lounge, mentally rehearsing his responses to the expected accusations. Petrie was early, too, a conservatively dressed, undistinguished man but unlike Burcher someone who occasionally attracted the sort of attention Burcher shunned, exuding the confidence that came from being imbued with power. It occurred now in the quickness with which a waiter was at their side, before they'd finished shaking hands. They ordered coffee. Burcher had selected a table and chairs beyond the hearing of anyone else in the lounge.

Petrie said: 'We're getting some worried calls, from around the country.'

'The Deliocis made a total mess,' said Burcher, deciding upon attack for defence. 'Their *capo* didn't even go personally to make the collection from Northcote.'

'Do you tell him to?'

Careful, thought Burcher. And then, quickly, came up with the perfect response. 'I didn't have the authority to *tell* them, when I arranged the collection . . . that would have been disrespectful.' He was sure the smile was properly apologetic. 'Which I'm afraid I was, when I heard what happened.'

Petrie shook his head, dismissively. 'How's it all going to be sorted?'

Burcher accepted he was going to have to commit himself. 'Before he died, Northcote told them his successor knew all about it. Which is perfect. He just carries on where Northcote literally stopped. Everything goes on uninterrupted.'

Petrie smiled. 'That's good. This is why I called you, to hear how it goes on. We've got other outside accountants, sure, but no one with Northcote's overview. You think Northcote trained the new guy up?'

Now it was Burcher who shook his head. 'No. As we've already said, when we met that last time he was stupid. Said he'd held things back that would be embarrassing for everybody and that it was his insurance against the firm being involved any more. I told him not to be ridiculous and that he had to return everything he'd kept. He said he was going up to the country, so I told him we'd pick it up there.'

'Our accountants inside should have picked up what he was doing,' conceded Petrie.

'It was too sweet for too long,' said Burcher. 'Everyone got sloppy.'

'How you going to bring the new guy into line, if he thinks he can say no?'

'Working on it,' said Burcher.

'There's another problem,' announced Petrie. 'Doesn't involve you but you should know about it. Like you said, people were getting sloppy. There's been a tightening up. One of our electronic whizz-kids picked up someone trying to hack into our subsidiaries. Happens a lot but this seems to have happened too much, like they were being targeted.'

'Where's the hacking from?'

'England. But our guys don't think that's the origin.' He shrugged. 'I don't understand what the hell they're talking about. They say they can find out where, though.'

'I thought there were ways of making that impossible?'

'So did I. It's a problem, people not doing the job they're paid to do.'

Nine

The entire Litchfield staff, under the autocratic command of Jack Jennings, was already assembled at the lawyer's office when Carver and Jane arrived, also early, for the reading of the will. The atmosphere in the shuffling, near-silent ante-room was palpably a mixture of uncertainty, self-recrimination and embarrassment.

At once Jane said: 'Let's get a few things out of the way, before we go in. Firstly, the robbery – what's happened – up at Litchfield is not anybody's fault or responsibility. I brought you back here and I am glad I did: people who did what they did to Dad's home would have badly hurt anyone who had been there, in their way . . .'

Not hurt, thought Carver. *Killed.* If there'd been a caretaker – despite whatever had been published in the newspapers – who'd emerged at whatever period of the invasion, he or she would have been killed. Feeling he should contribute, Carver said: 'That's absolutely right: we – you've – been lucky, by not being there . . .'

'Like I said,' Jane cut him off. 'That's the first thing. Here's the second. It gets rid of the place, which I would obviously have done anyway . . .' The pause was perfectly, theatrically, timed. 'You're here to hear my father's gratitude, which I want to extend. Thank you for looking after him as well and as faithfully as you did, for so many years. He loved you all as much as you loved and cared for him . . .' The next pause was just as well staged. 'Now we come to the third point I want to make. No one's job goes. You're all going to be absorbed between our place here, in Manhattan, and our place in Litchfield. We all stay together, OK . . . ?'

The relieved acceptance was as palpable as the earlier ambience.

'That's how it's going to be. But if any of you wish to leave, after today, then of course you go with our love and best wishes. And with the best references it's possible for me to give you . . .'

Before there could be any response Burt Elliott's secretary appeared to usher them into a room in which chairs were already set out in rows. The lawyer came forward at once to greet Carver and Jane and personally led them towards two larger, wide-armed and high-backed chairs which segregated them from everyone else. Carver sat self-consciously. Jane showed no discomfort.

Elliott, a large, bulbous-featured man, began with the prepared expressions of sympathy and regret, to which Carver closed himself off, not hearing the words but watching the man and his attitude, particularly towards Jane. Burt Elliott could be the person with whom Northcote had deposited the firm's escape. Nothing Elliott could read, obviously. A discreet sealed envelope or package. That's what lawyers were for, discreet exchanges of discreet information. Jane would demand to know what it was if he were handed something today. There would be an evasion of sorts in his dismissing it as something involving the firm, although logically that would have been deposited with the firm's lawyer, not Burt Elliott. Personal insurance that protected the company, mentally snatched Carver: it wasn't good – hardly good enough at all, confronted by Jane's newly emerged attitude – but he arranged such schemes every week and he was sure he could talk convincingly enough to satisfy Jane's curiosity.

Elliott had got to the bequests now, itemizing the individual legacies. The housekeeper and the cook were already crying and Jennings broke down too when the amount of his gift was declared.

'There are individual, personal letters of gratitude to each of you, from Mr Northcote,' said the lawyer, offering envelopes to each. There were still some remaining when he finished and the lawyer said to Carver: 'There are also some bestowals for his personal staff at the firm, with instructions that they should be handed to you to be dispersed.'

'Of course,' accepted Carver, needing physically to stop himself grabbing out for the envelopes and further restraining himself from at once searching through for one addressed to him. He delayed until a disruption was caused by the staff withdrawing, at Elliott's suggestion, to the ante-room while the family details of the will were read. There were envelopes for Janice Snow and Northcote's secretarial staff but nothing in Carver's name.

The rest of the meeting was brief. Jane, who already knew, accepted without any reaction whatsoever that she was a millionairess in her own right. Carver's instinctive thought at the declaration of his gift was that Northcote, the consummate accountant, had taken every measure to prevent either he or Jane paying more than the absolute minimum in tax.

Carver seized his opportunity when Jane preceded him out into the ante-room, to more tears and individual thanks from the still-assembled staff. He stopped at the communicating door of the office, blocking the escorting Elliott, and said: 'Wasn't there anything else for me?'

'Anything else?' frowned the lawyer.

'A package maybe? An envelope?'

Elliott shook his head. 'You've got all there was. What were you expecting?'

'Something to do with the firm,' said Carver, using the avoidance he'd planned for Jane.

Elliott shook his head again. 'Sorry.'

Carver got to Jane's side as Jennings was announcing that with almost twenty-four hours before the funeral he intended returning to Litchfield, with the housekeeper and the gardener, to continue the clearing-out.

When he asked if she were quite sure she wanted everything thrown away Jane said: 'I never want to see the place again. Or anything that was in it.'

As they drove back to Wall Street, Carver said: 'You didn't tell me we were going to take everyone on.'

'I didn't decide myself until we were on our way to hear the will. We're stretched, with our own place at Litchfield as well as the apartment here.'

'We've managed well enough so far.'

'There'll probably be a lot more entertaining, now that you've properly taken over. Before we were married and I was living at home there were times when we had people in every night.'

Would Northcote's real paymasters have been among the guests, wondered Carver. 'They can't all live in, here in Manhattan.'

Jane turned more fully towards him. 'Is there a problem?'

'None. I just think you might have mentioned it to me first.'

'I told you, I didn't decide until we were on our way to Burt Elliott's office. I'm sorry.'

She didn't sound it, thought Carver. 'So where will they live?'

'We keep on the apartments Dad set up for them here in Manhattan. It's tax-deductible, isn't it?'

'I'll have to see the scheme he used.'

'If Dad devised it, it works. So we're agreed, there's no problem.'

'OK.'

'What were you talking about to Burt as we left?'

'Thanking him, that's all,' said Carver.

* * *

Carver endured more tears and gratitude from Northcote's office staff and asked Janice Snow to stay when everyone else began filing out of the office, their bequest envelopes in hand. Janice said: 'I'm glad we can talk. The girls are worried about what's going to happen to them . . . and I'd like to know what's going to happen, too . . .'

He should have anticipated it, accepted Carver. But it was a convenient opening. 'I haven't had time to discuss it with the other partners but I'm not planning to let anyone go. Most certainly not you. You're going to have to help me a whole lot for the transition to be as seamless as possible.'

'What about Hilda?'

'We'll have to work it out,' improvised Carver. 'Off the top of my head I don't see why you can't both work in tandem. The work's going to be there.'

'I'm grateful. Very grateful. The girls will be, too.'

As she made to stand Carver said: 'That's not all I want to talk about . . .' and placed Northcote's three unidentified keys on the desk between them. 'You recognize any of these?'

The woman did get up, to pick through the tiny collection. She at once separated one and said: 'That's his personal safe key, in the vault downstairs . . .' She isolated another. 'And that's my safe key, here in the office. I'd got another from security, thinking I'd lost it. I don't know what he was doing with it . . .' She smiled up. 'He was getting very absent-minded about things lately . . . leaving things unlocked.'

Didn't he know it! thought Carver, feeling a warmth of satisfaction surge through him. Everything had to be in Northcote's personal safe! That's where he'd seen the inflated draft accounts for Mulder, Encomp and Innsflow and that's where they'd still be. When he found . . . With difficulty Carver halted the thought, bringing himself back to the woman, who'd sat down again. What he'd imagined at Litchfield to be a security key remained unidentified on the desk. 'You don't know that one?'

'I've never seen it before,' said Janice, positively.

Genuine ignorance or what he'd suspected to be avoidance on the telephone? Carver breathed in deeply, preparing the new approach. 'I want to talk some more about those three companies that George kept very much to himself.'

'There were others,' announced Janice at once. 'One's called BHYF, the other NOXT.'

She wouldn't have offered them like that, if she were part of it, Carver thought. 'Five, in all?'

'That's all. I've checked.'

'Anything retained, of George's copies?'

'Not on the computer: I did the computer filing for him, remember? I would have known.'

'What about hard copies?'

'They'd be in his personal safe, in the vault, if there are any. He would have run them off himself if he'd wanted to.'

'You haven't looked?'

The woman shook her head. 'With so much uncertainty now I waited for you to come back.'

'Good,' nodded Carver. 'To do the independent audit George would have needed the books . . . invoices . . . how did they get here?'

'I don't know,'

'You don't know! You dealt with all his mail . . . all his deliveries, didn't you?'

'I never received anything in the mail. Or by personal delivery. Mr Northcote met a lot of clients personally. I told you that on the telephone. I always assumed that's how he got the accounts, handed over personally.'

'You handled his appointments diary – which I need to go through with you – so how often did the Mulder people come here to see George?'

'I don't remember anyone actually coming here, to the office. Although it could easily have happened. People often gave just their names, without saying who they represented.'

Or even initials, like S–B, and rarely lunched with Northcote in the same place twice, thought Carver.

'Why are you asking me about these special clients?' Janice demanded, abruptly.

'Because they are special: different from the rest,' said Carver, deciding he was giving nothing away by being honest. 'I need to know why they were dealt with like this, which isn't usual.' He hesitated. 'I got the impression that George was thinking of ending the firm's association. He say anything about that to you?'

'Never,' said Janice.

He was trying too hard, too quickly. Unless, that is, Janice Snow was part of the conspiracy. It would make sense to have someone else in the firm, ensuring Northcote stayed in line. And explain her vagueness now, despite her earlier giving him the names of the last two companies. Who had been Northcote's PA before Janice? And how had Janice Snow come to be employed? Personnel would have her records. Maybe even those of her predecessor. And if . . . Carver once more consciously halted the drift, realizing how easy it was becoming to make shapes out of shadows. George Northcote's personal office safe wasn't in the shadows any more. The key was right there in front of him on the desk, waiting to be used. He said: 'It's going to take a while for me to understand how George worked: to understand his special relationship with his special clients. Time we haven't got today. Why don't you go and tell the girls that they're all OK? And try to remember some names. You think you could do that?'

'I'm sure I could,' promised Janice. 'And thank you again.'

It was not until he actually got to the gates of the vault that the analogy occurred to Carver. They were exactly that, floor-to-ceiling metal-barred gates that looked, unnervingly, like the cell doors in every prison movie he'd ever seen, quite often with a man shouting through them that he was innocent or had been framed. For the first time Carver realized that George Northcote's personal safe was an old-fashioned, key-operated twin to that in Litchfield, differing only in the shape and cut of the key that opened it. All the other safes worked by combination – standing like an honour guard beside it in the vault.

Carver had every right to be going through Northcote's personal records but he still looked uncertainly around the vault, even though he already knew himself to be alone, and even turned to the similarly empty corridor before turning back to the heavy safe casing secured to the floor. The door swung easily, soundlessly, open to reveal a half-filled interior, the shelves much more tidily arranged than he remembered from his accidentally stumbled-upon discovery a few short days ago. The files then for Mulder Inc., Encomp and Innsflow International had been strewn haphazardly upon the uppermost shelf. They weren't now.

Carver worked his way methodically through everything, page by individual page, to ensure a cover or a section hadn't been utilized to hide what he was looking for. None had. Refusing to accept defeat – refusing in his switchbacking desperation to accept Northcote had denied him yet again – Carver went just as carefully through every manila folder, binder and paper yet again, recognizing each totally legitimate client.

Carver slammed the safe door closed so violently that it bounced open again, unsecured, and was at once embarrassed at his own petulance, although the fury still burned through him. As he closed and locked the door more properly he thought, why? Why, having promised – given an undertaking at least – to provide the documentary protection, had Northcote reneged, exposing them all to danger? Because he'd thought he had time, Carver supposed. Insufficient. Everything was insufficient. What he knew – or didn't know – was insufficient and ways to find what he didn't know and how to protect the firm and Jane and himself were insufficient. Alice, too, he supposed, although she was not directly in danger. What about the handwritten, still unread notes in Northcote's nightstand? Hurriedly, angered at himself for not including it in his previous searches, Carver went yet again through everything in the safe, seeking references to companies named BHYF and NOXT. Once more, there was nothing. Nothing, that is, in this half-filled safe. There might – just might – be in the firm's records, though. There were still places to look, computer avenues to follow, and a computer in Northcote's office along which to travel them.

But Jane was waiting there when he got back upstairs. She said: 'I've gone through everything for tomorrow with the funeral director, arranged for the insurance company to send their inventory for Litchfield and arranged a meeting there with the loss adjuster the day after tomorrow. I'm seeing the realtor then, too. And I'm up to date with the condolence letters.'

'Don't you think you should slow down just a little?'

'I'll slow down when everything's done. We should leave now if we're going to be on time for tonight.'

He'd forgotten the rescheduled dinner, Carver realized. 'I'm ready when you are.'

As they got into the elevator Jane said: 'Janice told me you're keeping all Dad's office staff on.'

'They can be absorbed through the firm easily enough.'

'I'm glad you've done that.'

It was almost as if Jane saw herself with a place in the firm. Carver said: 'I thought you would be.'

Jane came to an abrupt stop at the door to their car that the driver held open on the pavement outside the Northcote office block. 'I forgot! Janice said she didn't know what to do with the valise you'd left in Dad's office. I told her to put it in her own office safe. Was that right?'

Carver's sensation was of his stomach being hollowed out. 'Fine,' he managed.

'That the one you brought back from Litchfield?'

'Yes.'

'You never did tell me what was in it.'

'Some stuff he'd taken home to work on.' Would it still be there if Janice Snow was involved in it all?

Alice Belling didn't have it all – didn't think she had half of it – but she had the exhausted satisfaction of believing that she had almost enough to understand. And the other linked companies. She'd abandoned the repeated efforts to get into the Mulder Inc. subsidiaries spread throughout America, instead using the local tax offices and local company registers in twenty-six of the states she'd so far covered. In Abilene, Kansas, she'd found another reference to the Rome-based BHYF International. Independence, Missouri, had given her NOXT, again headquarters in Cheapside, London, England. And as with BHYF it defeated her attempts to hack into it.

As she paid, the persistent manager said: 'Changed your mind about that drink, Alice?'

She shook her head, smiling. 'Got a big day tomorrow.'

'More to do here?'

'A funeral.' She had every reason to go. She'd met George Northcote. And liked him. She supposed she should have warned John, but she hadn't decided when he'd called from East 62nd Street and now there was no way she could call him back.

'Anyone close?'

She shook her head again. 'Someone I thought I knew.'

'*Thought* you knew?' queried the man, frowning.

'Mis-spoken,' she said. It actually wasn't mis-spoken at all, she thought.

Stanley Burcher decided it was time to identify John Carver, who shortly was to become his obedient marionette, dancing whenever he pulled a string. And what better – and more unobtrusive – way than becoming a mourner at a funeral that would be attended by so many. It was even right that he should attend. Burcher decided he had known – *properly* known – George Northcote better than anyone who would be there.

Ten

Alice was at the rear of the cathedral and Carver saw her the moment he entered, Jane at his side disdaining his supporting arm as she'd rejected Dr Newton's offer of tranquillizers, either for the earlier private entombment or for this very public ceremony. Alice smiled faintly. Carver showed no recognition, although he could have done: they'd officially – publicly – met, more than once, during her article preparation on Northcote. He realized it was the first time that the two women he loved had been together in the same place. The first time, also, that Alice had seen Jane, although that might be difficult, through Jane's dark veil. Despite the rationalizing, he waited for the discomfort. There wasn't any. He wished he'd responded to Alice's smile but it was too late now. He was long past her pew, more than halfway along the nave. An estimate was difficult but Carver guessed there were at least a thousand mourners. Maybe more. Maybe among them were . . .

He hadn't paused, at seeing Alice: hadn't needed to. But he came close now, the briefest, easily hidden, stumble. Of course they would be here, somewhere: whoever *they* were. What did they look like, mob guys? Did they wear five-hundred – a thousand – dollar suits? Permanent dark glasses? Not move without 300lb bodyguards around them? Or were they – or those who represented them – quite ordinary, the sort of people you never noticed on the streets or on the subway: never saw anywhere, anywhen, because they were professionally and physically so inconspicuous as to be invisible? Carver actually looked around, more intently at the crowd than he'd looked at Alice. And saw no one, no face he could have remembered, no thousand-dollar suits, no dark glasses. Nothing. But he was sure they'd be there.

He was so enclosed in his own thoughts that there was almost another stumble when he momentarily failed to recognize their pew, from which he only recovered by ushering Jane in ahead of him. But so engrossed did Carver remain that everything – the service and the hymns and the eulogy – seemed to be on a suspended, out-of-body level until it was his moment to give the second of the readings, from Corinthians.

It was as if his steps, ascending to the pulpit, awoke him, although it was only when he started reading that he appreciated the hypocrisy of the passage. He began: '*Render therefore to all their dues: tribute to whom tribute is due* . . .' The cough was disguisable, like everything else. '*Fear to whom fear; honour to whom honour* . . .' Carver managed to complete the full text without any further hesitation, wondering as he spoke how many sharks out there in the sea of unseen faces were recognizing, as he was recognizing, the irony of the meaningless words he was mouthing. When he got back to his place Jane felt across and squeezed his hand and whispered: 'That was wonderful, darling. Thank you.'

There was a second eulogy from the bishop, in which he referred to Northcote's financial support for a drug rehabilitation centre in Harlem of which until that moment Carver had been unaware, and two more hymns before the procession out of the cathedral. As he passed where Alice stood Carver smiled at her. Now she remained expressionless towards him.

Stanley Burcher stood, anonymous as always, within the crush of people, watching the man he now knew to be John Carver caringly although not touchingly escort his wife from the cathedral. Not as dominantly commanding as George Northcote, not as physically big, but certainly imposing, tailored to illustrate the broad-shouldered, straight-backed stature. Tight, crinkled hair like a tight cap, heavy-nosed face, no jewellery, not even a wedding band. In closer proximity Burcher guessed Carver would emanate the same instinctive ambience of power that came from Charlie Petrie. Burcher was turning, with the existing procession, and intently studied the congregation to try to locate whoever it was to whom Carver had so briefly smiled. If the Deliocis had done as they were told there should be somewhere among this train of people someone preparing for him as full a profile as possible upon John Carver. He hoped he was wrong, about his impression that the man had the arrogance of power. He'd declared himself – and his idea for continuity – now. He'd lose face if he didn't come through. But then how could he fail to come through, with the backing he had. He didn't need to go to the wake. He'd shown sufficient respect for George Northcote's passing. If the stupid bastard hadn't behaved in the totally unexpected way that he had, he'd still be cutting the grass of his Litchfield pastures.

The receiving line at the Plaza was so interminable that Carver decided he'd miscalculated his one thousand mourners estimate by at least half and he stood, constantly, surreptitiously, looking beyond the person he was immediately greeting and introducing to Jane for the initial sight of Alice, for the first time – at last – experiencing a discomfort he expected to become guilt, which he knew – although he didn't want to accept – was a feeling he deserved. But never felt, because Alice never appeared in the line. Discomfited though he was, Carver still felt a lurch of disappointment, which increased his discomfort even more.

He and Jane split, to circulate, which Carver realized he would normally have accepted as a necessary duty – which it still was, because the majority of the people with whom he exchanged empty pleasantries were existing clients – but now his concentration was absolute, entirely different from what it once would have been. He was intent upon every name, trying to remember it from the client list, and when he didn't know one he stopped longer, waiting for one of the company names constantly echoing in his mind, not knowing what he would do if he heard it. Which he didn't.

It was almost thirty minutes before he reached Jack Jennings, grouped with the house and office staff. Carver only intended a passing greeting but Jennings separated himself from the others and said: 'Everything's out of the house, for when Mrs Carver needs to come with the realtor.'

'I'm grateful,' thanked Carver.

'And sheriff Hibbert stopped by. He says he can't understand it, but his forensics guys haven't picked up a single clue from the way the house was trashed. He asked me to tell you: tell you he was sorry and that he'd see you up in Litchfield.'

There was really nothing Hibbert could have told him, thought Carver. He looked beyond Jennings, to the office staff. 'Where's Janice?'

'She got upset at the service,' said Hilda. 'She's gone home.'

Security would have the combination code to her safe, Carver guessed. He couldn't wait until the following day to retrieve the valise. Or finally to go through its contents to understand, if he could, the importance of BHYF and NOXT.

Carver tensed for Jane to say she would return to Wall Street with him but she didn't, accepting his promise not to be longer than an hour. Security did have the code and Carver's relief began at the sight of the valise and settled when, inside his own locked office, he found what he initially believed to be everything intact. It only took him fifteen minutes to realize it wasn't. He'd counted the folios he had taken from Northcote's nightstand and the six spreadsheets were there but they, in themselves, were incomplete for both BHYF and NOXT. There was, though, a pattern. It was classic double-accounting, with sufficient reworked figures to see that already-substantial profits were being hugely inflated, doubling or even trebling the returns. Which didn't make sense. These were the sort of massaged, fraudulent figures that he'd accused Northcote of creating when they'd had their confrontation over the three other companies, meant to be produced at a stockholders' meeting or just prior to a flotation, to boost share prices and investors' confidence. But BHYF and NOXT were clearly shown on the papers in front of him to be private, non-stockholder companies with inaccessible registrations in Grand Cayman, certainly not businesses about to offer themselves on a publicly scrutinized, monitored market. It was a jigsaw. A jigsaw with too many pieces still missing. He'd only skimmed the other spreadsheets in Northcote's safe, everything far too brief to learn what he needed to know. His linking denominator in all five companies was this inexplicable inflation. Where was the bridge, the conduit joining it all together, making it understandable? Still hidden, he answered himself.

Geoffrey Davis, the firm's lawyer, answered the internal telephone himself and said at once: 'I didn't expect you back this afternoon.'

'One or two things to look at,' said Carver. 'Let's talk about the Chase.'

'What about it?'

'Do we have a safe-deposit facility there as well as the firm's account?'

'George did.'

After so many blocked alleys Carver's feeling was more of hope than expectation. 'In his name? Or the firm's.'

'The firm's.'

'So I've authority to access it?'

'Might be an idea to advise their security director. You want me to do that?'

'Right away,' said Carver.

'Too late today. Tomorrow OK?'

'First thing,' said Carver.

It was time to get back to as much normality as possible, Carver decided, replacing the telephone. Hilda had to re-establish his diary. And devise a way for her and Janice Snow to work together. And he had to see Alice, with more reason than normal. He needed to hear what she was so excited about. She must have been directly beside the telephone from the quickness with which she picked it up.

'I'd hoped it would be you,' she said. 'Kind of expected it.' She wouldn't tell him on the phone how much more she'd discovered. One of the few rules between them – the most important rule of all – was always to be honest and she hadn't been: not exactly dishonest, not talking to him about how she learned some of the things that had made her successful. Still, better disclosed when they were face to face.

'I certainly didn't expect to see you there today.'

'Jane's very beautiful.'

'I don't want to go this route.' Alice's phrase, he remembered.

'Sorry. You OK?'

'No. There's a lot I want to talk to you about.'

'A lot I want to talk about to you, too.'

'Tomorrow?'

'When?'

'Early. I've got to go to the Chase in the morning. I could come straight on from there.'

'Still nothing?'

Carver hesitated. In some manner, somehow, she'd involved herself, obviously wanting to help. But potentially endangering herself, which in every way – at all costs – he had to stop her doing. 'Things still to check out. You haven't done anything more, have you?'

Now the hesitation was from her end. 'I'm looking forward to our talking tomorrow.'

'That isn't an answer.'

'I think I know how it's done.'

Which was more than he did. 'You told me that already. And I told you to stop.'

'What time tomorrow?'

'Just stay in the apartment until I get there. And don't do anything else until I do.'

'How about I love you?'

'I love you. So please do as I ask.'

'I love you too.'

That wasn't a proper answer either, thought Carver. He was soon to find others, though. Some of which he wanted to know and others which he didn't.

Jack Jennings was waiting at Northcote's West 66th Street apartment, as they'd arranged, and said at once: 'I think I've found what you're looking for,' which he had.

The safe was in Northcote's study, fitted behind a cupboard as it had been in Litchfield. This was a much more modern model, although still key-operated, and the last remaining unidentified Litchfield key, the odd red one, fitted perfectly. It contained far more than Litchfield, although it took Carver far less time to absorb. There were a lot more photographs of Northcote and the unknown Anna, whose surname he discovered from three of the accompanying documents to be Simpson, and other photographs he looked at intently but failed to recognize. And there were five spreadsheets which he guessed, without comparing, to be part of what he'd found in the nightstand at Litchfield.

Carver sat at Northcote's desk almost too long, the BHYF and NOXT material of least interest, as he realized it couldn't be taken from here, not tonight at least. When he told Jennings he'd be back early the following morning the butler said he hoped everything was all right and Carver said he hoped it was, too.

*　*　*

With the extra staff, and the nurses who were still there, the East 62nd Street apartment seemed very overcrowded: when Carver went to enter the dining room that night, one of the Litchfield maids helping Manuel stood aside to let him in as he held back to let her out and Manuel completed the confusion by colliding into her, from behind.

Jane said: 'I'm taking four back to Litchfield with me.'

'That'll help.'

'They can live-in there but you need to check the apartments here.'

'I know.' He'd actually forgotten. Remembering was part of returning to normality, he told himself.

Manuel led the maid back in with the serving trays, his irritation obvious at what he clearly regarded as an intrusion on to his territory.

Jane said: 'I thought meat loaf was the easiest: I didn't know how today was going to turn out.'

'Meat loaf's fine.' Carver took a token portion to rearrange on his plate.

'I talked with Rosemary when I got back this afternoon.' Rosemary Pritchard was Jane's gynaecologist. Alice's, too. Upon John's recommendation, when she'd had an irregularity problem which Rosemary Pritchard had rectified to the point of Alice's complacency.

It would have been fatuous to ask what about. 'What did she say?'

'That there'd have to be some tests, obviously. But if they're OK I can start IVF right away . . .' Jane ate with her head over her plate, not looking at him. 'She asked what you thought about it.' She looked up at last. 'So how *do* you feel about it?'

Carver sipped his wine, delaying. 'About our having a baby, I feel fine. About rushing into it now, as if we have something to prove, like it's a race, I'm not so sure.'

'Rosemary told me it nearly always takes time, so we're not rushing into it.'

'Maybe we should talk to Rosemary about it together. Other people, perhaps.'

'Other people like psychiatrists, perhaps?' she said, in echo.

'I didn't mean other people like psychiatrists,' he lied.

'What other people then?' she demanded, trapping him.

'I wasn't thinking any further than Paul Newton.'

'Who's a medical doctor who's overcrowded this apartment with nurses I don't want or need and who are leaving the very moment their seven days are up.'

Carver pushed the meal away. 'I won't let this get into a fight. It's not a situation to fight *about*. I'll come up to Litchfield at the weekend and we'll talk more about it and then we'll go to see Rosemary together and work it out.'

'You . . .' started Jane but stopped.

Carver waited but she didn't continue. Instead she said: 'I forgot you didn't like meat loaf.'

'I wasn't hungry anyway.'

Stanley Burcher heard his telephone as he walked along the corridor to his room and finished at a run, snatching it off its cradle at what he guessed would have been its last ring. The voice he recognized at once to be Enrico Delioci's said: 'She knows too much. She . . .'

'Stop!' insisted Burcher. 'Where are you?'

'With her, in her apartment.'

'Using her phone?'

'Mine. Cellphone,' said the other man, heavily patronizing.

Burcher breathed out, heavily. There'd still be a trace to the Algonquin, on the cellphone. 'What's she know?'

'The names of all the companies. That records were never kept after she wrote up the official returns from Northcote's handwritten originals. She also told us Carver brought a bunch of stuff back with him from Litchfield. Needed a valise to carry it. And he's been asking her questions about it all.'

Burcher's mind was leapfrogging ahead of all that was

happening, trying to keep everything in its proper order. This looked like another fuck-up, worse maybe than Litchfield. 'She hurt?'

'You told us to find out what she knew. She wouldn't tell us at first.'

The bastards were setting him up, making him responsible! 'There has to be another accident. Get it wrong and there'll be a lot more.'

Eleven

Carver carried the coffee that Jack Jennings had waiting for him into the West 66th Street study, where the previous night he'd made the most unexpected discoveries of all, and sat sipping it at Northcote's desk, looking more carefully through everything he took once more from the safe. It was easy to divide the papers between the two attaché cases Carver had brought, having been mentally able to plan overnight. The personal material and photographs took up more room in one than the additional inflated calculations for BHYF and NOXT in the other and Carver gave himself time to finish his coffee and study them more carefully than he had the first time. They unquestionably formed the missing section of what he'd found in the Litchfield nightstand and Carver wondered why Northcote had worked like this, piecemeal, leaving documents behind him like a paperchase, which, in fact, it was. And then he remembered Northcote's difficulties at the end with holding thoughts and words and decided the older man's problems had been greater than any of them had suspected. Or maybe it was intentional, dividing what he'd withheld to save some if he lost – or was forced to surrender – part. Whatever, it was time-wasting speculation. With what he now had – and whatever Alice had possibly unearthed – he now had virtually all he needed to get rid of the unwanted clients and protect the firm.

There was an internal email from Geoffrey Davis when he arrived in Wall Street, advising him that the Chase Manhattan security manager was expecting him at ten and reminding him that he would need the second key, for the unlocking procedure. It was the same, customary, system for his safe-deposit facility at Citibank, just two blocks further up along Wall Street – the key for which was already in his pocket – but Davis's reminder surprised him.

'I've got no keys unaccounted for. I thought it would be here,' he told the lawyer on the internal telephone.

'I don't have it. Maybe Janice keeps it,' suggested Davis.

Which was how Carver learned from Hilda Bennett that Janice Snow had not arrived for work that morning.

'You said yesterday she was upset. Maybe she's taking the day off.'

'I called. There's no reply. And no answering machine, to leave a message.'

'Call again now. I'm looking for a key.'

Hilda did, hanging on for a full five minutes, before shaking her head and replacing the receiver. Hilda identified all the keys they found going through Janice's desk drawers and finally, impatiently, Carver called Davis back and told him to alert the bank security manager that he did not have the necessary duplicate. Before he left his own office Carver carefully locked the two attaché cases into his private safe.

Carver arrived at the Chase Manhattan imagining that the warning in advance would be sufficient but was irritated at the extent of the officialdom. Even though the vice president in charge of the division had met Carver both in the Plaza receiving line and later during Carver's dutiful mingling at the reception the man still insisted upon Geoffrey Davis personally bringing from the Northcote offices the most recent boardroom minutes unanimously accepting Carver's appointment, and even then he weakly protested that there should have been supporting legal proof of Carver's accession before a duplicate key could be issued. The approval was finally agreed when a senior vice president accepted Davis's argument that he physically represented legal proof. Carver thanked the lawyer for his help but said there was no need for him to stay for the opening of the box.

It contained half a million dollars, in easily counted one-thousand-dollar bills individually bound in ten-thousand-dollar bundles, yellowing certificates and diplomas confirming George Northcote's professional qualifications, two photographs, along with the lease, of Northcote's original Wall Street building before its demolition for replacement by the present skyscraper, and three more prints, with handwritten annotation, of Anna and Northcote's Italian and Spanish visit. Each yet again showed, to Carver's eye, two people blissfully in love. Unlike those he'd discovered in Litchfield, each of the three clearly showed Anna wearing a wedding ring.

There was nothing else.

Despite the West 66th Street findings, and his deciding earlier that morning that he had sufficient, Carver was disappointed that the box was empty of anything other than more personal memorabilia. Had Anna Simpson been in yesterday's cathedral congregation or the later receiving line of a thousand empty faces, the one mystery figure who, from all the photographs he'd now seen, he might have identified? What could – would – he have done, if he had recognized her? There would have been nothing he could have done in the church: little, with Jane so close beside him. But there would have been a chance for something as he moved about the room. An urgent whisper, for her to call him: an equally urgent demand, for a way to contact her. For what? Far better left in the past, a successfully – and properly – lost secret. He had to decide what to do with all the personal material, once he'd resolved the more important problem.

Carver straightened from the box but paused, uncertainly, before taking out the photographs and putting them into his briefcase. He secured it and rang for a security official to complete the necessary double locking and let him out of the vault. It was the vice president in charge of the division who responded, a young, fair-haired man.

As they went through the procedure, the man said: 'I was not being intentionally awkward earlier, Mr Carver. I was strictly following regulations.'

'You should always do that,' said Carver.

'We value your business, here at the bank.'

There'd probably been some rebuke. 'That's good to hear.'

'Is there anything else I can do?'

'Nothing, thank you.'

The man smiled. 'Just one more regulation. You need to sign yourself out on the register against the box number.'

It was not until he was bending over the bound book that the idea came to Carver and he covered the quick examination by pretending to fumble with the pen.

'It's ten forty-five,' offered the young man, for the required departure time.

Carver nodded, intent upon George Northcote's signature at the bottom of the preceding page. George Northcote's departure from the safe-deposit vault was timed at eleven-fifty-five and dated five days earlier, the day he'd had lunch at the Harvard Club with a person or persons designated in his diary as S–B.

Alice said: 'It's been longer before, but this *seems* the longest.'

Carver said: 'It's been a lifetime, in days.'

They stood strangely awkward in front of each other. Carver reached out and she came to him and they kissed and held each other for several moments before separating again.

'There's coffee. Or do you want something else?'

It still wasn't noon but Carver said: 'Something else.'

'I mixed some, just in case.' She poured the Martinis straight, without ice. As she handed him his drink she said: 'You found anything?'

She had to be kept out of it: kept out and kept safe. He was the only person capable of sorting everything out: of keeping everyone safe. Carver shook his head. 'Nothing that properly helps. But you told me you knew what it was all about.'

Now Alice shook her head. 'I'm only guessing what it's all *about*. I think I know how it works.'

Carver sat, drink in hand, waiting. He had to get everything there was to get from her. And then work from that foundation.

'You're going to be angry. Disappointed in me. Please don't be.' She drank, deeply, the Martini made more for her benefit than for his.

It was an attitude, a meekness, Carver hadn't known in Alice before. 'Why don't you just tell me?'

She'd rehearsed it, several different ways, but the admission of her hacking still came disjointedly and when she had finished Alice wasn't sure that she'd explained it as fully or as understandably as she'd intended.

Carver remained unspeaking for several minutes, his own Martini untouched. Then, quiet-voiced, he said: 'For two days, longer, you've been hacking into their systems . . . into IRS records . . . company registrations . . . not just here in America . . . in other countries, too. . . ?'

'Yes,' she confessed, simply.

Carver shook his head, in genuine disbelief, his thoughts still coming out in bursts. 'I can't begin to guess . . . no one can . . . how many laws you've broken. Not just broken here . . . broken internationally . . .'

'No one will ever find out . . . can ever find out,' she insisted. 'It's going to be all right.'

Carver wasn't angry. Disappointed, either. And although he'd said it, as if it was his major fear, he wasn't thinking of the law, either. 'What if they detected you . . . the people who did what they did to George?'

'I told you how I've made sure they can't.'

'One hundred and one per cent, no-possibility-of-being-wrong sure?'

'Absolutely.'

'I've read, heard, that it's possible for hackers to be caught . . . that there are devices.'

'I didn't use my own terminal, here. I used the double cut-out of a computer cafe. And someone else's system, further to hide myself.'

Carver didn't properly understand what she was telling him but he thought – because it was what he wanted to think – that maybe it would be OK. It sounded as if she knew what she was doing. Kids of fifteen had got in and out of the Pentagon and NASA systems without being detected. 'No more. Promise me – give me your word and mean it – that you won't do any more.'

'I promise.'

'Mean it this time,' he insisted. 'Not like before.'

Alice didn't want to stop. There really wasn't a chance of her ever being discovered and to prove she'd guessed the scam correctly she needed to get into one of the systems so far denying her entry. 'I won't do it again.'

'So what is it?' he finally demanded.

'Money laundering, pure and simple. But absolutely brilliant.'

'Show me.'

She did, literally, leading him to her desk, upon which she had all the computer printouts sequentially arranged country by country, America dominant with Grand Cayman at the very pinnacle. 'We'll go left to right, read it like a book, which I think we can,' she declared. 'What we're looking at is a global shell game, things being moved so far so fast there's no chance to see which cup the pea's under. We start with five organized-crime – Mafia – offshore companies, out of reach and out of sight of any law, criminal or civil. Into them we have to channel – also out of reach and out of sight – all the illegal proceeds of every crime the Families commit: drugs, pornography, prostitution, loan sharking, protection, the lot. And if my theory *is* right it is a lot. Billions of dollars. You with me so far . . . ?'

Carver nodded, pouring fresh drinks for them both, following the electronic footsteps through the printouts.

'Here's how they do it,' Alice picked up. 'Mulder Inc., Encomp and Innsflow International establish dozens of subsidiaries, here in America, state by state, internationally, country by country. The trick – and I think initially it's a quite legal trick – is trading only between each other, state by state and country by country. But never through their *own* subsidiaries. Mulder switches through Encomp, Encomp through Mulder and each through Innsflow. To do that, they need a conduit, again quite simply a very efficient, internationally established import–export organization. Which they've done with BHYF and NOXT, whose records and near-incalculable profits are also, ultimately, lost in the golden sand of the Cayman Islands, using the same shell-game technique. By constantly juggling the deals they avoid the legal requirement, particularly necessary in England, to record the tradings as a "related-party transaction". Isn't that brilliant?'

The missing parts of his jigsaw, identified Carver, excitement moving through him: and interlocking perfectly with the handwritten, incomplete calculations from Northcote's nightstand. 'Offshore is tax evasion and avoidance but they don't *care* about paying tax!'

'Not in the process,' smiled Alice. 'Virtually everything Mulder, Encomp and Innsflow – and their subsidiaries – trade in is consumer-orientated, cash-orientated . . .' She smiled again. 'And all sharing two remarkable similarities. There are sky-high supply costs which continue to soar all the way along the state-by-state, country-by-country supply route. And matchingly high management, building and plant maintenance and depreciation costs.'

'To account for the dirty money being pumped in?' anticipated Carver.

'Exactly,' said Alice. 'The genuine cost of what they're moving between subsidiaries and states and countries has to be a fraction of what the books show, on every record I've managed to get into. Take blank videos, for instance: they start *off* charging one dollar each for bulk orders of up to ten thousand cassettes. By the time it passes through BHYF or NOXT, it's up to seven dollars, sometimes even ten. No bona fide business could afford to buy or trade at supply costs like that: no bona fide business would accept supply costs like that. But Mulder, Encomp and Innsflow do . . .'

'Buy for cents – fractions of cents – and pad it up into dollars and then tens of dollars and then hundreds of dollars, all the way along the chain,' accepted Carver. 'They boost true costs of say ten thousand dollars up to an inflated hundred thousand, pay forty thousand in tax . . .'

'And they've laundered fifty thousand dollars worth of dirty money,' completed Alice. 'Multiply that by the number of subsidiaries throughout every state in this country and all the international locations – just those that we know about, by the way – and you've got your billions.'

'Or more,' agreed Carver, reflectively. Until that moment he'd had no conception of how big, almost literally how cosmic, the operation was.

'You think George devised the whole thing?'

Carver decided against a third Martini. 'He said it had taken a long time to set up. But although it's simple, like you said, no one man could operate and control such a system. And there are different tax laws in different countries.'

'It wouldn't take many,' suggested Alice. 'Remember it's basically done in-house, by their own accountants. They only need to go outside for the legally required independent audits, to keep the wheels moving. And those wheels move damned fast. The subsidiaries never deal with each other *within* the states in which they're established. They're spread – oh so very cleverly spread – throughout the regional centres, none impacting in such a way to enable cross-referencing. So no one local tax authority sees a return that can be compared to show how the costs are being inflated with dirty money.'

Carver snorted a humourless laugh. 'I wonder if they'll use what happened to George – what they did to George – as an example to any others who want to get out?'

'Something else we'll never know,' said Alice. She left the desk and her printouts, leading Carver back to the couch. She nodded to the Martini pitcher. 'You want any more?'

'Yes, but I won't,' he said.

'So where does all this take us?'

It takes you nowhere, decided Carver, positively. Where did it take him, coupled with everything else he'd assembled? The squaring of the circle. It was unquestionably enough to give to the FBI to initiate an investigation into off-sheet, double accounting. But as he'd known from the beginning, doing that would destroy in ignominy and disgrace the firm of George W. Northcote International. It would also mean Alice's arrest on countless charges, a second reason why the FBI was not an option. But he could meet the men who'd controlled and manipulated George – if such an encounter ever occurred – with the ground level, knowing enough to confront them, and if it got bad make the *threat* of going to the FBI. Create a stand-off, on his own terms. Could, that is, if he had the courage to do so. And he did have that courage and that determination. George had failed because George was old and failing and fallible. Not up to confronting anyone. But he was, Carver knew. It wasn't the arrogance that Alice – even Jane – sometimes accused him of. He was the only person who was up to it. Could do it.

He limited his answer to confirming that he'd found incomplete, out-of-date BHYF and NOXT spreadsheets, missing out any mention of the photographs of Anna.

'If there was anything else at Litchfield, it would have been found?' she persisted.

'Unquestionably.'

'So everything could be all right? If they found whatever they forced George Northcote to disclose – lead them to – they've got no reason to pressure you or the firm?'

How many times had he tried to reassure himself with that thought? 'They're still on the client list.'

'Which you're having to adjust and reduce, because of George's death: you've had that as your out from the beginning.'

Would he really be able – brave enough, strong enough, convincing enough – to meet the situation if it came to a confrontation? Pre-empt it, he thought. There were the post office box numbers in Georgetown, on Grand Cayman, on the client list, against all five companies. He'd write that afternoon severing all and every connection. It didn't need to come down – or more accurately escalate – to confrontation and threats: just a simple business disassociation, the sort of thing that happened all the time. He said: 'I want to take everything you've turned up.'

Alice looked back to the desk. 'Why?'

To prevent you being a target, Carver thought. And then he thought, why not be honest? 'You've stopped now, haven't you?'

'Yes,' said Alice, only just avoiding the hesitation.

'There are some things I haven't had time properly to look at – assess – yet. It might interface with what you've accessed and downloaded: make everything complete. I won't know if it does unless I have your stuff.'

'Why not bring what you've got back here and we'll go through all of it together?' Alice attempted to bargain.

'You know why.'

'I *am* involved!'

'Not any longer. People this clever, they've got ways.'

'That's ridiculous!'

Their first argument, about anything, recognized Carver. He wondered if Alice recognized it, too. He said: 'I want to take away with me everything you've got. We've already agreed – at least I've decided – that we can't count the number of laws you've broken, getting what you have, let alone the other risks there could be. I don't want any arguments about no one ever being able to find out and trace you . . .' He hesitated, deciding to continue the honesty. 'I'm not angry or disappointed. I'm frightened. Very, very frightened and I don't even know completely what I'm frightened about. At the moment all I can think of is containing things. And containing – taking away from you – all that's on that desk over there is the most important containment there is at this precise moment.'

She could get it all again, thought Alice. That and more. It would be tiresome and time consuming but she knew the electronic doors through which she could go in and out as she pleased. And just to allay his fears – not that he'd ever know – when she finished she'd leave behind a trigger word to self-destruct her hidden presence when it was entered into the machine. She got up, gathered together everything from the desk and silently handed it to him. Then she said: 'That was our first row.'

'I already worked that out.'

'I'm glad it wasn't a serious one.'

'So am I.'

'Can you stay longer?'

'Tonight. We'll eat somewhere in the Village.'

'Tonight then.'

'Leave it alone now, darling. I thank you – love you – for helping. For working it out when I was approaching from entirely the wrong direction. But now I don't want you to do anything more.'

'I already promised,' said Alice. When she was a child and made a promise she knew she wouldn't keep she'd crossed her fingers behind her back, because then broken promises didn't count. She crossed her fingers now.

Carver walked back to the office, glad he was on foot because as usual SoHo was virtually gridlocked. It still took him almost half an hour, because the sidewalks weren't much better.

The ground-floor receptionist said: 'People are looking for you, Mr Carver,' and Hilda, red-eyed, was waiting outside the elevator doors when it reached his floor. 'Your cellphone's off.'

'What?' he demanded.

'Janice hanged herself,' said the woman.

There *wasn't* any risk of her being discovered, which meant there was no reason for John to be frightened. She hadn't liked his admitting being frightened. She'd recognized he'd been overwhelmed by George Northcote but George Northcote had been a physically overwhelming man. And being overwhelmed wasn't being frightened. It was still only one fifteen: more than enough time to duplicate what she'd surrendered and carry on pricking at the sites and their local tax and company registration offices, to colour in more of the incomplete picture.

'Thought you'd deserted me,' protested the Space for Space manager.

'Never,' Alice flirted back.

'Feeling thirsty yet?'

'You never know. Depends how hard I have to work.'

Her favourite station, the one at the end of the line where there was least chance of her screen being read over her shoulder, was empty. She logged on, dialled the hotel reservation chain, fingers poised to complete her entry with her Trojan Horse password. And was confronted on the screen by the message 'Remote-Requested Access Refused'. No problem, she told herself: inexplicable glitches happened all the time. But rarely four more times. She tried one more time before quickly disconnecting. Their mainframe could have crashed. Or there could have been a power interruption, although in the past she'd found the English grid system more reliable than American electricity suppliers. The screen glowed at her, invitingly.

From his counter the manager called out: 'You gotta problem?'

'No,' denied Alice.

She used the Google search engine to find that the local newspaper was the *Basingstoke Gazette* and accessed its website in seconds. Its front page was dominated by a photograph of a fire-blackened shell. Police were treating as murder the deaths of a caretaker and two early-shift cleaners in the arson attack that had totally destroyed the European headquarters of the hotel chain's reservations site. There had been four different seats of fire, all caused by explosions of what forensic experts had already established to be incendiary material, most likely phosphorous. The possibility of terrorism had not been ruled out, although there was nothing to explain why the building or the hotel corporation had been targeted.

Alice turned off the machine and fumbled for her user's fee.

The manager said: 'What's the problem here?'

'Something unexpected came up,' said Alice.

Throughout his journeying up and down town Carver had been unaware of the two men alternating their surveillance, but then they were professionals, both former policemen. It only cost one of them $50 to learn the name of Alice Belling from the janitor at Princes Street. Their instructions were to pursue Carver, which meant neither followed Alice to the cybercafe to get a visual identification.

Twelve

Carver waited two hours and was about to follow Geoffrey Davis and James Parker, the personnel director, out to Janice's Brooklyn apartment when the lawyer called to say they were on their way back into Manhattan. It was another thirty minutes before they arrived. Davis's normally florid face was pale. Parker's was ashen.

As he came into Carver's office Parker, a thin, bespectacled man, said as if he needed to explain: 'I've never seen a dead body before . . . not dead like that.'

Davis said: 'We stayed on to identify the body, to save Janice's mother. Although it was she who found Janice.'

'From the beginning . . .' insisted Carver.

Parker looked to the older man and Davis said: 'Janice didn't come in this morning, as Hilda told you. Hilda kept calling and getting no reply. Then she got a call from Janice's mother. She'd gone around to Janice's apartment when she didn't get a reply either. She let herself in with her own key and found Janice dead . . .'

'Dead how?' broke in Carver.

'Strangled, according to the medical officer. Although it's obvious she tried to hang herself, from some loft-bed stairs.'

'The rope broke,' said Parker. 'That's how she got injured.'

Carver shifted irritably. 'You think we could get some coherence into this! I want to know what happened and I'm finding it difficult.'

Davis looked surprised. 'Last night Janice phoned her

mother, in tears. She was upset by the funeral: said she didn't know what was going to happen to her . . .'

'She knew what was going to happen to her,' interrupted Carver, again. 'I told her she was being kept on, working with Hilda . . . that no one was being let go.'

'Hilda told me,' said the lawyer.

'And I got your memo, with a confirming copy to her,' said Parker.

'People get confused in grief,' said Davis. 'She'd been with George for a long time: knew his ways.'

Perhaps she knew more than his ways, thought Carver. Her being upset certainly wasn't because she was frightened of losing her job. 'The mother gets into Janice's apartment with her own key? It wasn't locked . . . chained . . . from the inside?'

'Apparently not,' said the lawyer. 'Janice hanged herself from a rope knotted to the topmost rung of the loft ladder. It was there that the rope snapped, quite close to the top. The medical examiner doesn't think it happened immediately: his sequence is that she kicked away the stool she'd stood on and for a while the rope held: that's how she strangled herself. He thinks she probably struggled, the moment she did it: according to the medical examiner people do that when they begin to strangle. The rope only broke when she literally became a dead weight.'

'What injuries?' prompted Carver.

'Surprisingly extensive,' said Davis. 'She came down awkwardly. Trapped her left arm underneath her, breaking it. And three fingers on that hand. And her left leg. That twisted under her, too.'

'How high's the stool?'

Davis looked at Parker, to be reminded. Parker said: 'Eighteen inches, two feet maybe. I didn't pay much attention to it.'

'Neither did I,' admitted Davis.

'From a drop of eighteen inches to two feet she breaks an arm, a leg and three fingers?' queried Carver.

Davis frowned. 'What are you suggesting, John?'

'That the extent of her injuries really is surprising.'

'The doctor says strange things happen sometimes,' said Parker.

'It certainly did here!'

'Janice left a note,' disclosed Davis. 'She must have written it soon after she spoke to her mother. She'd been dead for almost twenty hours before she was found. She wrote that she was sorry for what she was doing but that everything was going to be turned upside down by George's death. She repeated that she didn't know what was going to happen to her: that everything was over.'

They would have been standing over her: had probably already started the torture, breaking the fingers of her left hand but leaving her right, so that she could write what she was being told. 'What was the apartment like?'

'Like?' Again the lawyer frowned.

Carver stopped just short of using the word trashed. 'Tidy? Or untidy?'

'I didn't pay much attention to that, either. But it seemed pretty together to me,' said the personnel director. There was some uncomfortable body language.

'That's my recollection, too,' said Davis. Then he said: 'You implying something different from what the police say it is, the suicide of a mentally upset woman? Which I also believe it to be, having been there and talked with them.'

'A mentally upset woman who didn't bolt or chain her door?' Carver once again felt restricted – physically strait-jacketed – by an impotence far worse, far different, from that he'd felt with Alice after discovering Northcote's criminality.

There was another expression of surprise from the lawyer. 'A woman intending to kill herself who knew people would have to get in to find her!'

All so logically, so easily acceptable by police probably working ten – a hundred – more obvious homicide cases. Would Janice, brutalized, bewildered, already grief-stricken, have told them – given them – what they wanted? Had she known it – had it – even? She surely wouldn't have endured so much torture if she had. It proved, he accepted, that she hadn't been part of any mob-orchestrated conspiracy. There was a sudden, physical chill. It proved even more positively that they hadn't found whatever it was – of which the night-stand contents could be a part – when they'd ransacked Northcote's house in Litchfield. And if Janice hadn't had it, then they'd go on looking and torturing and killing. The chill became even more physically intense at a sudden new awareness. Would she have told them of the valise he'd brought back from Litchfield, before the burglary? Carver thought he would have done, if his fingers and arms and legs were being broken. Forcing himself on, he said: 'How old's the mother?'

'Old,' judged Parker. 'Mid eighties, I'd guess.'

'Married or widowed?'

'I don't know,' admitted Parker.

'Find out,' ordered Carver. 'Find out if Janice financially supported her, too. Look after the funeral, everything . . .' He looked to Davis. 'If there's a will, ensure it's administered. If there isn't, apply to administer what there is of Janice's estate. We'll switch Janice's pension to the mother.'

'That's a very generous package,' said Davis.

'No reason why I can't do it, is there?' Carver was aware of the truculent bravado.

'I think you might run it by the other partners,' suggested the lawyer.

'I will, but start on it right away,' said Carver. 'Can we get the medical report on Janice?'

Davis shook his head as much in a gesture of bewilderment as in refusal. 'We're not next of kin. And in these sort of circumstances I'm not sure that even next of kin are allowed access: few of them would want what you're asking for.'

'Try. I want to see it.' Why, he asked himself: to what purpose? 'Something else,' he added, looking back to the personnel director. 'I want to see Janice's file. And that of her predecessor, if we still have it.'

'I don't think we would have it,' said Parker.

'Look, just in case,' ordered Carver.

'You sure there's nothing you want to talk to me about, John?' demanded Davis openly. 'You imagining there's some link with the Litchfield robbery? Because if you are, I can't see where you're getting the slightest connection from.'

No one was supposed to, thought Carver. 'Just both see what you can do, OK.'

'I'll try,' promised the lawyer, doubtfully.

'So will I,' undertook the younger man.

Shouldn't he have told Geoffrey Davis? Set out all he knew – shown the man Alice's printouts and the roughly worked inflated calculations from Litchfield – to explore all or any legal salvation there might be? *I think you might run it by the other partners* echoed in Carver's mind. That would be the lawyer's inevitable, responsible reaction. After going through – and realizing and agonizing over – all the devastating implications of exactly what he was being told: seeing, and realizing, that there wasn't any blinding light to mark an end to the tunnel but only that of the approaching train. To insist upon telling the partners would, in fact, be Geoffrey Davis's personal and professional salvation. Initiating, in turn, the personal and professional salvation of them all. They provably didn't know and were therefore provably, legally innocent of any misdemeanour or crime. Their recourse would be, could *only* be, to call in the police – and the FBI, he supposed – and the Security Exchange Commission and anyone else they could think of. And then stand up dazzlingly white in the equally dazzling light of the hurtling train, having done the right thing as well as having exonerated themselves from any misconduct, guilt or censure.

Which he could still do, Carver thought. At that moment *wanted* to do, to walk away, to escape and start again. Could he – could any of them – start again? Wouldn't there always be, despite any and every exoneration, the stain of association upon them? Did he, personally, *need* to start again? He was a millionaire, in his own right. Jane was a millionaire, in her own right. He could, quite literally, walk away from it all. The deafening warning bell sounded once more in his mind. Walk away with whom? Not with Jane. With Alice, certainly, easily, but not with Jane, who, as he'd decided when it had all first begun – seven days ago, seven years ago, seven hundred years ago? – would hate him and abandon him if he exposed the firm and her father. And he didn't want to be hated or abandoned by Jane, as he didn't want to be abandoned by Alice. Another circle squared. Why had he allowed himself the reflection, knowing its conclusion before he started? Desperation, he supposed. Not knowing – not properly, safely knowing – where to look, where to go, what to do. Not being, not feeling, adequate. But that was how he had to be, adequate. Not with Geoffrey Davis's involvement, help or advice, or the partners' involvement, help or advice. Not with anyone's involvement. Clang went the bell. Alice was involved. If she hadn't involved herself as deeply, as cleverly, as she had, he wouldn't have been able to confront an approach he hoped never to meet. But *they* didn't know about Alice. Never would. So it came back, as it would always come back, to him. Back to how strong he was capable of being.

When she responded to his summons Carver let Hilda say what she wanted to say about death and tragedies and not knowing people at all when you believed you did, before dictating the severance letter already so well rehearsed and prepared in his mind to BHYF, NOXT, Mulder Incorporated, Encomp and Innsflow International. He said: 'And erase them from the clients list.'

'Today, you mean.'

'Today,' confirmed Carver.

'My mother always said misfortune came in threes. I hope she was wrong.'

'So do I,' said Carver.

Alice said she didn't want to go out to eat and was thinking of omelettes and Carver said there were things to talk about first.

Until that moment Alice had wavered, undecided. Now, abruptly, she blurted: 'I've got something to tell you, too.'

'You first.'

'No, you,' she refused, already regretting her decision, wanting to get out of it. But stood unmoving, wine unopened in her hand, as he told her. When he had finished she handed him the bottle and the corkscrew. She said: 'You think she was murdered, like George?'

'Of course she was,' he said, almost impatiently. 'Tortured to begin with.'

'Jesus!' It was right that she tell him about the bombing in England. She said: 'They would have known who she was, from George. Seen her if they ever came to the office. They could have thought she knew more than she did.'

'Perhaps she did know more than she admitted to me.' He drank deeply. 'There were some things I brought back from Litchfield, in a valise. Janice put it in her office safe one night . . .'

'If she was tortured she would have told them,' said Alice, at once understanding.

'Yes.' As well as telling them about his specifically asking about the five companies, he thought.

Alice momentarily couldn't speak, her already existing terror doubled. She said: 'Oh shit!' and then she said, 'What a stupid, ridiculous, thing to say!'

Carver said: 'You had something to tell me?'

She did, as calmly as possible, but hearing the words reverberate in her ears and thinking, you caused it to happen, you caused it to happen.

He said: 'Three people died?'

'I killed them: caused them to be murdered.'

'You said it couldn't happen, for fuck's sake! That no one would ever find you!'

'Ordinarily they're not supposed to be able to.'

'What about *extra*ordinarily?'

'You need to be brilliant to recover an Internet protocol.'

'These people *are* brilliant! Absolutely fucking brilliant . . .' There was a hesitation, of awareness. 'How do you know?'

'I wanted to find out more: to get through their firewalls.'

Carver looked at Alice, letting the silence widen between them, and when she finally looked away he said: 'You gave me your word!'

With my fingers crossed, she thought, which now seemed – *was* – so fatuous. 'There wasn't enough.'

'I *have* enough.'

'So you lied to me, too!' she seized.

'I was trying to protect you: to keep you safe.'

'I was trying to protect *you*: to keep *you* safe,' she echoed.

'We don't know what we're trying to do, do we?' asked Carver, rhetorically. 'They're better – bigger – than we are. And I always thought there wasn't anything I couldn't handle.'

'You know what I think?' demanded Alice. 'I think we've still got time to go clean. Get out. Get help and protection. You're right. We're in way above our heads, so that's what we need. Help and protection.'

'You'd go to jail.'

'I'd get a deal.'

'I don't know if what you've got – what I've got to go with it – is sufficient for a fuller investigation.'

'What *have* you got to go with it?' she pounced.

He didn't immediately reply. 'Calculations: some of George's rough calculations.'

'Where?'

'Safe.'

'Where?' she repeated.

'Where it needs to be to protect us.' Was his office vault secure enough? For the time being, until he could think of something else: something better.

'Darling! George, who thought he had something – whatever it was – to protect himself, is dead, his face literally chopped meat! Janice is dead, because she wouldn't tell you what she knew, if she knew anything at all. Or tell them, if she knew anything at all. In some half-assed English town or village or whatever the hell Basingstoke is, three people are dead, leaving kids and husbands and wives. We can't do this by ourselves any more. We're not good enough. Clever enough. We've got to go to . . .' Alice stopped, still not sure what they had to do to guard themselves. 'The FBI! They'll do a deal with us in return for our evidence! We go to the FBI, tell them what we know. I'll admit everything I've done and do the deal.'

Carver gave himself more wine, accepting so much – too much but not enough – of what Alice said, like their not being good enough or clever enough. 'I told you I am not sure what we have is sufficient for an FBI investigation. What you got illegally hacking into IRS offices and company registration records can't be the basis for an investigation: a defence from people this good would have it ruled inadmissible before it got anywhere near a court or a grand jury. What I got from Litchfield – although explaining your inadmissible findings – isn't sufficient by itself. Whatever – whichever – way an FBI investigation went, the firm would be destroyed. Whatever deal you cut with the Bureau, your career and reputation would be wiped out . . .'

'I'd be alive, for fuck's sake! You'd be alive.'

'I don't want to say the rest.'

'You don't have to say the rest. OK, Jane would be devastated but she'd be alive!'

'All three of us with different identities, living – existing – in some godforsaken country, never sure when they might find us.'

'We're not sure now, for Christ's sake! We're totally unsure and terrified. I am, at least.'

'The five companies we know about were all George kept, in the last six months.'

Alice sat, empty glass in hand, waiting.

'So there aren't any more,' continued Carver.

'What's your point?'

'I severed the firm's connection with the five today.'

There was another moment of silence. Then Alice said: 'How?'

'Official letters.'

She regarded him with further disbelief. 'You think that's it, if Janice told them about a valise you brought back from Litchfield, where they clearly found nothing! What are you saying – trying to say – John?'

'I'll give it to them.'

More silence, longer than any before.

Spacing her words Alice said: 'Give them what?'

'What they were looking for at Litchfield but which I found first.'

'Was that all you found, just rough calculations? What about George's bank?'

'I haven't been to his personal bank. You know I went to the Chase this morning. There was . . .' Carver stopped, shaking his head.

'What?' she demanded.

'Nothing that helps. Just some personal things.'

'What personal things?' she insisted.

'Photographs. No one I recognized. They were old.'

'Maybe it's someone the FBI would recognize!'

'It was a woman. Her name was Anna, Anna Simpson. That's all I know.' Why had he told her that, if keeping things from her was her protection? He was flaking, coming apart.

'I want us to get help, John. Proper, official, professional police help.'

'Let me think.' He actually had an idea but decided against sharing it with Alice. She knew too much already.

'There's nothing to think *about*, apart from staying alive!'

'What's an Internet protocol?' he suddenly demanded.

'The address – the trace – of whoever's got into your system. The fingerprint, if you like.'

'I don't like,' said Carver, turning her expression. 'What are the chances of them finding you – where you worked from – through the English place they bombed?'

'I don't know,' admitted Alice, honestly.

'Out of ten, give me a figure.'

'A two.'

'That's good. And even then it wouldn't get them to you, personally, would it? Just to the cafe. And no one there knew what you were doing, did they?'

Alice felt a sweep of nausea. 'They've got to be warned.'

'No one knew what you were doing?' insisted Carver.

'Of course not.'

'How did you pay?'

'Cash.'

'No credit cards or cheques?'

'No.'

'So no one ever knew your name?'

The memory echoed in her mind. *I'm Bill, by the way*. And her automatic response. *Alice*. She said: 'No.'

'Then there's no way you can be identified, even if they did trace back to Manhattan.'

'What about a warning?' said Alice.

'I'll think of something.'

'There's nothing to think about. An anonymous call's all it'll take.'

'Leave it to me,' demanded Carver. 'And I really mean that. Leave – it – to – me!'

'OK.'

'I don't feel hungry,' he announced.

'No.' She paused. 'We could go to bed.'

They did and there was the aphrodisiac of fear for both of them and for a long time afterwards they lay silently, exhausted, together.

At last he said: 'I've got to go up to Litchfield tomorrow. I'm not sure yet what time I'll be back.' When he'd telephoned to tell Jane of Janice's death she'd been trying to fix the realtor's inspection visit for noon. He should have called her again before now.

'I'll wait to hear from you.'

After Carver had gone Alice stood with her wine in her hand, staring out over the bustle of SoHo in the direction of the cybercafe. The risk was minimal. But she hadn't believed they'd locate her Trojan Horse in the hotel chain's booking system.

The telephone was picked up at once and the voice said: 'Here we are, ready and waiting to help you!'

'Is that Space for Space?'

'It is and it's Bill and I know that's you Alice 'cos I got an ear for voices. Tell me we're going to have that drink at last, Alice?'

Alice hurried the receiver back on its rest, the feeling of nausea again blocking her throat.

Stanley Burcher extended his hand towards Enrico Delioci and said: 'I'd like the phone.'

The Don's son frowned, in feigned misunderstanding. 'What?'

'The cellphone you called me on from the woman's apartment.'

'The fuck you talking about?'

'The phone,' insisted Burcher, soft-voiced as always and as always hating being on this Queens film set. 'I want the phone you called me on, from Brooklyn.'

'Why?' demanded the younger man, truculently.

Burcher turned away from him, towards the father. 'Don Emilio, this isn't going well for any of us. I appeal to you!'

'Do you not trust us, Mr Burcher?'

'I trust you and your son and your Family totally and implicitly,' lied Burcher. 'What we can't trust – predict – is the use the law would make of whatever is stored within the phone's memory.' He slowly reached into his pocket, to produce a new cellphone, a very recent introduction on to the market, from which it was possible to transmit photographs, and offered it to Enrico. 'There! A replacement.'

'We'll destroy the old one,' said Paolo Brescia.

'I want it now, its memory card or battery or whatever it's called, intact.'

There was total silence within the room. Alert though he was, Burcher did not detect the gesture from father to son. Enrico Delioci rose, left the room and returned again within minutes, offering the instrument in a hand shaking with fury. Burcher said: 'Thank you.' There was no guarantee that what he'd been given was the telephone upon which he'd been called from Brooklyn and upon which he'd given the order to dispose of Northcote's assistant. The silence stretched on. Burcher said: 'Now tell me what I need to know about John Carver.'

It came, tight-lipped, from Brescia again. Burcher listened dispassionately, wishing there were more but conceding there was enough for his intended confrontation with the accountant. It wouldn't be the only confrontation, Burcher decided at that moment. When he'd established his personal control over John Carver, he'd enjoy telling these people that their usefulness was over.

There hadn't been any prior telephone call, which there always had been before, so Burcher's surprise was tinged with alarm at finding Charlie Petrie waiting for him at the Algonquin.

'You come about Brooklyn?' Burcher anticipated.

Petrie shook his head. 'You seen Carver yet?'

'Going to surprise him tomorrow.'

'We thought you should hear about the hacking first.'

Thirteen

It was more practical – his decision, about which there was later some ironic, even irritated, reflection – to meet Jane at her father's estate, which is what Carver did rather than put down at their own country home to drive the ten miles around the separating lake. Jane hadn't arrived but Jack Jennings was already there and together they toured the house. There wasn't the slightest trace of damage anywhere. All the jack-hammered doors had been replaced and those torn off their hinges rehung. New refrigerators and freezers gleamed in the recesses. Cracked or too badly stained tiles had been relaid and overbalanced wine racks rebuilt and re-labelled, although there was obviously no wine. George Northcote's bedroom and dressing room had been re-carpeted. The only hint of the work that had gone into redecoration was the faintest smell of paint and a lot of windows open to dispel that.

Carver said: 'In the time you've had you've worked miracles, Jack.'

'Mr Northcote was well liked around here. I called, things got done right away. The outhouses are the same. Everything fixed, all the damaged machinery gone . . .' The man gestured in the direction of the hollow into which the tractor and cutters had flipped. 'There was . . .' He stopped, seeking the acceptable words. '. . . some stuff, mess, there. We cleaned that up, too.'

What might there have been for a proper forensic examination to find, wondered Carver. 'You've still done damned well. Thank you.'

'I heard about Mr Northcote's PA. It's terrible, poor woman.'

'Terrible,' echoed Carver. He wished Jane would arrive, so they could get it over with and he could get back to New York. In the circumstances he supposed he had to be here, supporting her, but he'd had again to reschedule his already rearranged appointments – which actually took away the need for any hurried return – but he felt cut-off here, too far away from things. Wasn't that what – and where – he wanted to be, he asked himself at once: away from it all, where no one could find him? In truth – truth which he forced upon himself – Carver didn't properly know any more where he wanted to be or what he wanted to be doing. There wasn't a road that wasn't blocked, no half-formed hope that stood up to examination. There was the one hope he hadn't explored, he corrected himself: the one that had come to him the previous night, when he had been with Alice. Which wasn't new. It was the one, the last one, that he'd inexplicably forgotten but which to pursue, as he had to, could be as destructive as everything else closing in around him.

'Here they come,' announced Jennings, from the newly restored front door.

Barry Cox was the senior partner in the real-estate firm that bore his name, a squat, quickly moving man able to smile and talk at the same time, which he did constantly. He, not Jane, led the tour of the property, making quick entries in a small notebook and frequently having Jennings secure one end of a long, spool-retracting tape to measure the main rooms.

As they followed the man around, Jane said: 'I'm coming back to New York with you. I had Barry drive me over, so we can leave right away.'

'You didn't say, last night.' He'd somehow make time to see

Alice. He was glad after all that his diary was clear for the afternoon.

'It hadn't been fixed then.'

'What hadn't been fixed?'

'Our first meeting with Rosemary. She got a cancellation so she called me. I tried to catch you at the office but you'd already left to come here. Hilda said she thought it would be all right. And there's some more replies to condolence letters I need to sign, apparently.'

'In future will you personally clear things with me first?'

She looked at him curiously, frowning. 'What's the matter?'

'I haven't done any worthwhile work since I can't remember when, in a firm I have now to run. I intended trying to fit some things in later today.'

'I tried calling you! You weren't there!' she said, stiffly.

'You knew I was coming here. You should have waited.' There was no purpose in exacerbating it into an argument but he was irritated by her increasingly taking him for granted. It occurred to him to tell her that he was in charge of the firm now, not her, but decided against it.

'I'm sorry!' she said, in a voice that didn't sound it.

'Let's leave it.'

'All done,' declared Cox, emerging from the main living room at the opportune moment. 'Time to talk.'

Jane said to Jennings, who was already withdrawing, 'Will you transfer my stuff from Barry's car to the helicopter?' and then to the realtor, 'How long will it take to sell?'

The man gave a professional non-committal shrug and went into a well-rehearsed speech about market difficulties in an economic recession, concluding that it was a very valuable property, in the three-to-five-million band, which was a big commitment for a person to make.

'Not for a person with five million,' said Carver. 'And people who haven't got that sort of money don't look at this sort of property. You're going to concentrate upon the city?'

Cox had three offices there and the reputation of being the best country-house salesman operating out of Manhattan, which was why Jane was employing him.

'I'm going to offer it to as wide an audience as possible, Mr Carver,' said Cox. 'The Net, with a picture display and digital viewing, major prominence in the housing mags all along the East Coast right down as far as Florida. Might even consider the Caribbean: lot of money in places like Antigua and the Caymans.'

'What?' broke in Carver, sharply.

Jane and the realtor looked at him with matching frowns.

'I'm sorry . . .?' questioned Cox.

'Why did you suggest the Ca . . .?' Carver only just managed to switch to Caribbean and knew he sounded as stupid as he looked.

'There's a lot of money there,' repeated the man. 'It's a good marketplace.'

'Advertise it wherever you judge the most likely places to get a sale,' instructed Jane, impatiently. 'Put it on for three.'

Now the realtor frowned at her. 'That was my bottom figure, Mrs Carver. I think we should begin higher. People like to bargain, think they're getting a deal. Starting at three-seven-five would build in the drop to make a buyer think he'd got his deal and cover your costs and fees.'

'Three,' insisted Jane. 'Thanks for your time, Mr Cox. I look forward to hearing from you.'

In the helicopter, their conversation unheard by the ear-phone-wearing pilot, Jane said: 'What was all that about back there?'

'Just clarifying some things,' said Carver, inadequately.

'Sounded more like confusing some things.'

'You're giving the place away, you know.'

'It's mine to give away, OK?'

'OK,' accepted Carver. He didn't like the new Jane, he decided. At once he contradicted himself. He loved her as much and as deeply as he'd ever done. What he didn't like was the new attitude. Perhaps his own wasn't much better.

Rosemary Pritchard was a diminutive, sharp-featured woman with the sort of commanding presence that reminded Carver of the matronly, no-nonsense Hilda Bennett. The clipped voice fitted, too.

Jane said: 'Thanks for fitting me in.'

'Fitting you *and* John in,' qualified the gynaecologist.

'OK,' said Jane, with a touch of renewed impatience. 'Can you help me . . .' The break was a speed bump. '. . . help John and I, to have a baby?'

'Does John want a baby?'

Rosemary's quiet-voiced question startled both of them. Jane began: 'Of course John . . .' before Rosemary in turn, but much more definitely, blocked the response.

'It wasn't your question, Jane. It was John's.'

No! thought Carver, at once, and was just as quickly surprised at his reaction. Of course he wanted a child: children. He and Jane had talked about it – planned it or thought they were planning it – until the months had stretched into years, sixteen in fact. But he didn't want a baby now: not at this precise moment with so much hanging over them. Jane had insisted – arranged without discussing it with him – that he should be here. Invited him, in fact, to have his own voice even if she hadn't anticipated what he would say. 'I think we're rushing things. Because of what's happened.'

He was conscious of Jane twisting towards him. He didn't look back at her. She moved to speak but before she could Rosemary said: 'What do you think of that, Jane?'

Strangely, for someone who'd been about to respond so quickly, Jane didn't answer.

The gynaecologist said: 'How long have you both been thinking about in vitro fertilization?'

Hurrying ahead of her husband again, Jane said: 'A year, at least.'

Once more Carver ignored her demanding look. He said: 'The question was *both*. We haven't *both* been thinking about it for a year, at least.'

'Jane?' prompted Rosemary.

There was still a hesitation before Jane said: 'It's time we started a family!' And maintained the bloodline of a wonderful man, she thought.

'Is *this* the time?' demanded the other woman.

'I came here to talk about having a baby!' said Jane. 'Not to be psychoanalysed!'

'That's good,' said Rosemary. 'It's easy to cross boundaries, in this job.'

'Can we just talk about IVF?' asked Jane.

'Sure,' agreed the other woman, easily. 'What do you want to know?'

'How quickly – easily – can I become pregnant?'

The gynaecologist let some silence come between them before, straightening and picking up her pen, she said: 'I put you on the Pill to regularize your periods: hopefully to make them more comfortable for you?'

'When my periods became easier I found I didn't need it,' said Jane.

'I didn't know you'd stopped,' intruded Carver.

'You didn't talk to John about that?' demanded Rosemary.

'No,' Jane admitted.

'And you didn't tell me, either, did you?'

'No.'

Everyone lies – or avoids the truth – with everyone else, thought Carver. Until now he wouldn't have believed it from Jane or Alice but now he knew both had avoided the complete truth. The rushed awareness of his own hypocrisy – at least towards Jane – surged through him. What had he been doing, for the past eighteen months? Not lying, certainly, because the question had not been put to him. Nor avoiding the truth, he supposed, because again there had been no challenge. But he was certainly morally guilty of lying to Jane by having the affairs with Alice. Or was the moral lie the one to Alice, prepared though she insisted she was to live with their arrangement? Another to join the never-ending list of unanswerable questions.

'Do you properly know what in vitro fertilization involves, beyond what you've read in newspapers?' asked Rosemary.

'No,' managed Carver, just ahead of Jane, who almost as quickly said: 'Yes.' Anxious to cover the awkwardness – genuinely to help Jane – Carver said: 'I'd certainly like to know.'

'The first – the most important thing – you've both got to understand is that IVF is not the absolute guarantee of pregnancy,' said the specialist. 'Despite all the claims, only one in ten women successfully becomes pregnant at the first attempt, by which I mean actually *having* a baby. My personal experience – success rate – is that just a quarter of my patients *ever* achieve a full pregnancy that produces a healthy child . . .'

'What's it involve?' demanded Carver. He had to find an escape, not from ever having a baby – a dilemma he had until now refused to contemplate – but from even considering it at this time.

'For you, a series of tests,' replied the woman. 'Neither of you have undergone fertility exploration, have you?'

'No,' said Carver, quickly again.

'A sperm count for you is the most obvious. For you, Jane, a fallopian-tube examination and ovulation monitor . . .' She hesitated, looking directly at Jane. 'At this moment – maybe for some time in the future – I'm not convinced you two can't create a baby in the normal, unaided way. And until I am, I'm not even going to begin to consider IVF. Doctors don't fix arms and legs *before* they're broken . . .'

'If John and I were able naturally to have a baby, I'd have become pregnant by now,' insisted Jane.

'There's no logic in that whatsoever,' dismissed Rosemary. 'You've a history of menstrual difficulty. Simply coming off the Pill, for however long you have, doesn't automatically mean you're going to become pregnant. We'll run the tests, on both of you. If there's a problem that we can't fix, then we'll move on to IVF.'

'When?' demanded Jane.

'When we've discovered if there *is* a problem. Rushing into IVF if there's not could actually lessen rather than increase your chances of becoming pregnant.'

'When can we start the tests?' persisted Jane.

'All we initially need from John is a specimen. I could start with you, Jane, next week.'

'It's fixed then,' decided Jane.

'We're beginning a procedure,' said the gynaecologist. 'We don't yet know there's anything to fix.'

'When next week?' said Jane, rising.

'Tuesday, ten,' said Rosemary. 'And Jane . . .'

'What?' said Jane, already on her way to the door, Carver following.

'I *am* a psychologist, as well as a gynaecologist. Why don't you and John really talk this through?'

Jane held back until they got outside. Then she whirled on Carver and said: 'Thanks a whole lot!'

'Don't blame me for what happened back there! You fouled it up, not me!'

'You didn't help!'

'You heard what she said – why don't we really talk this through? Which we didn't. And haven't. This is irrational, Jane. I know your grief and I know your loss. But this isn't the way to compensate.' He was aware of curiosity from people having to manoeuvre around them on the sidewalk. Aware, too, that this wasn't the time to ask her about any safe-deposit facilities in her father's private bank, Carver's last hope of a more complete dossier.

Jane began, at last, to cry. But silently and, unlike the first day, with no racking sobs. She let the tears run, unchecked. Her nose, too, and Carver gently wiped her face, angry at the now greater curiosity of passing people. She said: 'I'm trying to hang on, John. I'm looking for something to hang on *to*.'

'How about me?'

'Yes,' she said. 'How about hanging on to you?'

Carver had the cab detour to East 62nd Street, glad Jane changed her mind about returning with him to the office. Having tried three times to call Alice he didn't understand why the message on her answering machine had changed. Or why, even more worryingly, she hadn't replied. He tried a fourth time from the back of the taxi and got the same strange-voiced reply – strange-voiced but to him easily identifiable as her – and couldn't comprehend why she didn't confirm her name or number in her message: she was a working journalist to whom the telephone was a major source of commissions.

He was even more unsettled by Jane's kerb-side collapse and her unarguing acceptance of the nurses' help when they'd got to the apartment. How close was Jane to a much more severe breakdown? By finally acknowledging the need for nurses, Jane was acknowledging a problem. Would she also acknowledge the need for a psychiatrist? He could talk to Dr Newton, from the office. Have Newton make a visit to the apartment and, if he considered it necessary, the doctor could broach the idea, to put the thought into Jane's mind ahead of his suggesting it.

If there was some mental condition, could he risk talking to Jane about safe-deposit boxes? Not that there was a risk in *talking about* such boxes. The danger, in Jane's fragile state, was what those boxes, if they existed, might hold. And Carver wasn't thinking at that precise moment of incriminating evidence of long-term and massive money laundering. He was thinking about photographs of a beautiful, laughing girl named Anna. If Northcote had left the photographs so easily discovered at Litchfield and at West 66th Street – needing nostalgically to remind himself, Carver presumed – or in the firm's vault, what was there likely to be where Northcote would have believed only he would ever have access? But he had to get to it, if it existed. And for precisely that reason. The more he thought about it the more logical it was that a personal safe deposit was the only place Northcote would have believed secure and secret from everyone except himself. And there had to be one, Carver decided, letting his speculation run on. He knew from the Chase Manhattan ledger that Northcote had been to the firm's vault on the day of his Harvard Club encounter. And if he'd handed over then what he'd retrieved he – and Janice Snow – might well still be alive. So where else but to his own bank would he have gone, in between the Chase Manhattan at 11.30 a.m. and the Harvard Club, at 1 p.m.?

So engrossed was he that Carver physically jumped at the sound of his own cellphone, almost dropping it as he fumbled it from his pocket.

'Mrs Carver told me you would both be coming back,' said Hilda.

'She's not, after all,' said Carver. 'I'm on my way, though. Five blocks maybe but the traffic's like it always is.'

'I took it upon myself to arrange something, knowing you'd be here around this time.'

'What?' demanded Carver, apprehensively.

'There was a call from a lawyer, representing those companies Mr Northcote kept on,' replied Hilda.

'What's the name?' demanded Carver, hearing the crack in his own voice.

'He didn't give one, although I asked, obviously. He said it was extremely important that he talk to you as soon as possible but that he was leaving New York tomorrow. So I gave him an appointment at five this afternoon. You'll be here well in time for that.'

Run, instinctively thought Carver. Then, delay: delay at least until he could prepare himself. Get to Northcote's personal box. 'He leave a number: a way to contact him?'

'I asked him for one, of course. Just in case. He said he was moving around the city and couldn't be reached.'

Carver looked at his watch. He had just twenty-five minutes, he saw. Abruptly, ahead, the traffic cleared.

Fourteen

By the time Carver reached the office he had fifteen minutes left and the only precaution upon which he had decided took just five of them, because everything was already set up. All that was left for him to do was wait and try to anticipate, which he initially did but quickly gave up because he wasn't anticipating he was imagining and the image upon which his mind settled was the near-faceless body of George Northcote. Carver forced the panic back, consciously breathing deeply as if pulling the courage into himself. He could do it, if he didn't panic: if he didn't conjure up mental horror pictures. His stomach churned, physically, and a few times audibly. There was no visible shake when he looked down at his hands, lying before him on the desk. He lifted them, holding them out straight in front of him. Still no shake. He felt his face. He wasn't sweating, either, although he felt hot. He wiped a handkerchief across his face all the same, knowing he wouldn't be able to do so later. He didn't know – which was the root of his fear – what he was going to be able to do later.

The lawyer who hadn't left a name arrived precisely on time and as Hilda ushered him into Carver's room Carver thought at once of his memorial service reflection about professionally invisible people. In a crowd this man would have been practically see-through. He was medium height and slightly built and everything about him was muted: muted grey, single-breasted suit, grey-on-grey patterned tie, a white shirt.

It was impossible to gauge the man's age from the expressionless, unlined face. There was a strange, oddly unmoving smoothness in the manner in which he walked, a progress rather than an actual walk, the glide of an invisible, ghostlike – or was it ghost-making? – man. Carver had intended to remain seated, as Northcote had shown his superiority at their confrontation, but had hurriedly to scramble to his feet – totally losing the planned impression – when the inconspicuous man stopped the offered handshake halfway over the desk, making Carver rise to it. He at once turned to examine available chairs, to take the one that put himself directly – confrontationally – across the desk from Carver, and said: 'It's good of you to see me at such short notice.' The polite, ingratiating voice was soft, worryingly close to being inaudible, with no discernible accent.

'Particularly as you weren't able to leave a name.' Carver was pleased at his own hopefully forceful tone, evenly pitched but demanding, someone unaccustomed to being treated inconsiderately.

A reasonable attempt at playing the affronted man, Burcher decided. But only just. He rose, taking a prepared card from his top pocket, but offered it across the desk in such a way that Carver had once again to stand to accept it.

He was going up and down like the other man's marionette, accepted Carver. The two-line inscription on the plain pasteboard read *Stanley Burcher, Attorney at Law*. There was no address or contact details. Carver at once remembered the regular entries in Northcote's diary, S–B. Could he have misread the intervening squiggle as an ampersand to mean Northcote was meeting two people when it had only been this man, Stanley Burcher?

The lawyer said: 'The name wouldn't have meant anything. I knew the company names would.' He was unsure how long to permit the accountant to imagine his superiority. It was important not to begin wrongly. They were going to have to deal with each other for a long time, years, so there had at least to be an amicable working relationship, if not friendship. Until the very end Burcher had imagined something approaching friendship between Northcote and himself. Mutual respect, certainly.

What, Carver wondered, was the other man's real name? And how many other people had ever posed themselves the same query? Impossible, probably, to guess: as so much else – everything else – in which he was so suddenly and so unwillingly caught up was impossible to guess or to comprehend. The thought was abruptly replaced by another, far more relevant. There had not been time for his severance letters to have reached Grand Cayman. So what had brought this man here today? 'How can I help you, Mr Burcher?' Bullshit politeness to bullshit politeness – we're quietly talking murder, you know, your murders, yes I know, good of you to put it so discreetly.

Burcher allowed a momentary but perceptible hesitation, for Carver's benefit, and Carver was pleased, misconstruing it as he was intended to. Then Burcher said: 'I don't think either of us needs to perform, do we, Mr Carver?'

'I don't understand that remark.'

'I know we can speak openly,' declared Burcher. 'George Northcote told my clients just before he died that you knew everything in which he and my clients were involved. Which is convenient for us all: it involves you. Makes you complicit.' After softball comes hardball, to let the man know how irrevocable, inescapable, his position was.

He had to tread – but more importantly, to speak – with extreme care, Carver reminded himself. 'I have learned certain things, in the last few days: things that greatly concern me. That knowledge, in itself, in no way involves me. Nor makes me complicit, with anyone or in any way, in anything.' He felt good, equal in this confrontation: stupid to have hollowed himself out, near mentally as well as physically. His stomach most definitely wasn't in turmoil any more: all his arguments were ready, logical. There was an immediate lurch – a twitch – of contradiction. How far from the whirling blades had Northcote's face been when he'd talked – screamed in the frantic terror of realization – of long-kept secrets no longer being secret?

Too obviously rehearsed but not a bad attempt, allowed Burcher. 'We both know what we are talking about, Mr Carver.'

'We do indeed, Mr Burcher.'

'I hope this is not going to become a difficult situation,' said Burcher, the voice still politely soft, perfectly modulated. Surely this man wasn't going to be stupid!

'I see no reason why it should,' said Carver. He was driving, choosing the route.

'There *is* no reason.'

Carver recognized the beginning of a who's-going-to-blink-first contest. 'You're obviously not aware of my letters.'

Burcher was put off balance by a remark he did not understand but he betrayed no reaction. 'No. Tell me about your letters. And what they said.'

'I yesterday sent letters officially severing all connection between George W. Northcote International and Mulder Incorporated, Encomp, Innsflow International, BHYF and NOXT,' enumerated Carver, with what he judged to be the necessary formality.

'I most certainly didn't know about those letters,' easily admitted Burcher. 'It would have been far better if we'd talked before they were sent.' It looked as if moulding Carver as the man had to be moulded was going to be more difficult than he'd imagined. It had been a mistake to imagine otherwise and Burcher didn't like conceding mistakes.

He was still in charge, decided Carver. 'I don't see any benefit in my having done that. I didn't, after all, have any idea we were going to meet. But why, not already knowing of my firm's disassociation from your clients, are you here today?'

Very definitely not as easy as he had imagined, Burcher recognized. 'Those whom I represent no longer appear on your computerized client list. I was asked to find out why,' Burcher improvised.

Now it was Carver who was tilted, hesitating, unsure which way to take the conversation. Cautiously he said: 'I've just told you I've ended my firm's involvement with your clients.'

'And immediately – before any discussion – erased them from your records?'

'I don't see any point – any purpose – in our discussing it further. The decision has been made. It's irrevocable.'

'I think there is need for further discussion, Mr Carver.'

'I repeat that I don't, Mr Burcher.'

'There could be some resentment from my clients.' He had to hear Carver out, fully discover the reason for the man's confidence, knowing as he clearly would what had really happened to Northcote and to the woman in Brooklyn.

'As I have some resentment at learning that your clients have been illegally monitoring my firm's computer system.'

'Learning that is most definitely a cause for concern,' picked up Burcher, heavily.

'I'm glad you agree with me.'

'I'm not agreeing with you, Mr Carver.'

'Then I don't understand.'

'My clients regard their security – the security of their affairs – as extremely important.'

'As I do, with my firm. Hence my irritation.'

'My clients are more than irritated – far more than irritated – at discovering that very concerted attempts have been made illegally to enter their computerized records both in this country and elsewhere.'

There was an echoing thunder of words in Carver's mind – no reaction, facial or verbal, no reaction, facial or verbal . . .

Even-voiced, sure he remained as expressionless as the man facing him, Carver said: 'Then they'll understand how I feel about their illegal entry here. I obviously need to update security.'

Burcher let a silence grow between them, staring directly at Carver, who stared directly back. The lawyer broke it. He said: 'Are you surprised to hear that efforts were made to intrude into my clients' affairs, following George Northcote's death?'

Carver was chilled – physically cold – but sure he gave no indication. 'As surprised as I was to learn that your clients have been intruding into mine.'

'*Theirs*,' pointedly qualified Burcher, at once.

'As I am sure you were more aware than I was, until very recently, no records of your clients' affairs were retained here . . .' Now Carver let in the pause. 'Which is extremely unusual and not a manner or a practice in which this firm will continue, now that I am in control of it. The fact that it has been allowed to exist, until now, was a major factor in my decision to disassociate from your clients.'

'We are moving ahead of ourselves, going off at tangents,' protested Burcher.

'I don't see that we are.'

'We were talking about illegal computer entry. Hacking.'

'I did not think there was anything further to talk about on that,' said Carver, the coldness moving through him again. 'But the fact that your clients considered themselves able to do it – and you felt able to admit it so readily to me – provides a further reason for our parting.'

'The hacking attempt upon my clients – quite a lot of which they believe to have been successful – originated from here, from Manhattan,' announced Burcher. 'My clients are confident they'll very shortly find out from where. And by whom.'

'Which should enable you to complain to the FBI.'

The face confronting him remained unmoving. 'You disappoint me. That wasn't a very clever remark, Mr Carver.'

'It depends upon your point of view. Mine is that there is nothing to be gained for either of us by continuing this conversation. I've made my decision, communicated it to your clients, and consider my letters to be the end of the matter. It's unfortunate that you've had a wasted journey.'

'I am not at all sure that it has been a wasted journey. Or that it is the end of anything.' He was arguing, as if Carver had an argument to put against him, Burcher realized, astonished.

'Mr Burcher, I have told you – and tell you again, now – that the firm of George W. Northcote International will no longer act for your clients in any capacity or in any way whatsoever! That, surely, is clear enough!'

There was another long silence. Briefly, for the first time, Burcher broke the fixed gaze in which he had until that moment held Carver, to look unseeingly down at some spot near the bottom of the desk, as if in contemplation. He'd been badly wrong, believing that John Carver would roll over at a frontal approach. Coming up again after several moments, the man said: 'The computer intrusion is not my clients' greatest concern.'

Carver waited, actually imagining the beginning of a renewed confidence.

'What did George Northcote tell you of his working relationship with my clients?'

He'd be losing control – temporarily at least – by replying to such a direct demand but there was advantage in his doing so, Carver decided. 'Nothing, apart from confessing that for a very long time he had acted for companies controlled by organized crime. He did not provide any identities. I told him I had no intention of continuing – which I've also told you, today – and he said it was a situation that would not arise: that his retirement ended the firm's association.'

'George Northcote profited very greatly from his firm's connection.'

'A benefit limited absolutely between himself and your clients.'

Burcher nodded, although Carver wasn't sure with what the man was agreeing. The lawyer said: 'At the end of his life, George Northcote proved himself a very stupid man. I hope – my clients hope – that you are not going to make the mistakes that he did.'

'Repeating the mistakes of George Northcote is precisely what I do *not* intend doing.' Carver was satisfied with the retort but the confidence wasn't there any more.

For the first time there was what Carver guessed Burcher intended to be a smile, lips drawn back from sculpted teeth like the brief opening and closing of a curtain. 'That's good to hear. Northcote's mistake was breaking a long-established understanding. No records were ever kept here. But towards the end, maybe over as long as five or six years, my clients estimate that Northcote retained what built up to be a substantial dossier of original material. This should have been prevented by our own people, of course. But after such a long and satisfactory association, they'd grown complacent. Which was their mistake.' Burcher stopped, waiting.

Uncertainty about what to say – what to admit and what not to admit – surged through Carver. Momentarily he had another mental image of a crushed, near-faceless body. He said: 'George told me they were to guarantee the end of the firm's links with you.'

'Aah!' said Burcher, stretching the exclamation as if a profound mystery had been explained. Then, after another pause, he said: 'How, exactly, did he intend achieving that guarantee?'

The thin ice was creaking beneath Carver's feet again. 'He didn't make that clear. I remember him saying that there wasn't going to be a problem.'

'Wasn't going to be a problem,' echoed Burcher, spacing the words to make them into an obvious threat. 'But there was. And is. A very big and very real problem, Mr Carver. My clients gave George Northcote the guarantee he asked for. And in return he promised to return everything he'd retained. But he didn't. My clients have gone through everything, back more than ten years. And they know there is still material missing. And have even had it confirmed.'

Janice Snow, thought Carver, immediately. 'How was it confirmed?'

'You brought a valise back from Litchfield. My clients believe that valise contained missing documents that belong to them. They will be most distressed if, this time, they do not get them back . . . *all* of them back.'

It was not the admission about Janice Snow that Carver had hoped for but this man was too clever for him to try to get it more obviously with another question. Carver decided he'd played enough and achieved enough. He said: 'I believe there are some things belonging to your clients . . . not a lot but some . . .'

The curtain was briefly parted for another grimaced smile. Burcher thought that maybe it wasn't going to be so difficult after all. 'I am so glad this is going to be resolved amicably. Sensibly.'

'You spoke of your clients having given George guarantees?'

Burcher nodded but said nothing, forcing Carver reluctantly on. 'Which was the return of the documentation on the understanding that all links between this firm and your clients are ended?'

There was another nod, no words. Burcher decided it wasn't going to be resolved today but then what was the hurry? He and Carver had a long life ahead of them.

Carver stopped speaking, waiting. Tensed, too, against his stomach turmoil becoming audible again. There was still no visible shake in his hands, seemingly easy upon the desk in front of him. He didn't want to risk lifting them from the support, as he had before.

Burcher again broke the impasse. 'There is a great deal of annoyance.'

'Of which – in which – I am in no way involved. Nor is the firm, only by title, which has no relevance any more.'

'I'll make the argument,' promised Burcher.

Could he make his own argument, Carver asked himself. And followed with the other questions. Was he brave enough? Strong enough? Did he have incrimination enough? 'I need the guarantee.'

'I need the missing documentation,' declared Burcher, flatly.

'I know that.'

'*Everything*,' insisted the lawyer.

'Everything,' agreed Carver.

'Have you told anyone? Your wife, for instance?'

Carver wasn't sure how much longer he could hold on. Minutes. No more than minutes. He moved one hand to cover the other. His skin was tingling, sensitive to the touch: unreal. It was all unreal, so totally disorientating. Forcing the steadiness into his voice, he said: 'Of course not! Tell his daughter what her father had done!'

'What about Alice Belling?'

Carver later thought – although never admitting it – that if he had not been sitting he might actually have had difficulty in remaining upright, staggered at least, at the numbing awareness of how completely he was trapped. It would be ridiculous to pretend – to question. 'Absolutely and most definitely not.'

'I want you to understand, Mr Carver, my clients' determination to recover what is rightfully theirs.'

He had to end it soon! Very soon! 'I hope you understand my equal determination for separation between us.'

'I'd be better able to discuss that with my clients if I left today with what they want.'

Carver indulged himself – tried to recover – with a hint of derision. 'Do you honestly imagine that it would be here?'

'I'd certainly imagine that you have safes here. A security vault.'

Not imagine, thought Carver. He'd know. Know from a bewildered, terrified, tortured Janice Snow. 'What you want is divided between bank safe-deposit boxes. And the banks are now closed.'

'I've talked about mistakes, Mr Carver. Too many totally unnecessary mistakes.'

'Which I've heard.'

'I hope you have, Mr Carver. Sincerely hope you have. You already appear to have a complicated personal life: it's not one to complicate further. This is a situation to be ended.'

'As is our connection,' persisted Carver. 'I've given you my guarantee. I look forward to yours.'

'I want it all by tomorrow,' demanded the man, letting the artificial politeness slip for the first time.

Carver's only need – a physically aching need – was to end this confrontation: end it and escape. 'Where can I reach you?'

'You can't. I'll reach you here, tomorrow. Noon.'

'You're coming here at noon?'

'I didn't say that. I said I'd reach you here, at noon.'

'I'll be waiting.'

'We both will.'

It was three hours before Carver got to Princes Street, almost one of them spent practically unmoving – initially slumped – in his chair in the darkened office, recovering. He was exhausted by the encounter and further drained, more so mentally than physically, by analysing it all and what he had to do as a result of it.

He'd telephoned, warning her, and when he entered her apartment Alice said: 'Jesus!'

'I know,' he stopped her. 'Shit on a stick.'

'Not even close.' She poured her prepared drinks, spilling some in her own nervousness, and said: 'So it was bad?'

Carver stared into the Martini. 'That's the funny thing. It didn't seem so, when it was happening. It was only afterwards, thinking about it all. Listening.'

'Tell me.'

He did, rehearsed, word-perfect, and Alice put her drink aside, head bowed. She didn't immediately speak when he finished and Carver didn't try to prompt her, his mind once more analyzing what he'd said, trying to think of what he might have overlooked or misinterpreted, finding nothing. There was, though, still the denouement.

Alice said: 'He knew about me? *They* know about me?'

'By name. Involved with me. He didn't associate you with the hacking.'

Alice hadn't once personally answered her telephone since the Space for Space manager's recognition of her voice, tensed for the man to call back after tracing her number by dialling the 69 'last-call' identification code. He hadn't. Her line had gone five times that day, twice Carver trying to find her – the last time warning of his arrival – and twice with editorial queries on articles she'd written. The fifth caller had ominously disconnected, without leaving any message. She'd been too frightened to dial 69 herself, to learn who the caller was. 'What *did* he say?'

'That they knew the intrusion originated from here, from Manhattan.'

'That all?'

'That they were going to find out who it was. Which we know they can't, because you didn't leave any identification, did you?'

Alice was on the point of telling him, but decided against it. 'What about you and I?'

'The threat was there, as it was in everything else he said.' It was the moment to tell her, to reassure her. 'In fact, he said far too much.'

Alice retrieved her drink, frowning across at him. 'What do you mean?'

'I recorded everything. We've had the wired-in system for years, for client interviews.' He smiled. 'I pressed the button and got it all: I've even made a copy, before I came here tonight. And we've got his name: or at least the name he's using. He might even be the conduit through whom George dealt. Combined with everything else, it's the dynamite that'll blow them away.'

Alice smiled back. 'And there's going to be a meeting tomorrow?'

'He's contacting me at noon, to arrange a place.'

'Which makes it perfect. He tells you, you tell the Bureau and they pick him up, with the evidence, when he makes the meeting.'

Carver looked at her for several moments before saying: 'No.'

'What do you mean, no?'

'That way I lose it all, the firm, us, Jane. We've talked about it.'

Alice put her drink aside again to come over to where Carver was sitting. She knelt at his feet and took his glass from him, so that she could take both his hands in hers. She said: 'No, John.' Then, spacing the words: 'No! No! No! We've also talked about how they're too big for us to fight. They killed George and they killed Janice and they'll kill you . . .'

'Not when they hear the tape. And I tell them I've got a copy of it as well as duplicates of everything else.'

'John, you can't frighten *them*!'

'I'm not trying to frighten them. I'm not going to threaten them. All I want is severance. This is my insurance. Our insurance.'

Alice felt a sweep of helplessness: of not knowing what to say, what to do. And then, abruptly, she did know. 'I want you to promise me something. I want to know where you're going to meet this man Burcher.'

'Why?'

'I want to know where you're going to be. That you're going to be safe. Make it somewhere open, the park maybe, with people all around you. Not an enclosed office or an apartment. Or a car where they can take you anywhere they want.'

'All right.'

'Mean it!'

'I mean it.' The demand had been reversed, Carver realized.

'Can you stay?'

'Not with Jane the way she is.'

'Call me then, when the arrangements are fixed.'

'OK.'

'I love you.'

'I love you, too. It's all going to work out fine.'

'I know,' said Alice. And believed she did.

Stanley Burcher's irritation was soon subdued by his inherent objectivity. He knew what he was going to do and wished he didn't have to use the Delioci Family to achieve it but his brief, final involvement with them wouldn't give them any continuing rights.

Fifteen

What sleep she managed was fitful, half-awareness briefly broken by horror dreams of men hitting and beating and torturing people, of trying to run or escape: once it was John very clearly in her mind and another time it was herself and it was so real, so painful, that Alice woke crying out at the hurt. She felt physically sick when she finally, properly, awoke, and then she *was* sick, needing to run to the bathroom, and as she retched she decided that it was scarcely surprising, knowing – but even more frighteningly, not knowing – what she was that day going to start. The nausea wasn't helped by her having finished off the Martini pitcher without bothering to eat after Carver had left the previous night. She couldn't remember eating lunch, either. She forced herself now to eat toast she didn't want and drink coffee that she did, to take a headache pill.

What *was* she going to start that day? Too much yet to comprehend or imagine. Total, devastating upheaval, the most devastating of all, destroying her life with John. And it would be destroyed, Alice forced herself to admit. What was actually involved in entering the Witness Protection Programme was another thing she couldn't anticipate, apart from being given an entirely new identity, possibly in an entirely new country, but she didn't believe there would be any chance of retaining contact with John. More importantly, she didn't believe he would want to be with her, know her, because what she was going to do would end the firm of George W.

Northcote International, and with it most likely John's marriage to Jane, from the humiliating exposure that would result. Alice accepted – although it was the last thing in the world she wanted to accept – that he'd hate her, for making all that happen. Despise her, for wrecking – desolating – all their lives.

But at least they would *have* lives. Not be crushed or defaced or throttled. And maybe, even, he would have Jane. The humiliation of knowing what her father had been and done would not be public, in front of all her friends, because she wouldn't be able to have those friends any more. If she and John could make their peace they could still have each other after all.

What of her peace? Alice asked herself. The most unknown of all the unknowns. She guessed it would take a long time, if she ever found it at all. So was she prepared to take the first, irrevocable step upon the journey on which she was about to embark? No, not if there had been any other choice. If there had been the slenderest of straws she would have grabbed, not just clutched at it. But there wasn't. There were already two tortured bodies to attest to that. She'd make a third, she supposed, although mentally agonized, not physically broken. She hoped. It still wasn't fixed yet. Nothing whatsoever was fixed: not in place as logically, sequentially, as it was in her mind. It could actually still go wrong, even when it was fixed. Not go sequentially at all, like it did in movies. She had to ensure everything was right, first time. There'd be no chance – no action replay, take two, take three, rewind – for it to be got right, as it had to be got right. Alice was terrified. Physically, mentally, in every way possible, absolutely terrified.

Which she couldn't be. If she let herself be motivated solely by fear – another way of saying unthinking panic – it wouldn't be right first time. Disaster would implode upon disaster. She would have liked a stiffening drink, even with the orange pinkness of dawn still smearing the faraway horizon of New

Jersey, but the thought brought her again too close to retching and she put the unthinkable thought aside, because it was unthinkable. Booze wouldn't help. The reverse. The only thing – the only person – who could help her was herself, keeping in their strict and proper order in her mind what she had to do and how she had to do it. Another intrusive, irrational thought came to her and she thrust that aside, not because it was unthinkable but because it was dangerous and the last thing she could risk was any more danger than she already knew she faced.

Alice carried her coffee from the kitchen to her office to get the telephone number of the FBI's Manhattan field office on Broadway's Federal Plaza from the telephone directory and used a street map to trace a zig-zag route back and forth across the city. She was unsure whether it would be quicker – better to keep her on schedule – to use the subway rather than risk buses on gridlocked streets, and decided she had an easy choice of alternatives if above ground proved more difficult than below. It might, actually, make sense to dodge up and down. *They* knew she'd hacked from Manhattan. Were looking for her here. They knew her name was Alice. So did the over-friendly manager of the cybercafe, who might have got her number from the call-back service even if he hadn't used it yet. But who would volunteer it soon enough – scream it over and over again – under whatever torture he was subjected to. She couldn't wait until the protection programme to disappear. She had to do it now. That realization prompted another, which she at once recognized was going to tighten up her schedule because she'd decided she had to be back in Princes Street by eleven thirty that morning, but it was a precaution she most definitely had to take. She was pleased it had occurred to her now, in time, and not as an afterthought when it might have been too late. She checked her balance and calculated that even leaving sufficient for her regular payments to be met she had slightly over $17,000 if she withdrew from her savings as well as her checking account. Her branch was downtown, which would increase the dangerous, unnecessary temptation. Once more she put it to one side.

Alice sat for a long time upon her remade bed, knowing she had to make herself invisible as, according to John, the quiet-talking Stanley Burcher made himself invisible. She chose scuffed gym shoes, jeans, a white T-shirt and a kagoul with an all-encompassing hood. She posed in front of the closet mirror – raising and lowering the hood several times – to satisfy herself that with it raised she became a wallpaper person. She finished the effect with dark glasses and was even more satisfied. She decided the necessary satchel completed the impression of an indeterminately aged student.

It was only when she was actually inside the elevator, reaching out for the button, that she corrected herself, switching from ground to basement level, to use the janitor's stairs and the delivery entrance to emerge not directly on to Princes Street but into the side alley which connected with the service lane to Greene Street. She walked with the hood up, head bowed, dark glasses in place but unhurriedly because she'd read somewhere that in observation surveillance a hurrying person attracts more attention than one walking normally.

Alice had known she would do it, from the moment the idea first came to her. Like the proverbial moth to the proverbial flame she flitted through the downtown side streets until she reached that of the Space for Space cafe, only hesitating at the actual moment of emerging on to it. Then she did. Her immediate relief – absurd because she would have known from the publicity if it had been attacked – was that the cybercafe was still there and, from what she could see through the window, was as busy as ever. She couldn't pick out the persistent Bill. Or anything – a parked vehicle, loitering people – to indicate the place was being watched. At once Alice, proud of believing that she totally knew herself and impatient with pretension, accepted that she was posturing.

How could or would she know if the place was being watched! She had no special ability: no training. She moved past, forcing the normal pace instead of hurrying, which she was desperate to do, hunched inside the hooded concealment. It had been ridiculous, coming here! The very opposite of what she'd determined, not an hour earlier in Princes Street, that she had never to do. She turned at the first available intersection and took a circuitous route to get her back towards her bank.

She chose a desk assistant to make the withdrawal, relieved she'd anticipated the request for additional proof of identity and brought her passport. Which from now on, she decided, she needed permanently to carry.

'That's a lot of money, Ms Belling,' said the man, as he counted it out.

'Yes.'

'Don't you think a bearer cheque would be safer?'

'It has to be cash.'

'You be careful now.'

'I intended to be,' said Alice, a remark for her own benefit more than for the man.

The need occurred to her as she stacked the last of the money into her satchel. 'And I need coin.'

'Ma'am?' frowned the desk assistant.

'Nickels and quarters. Five dollars worth.'

'Five dollars worth is a lot of coin.'

'I'm on a tight schedule,' urged Alice.

The man was back in minutes from the counter. 'You sure about a cheque?'

'Positive. And thank you.'

'You be careful now.'

'You already said.'

Alice crossed towards the river and then cut uptown, consciously passing three telephone pods, knowing she was delaying the moment of commitment from which she would not be able to withdraw. The satchel, which she wore strapped across her chest, was heavy and the coin made a pendulum in her purse, banging against her leg as she walked. The next telephone, she promised herself: she'd make the call from the very next telephone. Not put it off any longer. She saw the pod on the corner of 31st and Eighth, by the post office. And walked on by. She was being ridiculous, she told herself. And getting tired, with the city still to criss-cross. And it was already ten twenty. She was behind schedule: not a lot but behind. She'd definitely begin at the Port Authority bus terminal.

Alice found a closed booth and wedged herself in, relieved to squeeze out of the satchel, and counted some coin on to the ledge. She hesitated, breathing deeply to calm herself, but didn't manage to, not in any way she could feel. She was hot and had the sensation of hearing her own heart beating: it sounded fast. Abruptly she pumped a quarter into the box, almost dropping it on her first attempt with sweat-greased fingers.

'This is the Federal Bureau of Investigation.'

It was a woman, black, Alice guessed from the tone. 'I want to speak to the agent-in-charge, please.'

'Can I ask who's calling?'

'No. I want the agent-in-charge.' Her voice was close to catching, at the end. Hearing the thump of her own heart was disorientating.

'I'm not sure if he's available right now. Can I ask what the subject matter is?'

Alice breathed in deeply again. 'Organized crime. Murder. Money laundering.'

'Can I ask you to hold on for a moment?' said the woman, still flat-voiced. Before Alice could respond the line went dead.

A minute, Alice decided, able to see the station clock. That's all she'd give them. She didn't know how long it took to put a trace on a call but as computer canny as Alice was she guessed it wouldn't be long – only minutes – with sophisticated electronics. And the FBI would surely have the latest sophisticated electronics. Thirty seconds had to have passed. Alice waited for the large hand to drop, easing down to pick up the satchel.

'Ma'am?' came a man's voice.

'Am I talking to the agent-in-charge?'

'Can I ask who you are?'

'I want the agent-in-charge. Someone in authority.' Two minutes had to have gone by now.

'My name's Gene. Do you want to tell me yours?'

'We'll use Martha. Be ready for that name when I call back,' demanded Alice and put the receiver down.

Alice boarded the first cross-town bus she came to, easing herself close to the door, not bothering to look for a seat. West Street seemed surprisingly empty, which was good. She eased the satchel between herself and the side of the bus, making it impossible to pick, checking her watch as she did so. Ten thirty. If she was going to keep to her eleven thirty downtown return to Princes Street, to be in more than good time for John's call, she reckoned she had time for two more calls – three at the most – to Federal Plaza. She got off at the New York Public Library, stopped at the first street phone she came upon, with no hesitation this time.

'Hello, Martha,' greeted the voice of Gene. 'What is it you've got to tell us?'

'You aware of the funeral of George W. Northcote?' Alice stood with her satchel protectively entwined between her feet, her wrist tilted to time herself, glad that unlike the station clock her sportsman's watch had a calibrated sweeping second hand.

'Hard not to be.'

'Unknown by anyone else in the firm, he laundered huge amounts of money – billions – for organized crime over decades. He was murdered up in Litchfield – it was disguised as an accident – when he wanted out.'

'You got a Family name?'

Two minutes, calculated Alice. 'Northcote had a personal assistant. Janice Snow. She was killed – again disguised as an accident – out at Park Slope in Brooklyn. They thought she had what they want.'

Two minutes, thirty seconds. 'What do they want, Martha?'

'The proof that Northcote kept back, believing it was his leverage to bargain a way out.'

'Let's take this nice and slow,' said the man.

'We're taking it too slow,' said Alice. 'Wait for my next call. Get on to Litchfield – the sheriff's named Al Hibbert – and on to Brooklyn.'

'Martha . . .!' but already Alice had replaced the telephone and started to walk with her satchel restrapped across her chest.

Second Avenue wasn't as congested as cross-town and Alice rode the bus past 34th Street, automatically looking towards the East River and the bee-like rise and descent of helicopters that since Northcote's killing had been so much of John Carver's life. Where would John be now? Doing what now, in his naive and misconceived belief that he could win where – and what – George had lost. Was that it! she asked herself, incredulous at the thought. Surely John – whom she'd long ago uncritically judged to be in awe of his father-in-law – didn't imagine what he was attempting today was a who-could-survive contest between a dead man, who horrifically hadn't, and himself, believing that he could? Surely not, she thought again, the rhetoric that of anxiously needed reassurance rather than a positive answer, which she couldn't anyway have provided. And for what? To prove what, apart from his own stupidity? If they were ever together again, properly – miraculously – together after he and Jane had been taken out of danger – would there be any way she could explain to him that he didn't have – hadn't needed – to prove himself? Would there be any benefit – any reconciliation – in trying? Of course not. By then it would be too late.

She got off at 14th Street, checking her watch once more as she did so. Ten fifty. In good time. Ahead of schedule now. The handset had been ripped from the wall of the first pod she came to approaching Union Square Park. There was one that worked at the Sixth Avenue junction.

Gene answered the call on the first ring. He said: 'I think you're jerking us around, Martha.'

'If you believed that, you wouldn't have taken this call yourself. I'm not one of your crazies and you know it.'

'I want you to come in.'

'*I* want to come in. But not yet: I can't, not yet.'

'Why not?'

'I want to give it all to you. The proof. Their negotiator. Everything.'

'You've got that!'

'I'll have a meeting place. The meeting place where it's being handed over to their negotiator, who doesn't know everything's been duplicated.' She'd keep the name of Stanley Burcher back. John was most probably right, about it being phoney. If the Bureau checked and couldn't find the name it would be a further reason to dismiss her as a crank.

'Handed over by whom?'

'Someone who's totally innocent. Who thinks he can handle it all by himself.'

'He can't!'

'That's why I'm talking to you.' Three minutes, Alice saw. Too long.

'What's your involvement, Martha?'

'Complicated. You'll have to wait for that, too.'

'How long?'

'Today. That's why I'm doing this. You've got to be ready.'

'You know the penalty for wasting Bureau time?'

'You spoken to Litchfield? And Brooklyn?'

'That's not an answer.'

'Be ready, when I call. There might not be a lot of time. The name's not Martha, by the way.' It was, in fact, her mother's name.

'I never thought it was. Mine's Gene, though. Gene Hanlan.'

'Wait.'

'We'll wait. Just make sure it's worth our while.'

The tension, although not the fear, went from Alice as she rode downtown, her money satchel secure on her lap beneath her cupped hands, glad that she hadn't needed to use the subway after all. She was by no assessment claustrophobic but she always had the vaguely uneasy impression of being too enclosed when she travelled underground. She was pleased, too, to be ahead of schedule. She hoped everything else worked out so well.

Alice was back in SoHo by eleven twenty and, uncomfortably remembering the perils of not eating, bought a tuna on rye and a pickle at a deli near the Guggenheim and still managed to get into her apartment, again through the delivery entrance, precisely on schedule. She made coffee to drink with the sandwich, realizing as she did so that she'd have to give the alerting call to Federal Plaza from her own telephone, risking identification. But that wouldn't matter, she further realized. By then, with the Bureau in place and able to make their seizures, she'd *want* to be taken in. It was only the thought of telephoning that prompted Alice, belatedly, to look at her answering machine, upon which one call was registered. Panicked, imagining that Burcher had made the arrangements early, Alice jabbed at the reply button. There was audible breathing, vague, discordant music, but no words before the blank of disconnection. Alice felt sick again.

John Carver was more confident than he had expected to be and was grateful: relieved. The feeling was largely predicated upon the early morning meeting with Paul Newton, after the Manhattan physician's examination of Jane.

Newton's prognosis was that Jane's symptoms were entirely predictable in someone who had been as close to her father as Jane and did not indicate any more deeply rooted mental problem needing psychiatric help. He'd prescribed something called chlorpromazine, which he described as much stronger than the tranquillizers given to her by Dr Jamieson, and in Carver's presence briefed the nurses, whose attendance Jane was no longer resisting, upon the possible side effects, including disorientation and verbal communication difficulties.

'The idea,' Newton had told Carver, 'is to block the recent, most painful memories.'

'You sure she doesn't need a psychiatrist?' demanded Carver.

'It's your choice, of course,' said the doctor. 'I intend to monitor her every day. If, on any one of those days, I – or any of the nurses – see any change, then naturally we'll react to it. At the moment all Jane is suffering from is extreme but postponed grief. She's run herself dry, mentally as well as physically, trying to do all that she has since her father's death.'

'How long?' asked Carver.

'I'll judge it on a day-to-day basis,' said the doctor. 'Maybe as little as a week.'

'Anything else I need to do? To know?'

'Avoid Litchfield, going there or talking about it: certainly any discussion about the sale of the estate. That's where the awfulness happened: it's that awfulness she's got to adjust to in her mind and therefore, this early, she doesn't need any reminders.'

Carver's mood was also buoyed by listening to the tape, which he'd played and replayed in his locked office as soon as he'd arrived in Wall Street. The tape was the last thing he duplicated after copying everything he'd retrieved from Litchfield, West 66th Street and from Alice. There was no way Burcher or those the lawyer represented could do anything but agree the separation. And keep that agreement to the letter. Carver telephoned the securities manager that he was on his way and easily walked the two blocks to Citibank, still arriving by nine forty-five. Determined to avoid any oversight Carver used the entire table in the private safe-deposit room, laying everything out in two individual piles. The third collection was of all the personal and legal documents and photographs concerning Northcote and Anna Simpson and Carver was slowed by it, wondering if Northcote had been as happy with Anna as *he* was with Alice: wondering, too, if Northcote had rationalized his relationship with her and his wife as *he*'d rationalized his with Jane and Alice. Intriguing but unanswerable speculation, he acknowledged yet again. And therefore pointless. Just as it was pointless keeping it all. He wouldn't, Carver decided.

He'd get today over, removing each and every threat. Ensure that Jane fully recovered, even if she needed a psychiatrist, which, despite Dr Newton's assurances, Carver still suspected she might. And then destroy this personal hoard in front of him, as Northcote should have destroyed it when it was no longer relevant.

He replaced the uncopied material and photographs in the security box first, before moving the briefcase alongside it. He loaded them one by one, original in the briefcase, copy back into the box. Again, the last item in each was the tape.

Carver went perfunctorily through the duplicate key relocking and signing out procedure, thinking now about Alice. He wouldn't call her until everything was over. She'd compounded their problems by her computer trawling – and ignored him when he'd told her to stop – and he was suspicious of her demands the previous night to know precisely when and where he was meeting Burcher. More than suspicious. So, if she didn't know, she couldn't interfere, maybe to put everything at risk.

He strode purposefully out on to Wall Street, with more than sufficient time before noon to walk the two blocks to his office, his mind switching back to Jane. Your choice, Newton had said. So he'd make it. He'd call the doctor and tell him he wanted a second, psychiatric opinion: the best available. He wanted Jane well – properly, completely well – as soon as possible.

'Good to know that everything's going as it should, sensibly,' said a voice Carver recognized at once, on his left. He was conscious of a close presence at his right, too. And behind.

'Here's the car,' said Burcher and before there was a moment for Carver to resist – cry out even – the inexorable pressure of the three surrounding men turned him towards – and then into – the open door of the vehicle that pulled up.

'There!' patronized Burcher. 'Now's the time to talk properly.'

Sixteen

'Heads up,' demanded Gene Hanlan. 'What have we got?'

'A crazy,' dismissed Ginette Smallwood, disillusioned from wasting the past four months investigating tip-offs from Federal Plaza walk-ins who'd turned out to be exactly that, initially convincing crazies who'd evolved good-sounding stories to get their fifteen minutes of fame. And to get her the reputation of someone who couldn't differentiate fact from phoney if she'd had Pinocchio on her shoulder.

'Doesn't sit right,' dismissed Hanlan. He twisted to the permanently displayed street map of Manhattan on the board behind his desk, upon which red marker flags were already displayed. 'We start at the Port Authority terminal . . . maybe she's an out-of-towner . . .'

'Or maybe she's an in-town, uptown girl who chose the terminal for good reason,' interrupted Patrick McKinnon, the rotund, retirement-planning third field agent.

'Maybe an in-town girl indeed,' accepted Hanlan, still at the wall map. He tracked his finger along the electronically traced route that Alice Belling had taken. 'Sure as hell knew the city's transport system, according to the timings . . .' He turned away from the wall chart, gesturing to the separately marked tapes: the only incomplete one was Alice's first, before they'd been ready. 'We need to get the official opinion from the mumbo-jumbo thumb-suckers at Quantico but I don't hear any of that as a crazy. Stressed, sure. If I didn't think that, I *would* mark her as a crazy and we wouldn't be sitting around here now, talking about it.'

'Let's hold for a moment on Quantico,' suggested Ginette. Among its several disciplines, Quantico was the FBI's Maryland installation for offender profiling, where most of the psychological ancillaries were concentrated, including voice-print analysts.

'We're holding on everything for the moment,' assured Hanlan. 'But I've got a gut feeling. The Litchfield shit-kicking sheriff admits George Northcote's death is odd, despite what the coroner says. The house gets invaded like Baghdad on open day. And anyone here remember a hanging suicide breaking so many arms and legs from a two-foot fall?'

Neither of the other two answered the question. The querulous woman said: 'If mysterious Martha knows so much, how come she doesn't have a Family name?'

'Because she doesn't have a Family name!' threw back McKinnon, irritably. 'You heard what she said. I read it that she knows some but not all. Which I also read as meaning we need to get involved here . . .' He paused, for the effect. 'Organized crime . . . murder . . . money laundering . . . You really need me to spell out the career advantages of having our names at the top of the list of this sort of investigation?' His pension increased by $150 a month if he got promoted one more grade.

'Not for a moment,' grinned Hanlan, whose mind had begun to calculate that as early as Alice's second telephone contact.

'What's the essential for the perfect con?' challenged Ginette.

'For fuck's sake!' exploded McKinnon, who'd spent an unconsummated month hitting on the girl – and his ex-wife's entire month's alimony on dinners and Broadway theatres – before she'd told him she was gay. 'You've struck out three times in a row. Shit happens. This could be how you get off the bench and up to bat.'

'So what do we do?' accepted Ginette, reluctantly. She needed an impressive recovery.

'Put everything else on hold, for today at lease,' ordered Hanlan. 'Go through the case notes of Litchfield and Brooklyn if they're wired soon enough, which was the promise from both . . .'

'When's the last time a local force – certainly a local force who've already made up their minds and closed the case – co-operated with the Bureau?' demanded Ginette, who was thirty, model-thin, blonde and not gay, just resentful of the automatic chauvinistic expectation of office affairs.

'Northcote was high profile,' picked up Hanlan, ignoring the interruption. 'Let's see what's in the public domain.'

'That route,' said McKinnon, nodding to the map behind the agent-in-charge, 'goes in a square circle.'

'You want to help me with that?' invited Hanlan.

'Starts on the west side, crosses east, goes downtown, back west, always using phone boxes. And obviously public transport. She's definitely a local, seen too many James Bond movies. But that's where she lives, somewhere downtown. She was hurrying home.'

'Should be easy to find someone calling herself Martha who admits it's not her real name,' said Ginette.

'Downtown's financial,' said McKinnon. 'Northcote's office is on Wall Street. Martha could be a Northcote employee, stumbles upon where the secrets are hidden.'

'And the dead bodies,' agreed Ginette, less resistant. 'Janice Snow was an employee: maybe she shared what she knew with Martha.'

'Martha doesn't come back to us today, as promised, we call on George W. Northcote International tomorrow,' decided Hanlan.

'And ask what?' questioned McKinnon.

'To look at their client base?' suggested Hanlan.

'Northcote's top of the big-time pyramid,' warned Ginette.

'They got something to hide, they're not going to take kindly to us asking rude questions unless we've got due cause. Which so far we ain't.'

Hanlan reached over his desk for the third recording, fast-forwarding to where he wanted. The excerpt began with his own voice. *Handed over by whom?*

Then Alice's. *Someone who's totally innocent. Who thinks he can handle it all by himself.*

Hanlan said: 'It's someone in the firm: maybe two. Martha, our whistle-blower, and Mr Hard Guy, thinks he can face down the bad guys all by himself. Why's he doing that? The best guess, in my book, is to keep the firm squeaky clean. So he's high, a major player, maybe even a partner. Has to be, to have discovered whatever he has. We go in and we say we're not sure about Mr Northcote's death or that of his personal assistant, Ms Snow. Ask the partners, one by one, how they feel about it: if they've got anything they'd like to tell us. And watch the body language.'

'It's a way to start,' allowed Ginette, doubtfully.

'It's our best shot, we don't hear back from Martha,' insisted McKinnon.

Hanlan looked at his watch. 'Twelve. Whatever Martha's expecting to happen has got to be lunch time.'

'We hope,' agreed McKinnon.

'Shall I get the sandwiches?' offered Ginette.

'No,' said Hanlan. 'Like the lady asked, we stay ready to go the moment we get her call.'

Enrico Delioci, on his left, took the briefcase from Carver, without speaking, and handed it to Stanley Burcher in the front passenger seat. Burcher immediately opened it and started fingering through the contents. Paolo Brescia, on Carver's right, rode with his hand casually holding the courtesy loop, gazing out at the passing streets. He said to the driver: 'The Manhattan would probably be better than the Brooklyn Bridge.'

'Why pay a toll?' demanded the driver.

'Where are we going?' said Carver, glad his voice was steady. He wasn't sure if he was physically shaking from the fear pumping through him but hoped he wasn't. The men between whom he was too closely hemmed would feel it, if he were. They did wear dark suits but not shaded glasses. Like Burcher, they were inconspicuous, walk-by people.

No one replied.

'I asked where we were going,' Carver repeated.

'Somewhere quiet,' said Burcher, head bowed over the briefcase.

'Enjoy the ride,' said Brescia. He had an effeminate lisp.

Burcher turned at last, grimacing his version of a smile. 'I need to go through it in detail – talk about one thing in particular with you – but it seems OK. I knew we could work together.' He held up the tape cassette. 'What's this?'

'Something for us to talk about.' He'd made a mistake, Carver realized. A terrible, terrible mistake. Alice had been right. He couldn't face them down. But he had to now. The terrible mistake was also his only hope.

The curtain closed on Burcher's smile. 'So let's talk about it.'

'You're among friends. We don't have any secrets,' said Brescia.

Carver felt too threatened, squashed as he was by even harmless-seeming men in the back of the car. That impression brought the awareness that he was, in fact, physically bigger than any of the other four with whom he was incarcerated. Which didn't mean anything because he knew what they were capable of: what they had done to Northcote and Janice. He was going to feel threatened – *be* threatened – wherever he was with them, but he didn't want them this close – their bodies touching his – when he disclosed their entrapment. 'This ends your association with my firm, right?'

'That's something we need to talk about,' agreed Burcher.

'My people are extremely happy the way things are: how they've been – and worked – for such a very long time . . .' He patted the still-open briefcase, on the car floor at his feet. 'Even before you showed how well you understood priorities they asked me to tell you they didn't want things to end: that they saw every advantage for all of us in the arrangement continuing exactly as it's always been, to everyone's advantage.' Except, Burcher thought, the Delioci Family.

'I made it clear to you that that's precisely what I did *not* want. And wouldn't have.'

Enrico Delioci sniggered a laugh that emerged as a derisive snort. They were crossing the Brooklyn Bridge now, the pale sun dappling them with the shadowed patterns of the suspending superstructure.

Burcher said: 'John, this is the way it *is*. The way it's got to be. Look what George achieved: think about it. Think what you can achieve. All the respect and honour that George attained. More. You're set up, for a happy, contented life. Forever. People don't get things made the way you've got it made. Enjoy.'

They joined the expressway, made the left exit and almost at once took the turn-off towards the ferry terminal and turned once more into the lattice of narrow streets on the Brooklyn and Queens side of the East River. Once they've got you, they never let you go, thought Carver. There wasn't a definition – words that he could find – to describe how Carver felt. Frightened, certainly: acknowledging, finally, that he was out of his depth with these insignificant but supremely confident people who believed they owned the world. Which, Carver supposed, they did: their world, at their all-embracing level. But strangely – despite the definition and the words he couldn't find – Carver felt suspended above all those mixed impressions, beyond these people and beyond their danger. Making the tape hadn't been a terrible mistake. It was going to be his salvation because they couldn't hurt him – cause him any physical harm – while it existed: it was the connection – the provable link Northcote hadn't had – with the documentation at that moment lying beyond their grasp in the Citibank safe-deposit vault. 'We made a deal.'

'I promised to discuss it with my clients. Which I did. Now I'm telling you their decision,' lied Burcher.

'Which isn't my decision.'

They were in a car-abandoned, boarded-windowed labyrinth of rubbish-strewn alleys and streets, empty of life apart from an occasional scavenging dog or cat. Brescia sighed and said: 'Why don't we cut the crap! You're signed up, John, whether you like it or not. As Stan's told you, learn to like it.'

Did that mean that Burcher really had given his real name? It made it so much better if he had. 'And as I've told Stan, I don't like it.'

'We're here,' announced Burcher. 'We'll talk about it inside.'

The car made an abrupt left, then a right, and the street into which they emerged was suddenly clean, no longer an urban garbage dump. To their left was a high, chain-link fence sealing off a storage yard for dozens, maybe hundreds, of ship containers. A lot – the majority, as far as Carver could see – were marked with the names of the Mulder, Encomp or Innsflow companies. Beyond them, over the river, Carver could see the snag-toothed skyline of Manhattan. The car threw up a dust plume as it accelerated across the open strip towards warehouses, to which, as they got closer, Carver saw was attached a low office block. The sign on the side read *NOXT Inc. Export Specialists*. Cars were in tight formation in front but Carver couldn't see any people working outside. He did, through office windows, when he got out of the car. There was no obvious interest in their arrival. Carver was relieved to be free from the body contact of the men on either side of him. Burcher led. They went in through a door at the side and immediately up a flight of stairs into rooms fitted out as secretarial suites without secretaries or office staff. Burcher continued to lead, into a more expansive set of rooms, with leather furniture and decorative plants. The largest room was dominated by an impressive desk but everything looked sterile and unused, a stage set.

'Sit down,' ordered Burcher, contemptuously, not looking at Carver, who did as he was told. Burcher and Delioci went to the desk and unloaded on to it everything from the briefcase. From the top right-hand door of the desk Burcher took two sheets of paper, handing them to the other man, and together they compared every document against their list. Carver couldn't hear the mumbled conversation. It must have been fifteen minutes before they both straightened, turning at last to Carver. Delioci took the seat behind the desk and Carver wondered if his authority was greater than that of the lawyer.

It was Burcher, though, who did the talking. He said: 'You did good, John. We're pleased. Now the few things we've got to sort out . . . get right.' He made a hand gesture to the papers still lying on the desk before him. 'They're complete but there's something missing, isn't there?'

'That's everything I found, at Litchfield and at George's apartment, in town. And in his safe deposit at the Chase.'

'That's not what I'm talking about,' said the softly spoken lawyer. 'I told you my clients discovered there were a lot of attempts to hack into their computers. Some attempts that might have been successful.'

He had to protect Alice! Whatever happened – whatever threats were made – he couldn't disclose her name. Or her involvement. 'And I told you I knew nothing about that.'

'I know what you told me. My clients find that difficult to believe.'

Carver shook his head. 'I don't have anything to say to that, beyond what I've already told you, that I don't know anything about it.'

Burcher said: 'If we're going to work together, there's got to be trust between us. If we find you've lied, we're going to be very upset. And we will find out who did it. It's very important for us that we do.'

Carver no longer had the unreal impression of being suspended in mid-air because of all his conflicting feelings but the fear was stronger now, although not for himself. He hadn't expected the hacking demand: hadn't prepared answers, which he accepted he should have done. There was only one answer, if Alice were to be protected. Total denial. Which he'd already made. To repeat it could give the impression that he had some knowledge. 'I've also made it clear that we're not going to work together.'

There was another sigh from Brescia, who was sitting slightly behind Carver, between him and the door. Burcher said: 'John, you don't have a choice. That was made, years ago, by George Northcote. You've inherited his firm and you've inherited his responsibilities. Which you'll fulfil. This is the end of the discussion. There's nothing more to talk about. Except who got into the computer systems.'

The personal fear at last surged through Carver, at what he was about to do and say, the familiar skin-tingling, stomach-hollowing sensation. 'You haven't heard the tape.'

The two men at the desk stared, initially unspeaking, at Carver. Without breaking his gaze Delioci told Brescia: 'Go get a player.'

Burcher said: 'You stupid man. You idiotically stupid little man.' He still didn't raise his voice, just sounding each sound like a bell's funeral toll.

Brescia re-entered within minutes with a small cassette player and, unasked, fitted in the tape and pressed the start button. Burcher's voice echoed into the silent room. *It's good of you to see me at such short notice.* And then Carver's. *Particularly as you weren't able to leave a name.*

The recording apparatus throughout the Northcote building had been professionally fitted and the quality was perfect. Still no one spoke or moved, the lawyer and Delioci looking fixedly at Carver as the tape unwound with the identification of the companies and the quietly spoken and intentionally ambiguous innuendoes from Burcher. It was at Carver's denial of any knowledge of the computer hacking that Delioci stopped the tape with an impatient finger flick.

The roared shout – 'You're the total fucking idiot!' – at the lawyer and the fist crashing against the desktop was so unexpected that everyone physically jumped. Delioci rose, leaning towards Burcher, raging on. 'Like a fucking amateur you let yourself get wired like this . . .'

Burcher was ashen and there was a tremor in his hands, the middle finger on his left tapping against his thigh as if he were sending a signal. How could it have gone this wrong? How could everything – his coup, his dismissal of the Deliocis – go so wrong?

Delioci's head came around to Carver. 'So you've got a copy of the tape, which means you've got a copy of everything you've given back today and you're going to tell me that if we don't let go, you're going to turn it all over to the Feds, right?'

'I want the separation of my firm,' rasped Carver, hoarsely.

'Let me tell you what you're going to do,' said the man, controlled again. 'You're going to drive back into Manhattan, to the bank . . .' He nodded towards the finger-tapping lawyer. 'You're going to take him with you, right into the safe-deposit room and completely clear your box. I want everything . . .' He turned towards Burcher. 'You hear that? I said everything.'

'Yes,' said Burcher, almost a whisper.

The man came back to Carver. 'And when you get back here I'm going to tell you how you're going to work for us for the rest of your goddamn fucking life. But here's the thing I'm going to tell you right now, give you all the time you need to understand. You ever try – think of trying – another half-assed move like this and you'll get a choice. The choice will be who gets killed, your wife or your girlfriend. Yours to pick . . .' He switched to Burcher. 'And when you get back I'll have spoken to a lot of people who'll sure as hell want to speak to you . . .'

With only two of them in the rear of the car there was room for Carver to sit apart from Brescia and Carver did, as far as he could. Burcher hunched forward next to the driver, rocking very slightly back and forth.

Brescia said: 'You fucked up big time, Stan. Good job we're around to look after you.'

It was payback time, Burcher accepted. They were going to make him pay for every insult, real or imagined. 'It's going to be all right.'

'You'd better believe it,' said the other man.

Burcher stopped rocking, swivelling almost completely around in his seat to face Carver. 'Is everything in the box?'

Carver nodded, not speaking, his mind too jumbled to even think of words except those that echoed again and again in his head. *You're going to work for us for the rest of your goddamn fucking life*. And then: *The choice will be who gets killed, your wife or your girlfriend. You pick* . . . The car swept up on to the expressway and began going over the bridge, back into Manhattan.

'Everything that was hacked?' persisted Burcher.

'Everything I copied,' managed Carver. But the printouts were in the box! He'd have to say he did it, to save Alice. But they'd ask him how and he didn't know. Didn't know what Alice had meant about using English cut-outs – what a cut-out was, even – and they'd find out it was Alice and they'd kill her, because she had knowledge that could destroy them. And because they'd imagine it to be a fitting punishment for him.

'I suffer, you suffer, asshole,' confirmed Burcher. 'It all gets settled today. All of it.'

He had to fight, determined Carver. And then at once the questions. How? With what? The bank. That was the chance. His only chance. Last chance. Get Burcher into the vault with the security man, for the two-key opening procedure. Jump the lawyer there. Hold him and yell for the security man to help. Subdue Burcher and call the police, the Bureau, whoever. Get these other two in the car arrested. Then the shouting man back in the warehouse. Get protection. Alice had been right. The only way.

They turned into Wall Street. Carver could see the bank. He felt sick. He'd never fought anyone before. Not punched a man, wanting to hurt him. He wanted to hurt Burcher: hurt him as much and as badly as he could. And he could do it. He knew he could do it. He was physically bigger, stronger, than Burcher. It would help that he'd seen the security people, less than three hours ago. They knew who he was. Would react, when he called for help.

'You ready, asshole?' demanded Burcher.

Carver nodded. He was definitely ready.

The driver said: 'We get moved on, I'll go round the block.'

Carver saw the blue and white of the police car as he began to get out of theirs. It was coming in the opposite direction, slowed by other traffic. The decision was instant, unthinking, panic-spurred. He thrust the waiting Burcher as hard as he could out of his way, sending the man sprawling on to the pavement, and ran around the front of the car waving his arms and shouting, seeing the police driver and the observer turn in his direction, their lips moving, both frowning. Then Carver heard the bellow of the air horn behind him and twisted to see the truck for the briefest second before it hit him, knocking him beneath its tandem-mounted front wheels, which ran completely over his chest, crushing it far worse than George Northcote's had been crushed.

The frantically waiting Alice Belling saw the coverage on *Live at Five*, the story angled on the astonishing coincidence of the fatalities. She ran – literally – grabbing a case already packed. She didn't know how they'd done it to look like yet another accident: all she could think of was that they knew her name and that she would be next on the list.

Seventeen

The uniformed sergeant frowned up at Hanlan's entry, gesturing to a chair already set out, and said: 'The Bureau doing traffic accidents these days?'

'All kinds of things,' said Hanlan.

'Coffee?' The nameplate on the desk said Sergeant P. David Hopper. He was a small man bulged from sitting too long behind a desk and living even longer off relish-filled torpedo sandwiches.

'Coffee's good,' accepted Hanlan. It was like the hundred other police offices in the hundred other police precincts he'd ever been in, a scuffed, chipped, overused cell without bars in which people like P. David Hopper filled the drawers and cabinets with the stuff they brought from the previous scuffed, chipped, overused cell before moving on to the next. Hopper didn't have sufficient citations or plaques or souvenirs to cover all the clean patches left by previous occupants, leaving the wall pockmarked white. The coffee, from a percolator on top of a filing cabinet, came in an *I Love NY* mug.

'So what's all kinds mean?'

The apparent friendliness and immediate readiness to see him – rare from police to Bureau and vice versa – would be from curiosity, Hanlan knew. There'd been a lot of attention as he passed through the front hall and he guessed his presence would already be known about on the top floor. 'John Carver.'

Hopper shrugged. 'What can I tell you? Total mystery, why it happened, how it happened.'

'That's what I want to talk about, the mystery.'

The frown came back. 'I meant why a guy like Carver suddenly runs in front of a thirty-five-ton truck.'

'Doesn't it seem an odd coincidence that his father-in-law died in such a similar accident so very recently?'

Hopper shook his head. 'I don't know anything more about Litchfield than I've read in the paper and seen on the news. But I know about Carver because I've got the reports right here in front of me . . .' He patted some papers on the right of his desk. 'Which you're welcome to see and have a copy. I've got eight reliable witnesses – two trained squad-car cops from this very precinct whom I know and whose judgement I trust completely – all telling roughly the same story. For no reason, Carver suddenly runs off the sidewalk in front of a car, yelling and shouting, in the direction of the police car. The truck driver doesn't stand a chance. Can't be anything but an accident.'

'*Roughly* the same story?' pressed Hanlan.

'Couple of the witnesses thought they saw Carver push by some guy, knock him over.'

'The squad-car guys?'

There was another head shake. 'They only saw him when he started coming towards them. The two who saw the guy go over heard the first shout.'

Hanlan hoped that Ginette up in Litchfield and McKinnon, out in Brooklyn, were doing better than he was. 'What was the shout . . . the words?'

Hopper got up to refill his mug. Hanlan held up his hand against the gestured offer. Hopper said: 'No words. Just the noise.'

'What about the guy who might have got pushed over. Is he one of your witnesses?'

'No,' conceded Hopper. 'On balance I don't think there was

such a guy. You know how it is, situation like this. Guy gets squashed into the ground, everyone screaming and shouting, people's memories play tricks.'

'What about the car?'

'Car?'

'You said Carver ran in front of a car before he went under the truck. How come he didn't get hit by the car?'

There was the familiar head shake. 'Haven't thought about it. Had time to get by, I guess. But not the truck.'

'I don't see the sequence,' protested Hanlan. 'The truck has to be following the car, right? So if he gets clear in front of the car, how come he's hit by the following truck? Unless, that is, the car's stopped and the truck's overtaking. Any of your witnesses make that clear?'

'Gene, I'm trying to do all I can to help here. I truly am. So how about a little in return. You want to tell me why the Bureau's here, making traffic reports?'

Hanlan recognized the beginning of the usual resentment. 'We got a tip, sounded good. Big-time money laundering. The Northcote firm was referred to. We didn't get the promised call back, with more information, but the new head gets killed not a month after Northcote himself . . .'

'What workable evidence you got?' broke in Hopper.

'That's what I'm trying to find,' admitted Hanlan.

The uniformed man spread his hands. 'Best of luck getting into a firm like Northcote's. But you ain't going to do it with what happened on Wall Street. Like I told you, I don't know what made John Carver jump in front of a truck the size of Manhattan itself: I guess we never will. What I do know is that Carver's actual death was a one hundred per cent kosher accident . . .' That shrug came again. 'You want me to tell you amazing coincidence stories or do you watch them on television?'

'I've got an instinct about the tip.'

'Run with it then.'

'I need more.'

'Times like this I'm glad I do what I do and not what you guys do. You want I introduce you to our detective division along the corridor?'

'The crimes, if there are crimes, are federal.'

'Just a thought.'

'Anything comes up, you give me a call?'

'Nothing's going to come up, Gene. I got an arm-waving jaywalker didn't look where he was going.'

'Towards a police car, trying to attract their attention.'

'Best of luck. You've got my number.'

Hanlan offered his card across the battered desk. 'And here's mine.'

'Like to think I could help you by calling it,' said the other man.

Martha hadn't made contact when Hanlan reached Federal Plaza but George McKinnon was back from Brooklyn and Ginette Smallwood had called in to say that she was on her way from Litchfield. Hanlan and McKinnon were just finishing their review of the crime report on Janice Snow's hanging when Ginette came into the office and at Hanlan's insistence they went completely through it again in the hope that Ginette would isolate something they'd missed. She didn't. Every time the telephone rang they paused and looked up, hopefully, and every time got a mouthed 'no' in return from whoever in the support staff answered. It took them longer to go through the dossier on George Northcote's death, because the autopsy report was more detailed and there was the additional house-trashing burglary, which they studied just as intently.

There still hadn't been any contact from Martha by the time Hanlan reluctantly and finally pushed all the files aside, looking from one to the other of the two field agents for a reaction.

McKinnon said: 'Enough for a Saturday-night movie mystery, with some mighty jumps of logic to link it all together. But not enough, objectively, for us to initiate an official investigation.'

Ginette said: 'I agree. I don't know – but I'd sure as hell like to sweat Mystery Martha to find out – how and why she comes on to us two hours before John Carver throws himself in front of a truck . . .' She waved to the file Hanlan had brought back with him. 'But we can't buck the evidence of eight reliable witnesses, two of them police officers, that that's what happened. We've got more than enough for suspicion but not enough to move on it officially.'

'I still think we visit the Northcote office, see how they react to us,' suggested Hanlan.

'However and whichever way they react to us would be – or could be – explained as the shock of losing their founder and his successor, as they have,' insisted Ginette, who'd gone through all the psychological training courses at Quantico. 'We wouldn't be able to make any sort of assessment from whatever anyone said or did.'

'What sort of harassment or grief-intrusion action can you imagine they'd bring, if one of us said something just a tad wrong or out of line?' demanded McKinnon, his retirement benefits in mind.

Hanlan tapped the Carver file and said to Ginette: 'We got the addresses there of the two who say they saw Carver push a guy over. Go see them, talk to them again. Hear it the way they want to tell it.'

'OK,' sighed the woman. It was better than chasing all over Manhattan trying to catch Martha on the telephone, she supposed.

'I've got a feeling,' insisted Hanlan.

'Then take it to Washington DC,' said McKinnon. 'Set it all out, let legal counsel decide if we can risk looking at George

W. Northcote International. They say no, it's no. But it's not our asses on the line if they say yes.'

'Where the hell is Martha?' said Hanlan.

Alice Belling was, in fact, hunched foetus-like in a cushioned chair that smelled of too many previous users in a plywood-furnished room of a tourist hotel on Eighth Avenue where security guards confirmed key tags at a turnstile between the reception area and the accommodation and upon every floor of which there were CCTV monitors. She'd balled herself up in the chair with her arms clutched tightly around her, unsleeping, throughout the previous night, for most of it crying so hard and so uncontrollably that her stomach and ribs ached by early morning. Until then she had refused to think, her mind locked on a single awareness. John was dead. Arrogant, stubborn, stupid, wonderful, loving John was dead. Gone forever. She didn't have him any more. Would never have him any more. Gone. No goodbye. She couldn't remember if they'd kissed when he'd left her apartment for the last time. Never kiss him again. Touch him again. Feel his body again.

John was dead.

She had finally to get out of the chair to use the bathroom. When she moved her body ached more and she felt sick, from not eating. Something else she couldn't remember, when she'd last ate. Her mirrored reflection was almost grotesque. Her hair was straggled and lank around a face gaunt with grief, tear-red eyes sunk dark-ringed into sallow, greasy skin. It was almost difficult for her to recognize herself.

It was that thought which brought Alice back to something approaching reality, looking around the cheap room for the first time, trying to remember how she'd got there, why she'd chosen the place. She hadn't chosen it. Those first minutes, hours, had been driven by panic. There was the memory of the *Live at Five* coverage with the stills photographs of the partially sheeted-off truck and then a studio portrait of John and the commentary about the tragedy of coincidence and of the unique place in the city held by the firm of George W. Northcote. She had the recollection of fleeing the building, but not in blind panic, because she'd grabbed the packed case, still unopened on the bed beside the money satchel. How she'd got here was a blur. It had to have been by cab but she had no memory of it: of getting into this room or of trying to curl herself into the smallest ball and closing her eyes and hoping . . . Hoping what? That she'd go to sleep and never wake up again, to confront – exist with – what lay ahead.

Alice sat again in the unsteady chair, but properly now, with her back against its back so that her face wasn't against its tainted cushions. What did lie ahead? An impossible, far too complicated question. But she had to confront it. Not totally. That was definitely impossible. Isolate the priorities then. Staying alive, she thought at once, coherently at last. Whatever the empty, unknown future, she was going to live it. Exist in it. Endure it. Not curl up and die. Who would be pursuing her? John had warned her they actually knew her name. It was a miracle they hadn't already got to her, snatched her, whatever it was they did. Her salvation had to be that their total concentration until less than twelve hours ago had been John, not her. She'd had one miracle. She wouldn't get another. As she'd tried to get across to John, who hadn't listened and who was now dead – her breath caught and tears welled up and she strained against crying again – there'd only be one chance. So it had to be right. More than right.

She couldn't work it out here, in this flea pit where things were literally moving – noisily now – around her. The cabin was the place. The cabin which she believed now to have been somewhere in her mind when she'd fled Princes Street. The cabin was where she could safely hide until she'd completely worked out how to go on living.

Alice knew she should eat something to quell the nauseous hunger pangs but couldn't face the hotel's babbling self-service cafeteria. Instead she checked out, walked past the already assembling city tour buses and found a reasonably clean deli just past a news-stand where she bought the *New York Times*. Her coffee cooled and the Danish stayed virtually uneaten as she read the story and studied the photographs. The portrait of John was the same as that used on television the previous evening and she had to swallow heavily, using the cover of sipping her near-cold coffee, to keep down the emotion. There was something about the stills pictures of the scene that Alice believed should have some significance but she couldn't decide what and kept the paper with her, to study again later.

Alice was sure there was no possibility of her pursuers discovering her long-term parking facility for her precious Volkswagen, because she had been of no interest to them when she'd last used it, more than a month earlier. She still approached cautiously before recalling her embarrassment at trying to isolate surveillance on the Space for Space cybercafe but still she didn't hurry, lingering on the long-stay floor before directly approaching her car. She tensed at the slowness with which the engine turned but after two attempts it fired. She made the usual stop-start cross-town journey but the flow was easier on West Side Highway and she crossed the bridge before midday. She made Paterson her marker and reached it just before two. Before buying supplies she forced herself to eat scrambled eggs with milk at a drugstore diner. There was a newscast on television but this far from the city it was local.

It was four before she finally reached the cabin and the nostalgia engulfed her the moment she crossed the threshold. She let the packages stay where she dropped them, slumped in the all-encompassing chair in which she and John had wedged themselves together, just holding each other, the last time they had been there, and wept at the memories until she ached again. This chair smelled, too: smelled of him and his cologne and of them together. She said, aloud: 'I don't know what to do, darling. I'm so frightened. So very frightened.'

Gene Hanlan caught an evening shuttle to Washington DC, the appointment with the regional director and legal counsel arranged for nine the following morning.

They were back in the rear room of the Thomson Avenue restaurant in Queens but the atmosphere was very different and the phrase 'payback time' echoed in Burcher's mind like a litany. Emilio Delioci, strangely strong-voiced with no hint of asthma, conducted the meeting like a trial, which Burcher supposed it was, demanding individual explanations and questioning each of them with the expertise of a trial lawyer. Burcher recognized the trial lawyer's technique of patronizing humiliation in every demand directed at him.

'So in an unreachable New York safe-deposit box there's a bomb that could blow into oblivion our entire organization throughout the United States of America?' judged the old man, after an hour's inquisition.

'That's exactly it,' agreed the son, at once. 'It's a complete fuck-up.'

'Which might have been prevented if you'd gone back,' said the father, relentlessly. 'Just as the needless killing of Northcote might have been prevented if you'd moved your ass and gone up to Litchfield.'

Burcher stirred at the accusation, reading from it. Everyone else in the room was definitely treating this humiliation as his payback time. But Emilio Delioci was assessing it properly – as a Don should assess it – and acknowledged that what remained in Carver's safe-deposit box did have the destructive capability of more atomic weaponry than existed in the world's arsenals. With himself and his Family as the first potential casualties even before it all exploded. 'We have quite rightly had the inquest. It was an accident that should have been prevented but wasn't. That's in the past. Now we have to go forward.'

'We will go forward,' declared Enrico, looking at the lawyer. 'But without you. Northcote was ours. The operation was ours. We'll put it right.'

Burcher didn't have to force the derisive laugh. 'That's not a decision for you or for this Family. Don Emilio has quite rightly identified the potential risk that exists, to every Family in this country. It is they – in the form of the New York ruling Families – who should decide upon who should resolve the problem . . .' He staged the pause. '. . . and who should not. Which is why, before coming here tonight, I requested a meeting with those Family representatives. You will do nothing until you hear from them. Through me.'

No one was patronizing him any more, Burcher recognized. Just as he recognized that having made the challenge he had to survive it.

Eighteen

Jane Carver knew they were talking about her, could hear most of what they were saying and recognized from it that the stranger was irritated with Paul Newton but it didn't seem to matter, although she wished they weren't doing it as if she wasn't there, non-existent despite being propped up between them against supporting pillows. She'd never liked being ignored. She disliked even more how their faces kept receding, blurring like their words, and then coming back so that she could properly see and hear them again. It was important to hear what they were saying because it was about her.

'Mrs Carver?'

Jane turned towards the stranger, who'd sat by the bed. It was one of her clear moments and she could see he had a heavy, drooping moustache and very thick black-rimmed glasses. He was bald at the front but his hair was long at the back.

'Mrs Carver? Jane?'

'Yes?'

'Can you hear me?'

'Yes.' What sort of stupid question was that? Of course she could hear him now: she hoped the words wouldn't drift off, making it difficult to hear them again.

'My name's Mortimer, Peter Mortimer. I'm a psychiatrist.'

Jane smiled but didn't bother to say anything. She couldn't think of anything *to* say. Why was there a psychiatrist, as well as Paul Newton? He was their doctor in Manhattan, not somebody with a drooping moustache and long hair.

'What did I say my name was?'

Jane frowned. 'Mortimer.' Then she smiled. 'Cat's name.'

The man smiled back. 'That's good. I want to talk to you about something. Will you talk with me?'

'What about?'

'An accident. There's been an accident.'

Jane's face creased, briefly. 'I know.'

From the other side of the bed Newton said: 'I told her last night: tried to tell her.'

'What do you know?' asked Mortimer, ignoring the intervention.

'My father.'

'No, Jane. Another accident.'

'What other accident?'

'John. John's had a very bad accident.'

She shook her head against the pillow. 'No. It was my father. He's dead.'

'John's dead, Jane. A street accident.'

She shook her head again, wishing his face would come back so that she could see and hear him properly. 'It was Dad. Dad died. It was his tractor.' Where was John? She couldn't remember seeing him last night. Just the nurses fussing, holding her hand, stroking her hand, talking in low voices that she couldn't hear, giving her pills to take. She hadn't liked it. 'Where's John?'

'Dead,' insisted Mortimer. 'It was a bad traffic accident. A truck.'

'You're not listening to me!' Jane insisted back. 'It's Dad. *He*'s dead. What time is it?'

'Quarter of ten,' said Paul Newton, from the other side of the bed.

'John's at the office,' said Jane. 'That's where he'll be. Get him there if you want him.'

The man with the moustache stood and went to the end of the bed. Newton followed. Mortimer said: 'You see! She's blocked. Chlorpromazine was too strong.'

'I thought it was what she needed, in the short term,' said Newton.

'I can't hear you!' protested Jane. 'What are you talking about?'

'Your father,' avoided Mortimer. To Newton he said: 'Everything I've read in her file and that you've told me indicates Jane's a strong-willed, self-reliant woman. Chlorpromazine is entirely the wrong medication. On a strong-willed person it's like a medical lobotomy. I don't think Jane needs medication, apart perhaps from the mildest of tranquillizers. What she needs is counselling.'

'After losing her father *and* her husband!' demanded Newton, resenting the professional criticism, although it was he who'd called the psychiatrist in, as worried as the nurses at Jane's near-catatonic reaction to the drug. 'My diagnosis was that her grief needed to be suppressed.'

'It didn't,' rejected Mortimer. 'It needed to be faced, with the help of counselling. We should have talked first.'

'Now we are talking,' said the doctor, still hostile. 'What's your suggestion?'

'Getting her off chlorpromazine right away, which of course we can't,' said Mortimer. 'We've got to wean her off, gradually reducing the dosage.' He spoke now looking at the duty nurse. 'Make sure everyone on your twenty-four-hour roster knows. Reduce by a quarter each day. That understood?'

'Completely,' said the woman.

'I'll come in, every day, to monitor the withdrawal. I want to judge the time when she'll comprehend. Which she's obviously got to do by the time of the funeral.'

'I'll come in every day, too,' said the family physician.

'Anything else we need to do, apart from reduce the chlorpromazine?' asked the nurse.

'Get her out of bed,' said Mortimer. 'She's not an invalid, just mentally closed-down. Maybe take her for a walk in the park, introduce her to the outside world she's got to get back into.'

'There're no relatives,' said Newton. 'She's by herself now.'

'So are thousands of people in this city,' said Mortimer. 'Adjusting isn't going to be easy: I don't know – no one knows – how long it might take. But however long, that's what it's got to take. Adult, strong-willed adjustment, not chemical barriers. That's the way to dependency and irrational fixations. As closed-off as she is – and it's a judgement at this early stage largely based upon your case notes – I don't have Jane Carver in my book as a dependent person.'

She wasn't, decided Jane, who'd only heard snatches of the exchange and therefore didn't properly understand what they were talking about. Except that it was about her and that she wasn't included and that not including her was very definitely rude. She'd complain to John when he got home.

'So how'd it go?' greeted Patrick McKinnon as Hanlan entered the Federal Plaza office, forewarned it hadn't gone well because Hanlan hadn't called before leaving Washington officially to establish a formal investigation.

The agent-in-charge slumped down into his chair, his back to the cacophony of Broadway, seeking explanations and maybe justifications for himself. Hopefully, Hanlan said: 'Our girl called?'

'No,' said McKinnon, shortly.

Hanlan looked at Ginette. 'Washington is with you. She's a crazy, got lucky with coincidence. No sanction to proceed any further, unless she comes in with a whole bunch of incontrovertible evidence. No bullshit with newspaper cuttings or conversations with people she can't identify; the usual crazy stuff. Total refusal of any legal warrant application to look into the activities of George W. Northcote International.

Washington counsel say a firm with Northcote's clout would sue us from here to China, with tollbooths on the way.' He paused. 'It's political and it sucks.'

'Always,' agreed McKinnon

Ginette said: 'I found the two witnesses. They're good. Woman's a floor supervisor at Macy's, guy's a bank teller. Both say a guy was definitely pushed over . . .' She paused, smiling. 'That's their word, pushed deliberately, not accidentally knocked over when Carver ran past . . . and guess what?'

'What?' asked Hanlan, indulging her.

'The teller's positive Carver got *out* of the car that he ran around, in front of the truck, which was overtaking. *And* that the guy he pushed over was originally in the car, too.'

Hanlan came forward in his chair. 'You got statements?'

'Full and free, from both,' said Ginette. 'And both say – and this is independent of each other, not reminding each other – that Carver was yelling for help. The bank teller insists that's exactly what Carver was shouting – "Help me, help me!" '

'What about the guy who got pushed over? The car?'

'There's the confusion, when the truck sounds its air horn and Carver goes underneath. They're looking at that, obviously. But both say the guy gets up off the kerb, runs back to the car and the car takes off before the traffic gets blocked, which of course it did.'

'Make?' queried Hanlan.

'Blue Ford. No registration.'

'Shit! The guy?'

'Small. Nondescript. Both said they couldn't make any sort of image reconstruction . . . a description even.'

'You did good,' praised Hanlan. Better than *he* had, he conceded.

'Better than good,' prompted McKinnon. 'She's saved the best for last.'

'Tell me,' demanded Hanlan, wishing they hadn't need for the pretence.

'The teller works at Citibank, on Wall Street,' announced Ginette. 'Outside of which it all happened: he was on his way back in from late lunch. I went in, on a hunch. John Carver has an account there. And had already been there once that day. To the safe-deposit vault.'

'I should have waited,' admitted Hanlan. 'I went to Washington too soon.'

'You can always go back,' said McKinnon.

'Not without more than this,' refused Hanlan. He *had* knee-jerked too soon and now it was a matter of filed record and the only way to recover was to make the case for that second visit total and irrefutable.

Alice hadn't moved very much from the womb-like seat the previous night – just to the bathroom and on her way back to raid one of her dropped bags for a cracker from a convenient box – but eventually, she didn't know when, she'd gone to bed between sheets that felt damp from not being aired, and in which she'd last slept with Carver, and cried again, although not a lot, at that realization. And then, surprisingly, she'd slept uninterrupted until it was fully light, and outside she could hear the competing chirping and calls of birds she and Carver had bought binoculars and long-discarded books to identify – and failed – and leaf-shuffling moving things. She'd gone out on to the deck, in only the short nightdress she couldn't remember taking from her bag but which was all she'd often worn with Carver for their breakfast coffee, and she'd taken hers on the bench they'd always sat on looking over the narrow river and she didn't choke up at that memory, which she was glad about. The river would be cold, as it was always cold, because it fed from the Bearfort mountain tributaries, which they'd discovered when they'd tried, the first time they'd used the cabin, to skinny dip – and had never tried again.

Alice felt safe, alone, and wanted to feel that way forever.

Never wanted to see Manhattan – any city – again: hear its sirens and its jostling people and their noise. Stay here, with the birds and the scurrying in the undergrowth, and hide forever, live in the past forever. This past, this very special past only she and John had shared – intruded upon by no one else. Could they find her, all alone up here? The cabin wasn't in her name. Or John's. John rented it, paying cash for an entire year, from a distracted bookshop owner in West Milford: there had to be at least six months left on the rental. The phone was in the bookshop owner's name. So were all the other utilities. She'd be safe forever here: lost forever here.

Alice forced herself out of the fantasy, refusing its cocoon. There was only one way she could ever be safe – lost forever – and that was by becoming an entirely new person, with a new name and a new – but sustainable – background and a new passport and all the other new official documentation that said who you were, to those who felt it their business to know.

And who better than she to become a new person? Alice asked herself. She had no one. No family. No ties. And she no longer had John. No one. At the flick of a pen or a computer command Alice Belling could disappear forever – vaporize – to be reborn a new, ready-made, unknown person. Nothing to look back for. Nothing, either, to which to look forward. But there was something in the middle, something between what she was leaving behind – fleeing from – and the reborn future. Revenge. Alice wanted revenge. Each and every possible retribution upon whoever it was who had done what they had done to John. She was more determined totally to achieve that than she'd ever been to achieve anything in her so far totally achieving life.

And she'd opened the way: knew the way. That's why she was hidden up here, not to gaze out over a river and a forest, soon to become another memory, but to ensure she didn't make any mistakes guiding the FBI towards those who had to be punished. So what did she have to guide them? Not as much as she'd hoped: less in fact than she'd once had, because John had taken all her computer printouts. Could she risk trying to duplicate them, as she'd told herself she could? Not the companies. They'd have built stronger firewalls: almost inevitably set traps and snares to identify her more quickly, even if she tried to piggyback internationally as she had before. And caused the deaths of three innocent people, she reminded herself, unnecessarily. She was going to have to admit that, at some stage. And all the hacking. Not her immediate focus. Her immediate focus was upon convincing an unconvinced FBI agent in his Broadway office that she had evidence of a crime. Which she didn't actually have, Alice admitted to herself objectively. She had knowledge of crime but no way of proving it. Yes there was! Those local IRS offices – in which lay the proof of the step-by-step money laundering – didn't know they'd been accessed. No one was looking for her there, setting traps and snares. She could access them again and download everything she'd given to John. It wouldn't matter that illegally obtained material wasn't admissible in a court. She wouldn't be offering court evidence. She'd be handing it over as *her* proof, for the Bureau to confirm independently. And legally.

Alice felt a surge of confidence, a welcome difference from the hollow nausea it replaced. Because the IRS were unsuspecting, she wouldn't need the protection of a cybercafe, either. She could work from the cabin, although she'd take her usual precaution of making her Trojan Horse entry through someone else's system. All she needed was a laptop to replace the one she'd left in Princes Street in her panic to get away.

The thought of calling the Bureau's New York office came as she was driving back down into Paterson, to distance herself from the cabin before buying the computer. It was sensible, necessary, to keep in touch. She was going to need them very soon: need them to accept her the moment she made the request, which made it vitally important to convince them she was genuine.

It took Alice less than fifteen minutes to buy the computer system she wanted, a duplicate of the laptop and printer she'd abandoned in New York, and she stored both in the Volkswagen boot before re-entering the mall for the already isolated telephones. Once more she leaned so that her calibrated watch was in front of her, counting off the seconds.

Alice recognized the receptionist's voice from her first approach. She said: 'This is A . . .' and just stopped herself in time. '. . . Martha. I want to speak . . .' but before she could finish the line went dead and then she heard the other recognizable voice.

'I've been waiting for you, Martha,' said Hanlan. 'How come you haven't got back before now?'

'John didn't call, to tell me where they were meeting. That was our arrangement. That's what I was going to tell you, where the handover was going to be.'

'Where is it, the stuff that was going to be handed over?'

A minute, Alice saw. 'I don't know.'

'What about Citibank?'

'I don't know.'

'Martha! I think you know it's John's bank and that he was in the securities division earlier that day. And that you changed your mind about telling us.'

The photograph in the New York Times! That's what she'd failed to recognize, Citibank in the background! 'No, that's not how it was! He didn't tell me. That's what I was waiting for, for him to tell me.'

'Why'd he go back, with the others?'

A minute and a half. 'I don't know anything about any others.'

'I asked you this before and I'm going to ask you it again. What is it you *do* know? I don't want to go on screwing around like this. It's made me look stupid and I don't like being made to look stupid. I want you – with a proper name – and I want all this evidence that John had. That clear?'

'I'm going to get some of it. But I need to come into the protection programme. They know what I've done.'

'Who's they?'

'I don't know names, not yet.' It sounded bad, ridiculous, Alice recognized.

'What *have* you done?'

'Things.' On her way in from the cabin she'd thought she had everything worked out but it was all swirling in the wind again. They'd been talking just over two minutes. She shouldn't hang on much longer.

'You want to deal, we'll deal. But you've got to give me a lot before we even start. At the moment we're going around in circles and for most of it you're not making sense.'

'You've got John's murder as proof, for Christ's sake!'

'What I've got are five witnesses each of whom say John ran in front of a truck and died in a complete accident.'

Alice slammed the phone down, chest tight, feeling sick again. But she was sufficiently in control to see the news-stand.

Stanley Burcher tried to analyse the significance of the meeting being with the *consiglieri* of the five Families, not their Dons, but couldn't, not instantly. Perhaps, he thought, he'd get a guide during the discussion. They were in the park-view penthouse suite of an hotel on Central Park South in which the Genovese clan had a concealed investment, the six of them grouped around a table. There was an array of liquor and mixes on a smaller side table but no one was drinking. It would have been presumptuous for Burcher to have helped himself. Perhaps, he thought, it was presumptuous of him to have expected to meet the Dons.

Charlie Petrie said: 'It's a hell of a mess to clean up.'

'But it's got to be cleaned up,' insisted Vito Craxi, the

Bonanno counsel. 'There isn't a Family who haven't used the system and paid well for the facility. It's got to be kept intact.'

'Who's going to run it?' asked Burcher. There was still the opportunity of enormous power, being the liaison between these five and whichever accountancy firm was suborned into co-operating.

'It's being taken care of,' said Petrie.

'You asked for the meeting,' reminded Bobby Gallo, representing the Gambino clan. 'What have you got in mind?' He spoke as he got up to go to the drinks table. He did so without gesturing an invitation to Burcher.

'The only way in to Citibank security is through the wife,' said Burcher, discomfited at stating the obvious. 'She's the only one with the legal right. I might be able to use the severance with the firm's lawyer. And there could be an advantage in the girlfriend. Sure, Carver gave every indication of having everything at the bank but he could have split it up. Some guys do stupid things, pussy prowling . . .' He hesitated, unsure of the Delioci strength. 'I've called the apartment in Princes Street: left messages about an assignment. She hasn't been there. I guess she's run. We need to go into Princes Street. But not like Litchfield. If she is still around, I don't want her to know we've been there. If she has gone we need to know where she's gone *to*.'

The Luchese Family's Gino LaRocca, a thin, bespectacled man, picked up on the reference to Litchfield, needing the way in: the Queens-based clan had operated under the control of the Luchese organization. 'The Deliocis are out of this. Out of business. They fucked up big time, all the way. I've been asked to apologize.'

There were nods of acceptance, at the apology.

Petrie said: 'They'll be sore.'

'They try to do anything smart they'll be dead, starting with the old man himself and the son next,' said LaRocca. 'That's been made clear.'

'We don't want to draw attention at this time, taking out known small-timers,' warned Carlo Brookier, the Colombo Family *consigliere*.

'We all know that,' said LaRocca, irritably.

'I'm going to need people to do things, starting with getting into Princes Street. How can I do that, if Delioci isn't involved any more?'

'Through me,' announced Petrie. 'I want us to stay close on this.'

They didn't trust him any more, Burcher decided. They were excluding him from whatever new arrangements were being made and they were going to monitor everything he did. Channelling everything through Petrie put the Genovese family in total control of the money laundering.

Nineteen

Alice squatted cross-legged on the cabin floor, her mind back in synch, surrounded by the accounts of John's death, with the rest of the newspapers discarded unread. She'd been lucky, picking up *Newsday* at the Paterson mall. Its coverage was much fuller than that in the previous day's *New York Times* or anything else she'd snatched up. The photographs were reproduced bigger, too, so that it was easier to identify the Citibank building. The amalgamated stories fitted what she'd been told by Hanlan – certainly about it unquestionably being an accident, with witnesses talking of a mystery car that drove away – with the addition of John appearing to run towards a police patrol car.

It was pitifully easy for Alice to work out the sequence. John had met them somehow – she'd never know whether he'd intended to call or been prevented from doing so – and handed over what they wanted. And then tried to confront them with the threat of producing his copies. What threat would they have made in return? Jeered at him, so arrogantly sure of themselves, of their power? The most likely would have been to hurt Jane. Kill her even. Maybe, accepted Alice, for her to be hurt as well. They knew about her existence, although maybe not yet that she was the hacker they were hunting. Perhaps they hadn't even bothered with threats, mocking him, laughing at him. They wouldn't have been able to torture him – it was a relief, to realize that – because they'd obviously been taking him back to the bank. But there must have been some threat, she thought, changing her mind. Otherwise how could they have known Citibank *was* his bank? And that he had a safe-deposit facility there? Which was obviously where he'd thought what he'd kept would be untouchable by anyone except himself. How frightened he must have been, poor, optimistically brave John: knotted inside, believing in miracles when he'd seen the police car. Yards away from safety and protection, prepared at last – if he'd thought about it, which he probably hadn't in those few terrified moments – finally to sacrifice his precious inherited firm in exchange for his life. Which he hadn't saved and which was the bitterest irony of all. It hadn't even been necessary for the murdering motherfuckers to stage John's killing as an accident, as they had the other two.

For some reason she couldn't identify – didn't need to identify – it made Alice even more determined to exact her revenge. Which brought her back in more detail – attempted total recall – to the conversation with Hanlan. He was playing hardball, with every good reason. She'd realized as they'd talked how bad – how unconvincing – she'd sounded. How many times had she said 'I don't know'? Without intending any pun, Alice thought, *I don't know*, and didn't think it funny. It was difficult to recall the last time she'd found anything funny: ever would again. What *did* she know, Alice asked herself, unknowingly echoing Gene Hanlan's interrogation that morning. She knew how to get into IRS files with that unopened laptop over there on the desk. And how to download a paper trail of money-laundering tax returns for five Mafia-controlled companies, although she had no proof – nor way of obtaining proof – that they *were* Mafia-controlled. Incomplete though it was, would that be sufficient for the demanding Gene Hanlan, irrespective of it being obtained illegally? She wouldn't know until she retrieved them and tried to negotiate.

And she had time now, hidden away up here in the mountains where no-one could find her. It was good, to feel safe.

The feeling lasted until she began gathering up the discarded newspapers and on impulse turned to the public notice sections and found Carver's official death notice. The funeral was scheduled the day after tomorrow. She'd have to go, Alice decided. Whatever the danger, she had to go.

The return call from the telephone company came as they finished listening, for the fourth consecutive time, to the taped conversation between Alice and Hanlan. McKinnon took it, didn't say anything apart from thanks and turned back into the room. 'Paterson. She's taken to the hills.'

'The Catskills aren't our territory,' said Ginette at once and just as quickly wished she hadn't.

'I know what our – my – territory is,' threw back Hanlan.

'We could do a re-shoot of the Sound of Music,' said McKinnon, trying to lessen the tension. 'The hills are alive, to the sound of Martha, where are you, Martha?'

'Shut the fuck up!' said Hanlan.

'Gene!' soothed McKinnon, jerking a nail-bitten finger towards the latest tape, still in the player. 'You really want to hear it for the fifth time, hear nothing for the fifth time? I don't know what this gal thinks she's got . . .' He shrugged. 'Circumstantially, maybe a lot. Evidentially, we don't have diddly squat. Until she arrives outside here with a U-Haul packed with evidence – or points us the way – we're wasting our time.'

Now Hanlan indicated the tape. 'We almost had her real name there at the beginning.'

The other two regarded him solemnly, neither speaking, as if a mist distanced them from Hanlan.

Hanlan said: 'I'm not becoming paranoid about this.'

'Good,' said McKinnon. He thought that was exactly what

Hanlan was becoming and didn't want any foul-ups, even by association, between now and his retirement.

'But there's something here! I've got a gut feeling.'

'You keep telling us that,' reminded Ginette, as concerned as McKinnon.

The smoothly efficient burglary of Alice Belling's apartment in Princes Street did not produce as much as John Burcher had hoped, although the inscription on the back of the two photographs of Carver outside the cabin – 'Bearsfort. July' – gave them a possible although too wide-ranging direction in which to look. He was disappointed at Alice Belling's apparent modesty. Nowhere among any of the other photographs – all copied to hide any evidence of the entry – was there the sort of proud-parent studio portrait from which Carver's mistress could be positively identified. The best, ironically, was a thumbnail image that had accompanied her profile of George Northcote in her cuttings book, every clip of which had also been copied.

He picked his way painstakingly through the trawl, aware as he did so that the total, seemingly snatched-up disorder in which Petrie had personally handed over the package an hour earlier in the downstairs lounge wasn't snatched-up disorder at all. It would have been gone through – still be under examination, right now – by several people, each more than once, to ensure nothing was missed. But the responsibility for anything missed was his.

There was a substantial amount of business correspondence, none of it relevant, two letters confirming assignments that were still on her telephone answering machine, Burcher's attempts to make contact having now been erased. There were bank statements up to the previous month showing a comfortable balance and all the woman's utility bills were receipted as being paid in full before their due date. He was surprised at the total absence of any personal correspondence, not even a note that could have been construed to be a love message from Carver. Imagining themselves to be discreet, he supposed.

It was crumpled when he found it, crushed in such a way between two of the bank statements he was re-examining that Burcher didn't think it had been extracted for copying. It was a paid-in-cash receipt for access time upon a computer at a cybercafe named Space for Space.

Despite the well-remembered rehearsal of her first hacking expedition it still took Alice most of that day and well into the night to duplicate her IRS evidence, herding her Trojan Horses through the computer system of a Hertz car-hire outlet in Des Moines, Iowa. By the time the physical tiredness of unremitting concentration forced her to stop, just before nine, Alice was still short of her original trove and unsure if she might need any more.

Not a decision that needed to be made tonight, Alice thought, carrying her drink, more gin than tonic, to their once-shared chair. Time enough tomorrow. The following day. No hurry, now that she was safe. The refusal came at once. She wasn't safe, she was hiding: curling up like a baby, trying to make herself too small to be seen. To be found. There was more than enough in what she'd already downloaded to illustrate how accounts had been padded from subsidiary to subsidiary and from state to state and country to country. All she'd achieve by obtaining more – apart from postponing her committing, physical approach to the FBI – would be unnecessary repetition.

What if it wasn't enough, evidentially? Sufficient, maybe, for an IRS investigation but not for one by the FBI? It was an income-tax prosecution that nailed Al Capone, she reminded herself. But that had been in the 1930s, not now. Now she needed a Witness Protection Programme and only the FBI provided that. If only she'd had . . . Alice didn't complete the thought, her mind racing beyond it.

She hadn't been thinking properly, completely. Just selfishly, knowing that she was being pursued for her computer intrusion and desperate only to save herself. What about Jane? Jane was the one – the only one – who could get to whatever John had in the safe deposit at Citibank. And therefore the one at risk, as Northcote and John and Janice Snow had been at risk. All of whom were now dead.

Twenty

'I'm all right,' insisted Jane, relieved her voice hadn't wavered, because she wasn't, not as all right as she would have liked to be. But she didn't want anyone around her to realize it. There were still too many moments when her mind blanked, mid-sentence, and others when she suffered the audible and visual receding sensation that was the most disconcerting of all.

But she was sufficiently in control of herself and her surroundings to comprehend what she had been told the previous day and to prepare herself for what was going to happen today. John was dead. Today there was to be his funeral, in the same cathedral in which the ceremony for her father had been conducted, and after that the wake at the same hotel in which her father's had been held. And John's burial, later, when she'd decided upon where the interment was to be.

But most important of all she believed herself sufficiently free of the drug, now down to its one dose a day minimum, to understand – although perhaps not properly, fully, to comprehend – that she didn't have John any more. Didn't have anyone any more. That she was all alone. She'd never imagined being entirely by herself. Not having anyone to turn to, rely upon. She'd sat on charity committees – chaired some of them – and raised money to help people bereaved by tragedy or catastrophe and believed she'd had some conception of their loss. But now, despite the response-dulling effects of the medication, Jane accepted that she had no conception whatsoever. At this precise moment – probably for some time to come – it was too overwhelming for her to conceive, to rationalize in any way. Which was the easiest explanation for why she hadn't collapsed and wept the previous day or wept today, although she had awakened early, before it was fully light, with total recall of the conversation with Paul Newton and Peter Mortimer, and lain there for more than an hour, trying to envisage a future. And failed, remaining there mummified, thoughts, images, feelings, tears, refusing to come. It went blank again at that moment, so that she was not immediately aware of Geoffrey Davis talking to her.

'I said we could do away with the formal receiving line,' repeated the firm's lawyer.

'I don't want that,' said Jane, freshly insisting. 'Everything will be done properly, as it should be done.' John would have wanted that, for everything to be done properly. It was important to remember what John would have wanted. Expected. He would have come round soon enough to wanting a baby as much as she did. *Had wanted*, she corrected herself. Robbed of John and robbed of having his baby. Or was she robbed? Had he provided the specimen Rosemary Pritchard had asked for? She couldn't remember – there was still too much she couldn't remember – but if he had there was surely a possibility of it being used, to impregnate her, once the gynaecologist had corrected her problem. Something she had to call Rosemary about as soon as possible: today even, when she got back from the wake.

'We'll be there with you,' reassured Newton.

'I don't *want* everyone around me!' exclaimed Jane irritably, sweeping her hand to encompass the overcrowded East 62nd Street drawing room. 'I want you all to understand that I can manage by myself.'

'Jane, you can't stand there entirely alone,' protested Davis.

She couldn't, Jane at once conceded: it wouldn't be the

proper thing to do. 'You,' she decided, looking at the lawyer. 'You should represent the firm, with the most senior partner . . . ?'

'Fred Jolly,' identified the lawyer, indicating a balding, stooped man beside him whom Jane did not recognize, although she knew that she should.

'Sorry. Of course, with you, Fred.' She continued looking around the room. 'If my having some personal support is so important, Hilda can stay close to me: tell me whom I'm meeting, as often as possible. That all right, Hilda?'

'Of course,' said Carver's matronly personal assistant, who had organized this second funeral and who hoped at the actual service she'd manage the control Jane was showing. The reflection reminded her of the sobbing Janice Snow and she had to swallow heavily, tensed against breaking down.

Jane accepted that she might have difficulty retaining some of her thoughts but hoped the receding, blurred images or words were diminishing. 'But I don't think I need any support. Certainly not any further nursing, now that you've almost stopped those damned drugs.'

'*I* do. I really do,' challenged Newton, too quickly.

'What do *you* think?' Jane asked the psychiatrist, well enough aware of the bedside disagreement between the two men.

'You're nearly off the chlorpromazine now,' agreed Mortimer. 'You sure there aren't any lingering effects?'

'You're watching me, listening to me. What's your professional opinion?' demanded Jane, as the faces of those looking at her blurred. She was only distantly aware – but aware, which was all that mattered – of the psychiatrist.

Mortimer said: 'This isn't a consulting session.'

Jane's vision cleared. 'I've got live-in staff. And they have all your numbers. This is how I want it to be. How it *will* be. I appreciate all your care and all your concern. From now on I want to handle things by myself. And by *now* I mean just that.

Now.' It had been an effort to finish, but she was sure no one had detected her difficulty. She wasn't being stupid or arrogant. They'd weaned her off the medication because they'd decided she didn't need it, as she hadn't needed medication for her father's funeral. And if she didn't need medication she didn't need nurses to sit around and hold her hand. She didn't need anyone to hold her hand when she said goodbye to the best husband it had been possible to have. Which was the way to think, Jane told herself. Not to sink into a slough of self-pity but to think how lucky she'd been having him as a loving, caring husband for as long as she had. She'd need to spend a lot of time and effort having John's crypt designed: ensure it was a monument to him. And speak to Rosemary Pritchard. That was the first priority.

As they left the apartment Newton told Mortimer: 'Now it's you who've made the mistake.'

'We're going to be there, keeping an eye on everything,' said the psychiatrist. 'There can't be any problems.'

Alice hadn't tried to download any more evidence of cross-border invoice padding. She'd filled the intervening day tidying the cabin, eating properly for the first time since she couldn't remember when – but shunning alcohol – and driving yet again into Paterson to buy what she thought she needed for the funeral. If those hunting her knew her name she had to assume that they also knew what she looked like: had a photograph, even. Which made the need for a disguise more practical than melodramatic. The thought of adopting one still embarrassed her. The dark wig to conceal her blondness scarcely amounted to a disguise anyway. She added to it a hat with a veil longer than that Jane had worn at her father's funeral and remained unsure about dark glasses beneath it, deciding to wait until she returned to the cabin to make up her mind. The black dress would have benefited from some minimal lifting at the shoulders but without time for alteration – and doubting she'd wear it ever again – Alice hid the problem beneath a black jacket that fitted better.

It was only when she was driving back from Paterson that Alice finally confronted what she had been refusing, until that moment, to bring into the forefront of her mind, where it should have been from the moment she'd acknowledged Jane to be in danger. The obvious, immediate and seemingly *only* resolution was to involve the police and the FBI protection. But upon what evidence, came the recurring, taunting question. She'd already decided the IRS printouts weren't sufficient, quite apart from how she'd obtained them. From the attitude she'd encountered the previous day, the FBI wouldn't respond without considerably more – which she didn't have – and she'd never get by the desk sergeant in any Manhattan precinct house with accounts of murder masked as accident and accident fulfilling doubtless intended murder.

Jane, unaware of any danger, was the only person who could produce what was necessary to protect herself . . . what John had been taken back to Citibank to retrieve. Unaware, yet, where – or what – the secrets were that risked further shattering her already shattered life, as Alice was finally reconciled to hers being shattered. Was she thinking only of Jane? Alice asked herself, at last demanding personal honesty. Of course she wasn't thinking only of Jane. What Jane had access to, as John's wife, would provide her salvation, too. Was it the most obscene, unimaginably amoral cynicism, even to think as she was thinking? No, refused Alice. Jane's marriage – Jane's security, the fulness and completeness of her marriage – had never once been threatened by her affair with John. She'd genuinely, totally honestly, never seen herself competing with Jane. Alice would never expect anyone to believe her: she found it difficult, with total objectivity, to believe it herself. But without ever knowing it, without there ever having been a challenge, Jane had been the one who won. So it wasn't amoral or obscene or contemptibly cynical to contemplate – although until now, climbing the low foothills at last, she hadn't allowed herself to contemplate – how she could properly guarantee her survival. Which was all she was thinking about. Survival, for herself and for Jane.

So how was she going to achieve it? How was she going to get to Jane and talk to Jane in such a way – in such words – that Jane would not dismiss her as the FBI had so far dismissed her? Alice didn't know. She could think of no plan, no approach, that was halfway feasible. Jane would be in shock, grieving to breaking point. *Hello Jane, you don't know about me but I know everything about you. Your father, who worked for the Mafia, was murdered. John was going to be murdered and we've only got one chance to stop it happening to you and me. Oh, and by the way, Janice Snow was murdered, too. Now here's what we've got to do . . .*

As she turned off down the track, towards the cabin totally hidden in the riverside trees, Alice sniggered aloud at the sheer absurdity of it. But it wasn't – couldn't be – absurd. Somehow to keep them both safe she had to produce what John had hidden: to guarantee both their survival.

At the cabin Alice modelled her complete outfit in front of the full-length mirror, with and without dark glasses beneath the veiled hat, and remained undecided, glad of the hat because it lessened what she thought to be the artificiality of the ready-made wig, although after practice and careful pinning, again hidden by the hat, she became satisfied that it didn't look as artificial as she'd first imagined.

When she left the cabin, early on the morning of the funeral, Alice still hadn't thought of an approach to Jane that she considered remotely practicable and felt sick with the effort of trying.

Alice accepted she couldn't use the garage space reserved in her own name and it took her longer than she'd anticipated to find a spot in one on East 40th, although she still had time to walk to the cathedral. It was a bright day, which justified the dark glasses. She arrived with the bulk of the mourners and was grateful for their concealment. The two books of condolences, on either side of the entrance, created a congestion that stretched back to the outer steps but in which it was easy for Alice to mingle to avoid signing, although she couldn't isolate anyone standing too obviously close to either, checking names. Unwittingly echoing Carver's thoughts at Northcote's funeral, Alice told herself that those searching for her would be here somewhere, watching, looking. Would they have an identifying photograph of her, be comparing every woman coming in? The crush of people at that moment would make that impractical, she tried to reassure herself, although once past the condolence book bottleneck there was almost an immediate thinning-out in the vastness of the cathedral. She edged into a half-filled pew, relieved it was immediately filled behind her by other mourners, and at once bowed her head in cupped hands, further hiding herself in feigned prayer. She waited until she guessed from the noise that the pew behind her was occupied before raising her head. She stared directly ahead until she realized that the red cloth-covered stand in front of the altar was for the coffin and abruptly looked down at the order of service, her fogged eyes unable to focus on anything.

She sensed the family arrival from the movements of heads in front of her and turning with them she saw Jane, dressed as she'd been dressed for her father's funeral, upright and unaided by those around her, whom she recognized from her research visits to the Northcote building, although she couldn't remember the men's names. The other woman in the group was Hilda Bennett, John's PA. And then she saw the coffin following and her mind emptied and her eyes filmed and there was the rustle of everyone around her opening their service sheets and she automatically opened hers.

So did Jane. Who couldn't see the words either. All she could see – nothing receding and returning, receding and returning – in crystal clear, unwanted clarity was a flower-festooned box with burnished brass fixtures containing the body of the man to whom she had given herself completely, whom she loved completely, and whom she could not conceive being without. Not having. Any more than she had been able – was able – to conceive not having her always-commanding, always-controlling father. Two indomitable supermen to whom nothing was insurmountable. Leaving her alone. Bereft. She didn't know what she was going to do. How she was going to do it.

Jane anticipated the sitting down, without prompting. A man she didn't know, from the firm, she thought, but wasn't sure, ascended the pulpit and mouthed words she didn't hear because she didn't want to hear. She knew how wonderful John had been. She didn't need the contrived platitudes and hypocritical insincerity. She knew John. Fully and completely knew John, which no one else did. He would have made the most wonderfully attentive, adoring father. Which he could still be, from beyond the grave. Not physically attentive or adoring. But a father. A father for their child. She didn't care how many or what operations she had to undergo, what discomfort – pain – she had to endure: if John had left a sperm sample, she'd become pregnant by it. Was Rosemary Pritchard here: would she be at the wake? Urged by her own question Jane half turned, actually to look around the vast building, but didn't see anyone properly. Good today, if they could talk. Not essential, though. She could definitely make contact tomorrow. Begin everything tomorrow. If it was a boy – it *had* to be a boy – she'd obviously call it John. Create an archive of photographs and anecdotes and whatever had been written in the obituaries, so that John jr would know what a very special, unique father he'd had. She hoped so much to meet Rosemary today.

There was another ebb and flow of awareness but Jane

didn't need Hilda's supporting hand to rise for another unheard hymn or sit for another unheard reading or another unheard sermon about the cruel mysteries of God's will beyond mere mortal understanding. She wished she'd seen John's body: properly said goodbye. She wouldn't have been persuaded against doing so if it hadn't been for the god-damned drugs they'd fed her like candy, take this madam, take that madam. She wouldn't take anything, when she had John's baby. She wanted to feel everything, know everything. Like she knew how completely John had loved her, as she'd loved him. It wouldn't be an empty life, from now on. She'd have John's baby. Make him so proud of the father he'd never know. John Carver junior. It sounded good, strong, as John had been strong.

'It's over,' whispered the attentive Hilda, at her elbow.

'No, it's not,' smiled Jane, rising to follow the coffin from the cathedral.

Where was Martha, wondered Gene Hanlan, watching the procession from the back of the cathedral. She had to be here somewhere, among all these people. He'd spent the entire service studying the crowd without knowing what he was looking for, a woman crying, a woman furtive, a woman fitting his mental image of Martha, for whom he didn't have any proper mental image, which made his being there a waste of time. He'd still go on to the wake, Hanlan determined. It didn't make any more sense to do so than it had to come here but you never knew. There might just be something that would instinctively jar, although he couldn't imagine what it might be. He was curious at the faint smile on Jane Carver's face, as she passed. And wondered, too, why she was looking so intently from side to side of the nave, as if she were looking for someone. Probably the effect of tranquillizers. She'd need something to get her through the double whammy of losing a father and a husband like she had.

People rarely pluck a phoney name out of the blue: the psychological-profile training at Quantico was that somewhere there always had to be a subconscious connection, like people nine times out of ten choosing phoney names that began with their own initials. Would Jane Carver know who might call herself Martha? A long shot, among all the other shots so long they were virtually beyond the horizon. Certainly one he wasn't going to resolve today.

Hanlan moved as his pew turned to empty, emerging into the aisle at virtually the same time as Stanley Burcher, from the other side of the nave. Burcher hadn't seen anyone resembling the inadequate thumbnail picture of Alice Belling, although the crowd was too great for any proper examination or comparison. Not everyone in the cathedral would be going back to the wake at the Plaza. He hadn't bothered with Northcote's but there were a lot more pressing reasons for his going this time. Maybe he'd find Alice Belling there.

'Bearfort Mountains are New Jersey. Cavalcante territory,' identified Bobby Gallo. They were again in the hotel penthouse with the view over Central Park.

'They've used the system a lot,' said Charlie Petrie. 'Know its importance.'

'We should bring them in,' suggested the Luchese *consigliere*, Gino LaRocca. 'We get a better lead, they may have useful people on the payroll.'

'I think so too,' said Petrie. 'I'll fix it.'

'We've agreed the Northcote organization is finished,' said Vito Craxi, the Bonanno voice at the meeting. 'Who's going to take over?'

'I'm proposing a firm in Philadelphia,' said Petrie. 'We got pressure on the president and four directors. It's worked like clockwork for the past five years.'

'You want to use Burcher?' asked Gallo.

'I don't think we should,' said LaRocca. 'I've apologized

for the Deliocis but Burcher lost the handle on it, too. Let him work his usefulness out here but when it's sorted out I think Stan's time is up.'

'More than used up,' said Carlo Brookier, offering the Colombo opinion. 'This should have been settled – properly – a long time ago.'

'Anyone disagree?' invited Petrie.

No one spoke.

Twenty-One

Jane hadn't seen Rosemary Pritchard on her way out of the cathedral but there had been too many women in the congregation to isolate every one and a lot wore hats, some with veils like her own, although Jane didn't imagine the gynaecologist to be a hat-and-veil person. Hilda told her, when she asked in the car, that there wasn't an attendance list but they'd know later who had been at the service from the condolence books. Peter Mortimer and Paul Newton were among the first to arrive after her at the Plaza. Mortimer asked how she felt and Jane said OK, which she was. There had only been two ebb-and-flow sensations in the cathedral, both when she was sitting down, and none since. She was hearing and thinking quite clearly, knowing what she had to do, eager for everyone to arrive so she could find Rosemary. It wouldn't be possible for them to talk properly at the receiving line but she'd be able to tell Rosemary she wanted to see her later and that it was important. It was good to be able to think like this, not losing the thread halfway through. She told Hilda she didn't want anything to drink or to go to the bathroom. Why was it taking so long for everyone to arrive? Geoffrey Davis and the senior partner took their places beside her and Jane nodded to the parroted question about how she felt.

Hilda said: 'People are getting here now,' which they were.

Mortimer, standing drink in hand with Newton where they had an unbroken view of Jane, said: 'She's going to be just fine. The chlorpromazine didn't hit her as hard as it could have done.'

Jack Jennings was close enough, with the rest of the now dispersed Litchfield staff, to hear the remark and hoped the psychiatrist was right. He thought Jane Carver looked shaky.

Alice held back, wanting the concealment of the crowd that she'd had at the cathedral, desperately, anxiously, wishing she'd been able to think of a better approach to Jane. It hardly amounted to an idea at all but it might just get her to Jane, alone, which was as far as Alice had taken her thoughts. Get to Jane alone, today. Talk about documents she'd been promised by Northcote and then by John for the biography of Northcote she'd agreed to write. How was she going to persuade Jane – convince Jane – to open the safe deposit? She didn't know, not yet: hadn't worked it out. Just get them protected, that was all she had to do. Keep them both alive.

Stanley Burcher was using the concealment of the crowd, too, entering the room as part of the line but sidling away almost at once, not wanting officially to meet Jane Carver. Not yet anyway. If he determined upon the proposal taking shape in his mind it might be necessary only once, she being the only person with legal access to Carver's security facility. Could he turn that into a mere formality? Carver's severance letters would be on record in the Northcote building: the Families had the originals Carver had written to their registered Grand Cayman addresses. There was every reason for his officially approaching the Northcote firm, acknowledging the termination, and demanding the return of all documentation referring to the five companies, arguing that he knew they were being stored privately and not in the firm's vaults. The danger was that Northcote lawyers would examine what was in the box, once Jane had retrieved it. Could he extend client confidentiality and insist the contents be returned unexamined? They knew, from what Carver had produced in the NOXT building, what was duplicated in the Citibank vaults and Burcher doubted the woman would understand any of it. The Northcote lawyers would, though, when they went through it, as they inevitably would. Which way would they jump when they realized the significance? Like lemmings, over the self-exposing, self-destructive cliff, to the FBI? Or more practicably, and strictly within the law, gratefully accepting they were no longer professionally involved and even more gratefully thrusting upon him Carver's incriminating box? It was an impossible bet to call. But the sensibly practical route – the route Burcher would have expected any sensible, practical lawyer to take – would be the latter. Where in this milling reception room was the Northcote lawyer? Logically he – or she – had to be close to Jane Carver. Reluctantly, as he was always reluctant to enter any focus of attention, Burcher moved towards the receiving group. So, finally, although from a different direction, did Alice.

What the fuck was he doing here, Hanlan asked himself. Had he expected name tags, *Martha* in big letters? Imagined, in this babble, that he'd hear the voice he'd recognize when he wasn't sure he'd recognize it anyway? Stupidly – unprofessionally – he'd let this get to him: let instinct – gut instinct – cloud hard-assed reality. Ginette was right and McKinnon was right and Washington was right. Keep the door – or more literally, the telephone lines – open but don't invest this off-the-wall situation with importance or priorities it didn't have. OK, after this he wouldn't. Any more than he'd tell anyone else at Federal Plaza where he'd been or what he'd been doing. Just keep things in order of priority. File this at the back of the list. Hanlan still didn't move from where he'd established himself after also slipping out of the receiving line, token champagne in hand but undrunk, watching. Martha would be here, crazy or not. She'd have to be, according to every Quantico rule of psychological profiling. A big crowd. Rich crowd. No one – certainly no woman – looking out of place, particularly unusual or attracting attention. Most likely one of this sort of crowd then. But which side? The honestly rich side, who would have needed Northcote and Carver to keep them that way? Or the dirty organized-crime side, who according to Martha had found some way to make Northcote and Carver work for them? No way these days of guessing. Telling. Everyone – at this level – looked the same, behaved the same. Rich. Successful. Honest. A quiet voice said: 'Excuse me,' and Hanlan moved aside for Burcher to continue on towards where Jane Carver and her group were standing.

Jane let her mind freefall from everything immediately around her but intentionally, not from any legacy of the drug, her sole concentration upon finding one person, one face, which so far she hadn't seen. That's all she had to concentrate upon, only Mary . . . no, Rosemary . . . Pritchard. That's the only person she wanted to see: to talk to. Rosemary. Talk to Rosemary. Everything else was unimportant, banal. Trite words, trite responses. *So sorry . . . a wonderful man . . . tragic loss . . . we must keep in touch . . . lunch . . . Thank you . . . very kind . . . yes, keep in touch.* Where was Rosemary? Why hadn't she come? Jane felt tired, from standing, from shaking hands. Her back and legs ached and her hand, her fingers, hurt from being squeezed: people thinking the harder they pressed, the more sincere they appeared. *So sorry . . . a brilliant man . . . Thank you . . . very kind . . .*

'Jane?'

'Rosemary!' exclaimed Jane, then at once: 'No, not Rosemary.' She tried to focus but it wasn't easy to see a veiled face through her own veil and then abruptly the woman's image faded for the briefest of seconds. 'You're not Rosemary . . .? Who . . .?' Why wasn't it Rosemary? It had sounded like Rosemary.

'We have to talk,' urged Alice, conscious of the pressure from people behind. 'It's very important. About your father. And John. Both of them.'

'I thought you were Rosemary.'

'Can we talk? Can I come to see you, to talk? It's urgent.'

'Do you know Rosemary? Rosemary Pritchard?'

The pressure, the intervention, was now from the woman whom Alice knew to be Hilda Bennett. The woman said to Jane: 'Are you all right . . .? Do you want to stop . . . ?'

'No,' refused Jane, fully bringing herself back to where she was, what she was doing. 'What was it you said?' she asked Alice.

'We need to meet. About your father. And John.'

'Yes. Of course. Thank you. Very kind.'

Stanley Burcher was merged into another wall, studying Geoffrey Davis, who had been pointed out to him as the Northcote lawyer by a hovering hotel manager. Uncharacteristically Burcher was tempted to make a direct, personal approach, quickly dismissing the thought as unprofessional and in entirely the wrong circumstances. He thought Davis looked a practical, level-headed sort of man. But outward appearances were meaningless. He hadn't seen anyone resembling the magazine photograph of Alice Belling, who at that moment passed just twenty feet away as she left the reception.

Alice knew who Rosemary Pritchard was: John had recommended the gynaecologist to her. Why, at this moment in time and in these circumstances, was Rosemary Pritchard so important to Jane?

Jane was glad at last to be moving, relieving the ache in her back and legs and sparing her hand from any more crushing insincerity, which was still as crushing without the handshakes. *Appalling tragedy . . . so unfair . . . brilliant husband . . . brilliant father . . . you're very brave . . . couldn't be that brave myself . . . lunch . . . I'll call very soon . . . Thank you . . . lunch is good . . . I'll wait to hear . . .* She was learning how to control the ebbs and flows. It had come three times while she stood in the receiving line, though she was sure no one had suspected, because she was always sufficiently aware now in the very few seconds before they washed over her. Could compensate, say the words. *Thank you . . . very kind . . . so good of you to come . . .* Her back was aching again. Her legs too. She couldn't go on much longer. Wanted to stop. Finish now. Done enough. Done all she had to.

Hilda said: 'Do you want to go home now?'

'Have I done everything properly?'

'You've done everything exactly right.'

Jane was startled by Mortimer's reassurance, unaware until he spoke that the man was walking the room with her. 'Then yes, I'd like to go home.' No one knew, no one suspected. She had . . . Had to do what? Couldn't remember . . . She would though, soon enough. Just needed a moment. Get her thoughts together. What was it she had to do? It was important. More people in the way. *Fine man . . . brilliant mind . . . such a loss . . . Thank you . . . so kind . . . thank you . . .*

Jane couldn't remember getting into the car. They were going back across town. Hilda was talking. Just the odd word initially, then connected, making sense: '. . . a lot to do. Letters, things like that. Not tomorrow, if you don't feel like it. Whenever. But I'll get the condolence books now if you're all right for a moment. I'll go get them, then I'll come back.'

'I want that,' Jane heard herself saying. 'Like before.'

'That's what I thought. I expected that you would.'

'There must be other things I have to do . . .? Proper things . . . formal . . .?'

'Everything's on hold, until you're ready.'

'Not today.'

'No,' agreed the older woman. 'Nothing more today. Today you've done enough.' The car turned into East 62nd Street and Hilda said: 'Here we are. Home.'

Jane welcomed the sudden clarity, not aching now, not even feeling tired. 'Not home,' she contradicted. 'John isn't here any more.'

Alice hadn't intended to be there. She'd left the Plaza to retrieve her car and get back as soon as she could to the safety of the cabin in the Bearfort Mountains. It was only when she drove out of the lot that she decided to go to East 62nd Street, initially with no thought in her mind of actually approaching Jane, not knowing, even, why she was doing what she was doing. She tried the Melrose Hotel to isolate any obvious attention upon John's apartment building, from both the bar and reception, but couldn't see sufficiently from either. It was when she was outside in the street again that she saw Jane helped from her car by Hilda Bennett and sat undecided upon a bench at the Second Avenue junction and was glad she did because the older woman left after just fifteen minutes. Why not this afternoon? Alice suddenly asked herself. And just as quickly answered herself: *Why not?*

Twenty-Two

Neither was it a conscious intention – it hadn't crossed her mind – to say what she did until Alice entered the building and realized she had to negotiate reception security to get to the sixth floor, where she knew John's apartment to be. Nor, most stupid of all, had it occurred to her that there would obviously be CCTV cameras. The man smiled at her approach and asked who she was visiting and Alice said: 'Mrs Carver's expecting me. It's about Rosemary Pritchard.'

'She's just got back from her husband's funeral,' frowned the man.

'So have I.' What was she doing here, saying here! This was knee-jerk, unthought-out madness.

'Of course,' he said, looking more closely at Alice's veiled appearance. 'I was told to expect some people. Rosemary Pritchard, you say?'

'That's right.' Not a direct lie. By no means the truth, either. But the best – probably her only – chance of getting past the foyer to see Jane, who wouldn't have responded – had her staff respond – if she'd correctly identified herself. Which was unthinkable anyway. Which people were expected? She was thinking on her feet now, intuitively, snatching at each and any opportunity. Easy enough to claim a misunderstanding. It didn't matter. All that mattered was getting to Jane. She heard the man recite the gynaecologist's name into the internal telephone, her breath tight, and saw the man's unthinking nod of acceptance. 'You're to go up,' he told Alice, who was already moving towards the elevator.

It would have been Manuel who'd answered, she supposed. Or Jennings. John had talked of the staff transfers, after Northcote's death. Would either know what Rosemary Pritchard looked like? It was doubtful. As far as Alice was aware Rosemary Pritchard didn't make house calls. She'd get to Jane OK now. Nothing to stop her. To say what? She still wasn't sure. Retained research material didn't sound good enough any more, not now she was actually here. Never really had sounded right. So what was she going to say? She didn't know. Couldn't think of anything. Which could make this a bad mistake, ruining everything coming full frontal on to Jane like this with stories of murder and blackmail and Christ knows what else. Not *could* be a bad mistake. Would be a bad mistake, because she couldn't tell Jane anything of why she was here. Whatever story she tried to tell would be gibberish, the ramblings of a lunatic.

The elevator stopped at six, John's floor. Jane's floor, she corrected herself. John didn't live here any more. Never would, ever again. Or in Princes Street. Or in the cabin. The elevator doors sighed closed behind her but Alice didn't move. She most definitely shouldn't have come like this. This was panicked, ridiculous. Jane wouldn't understand a thing she said about being in danger. Have her thrown out, seized maybe by the security man downstairs. She should have gone from the funeral to Federal Plaza and surrendered herself to someone called Gene Hanlan and persuaded him to come here with her. That would have made the approach official, to be taken seriously. If, that is, Hanlan could have been persuaded and not gone on demanding convincing proof of her claims before confronting a widow on the day of her husband's funeral. Which Alice was sure he wouldn't conceivably have done.

There were three doors off the corridor in which she was

standing but she knew from John that the one into the apartment was directly ahead, at the corridor's end. It was pale green, Jane's favourite colour. Chosen by her, like the décor inside, pale green offset by cream, dark green for contrast in the carpets and drapes. John had liked it, too. Called Jane artistic. She should leave, Alice told herself. Call the elevator back and get out, before she was trapped by whoever else was expected. She couldn't have gained more than fifteen minutes, leaving the wake early. Insane to be here like this.

She had to take a chance with the FBI agent. It was her *only* chance. It might have helped if she'd brought the IRS print-outs from the cabin. Insufficient by themselves, but at least something. Perhaps not go to the FBI at all, not yet. But when? She wouldn't be gaining anything by waiting to get any more tax records. So she wouldn't wait. She had to live – survive – not wait.

The pale-green door was opened by Manuel, whom she recognized from John's description of the dark-haired, dark-skinned butler. A Mexican with a Mexican wife. Resenting the intrusion of others.

Alice said: 'The lobby called up.'

Manuel nodded and said: 'Rosemary Pritchard?'

'Mrs Carver's expecting me.'

'I was expecting Dr Mortimer. People from the firm.'

'I've come direct from the funeral.' Get out of the way, let me in!

As if aware of Alice's thoughts, Manuel stood aside, gesturing Alice towards a door to the right. The drawing room, Alice knew, holding back for the butler to open it for her but immediately thrusting past before he could block her way.

Jane Carver was in a chair by the window, looking across the verandah in the direction of the park. She turned at Manuel's voice, her features more squinting than frowning because at that moment Jane's vision was blurred, as much from a close-to-exhaustion half doze as from the persistent hangover from chlorpromazine. 'What . . .? Who . . . ?'

'Jane, we talked back at the hotel.' How long would it be before the others arrived, behind her? Minutes. Probably no more than minutes.

Jane's vision cleared. 'Yes?' She said, doubtfully. Something about her father. John. She wished she didn't feel so tired: so disorientated.

Alice was conscious of Manuel, hovering at the door, face creased in uncertainty. He said: 'Are you all right, Mrs Carver? Dr Mortimer's on his way.'

Jane roused herself, physically straightening in her chair. 'It's OK. I dozed off. I don't want anything, thank you.' As Manuel closed the door after himself, still frowning, Jane looked back to Alice and said: 'I'm sorry . . . ?'

It had to be the FBI, Alice decided. There was no other choice. Somehow, anyhow, she had to get Jane to Federal Plaza, talk and plead there until they took her seriously enough to put them both under some sort of protection until Jane could get the documents that were going to save them from Citibank on Wall Street. It could be done by tomorrow. By tomorrow they could be out of danger. 'I want you to come somewhere with me . . . it's very important . . . it's to do with . . .'

'Rosemary Pritchard!' exclaimed Jane, triumphantly. 'Yes, of course!'

Until that moment Alice had been unaware of the depth of Jane's confusion. She'd dismissed as understandable Jane's strangeness during their brief encounter at the Plaza, the bewilderment of grief and of being among too many people too soon, engulfed in that grief. But now it was obviously something else, something she'd been given to help her get through the ordeal. Dr Mortimer's on his way, Manuel had said. They'd be here soon, the prescribing doctor and people from the firm. She couldn't possibly explain to them: convince them. She couldn't be here when they arrived. 'Yes, Rosemary Pritchard.'

'Are you taking me to her?'

'Yes. That's what I want to do. Will you come with me now, right away?'

'Of course. I've been waiting.' Jane rose but swayed slightly, needing the support of the chair back. 'Still a bit fuzzy.'

'We've got to hurry, Jane.' How long had she been in the apartment? Five minutes, ten minutes? They had to get out. She was taking advantage of someone who didn't know what they were doing. She thought, forgive me, John. And then, forgive me, Jane. What she was doing was right, Alice told herself. It had to be.

Manuel must have used one of the side doors to get into the entrance lobby of the apartment. As they came out of the drawing room he said: 'People are on their way, Mrs Carver.'

'I need a coat, Manuel. We're going to see Dr Pritchard.'

'The others are coming,' the butler insisted. 'You should wait.'

'*They* can wait. Tell them that. Tell them to wait. Could you get my coat, please?'

The man didn't immediately move. He said to Alice: 'I thought you *were* Rosemary Pritchard?'

'No.'

'Who are you?'

'A friend.'

'Manuel! My coat please!' demanded Jane.

Alice couldn't believe the sudden lucidity: was worried it might suddenly bring Jane back into proper, questioning awareness.

Manuel said: 'I think you should wait, Mrs Carver. There are people . . .'

'Who can wait. I'll get my damned coat myself!'

Manuel got to the closet first. The coat was black, to match

Jane's funeral clothes. Jane took it but didn't try to put it on, instead throwing it over her arm. Alice's concentration was on the indicator board as they went down the outside corridor, alert for an ascending elevator, jabbing at the summoning button the moment she reached it. Manuel was at the still open door of the apartment, watching them.

'Everything's going to be all right,' said Jane, obscurely.

'I know it will be,' said Alice, who didn't.

The lobby was empty. The man at the reception desk smiled and said something Alice didn't hear. Jane smiled back at him but didn't say anything. Outside, Alice said: 'I've got a car,' and quickly turned Jane away from the direction from which vehicles would approach. Alice wanted to move faster but Jane was unsteady, scuffing her feet, needing a supporting arm. Alice could see the Volkswagen tantalizingly ahead, like a mirage, and for a moment, like a mirage, it didn't seem to be getting any nearer. But then it did and she bustled Jane into the passenger seat and tightened the safety belt around her. As she did so, close to the other woman, Alice saw Jane's eyes droop, then blink open, her head jerking back. Then it fell again.

Alice drove initially without thought, grateful she'd been facing east, making the right on Second Avenue and staying on it through four intersections before making the cross-town turn, wanting to avoid going close to the Plaza. She'd done it! She'd got Jane – poor, momentarily bewildered and confused Jane – and through Jane the FBI could get what George Northcote was murdered for and what Janice Snow was murdered for and what John had finally – too late – been so desperately running to the police to preserve. Which they could get now. Alice couldn't think, didn't want to think, beyond that. Whatever the uncertainties ahead, things were going to happen and when they did she had to face them, adjust to them.

It was when Alice was actually making the cross-town turn that Jane slumped heavily against her and when she was fully halted by the jam at the Fifth Avenue junction Alice turned to see Jane's head sunk deeply on to her chest, bubbling faint snores.

Loudly she said: 'Jane!' but Jane didn't stir.

'Jane!'

There was still no response.

It would be whatever Jane had been given, to get her through the funeral. That and the trauma of it all. Total exhaustion, as well. Alice felt close to total exhaustion herself. She wouldn't get what she wanted – the acceptance she wanted – taking a completely incomprehensible woman to the FBI. They'd most likely hospitalize Jane, separating them before there was any chance of even attempting to explain, which would make everything impossible.

Alice didn't turn downtown on Broadway but continued on straight across to Twelfth Avenue to go north, on to West Side Highway. She hoped Jane would sleep until they got to the cabin. She'd run into the first of her uncertainties, Alice realized. And still wasn't safe.

Gene Hanlan and the FBI became involved so quickly through a coincidental sequence of events. Geoffrey Davis didn't raise the alarm by dialling 911 but called Sergeant P. David Hopper direct, with a lawyer's recall that the man had been in charge of John Carver's accident investigation. And Hopper remembered Hanlan's unusual visit to the precinct house and called Federal Plaza after alerting his own detective division. Kidnapping is a federal offence and kidnapping had been the word Davis had used, in their conversation. And because it was the word Hopper continued to use, the NYPD detectives were led by a lieutenant, a short-cropped, trouser-suited woman whose ID badge said Barbara Donnelly. From the way in which they were trying to assemble people, with no interviews started, Hanlan guessed he was only five minutes behind the detectives.

'I didn't call you,' the woman greeted Hanlan, walking away from her team, physically separating him from everyone.

'So we're saving time,' said Hanlan. Sergeant Hopper had indeed been a rarity. This was the sort of instant and instinctive resentment to which he was accustomed.

'How'd you find out so quick?' The voice had a smoker's hoarseness.

'The Bureau already has an interest.' Hanlan felt he was due the exaggeration. If Jane Carver had indeed been kidnapped there should be a lot of people in the J. Edgar Hoover building eating crow within the next twenty-four hours.

'You want to explain that?'

Hanlan looked at the people now waiting on the far side of the apartment, close to the balcony window, and wondered if they could detect the antagonism between him and the woman in the exchange. It would worsen if he reminded her he didn't have to explain anything. Lowering his voice and putting his back towards them, Hanlan said: 'You know about the death of George Northcote, Carver's father-in-law, up in Litchfield? And of Northcote's personal assistant, out in Brooklyn?'

'Read something about it, after Carver got killed,' allowed the woman. 'So?'

'We've got an informant talking organized crime, money laundering and murder.'

'Shit!' she said, the hostility going from the manner in which she was confronting him.

'It's federal,' he pointed out.

'We've got pretty effective murder divisions here in the city.'

'If they were murdered – they've been officially accepted as accidents: Carver's most certainly was – they're out of NYPD jurisdiction.'

'We going to work together?' The woman was retreating further.

'I don't see any benefit in working against each other. Never did,' said Hanlan.

The detectives with Barbara Donnelly were shifting impatiently, knowing what was going on. There was some uncertain movement from near the window, too. She said: 'Let's just run through it, see how it goes.'

Hanlan turned to the waiting group, recognizing the two men and the woman who had stood in the receiving line with Jane Carver. There was one other woman, in a severely tailored suit, and three other men, one with a heavy moustache, another in the sort of black suit that staff often wore, and the third in a red blazer that also looked like a uniform. Hanlan introduced himself and asked for the general picture and at once Geoffrey Davis identified himself by name and position, taking control of the group as Hanlan hoped he was going to be able to take control of the law enforcement.

'Jane became very tired by the end of the reception: under a lot of stress. She asked to come back, so Hilda brought her. Arrangement was that we'd give her time to settle down, get rested, and then we'd come by to see she was OK. There's a few things I've got to see to. Will-readings, firm insurances and pensions that automatically revert to her . . .'

'I'm not getting a clear picture here,' protested Barbara, looking to one of the women. 'You Hilda?'

Carver's PA nodded.

'If you came back with her, how come you didn't stay until the others arrived?'

Hilda said: 'Jane told me she wanted to rest. That there was something she had to do later. She'd asked several times earlier about Rosemary Pritchard . . .' She hesitated, smiling towards the severely suited woman. 'This is Dr Pritchard. Jane wanted to know whether she'd been at the funeral. I told her that while she was resting I'd go back to the cathedral and pick up the condolences books . . .' She nodded to two bound volumes on a coffee table. 'We're going to need them, for the letters. When I got back, she'd gone.'

'With someone who pretended to be Dr Pritchard,' supplied a man in a blazer. 'Tom Reynolds, downstairs security. The woman said she was Rosemary Pritchard and when I called up, Manuel told me to let her on past.'

'But I was . . .' began the swarthy man in the black suit but Hanlan cut him off. 'OK, let's hold it there. Everyone can make their own contributions later but for the moment, let's get some continuity into this. You,' he insisted, pointing to Davis.

It came with a lawyer's precision and only took minutes. Davis finished by gesturing towards the gynaecologist and saying: 'Dr Pritchard was obviously the first person I called when I heard what had happened . . .'

'And I felt I should come straight over,' said the woman.

'We appreciate that very much. Thank you,' said Barbara. 'You had no appointment with Jane this afternoon?'

'No.'

'Nor arranged to be at the funeral: see her there?'

'No,' repeated the doctor.

'Were you treating her, for anything specific?'

'We're into patient confidentiality here,' refused the other woman.

'Dr Pritchard,' said the detective lieutenant, level-voiced. 'The way it looks, someone who knows you – or knows that Jane is a patient of yours – impersonated you and kidnapped her. We're not asking you to break any patient confidentiality. What we are asking is that you do all you can to help us find her and get her back safely.'

'I understand that: that's why I came as soon as I got the call.'

'Jane knew you: the woman couldn't have impersonated you,' said Hanlan.

'I asked her if she was Rosemary Pritchard,' intruded Manuel. 'She said she was a friend.'

'A friend of mine? Or of Jane?' demanded the gynaecologist.

Manuel shrugged and shook his head, unknowing.

'How was she?' asked Hanlan. 'She look frightened, as if this other woman was threatening her?'

Manuel considered the question. 'Not really.'

'What's not really mean?'

'She got angry, when I asked her not to leave until Dr Mortimer and the others got here. She didn't usually get angry.'

'Was Jane Carver under treatment by you, Dr Pritchard?' asked Barbara.

Rosemary Pritchard hesitated. 'I had recently seen her. And John.'

'How recently?' demanded Hanlan.

'A few days ago.'

'Let's try to get around this confidentiality problem by how I phrase my question,' suggested the detective. 'Because I've got a problem with Jane Carver coming home to rest after the ordeal of her husband's funeral then suddenly getting up and leaving, if she wasn't under any obvious pressure. Could whatever you were treating Jane for make her vulnerable? Behave in a way out of the ordinary?'

'Chlorpromazine could,' declared Peter Mortimer.

'What's that?' asked Barbara.

'What she was being given – wrongly given – to help her over the shock of her father's death,' said Mortimer. 'It can have bad side effects on certain people and in my professional judgement Jane was one such person. It had been stopped but there was clearly a residue.'

'What sort of bad side effects?' asked Hanlan.

The psychiatrist shrugged. 'Vulnerability, to repeat an already used word. Emotional dependency upon others. Fixation . . .'

'I think you're solving my problem,' said Barbara. 'All we need now is to know where she is.'

'And who she's with,' added Hanlan. He looked at the policewoman. 'You think your guys could get the initial statements?'

'Sure,' nodded Barbara. To her waiting squad she said: 'OK guys,' and followed Hanlan towards the window view, making room for the other detectives to start work. She said to Hanlan: 'You going to bring in a big team?'

'I don't know yet,' admitted Hanlan. 'What I don't want are any media leaks. If she's being held, we've got to avoid spooking whoever's got her into doing something in a panic to get rid of her. You warn your guys?'

'Sure,' agreed the woman again. 'But a thing like this, it nearly always gets out.'

'Let's just do our best. If it is a kidnap, there'll be ransom demands. We'll need to get this place wired: people here permanently. And the Northcote building, as well. Have negotiators there, too.'

Barbara Donnelly looked at him sceptically. 'And you want to keep it under wraps!'

'Let's just do our best,' Hanlan repeated. 'And . . .' He stopped, abruptly, looking back into the apartment. 'And at the moment we're a hell of a long way short of doing that.' He called out: 'Mr Reynolds? Dr Pritchard . . . ?'

The security guard and the gynaecologist crossed the room together.

Hanlan said: 'Downstairs, in the lobby. There's got to be CCTV?'

'Sure thing,' agreed the guard.

'And a viewing room?'

'Of course.'

'You mind coming with us, Dr Pritchard?'

No one spoke in the descending lift, but Barbara Donnelly was smiling faintly and when she glanced in his direction Hanlan smiled back, hopefully. There were four monitors in the viewing room but Alice was only on the loop of the primary camera, directed at the main door. The film showed her turning away immediately after her first exchange with Reynolds and Barbara said: 'She's trying to cover herself: seen there's a camera.'

Jane was between Alice and the camera as they left and the detective said: 'Here she's using Jane as a shield. And look, she's holding her arm, forcing her along!'

'Supporting, not forcing her,' qualified Hanlan. To the gynaecologist he said: 'Well? Do you know her?'

'I think I do,' said Rosemary Pritchard, although with doubtful slowness.

'Who?' demanded Barbara, eagerly. 'Give us her name!'

The gynaecologist shook her head. 'I don't have one. I'm fairly sure that I know her, that I've seen her or met her. But I can't *recognize* her: give her a name. There's something . . .' She shrugged. '. . . something, but I don't know what.'

On the second re-run Hanlan realized that he'd seen her, too. That morning, at John Carver's wake at the Plaza Hotel.

Jane had remained asleep, only occasionally stirring, during the drive up to the cabin and was very confused when Alice tried to rouse her, needing all Alice's support to get her into the cabin, so unsteady and still so half asleep that Alice continued straight on into the bedroom and laid Jane under the comforter, only bothering to take off her shoes. Jane snuffled and shifted for a position, but slept on.

During the drive Alice had tried to put some sort of reason into what she'd done and justified most of it, but not all, and the part she couldn't justify was the most important. But the major concern was Jane herself. However exhausted Jane might have been by the funeral it was surely unnatural, maybe dangerously so, to have slept for so long in a jolting car and to go on sleeping now, although the bed was far more comfortable than the Volkswagen's passenger seat. Jane should be seen by a doctor. Who would ask questions about medication which Alice couldn't answer. Want to know what Jane was doing there and maybe why. Alice reached out and felt Jane's forehead. Jane stirred at the touch but didn't wake up. She wasn't running a fever and was breathing quite normally. She'd wait, Alice decided. Sit where she was, here in the bedroom, alert for any discernible change in Jane. She'd definitely get a doctor if Jane became obviously ill but at the moment she wasn't obviously ill. Just deeply asleep. Which made Alice's other difficulty the most important thing.

She'd kept the radio on low, throughout the drive, tuned to breaking news for the first flash on Jane's disappearance, surprised she hadn't heard it. There'd be a panic, though, police and FBI: Gene Hanlan involved, almost inevitably. It would be a hell of a risk, calling from here, but she had to do it to stop the panic. Stop them thinking something bad might have happened to Jane. It would only take a minute, maybe two: it would be all right to leave Jane alone for just two minutes.

But Alice hesitated at the telephone, the Federal Plaza number beside it, and had to force herself to lift up the receiver. The moment she said 'Martha' into the mouthpiece Hanlan was on the line.

'You got her?'

The lobby camera, Alice knew. 'She's all right.'

'You know what you've done?' Hanlan certainly knew what he'd done, risking his entire career putting everything on hold in expectation of getting this call after seeing the CCTV film.

'Of course I know!'

'Why did you do it?'

'To get the evidence you said I needed.'

'She got it?'

'She can get it.'

'Now here's what you're going to do, Martha. You're going to come in, like I've been asking you to all along. Come in, and we're going to sort it all out. And now I want you to bring Jane to the phone so I can talk to her, hear that she's OK.'

'You can't talk to her. She's asleep.'

'Martha! You could be in a whole lot of trouble. Serious, criminal trouble. I'm keeping a very tight lid on everything to protect you but . . .'

'That's what I want, protection!'

'I know. And I promise I'll give it to you. All you've got to do is come in. Or tell us where you are and we'll come and get you.'

She'd held on the phone too long. 'I'll call again, later. I want to think.'

'Martha! Don't hang up!'

But Alice did.

The Bonanno's Vito Craxi said: 'I want to put things on notice here. We're looking at a fucking disaster.'

'A major fucking disaster,' endorsed Carlo Brookier.

No one was admiring the Central Park view or helping themselves to drinks.

Bobby Gallo, the Gambino *consigliere*, said: 'That's my Family's feeling, too. How we going to get what's in Carver's Citibank box? We don't get it, the system's bust. It's a collapse we don't want and can't have.'

Charlie Petrie knew clearly enough it wasn't general conversation. He, in particular, and the Genovese by unarguable association, were being held responsible. 'What about Burcher's idea, going to the firm direct, get back what belongs to us after Carver wrote his letters?'

'We can't be sure we know of everything Northcote held back. Who might be identified,' warned Gino LaRocca. 'We're over a barrel here.'

'We gotta shift something,' insisted Gallo.

'I'll speak to Burcher about a strictly legal approach,' undertook Petrie.

'I think it's dangerous,' protested Craxi.

'Let's vote on it,' suggested Petrie.

Craxi was the only objector.

Petrie said: 'I'll speak to him.'

Craxi said: 'After this, Burcher is superfluous.'

'He gets the stuff back from the Northcote firm, he provides a service,' said Gallo.

'He's still superfluous,' insisted Craxi.

'He gets the stuff back, *then* he's superfluous,' agreed Petrie. 'Right now he's got a use.'

Twenty-Three

Jane awoke in the half light of an uncurtained window, immediately aware of being fully dressed beneath the comforter, and that because of it she was far too hot. It was as she pushed the covering aside, her eyes adjusting to the deeply shadowed room, that she became aware of a woman slumped in a chair beneath the window, breathing heavily, asleep. There was a vaguely familiar smell, from the pillow or from the comforter, but she couldn't decide why she recognized it. There was no city noise outside, just the rustle of trees, ruffled by the breeze. Somewhere in the country then. But where? Who with? Why? Jane didn't feel any fear, any positive threat: she'd never known real fear or threat in her protected life. Her head was clear, which was good. No sensation of it being stuffed with cotton wool, her mind too thick to think properly. So think properly. John's funeral. People, a lot of people, at the hotel. A woman at the apartment. This woman? Maybe. Too dark to see her face. Couldn't remember her face. The woman said . . . Rosemary Pritchard! That was it! The woman was taking her to Rosemary Pritchard. Why was she being taken? Why not just go by herself? That didn't make any sense. Being here, somewhere in the country, didn't make any sense. Lying fully dressed in bed didn't make any sense. Whose bed? Whose house? Too much that didn't make sense. Jane was desperately thirsty. She eased herself off the bed, from the side furthest from the sleeping woman, steadying herself as she stood, locating a door, ajar, in the wall closest to her. She went out, pulled it fully closed behind her, orientating herself to the now shrouded room but at once wondered why she was staying in the dark, feeling out instead for the light switch and finding it alongside the door.

It was a country cabin, she instantly recognized, blinking in the abrupt light. Rustic plaid furniture grouped around a huge stone fireplace, logs stacked alongside, polished wood floor beneath rug throws. A computer, telephone and a pile of paper on a far-away desk by the door. That door obviously led outside. She guessed the one opposite was to the kitchen. It was only when she was crossing to it that she realized she wasn't wearing shoes. Looking down at herself Jane saw her clothes were concertinaed around her, from their having been slept in. She felt dirty, unwashed, too. Which she doubtlessly was. What the hell was she doing here? She'd wake the woman as soon as she'd drunk some water, find out what it was all about.

It was a functional kitchen, a stove, refrigerator, communal refectory table more than big enough for its six surrounding chairs. Salt, pepper and napkins sat on their island in the middle. Two napkin rings. Jane drank the first glass without pause, only bothering with ice on the second. She drained that too, like the first, and it came up again from a too quickly filled stomach, making her feel slightly sick. She filled the glass again but sipped this time. It was getting lighter outside. Through the kitchen window she saw a beetle-shaped Volkswagen, then she jumped, spilling some of her water, at a sudden animal scream, a victim of something larger.

Jane felt a familiar dampness and thought, damn. She was on her way back to the bedroom and the sleeping woman when she saw the corridor to one side of the fireplace and detoured along it. She found the bathroom first time, wondering if she would have to pad herself, relieved when she found one tampon remaining in its box in the bathroom cabinet. There were two toothbrushes in the bathroom cup and an electric razor, a Remington like John's, on a side shelf. And then Jane saw the cologne, the Cartier that John also used, and realized why she'd recognized the faint smell when she'd first woken that morning, beneath the duvet.

Jane jumped again, although less violently, as she emerged to the unexpected sight of the woman hurrying across the main room, towards the kitchen. Alice saw Jane at the same time and appeared just as surprised. There was a faint smile.

Jane said: 'I was coming to wake you.'

'I didn't hear you get up.'

'Obviously.' The other woman was blonde, about the same height and weight as she was. Probably around the same age, too. She wore jeans and a sports shirt and was barefoot.

'I'm Alice Belling.' There was no possibility of the name meaning anything so long after the profile of Jane's father. She hadn't rehearsed anything, worked anything out! She'd imagined being up, moving around, working up a passable story in her mind long before Jane awoke. Stupid – stupid! Stupid! Stupid! Stupid! Like so much – everything – else.

'I'm due an explanation.' Probably prompted by the reasons for her using the bathroom, Jane remembered why she was so anxious to talk to the gynaecologist.

'You became unwell after . . . after yesterday,' floundered Alice. 'I was taking you somewhere but decided it was better for you to come here until you recovered.'

She was definitely better, Jane decided. Her vision hadn't ebbed and flowed once since she'd got up and her head was still ice clear. 'When you're ill, you need a doctor, OK? Which is where you said yesterday you were taking me, remember?' She could remember! She was beginning to remember everything!

'I was going to get one. You went to sleep. I thought it was better to leave you . . .' Alice made a half gesture back towards the bedroom. 'I sat up.'

'And went to sleep. Where the hell are we?' This was unreal: totally unreal. She still didn't feel frightened. She was irritated, annoyed, at being bundled about without knowing why, like a child that didn't deserve an explanation. She'd always explain things to her child, treat it with the respect it deserved.

It wasn't difficult to find the edge to Jane's voice. Alice said: 'The Bearfort Mountains.'

'The Catskills!' exclaimed Jane. 'That's miles from New York! What *are* we doing here?'

Why hadn't she thought it out better! Something, anything! Forced herself to stay awake to get together some half-convincing story! 'Hiding.'

'*What!*' demanded Jane, incredulous. She shifted slightly, the beginning of uncertainty.

Alice recognized the movement, desperate for a way forward. It had to be a mix of all her half-thoughts and half-ideas and half-truths. 'Alice Belling,' she repeated. 'I wrote a long profile of your father, in *Forbes*. He was very flattering about it. Don't you remember the piece?'

'Kind of . . .' said Jane, doubtfully. The uncertainty was on her face now, her head intently to one side.

'He wrote me a couple of times, said he wanted a biography written. I began working on it, researching . . . I'd met John when I'd written the profile. The arrangement was . . .'

'You knew John?' Jane cut her off.

Alice coughed, to cover the need to swallow. Dear God make me think of something better than this! 'Like I said, we met when I was doing the profile: he handled any queries that came up after my interviews with your father. That was how it was to continue for the book, John acting as liaison when anything came up that your father was too busy to handle or . . .'

'Too busy to handle!' broke in Jane, again. 'My father was semi-retired, for a year!'

It was going horribly, appallingly wrong but it didn't matter. Jane was better now. All she had to do was get Jane back to Manhattan, to the FBI. Once they were safely inside the Federal Plaza building she didn't have to see Jane ever again. Or perhaps more importantly, Jane never had to see her ever again. Alice shrugged: 'It was the way we worked.'

'Hiding?' echoed Jane. She spoke loudly, making it a demand.

'Your father was tricked, a long time ago. The indications came up, in some papers I came upon. Old papers. They referred to some other documents that John found, through them. He put them in his safe-deposit box, in Citibank on Wall Street . . . The people who tricked your father want them back . . .' Alice needed to move, to get away from Jane's unremitting, suspicious stare. Alice started to pad towards the desk and her new computer, beside it the most recent printouts that had to go with the rest of the stuff already in the Volkswagen, ready to convince the Bureau. And abruptly saw the photograph! It was the one of John the fisherman, from their first visit, which she'd liked so much that she'd copied it for Princes Street. It was hidden at that moment behind the printouts but it probably wouldn't be if Jane moved any closer. Alice turned at the desk, wedging her hip on its edge, her body a barrier. An idea thrust into her mind and she grabbed it. 'I know this all sounds . . .'

'Preposterous!' refused Jane. 'My father and I were as close as it is possible for a father and daughter to be. John and I were as close as it's possible for a husband and wife to be. If my father had decided upon a biography, I would have known about it, from him or from John. If there was some problem with the firm, I would have known about it, from my father or from John . . . I don't know who you are or what you want

. . . what you're talking about, even . . . I am not frightened of you . . . You're going to take me to the nearest town from which I can speak to people . . . do you understand . . . ?'

'The FBI know you're safe . . . they want to speak to you . . .' The telephone was on the desk! She had to get the photograph away, before bringing Jane to the telephone.

'The *FBI*?'

Federal Plaza. That's all she had to do, get them to Federal Plaza! 'That's what John was doing, at Citibank on the day of the accident. Going to his safe deposit to get what he'd found, to pass it over to the FBI.' She was too far gone now to worry about – count even – the lies and the deceits. As much for Jane as for herself, Alice thought. Sorry John: I've made a mess of it but Jane will be safe. 'The agent-in-charge is named Gene Hanlan. It's too early to call him yet. You can speak to him first thing.' Get her out the room, on whatever pretext, just long enough to get rid of the damned photograph! Not a damned photograph. One of the few physical reminders she had of John. She'd take it with her, to her new life. She'd ignore them, whoever gave her the new identity, if they said she couldn't keep it: that she had to surrender and abandon all and every trace of her past. She had to have that positive memento of John.

'Whose cabin is this?'

Alice's mind was completely skewed by Jane's unexpected change of direction and without thought – without giving herself time to think, as she hadn't virtually throughout this disastrous confrontation – she blurted: 'Mine.'

'What about your husband?'

'I don't have a husband.' The sickness was there again, the churning low in her stomach, growing at the back of her throat.

Jane jerked her head back along the corridor. 'I had to borrow one of your things . . . I didn't realize I was due: so much happening, I guess. There was stuff in the cabinet, a razor. Cologne.'

The nausea worsened. Alice said: 'A partner. Didn't work out. It's only just happened. I haven't got around to clearing away the memories yet.'

'I haven't even begun to think about clearing away the memories yet.'

'I'm sorry. About John, I mean,' Alice forced herself to say. Today was the end. After today it would all be over. No embarrassment, about hypocrisy, about anything. Not the end, Alice corrected herself. This was the very beginning. The beginning of the rest of her life, lying, pretending, being someone she didn't want to be but had to be, saying things she didn't want to say, but had to say.

Jane looked down at her crumpled self. 'I need to clean up.'

Her escape, seized Alice. There was nothing she could do about the razor or the cologne but the photograph was the important thing. The only thing. Why the sudden change in Jane's attitude? It didn't matter. Getting Jane out of the room was all that mattered. 'You know where the bathroom is. And then we'll get going.'

'I need to make some calls, first.'

'I want you to.'

'I . . .' started Jane, but stopped.

'What?'

'Nothing.'

It took Alice only seconds to snatch up John's proud, joke-of-the-moment photograph and stuff it into a side drawer of the desk, beneath manuscripts and proofs of articles she had written and which she'd worked over, every time she and John had been here, all part of the fake domesticity, his reading by the amber, crackling fire while she did her job.

Alice was glad the main bathroom was en suite. She

couldn't have waited for Jane to emerge from the second one before being sick.

It had been a sleepless but productive night, the only potential problem a personal one for Gene Hanlan. Within an hour of his cut-off telephone conversation with Alice, Hanlan had organized an FBI plane to take him and a willing Rosemary Pritchard to Washington, for the CCTV loop to be photographically enhanced. It was while that was being done in the J. Edgar Hoover buildings that Hanlan endured the self-protective tirade from his regional supervisor, who'd failed to react to Hanlan's previous visit and who argued now that the Bureau was inescapably locked into a kidnap investigation that Hanlan had decided upon without superior authorization, which was against regulations, and that his career hung upon the safe return of Jane Carver. The confrontation was shortened by Rosemary Pritchard's positive identification of Alice Belling from just her features being brought up from beneath the veil, without needing to bother with hair colour change. The gynaecologist was, of course, able to provide the Princes Street address from her patient records and it was still early enough that night to obtain a judge's order to enter the apartment. Hanlan returned to Manhattan with a five-man forensic team and six seconded field agents to join the waiting Ginette Smallwood and Patrick McKinnon and the NYPD squad headed by Barbara Donnelly.

Hanlan had restricted the entry into Princes Street to just himself and Barbara Donnelly, in addition to the scientists, and assigned McKinnon to organize an incident room at Federal Plaza. By the time Hanlan and the woman returned there, ahead of the scientists, computers, desks and banks of pinboards had been installed in the conference room for the still-to-arrive clerks and support staff. McKinnon had already started the pinboards, fixing enlarged photographs of the Catskills range and then reducing the focus to the still extensive region dominated by the town of Paterson, from which they had already traced Alice's contact call.

There were also cots available for people to sleep in the mess.

It was 4.00 a.m. – by coincidence the time Jane Carver began edging out of bed in the Bearfort Mountains cabin – before the scientists arrived and a further hour before they produced the findings from their mobile laboratory facility. During that hour Hanlan declared the Bearfort Mountains their obvious target area, after seeing the location on the back of the now greatly enlarged photographs of Carver at the cabin.

'So Alice knew John Carver,' said McKinnon, examining the display. 'I've got five bucks says it was in a kind of a cosy way, too.'

'That put Jane at risk?' queried Barbara, at once.

'Might have done, from the jealous mistress syndrome, if Carver was still alive,' agreed Ginette. 'But he's not.'

'It's not unusual for a wife and mistress to know each other,' said the New York Police lieutenant.

'All she keeps saying is that they need protection,' reminded Hanlan.

'So why doesn't she come and get it, instead of running?' demanded McKinnon.

'Today could be the day,' suggested Hanlan, hopefully. To the man leading the scientific team, whom he thought looked young enough to be his son, Hanlan said: 'You got things to tell us?'

'Worrying things,' announced the man, at once. 'We got there second.'

'Shit!' said McKinnon.

'You sure?' asked Hanlan and wished he hadn't from the younger man's sour look.

'Very professional entry, one of the best I've seen,' said the scientist. 'We got picklock markings at the mouths of the mortice and the deadlock. We dismantled both. Very definite forced-entry groovings. The lobby mailbox had stuff dated more than two weeks ago. There's not one single message remaining on the answering machine. It's been wiped . . .'

'Careless,' remarked McKinnon.

'Not if there was a voice that didn't want to be recognized, trying to reach her,' said Hanlan.

'We're shipping the tape back to Washington. They've got higher specification audio equipment than we carry. They may be able to pull something up.'

'Fingerprints?' asked Barbara Donnelly.

'Just two sets,' said the scientist. 'Always together. All old.'

'One Alice's, one Carver's,' predicted Ginette.

'Inevitably,' agreed Hanlan. 'How about untouched valuables: stuff worth stealing?'

The scientist nodded. 'Some jewellery, a diamond ring, in an old setting, could be a family heirloom. Some gold chains. Television, video, computer . . . we're shipping the computer back to Washington, too, to get the hard drive looked at. People don't realize how much stays behind, even if you think you've deleted it . . .' The man hesitated. 'You want my guess, the guys who got in before us were doing what we're trying to do. Find Alice.'

'And Jane,' corrected McKinnon.

'And there's something that just might help,' offered the scientist, turning to the pinboard and the grinning photograph of John Carver. 'See this . . .?' he demanded, pointing to an image in the background, among the trees. 'Doesn't show so well, scarcely at all in fact, at the size of the prints in the apartment. Looks like a fallen branch. It isn't. That's the tail of a Volkswagen Beetle. Could be white or grey. Definitely light-coloured. Nothing else visible for a better identification.'

'Carver's not a Volkswagen man,' declared McKinnon, positively.

'No vehicle documentation anywhere in the apartment?' asked Barbara Donnelly.

The forensic expert shook his head and Ginette said: 'Responsible drivers carry their documents with them.'

Hanlan said: 'We're on to vehicle registration when the clock strikes.' Which wouldn't be for some hours yet, he realized.

'Here's how it looks to me,' said Barbara Donnelly, eager to prove herself. 'Crazy though it's sounded, it looks to me that Alice has been telling a reasonable story from the beginning. Carver's death might have been a definite accident but the other two've got questions. She talked about organized crime and we know now other people are looking. We've got to get to her – and Jane Carver – before they do.'

Hanlan decided to let the woman have her moment and hoped she hadn't seen McKinnon's patronizing smile. Hanlan said: 'And here's what we're going to do. We've got an identifiable picture of Alice, lifted from the loop. And we can get one of Jane. Paterson's our marker, with the Bearfort above it. This is the number Alice has, so I stay here. I want everyone else up there by the time people get out of bed, showing them the photograph. Obvious spots, stores, gas stations . . . Ginette, you stay here with me. Work the credit-card companies . . . gas cards . . . We find somewhere she's used more than once we've tightened our focus . . .' He jabbed at the map of Paterson and the mountains beyond. 'A lot of tracks but not a lot of roads. I'm going to put a Bureau prop up, something slow enough to be able to carry out aerial observation. Maybe there won't be a lot of old-style Volkswagens and we'll get lucky. When we get the registration we'll alert Highway Patrol, all the local forces, without telling them why. We draw blanks at Paterson, we move out, further up the mountains . . .' He isolated McKinnon. 'You co-ordinate it, Pat. You need more people, which you probably will, you call me . . .' He hesitated. 'And I'll call you if Alice comes on. You'll be right there, to pick her up.' Just like in the movies, Hanlan thought. Except they weren't in the movies, working to a script. Hanlan accepted that after the bawling-out in Washington he was going to need all the luck he could get. He had a defence and an appeal against anything the assholes there tried to stick on him but disciplinary procedures always left a stain, even if they were dismissed. And according to the book, which those at the J. Edgar Hoover buildings always went by, he had broken regulations. Hanlan looked around the assembled law-enforcement officers. 'Anything else?'

'Carver's safe deposit,' remembered Barbara Donnelly. 'That's where the Crown Jewels are supposed to be, according to Alice. Who can surely now be taken seriously? Why don't we go back to counsel about a court order, for access?'

'Good idea,' accepted Hanlan. With his bare ass on the line, why hadn't he thought of it first?

It was the first time they'd had a breakfast meeting, and an early one at that, close to seven, and Charlie Petrie at once apologized if it was inconvenient. He said: 'Got some business in Jersey. Want to get ahead of the traffic.'

'You got a lead?' asked Burcher, at once. Both men had chosen continental, bread and pastries and coffee.

Petrie shook his head. 'Covering bases. We've agreed your idea of making a formal approach to the Northcote firm.'

It would put him in an identifiable position, Burcher thought. He wished now he hadn't suggested it. 'It won't be easy.'

'You got a better idea?'

'Even if their lawyers go for it, they'll look to see what it is. They've got to.'

'And when they see what it is they'll realize how compromised they are. And have been for years. It can all be resolved sensibly, between reasonable men.'

'I'll work it out,' promised Burcher.

Petrie poured more coffee for both of them. Vito Craxi was right, Petrie decided. After this Burcher was superfluous. And he knew far too much. He said: 'We know you will, Stan. It's been a good and successful relationship.'

Stanley Burcher thought there was a finality in the way the other man spoke.

Twenty-Four

'Yes?'

The voice was relaxed to Alice's knock. Alice could imagine Jane lying back in the bath, soaking. 'I'm leaving some pants outside the door. A sweater. And some underwear.'

'That's kind.'

'We're about the same size.'

'Yes.'

'I'm going to get cleaned up myself now. Get ready to go.'

'All right.' Still relaxed.

Alice had run her own bath before collecting up the change of clothes for Jane. She lowered herself carefully, ribs aching, into the water, hotter than she normally had it, hoping the heat would ease away the discomfort of her retching. Where would she be sleeping, bathing, tomorrow morning? Not this early, she hoped. But safe. Both of them hidden away where no one could find them. She'd handled it very badly, Alice conceded. It was hardly a situation that could have been handled well but she should have done better than she had. Nothing she could do about it now. A pity that John had always insisted on showering and shaving in the second bathroom – *You need your space in the morning, because you're a grouch!* She didn't think she had been: hoped she hadn't. There was so much she wished for, so much it was impossible to turn back the clock to correct. Put right. Alice's mind butterflied, from thought to thought. When was she due? She couldn't remember. Hadn't bothered with notes in diaries because she was always so regular since undergoing treatment by Rosemary Pritchard, every twenty-eight days, almost always conveniently in the morning, maybe a passing twinge but never any serious stomach cramps. One of my luckiest patients, Rosemary Pritchard had called her. Warned her, too, sometimes, when she'd admitted being careless about her contraception, but she hadn't been careless, certainly not before John died as far as she could recall. Hadn't bothered, afterwards. No need to bother, ever again. She'd never go with another man. The idea revolted her, like so much else so easily, sickeningly, revolted her. Easy enough to understand why she was being sick. The fear from what she'd gone through. Was still going through – and she still knew what could happen to her, although at that moment she didn't feel frightened. She was, of course. Subconsciously. That's what it was, subconscious, justified fear. But all about to disappear today.

Alice felt fine, not sick at all, when she got out of the bath and put her jeans and sweater back on. A quarter before eight, she saw, when she restrapped her watch. She'd wait until eight, to ensure Gene Hanlan would be at the field office, although there'd probably be a contact arrangement to reach him at any time. Should she pack anything? It made obvious sense because although she was going to be protected there wouldn't be an opportunity to buy new things so quickly and she'd need fresh clothes, fresh underwear. Jane would be able to get what she needed packed for her, by one of the staff at East 62nd Street, and collected by someone from the Bureau. No cause to concern herself any more about Jane.

Jane was sitting in one of the fireplace chairs, barefoot like Alice, when Alice re-emerged into the main room, and Alice's first thought was that she *was* relaxed. If she had known, it would have all been different. Jane was looking around, her head moving with the intensity with which she was examining everything. Jane said: 'Pity it didn't work out.'

'What?'

'You and your partner. This is the sort of place a couple could be very happy in, hidden away from everyone, everything.'

'We were.' Alice's throat was dry.

'What did he do?'

'Architect,' said Alice, the first thing that came into her head.

'In Manhattan?'

'Trenton. He has his own practice.' It would only be for today but she had to remember, not change the story.

'He design this place? It's cute.'

'No,' she said. Then, hurrying: 'I've got eggs and some ham, although the bread's not fresh. You want some breakfast before we go?'

'I want to make calls before we go.'

'Yes, of course, we'll call the Bureau.'

'And Rosemary Pritchard,' insisted Jane.

'It wasn't intended as a positive deceit, although I guess it was,' said Alice. 'You'll understand when we get to the Bureau.'

'I need to understand now.'

'Let's get breakfast,' Alice tried to avoid.

'Let's get breakfast *and* talk now, so I'll understand,' insisted Jane.

Bizarrely, they prepared breakfast together easily, Jane setting the table and making the coffee, Alice putting out the ham and scrambling eggs, which meant she could talk mostly turned away from the other woman, concentrating upon the stove. Alice once more referred to Northcote being tricked into involvement and used the phrase organized crime and said the details had been in some office archives that had been made available to her. She'd immediately told John –

'Like I said, he was the liaison between your father and me' – and gave him what she'd found and she understood he'd put them in a safe deposit in Citibank. Alice listened to her own words and decided it was close enough to the truth and sounded a great deal better than her first stumbled attempt.

'What you call a trick, you mean my father did some work for gangsters, without knowing who or what they were?'

'That's what it looked like. As soon as I realized the significance I gave it to John, without reading it all.' Almost true, Alice consoled herself.

'A long time ago?' pressed Jane.

'That's what John thought, from some other stuff he found.'

'And which neither he nor my father told me about! But you know all about it.'

Alice saw her lifeline and seized it. 'I know about *some* of it because I was the person who came across it first: before I realized the significance I even made a few computer enquiries. It could have been embarrassing for the firm. That's surely why they didn't tell you, until they'd sorted it out.'

The look on Jane's face on the opposite side of the long table was quizzical but not as openly suspicious as it had been earlier.

'If all this happened a long time ago why are you – we – hiding now?'

There was an explanation here, too! 'I told you, before I realized what I'd come across I made a few computer enquiries. They must have picked them up.'

'Serious organized crime?'

'I don't know who they are. Names, I mean. But professional, certainly.'

'How do you know that, if you don't have names?'

'It's what John thought. Another reason for not telling you: not wanting to frighten you.'

'What reason would there be for neither my father nor John telling me about this book you're writing?'

The suspicion – the disbelief – was back! 'I don't know.' Pleading ignorance was all that she could do: all that it was safe to do.

'How much have you written?'

'None, yet. I was just collating material.' Alice hoped her face wasn't shiny from the sort of perspiration she could feel on her back.

'You got the material here? I'd like to read it.'

'It's in New York.' She had to stop this! Get away!

'Pity. I'd like to have seen it. Maybe some other time.'

'Maybe.' Alice thrust up from the table, collecting up her plate and mug. 'We should get moving.'

'There's a call I need to make.'

'Two,' said Alice. 'Mine first.' It was time to speak to Gene Hanlan. Get everything over with.

Alice was bewildered by what happened, how it happened. She was conscious of Jane behind her as she dialled the Federal Plaza number but didn't expect the abrupt hand over her shoulder to snatch away the telephone the moment she'd finished punching the number. By the time that happened – Alice close enough to hear the answering identification as the FBI herself – Jane had come from behind, to look down at her, and Alice saw the tension go from Jane's face.

'My name is Jane Carver. I want the agent-in-charge,' and then, instantly: 'I want to know your name.' Jane's face relaxed even further. She said: 'I am all right. She's told me who she is, a lot of other things.'

There was a pause, while she listened, and now Alice couldn't hear the other end. She rose from the desk chair, gesturing Jane into it. It wasn't important who made the contact, just that it was made and their being brought in was arranged. Jane sat. Alice watched.

Jane said: 'Was my father tricked? That's what Alice says,' and listened again.

Then: 'Was my father murdered? My husband? Janice?' There was some frowning head-shaking at whatever reply Hanlan gave. Jane said: 'Only me?' and then quickly: 'I'll call my lawyers, to block that. So don't try.' She smiled up at Alice and said: 'She's here,' and handed over the telephone.

Hanlan said: 'What the hell's going on?'

'You tell me. And I mean just that – tell me.'

Jane had walked away from the desk, to be near the outside door, but was looking at her intently.

'I told her we'd reopened the investigation into the deaths of her father and Janice Snow. But not her husband.'

'*Why?*'

'To get her in. To get you both in. We know you're somewhere around Bearfort: you marked your photographs at Princes Street. Someone got there ahead of us. They know you're there, too. They'll be looking.'

'We're leaving right away.'

'Don't! I'll have people at Paterson within an hour. Tell me where you are. We'll come for you.'

'Four miles out of West Milford, on the main mountain road. It's the fourth track, unmarked, on the left. There's a green mailbox. The name's Snelling. How long?'

'Two hours, tops.'

'Hurry!'

'Two hours. What's your telephone number there?'

Alice told him and physically sagged with relief as she put down the telephone, smiling up at the still expressionless Jane. 'They're on their way. All we've got to do is wait.'

'How long?' asked Jane, echoing Alice's question.

'Two hours.'

'West Milford is just four miles away. We could be there and back in less than an hour. There was only one left in your box.'

'Didn't Gene tell you there were people looking for me?'

'You any idea of the size of the Bearfort range? Less than an hour. Please.'

'You haven't made your call.'

'It can wait.'

There was something she could get from a pharmacy, too, Alice thought. It was worrying her.

'I don't believe it!' erupted Hanlan. 'I don't fucking believe it!'

'What?' asked Ginette Smallwood.

'Jane Carver! She doesn't think she's in any danger! And when I told her I could get a court order to open her husband's safe deposit she threatened to block me, in court!'

'I heard what you told her,' said the woman. And had believed it to have been a mistake as the man spoke. She said: 'You'd better tell Washington there'll be opposition, to cover your ass.'

'Let's bring them in first. I'll wait until then before speaking to Washington about court orders. Probably won't even have to, after I convince her I've saved her life.'

Hanlan's irritation deepened when he reached Patrick McKinnon on his cellphone to be told that the early morning rush hour had been worse than they'd anticipated and that the FBI team were still at least an hour short of Paterson, which made West Milford nearer two and a half hours away, without any allowance for finding the track to the cabin.

Ginette said: 'They're unpredictable, Alice certainly. Better warn them.'

Hanlan let the cabin number ring unanswered for five full minutes before slamming the receiver back on the rest. He said: 'Shit, they've run! What the fuck do they think they're doing?'

'The bad guys get them first, they're dead. We are, too.'

'Get back to vehicle registration,' insisted Hanlan. 'Tell them it's become a major emergency. I'll tell Pat.'

Which Hanlan did and which was how the Cavalcante Family, who'd had people using cellphone scanners since the identification of the Bearfort area, heard for the first time the name Jane Carver. They also heard, on Hanlan's second call, the repeated directions to the cabin four miles outside West Milford. And that Alice Belling was there, too.

The Cavalcante *consigliere*, Tony Caputo, was waiting impatiently for Charlie Petrie at the top-floor entrance to the elevator in the Family-owned office block overlooking the Delaware. The building was secure enough for Caputo to start talking even before they regained his suite. By the time they actually reached it Petrie knew every detail of the interception. He'd come all the way from New York because the escalating emergency demanded it but it made him appear like someone at the centre of everything that was happening, which was how he wanted to emerge.

Petrie said: 'You did good, Tony. Very good.'

Caputo, who knew very precisely just how well his organization had done, said: 'You didn't tell us the FBI were involved.'

'Because we didn't know,' admitted Petrie. It ratcheted up the stakes by at least a 100 per cent. There had to be an immediate *consiglieri* conference, as soon as he got back to New York: conceivably a full Mafia Commission gathering, attended by as many Dons as the *capo di tuttii capi* decreed. It would probably be most of them because most of them had used the Northcote laundry at one time or another.

'We get this wrong, we got a major, nationwide disaster,' said Caputo. He was a slightly built, compact man who enjoyed the trappings of his unquestioned authority, four gold rings to match the gold neck-chain and identity bracelet.

'We already knew that, before the Bureau involvement.'

'We've got people closer. We should get to the cabin first. What do you want we should do when we get them?'

Petrie did not respond at once, uncomfortable at being the man identifiably making the decisions on behalf of so many. 'Just get them away, from the cabin and the FBI. The Carver woman's our key. Literally.' But how to use her? Maybe he wouldn't need to, if Burcher got it right. He wouldn't tell the lawyer: let him go on as they'd decided that morning.

'What about the other one, Alice Belling?'

'We've got to sweat her, until she can't be sweated any more, to find out what she knows. Which we think is a hell of a lot. We've got to get it all, however long it takes and however hard – for her – it has to be.'

'OK,' accepted Caputo.

'And then she gets whacked,' ordered Petrie.

'OK,' agreed Caputo, again. 'You want to eat something? A drink?'

Petrie shook his head. 'I had breakfast.'

Twenty-Five

Alice drove as fast as was reasonably possible once they reached the twisting road, manoeuvring her wrist familiarly every so often to check the time. Jane saw the contortion and told her not to worry, that they had plenty of time, but Alice kept doing it, even though she knew the other woman was right. She got stuck behind a truck which looked similar to the one beneath which John had been crushed and wondered if the same impression had occurred to Jane. If it had, she didn't remark upon it. Instead, as they got closer to West Milford, Jane said: 'I had a stick shift once. An MG. It was fun.'

'I've had this since college. It's a kind of . . .' She hesitated, looking for the word. 'A souvenir, I guess.' The Volkswagen was the first thing she'd bought with her own money after her father's disgrace and suicide. It would have to go, along with everything else, she supposed. Would she be able to drive it back to New York? Probably not. She'd have to remember to take out the already packed IRS and company records printouts of the five Mafia firms. Her overnight case was ready, back at the cabin, the photograph of John protectively wrapped between two sweaters. That was the only souvenir she wanted, nothing more.

Jane said: 'You need gas.'

'I've got enough to get there and back to the cabin.'

'What about back to New York?'

'I thought we'd probably go in their car.'

'It would be a delay, if that's not how they plan it. Irritating.'

'I guess you're right,' agreed Jane, seeing the Shell sign ahead although on the other side of the road. She filled up and had to lean back into the car to take cash from her satchel.

As she got back into the car Jane said: 'That bag's full of money!'

'I left New York in a hurry . . . didn't know at first where I was going, what I might need . . . didn't want to use credit cards . . .'

Jane moved, as if to say something, but didn't.

Alice knew the pharmacy, attached to the small supermarket that she and John had used, in a mall on the outskirts of the small township. As Jane paid she said to Alice: 'I need to go to the restroom right away.'

'I'll wait,' said Alice, although she didn't. She'd already isolated the pregnancy-testing kits, picking the first on the shelf at random, and as an afterthought she took up a tube of toothpaste from an adjoining display.

'Bought something?' queried Jane when she emerged, nodding to the plastic bag in Alice's hand.

'Toothpaste,' said Alice, glad she had provided herself with the excuse.

'You know what?'

'What?'

Jane indicated her own package. 'False alarm. Just spotting.'

'Probably everything that's happened.'

'That's what I think.'

They walked back out into the car park side by side. Alice almost automatically checked her watch and Jane said: 'We've been gone exactly thirty-five minutes.'

'OK,' smiled Alice. That's how she could think now, she reassured herself. Of everything happening – and being over – in minutes.

Jane said: 'You want to do me a favour? Let me drive! That stick shift I had really was fun.'

'It's a pretty stiff box.' Still in so much danger it was bizarre standing here in a car park discussing gearboxes!

'Come on! It's only just up the road.'

'OK,' shrugged Alice. Just get everything over, that's all she wanted to do. Just minutes.

Jane couldn't get the car into reverse and ground the gears as she followed Alice's instructions and the Volkswagen shuddered unevenly backwards and then kangarooed forwards when Jane selected first gear. Jane said: 'Sorry . . . sorry . . .' and got into second and then third much more smoothly. She swung easily out on to the mountain road but almost at once, at the junction, made a left.

'No!' said Alice. 'This isn't the way to the cabin. This is the Stockholm road.'

'I know. I saw the sign on the way down, which is why I've taken it,' said Jane, accelerating, eyes fixedly forward. 'We're not going back to the cabin, not yet anyway. I think you and I have got much much more to talk about, don't you, Alice?'

When Alice didn't reply Jane said: 'When you next speak to Gene Hanlan you can tell him you were tricked. And that now it's you who's been kidnapped.'

The FBI spotter plane was disappointing. The pilot complained thermal updrafts made it difficult to fly as low as he needed, for a satisfactory search, which was further hampered by thick forest ground cover over wide tracts of the mountain range. Neither he nor the observer had seen a single vehicle resembling a Volkswagen. After two flights Hanlan suspended the aerial search but kept the plane on standby.

It was not until just after nine thirty that Hanlan was finally able to relay the licence number and specifications of Alice's light-grey vehicle to Patrick McKinnon, who estimated that they were still thirty minutes short of West Milford. Hanlan duplicated the vehicle details to the relevant Highway Patrol offices and all police forces in a twenty-mile-wide arc between Paterson and West Milford. He also copied everything to Highway Patrol and state police headquarters at Trenton.

When McKinnon came back on the line Hanlan was telling the Northcote firm's lawyer Geoffrey Davis of his conversation with Jane Carver, anxious to discover if she had instructed the man to oppose legal access to the Citibank safe deposit, which she hadn't. Hanlan said he'd call back.

'They were ahead of us again,' announced McKinnon. 'They took down the Snelling mailbox marker: we overshot first time. Place has been ransacked. Not as bad as the photographs we saw of Litchfield but close.'

'Any signs of violence . . . blood . . . ?'

'None. There should be forensics, though. We've driven over their car tracks but there should be something left.'

'I'll send up the guys we brought back from Washington,' said Hanlan. 'They're due to finish what little was left at Litchfield and Brooklyn. What about the Volkswagen?'

'Nowhere.'

'It would be there, if they'd been grabbed. They're still running, together.'

'Let's hope you're right,' said McKinnon. 'What do you want us to do?'

Hanlan wished he knew. 'Leave a couple of guys to see nothing gets touched. Make a base in the town, ready to move. I'll put the plane up again: hope something comes from the road checks.' He wished to Christ there was something more practical he could do than sit around hoping.

Barbara Donnelly said: 'Why have they done it?'

'Maybe it's a good job they did,' said Ginette, when Hanlan recounted his conversation with McKinnon. 'If they'd been there, we might have found bodies.'

* * *

The forensics team had finished what little was left for them to do. Because of the initial dismissal of both as accidents, the Bureau reinvestigation of the deaths of George Northcote and Janice Snow was largely restricted to autopsies, although by dismantling the lock of Janice's apartment – as they had in Princes Street – the scientists found unquestionable evidence of the lock having been picked. A Bureau pathologist at Brooklyn also established from the direction of the bone-splintering that it would have been impossible for Janice Snow to have broken her fingers falling from her supposed hanging. The beginning of decomposition made a positive finding difficult but from the detailed medical examination of George Northcote it appeared that the multiple lacerations to the face and head – wounds which were belatedly discovered to have blinded the man – were more likely to have been caused by a blade thinner and sharper than that of the cutting machine into which Northcote was alleged to have fallen.

'Nothing I'd like to go into court with but they weren't accidents,' the forensics leader told Hanlan. 'What are we looking for in the cabin?'

'Anything,' said Hanlan, exasperated. 'Anything at all. Just make it something I can work from!'

The two Mafia *consiglieri* had been informed of every word exchanged between Gene Hanlan and Patrick McKinnon because the Cavalcante searchers in the Bearfort Mountains were getting perfect scanner reception on McKinnon's cell-phone. It also gave them all the details of Alice Belling's Volkswagen, which were duplicated within thirty minutes of Hanlan providing them to the Highway Patrol headquarters at Trenton, where the Cavalcante Family had a paid informer in the communications room.

Tony Caputo said: 'We can't have missed them by much.'

'We still missed them,' said Charlie Petrie. He needed to stay here in Trenton, hear at once what was happening, but he was desperate to get back to Manhattan and convene a conference with the other New York Families. It was obvious what had to be done with the Belling woman. But how – what pressure could they use? – to get Carver's wife to retrieve what was in the safe-deposit vault?

'We won't next time,' promised the Cavalcante lawyer. 'We got everyone out there, waiting.'

'We've got to move quicker than that,' insisted Petrie. There was only one way he could think of and he had to know if it had already been set up. When Stanley Burcher immediately answered his Algonquin telephone Petrie knew that it hadn't.

'You spoken to Northcote's lawyers?' Petrie demanded.

'I'm still working it out.'

'What's to work out?'

'I've got to have every answer ready because they're going to have a lot of questions,' said the intermediary lawyer. The tiredness he felt from a long day had nothing to do with the 7.00 a.m. breakfast meeting. All he'd done since then was sit in his hotel room trying – but failing – to evolve an approach that would not bring him into direct, identifiable contact with the Northcote firm's attorney who had been pointed out to him at the Plaza Hotel.

'Stan, here's what you're going to do. You're going to call the guy, right now: this minute. You got to get whatever's in that fucking bank. You do that and you're going to be a rich and happy man for the rest of your life.'

He was already a rich man, Burcher reminded himself. And what sort of life would he have if he *didn't* get what Carver had copied? He could always run, Burcher told himself. It wasn't that he'd neglected the possible need for an escape route.

Alice tried at the beginning – once briefly breaking down in tears, although of frustration, not collapse, and then in annoyance that she'd broken down at all – but was finally silenced by Jane's total refusal to respond or acknowledge Alice's every insistence upon their physical danger, up to and including murder, with tortured interrogation in between. For almost an hour Jane refused to stop despite Alice's whimpering need for a restroom and by mid-afternoon they were way beyond the Paterson/West Milford arc that Hanlan had stipulated for his road watch. Jane's eventual halt was at a truck stop, like an oasis in reverse among the verdant pines and firs, a scoured-bald dust bowl of petrol and diesel pumps bordering the road and a stinking, cockroach-infested block of excreta-blocked toilets the stink of which made Alice's vomiting worse. No water came from the taps when she tried to rinse her mouth or wash her hands.

It was a further hour, close to four in the afternoon, before Jane pulled into another truck stop, although at this one an intermittently dead-bulbed sign boasted of a pay-in-advance, cash-only motel at its rear.

'Your treat,' Jane announced. 'Time to make those calls.'

The motel was a single-storey prefabrication of paint-stripped cabins, theirs a boxed, twin-bedded room with opaquely thin curtains and opaquely thin grey sheets beneath candlewick spreads. Both were patterned by long ago stains, mostly brown although sometimes black to match those on the threadbare, frayed carpeting. The one chair sagged out of any shape, its back black from the grease of a thousand unwashed heads. The bulb was missing over the processed-wood bureau, the mirror of which was whorled with verdigris. There was a urine smell from the open-doored, cockroach-scuttling bathroom.

Alice said: 'I'm not going to stay here! This is disgusting.'

Jane said: 'You'll stay because I say so. Because this is just the place for us to talk about the things we have to talk about. And where no one in their wildest dreams would think of looking for us, finding us. I'm protecting *you* now, Alice.'

Jane turned dismissively away, concentrating upon the

number she was dialling, instinctively smiling at the immediate connection but at once frowning, impatiently talking over the babble from the other end the moment she identified herself.

'I know . . .! I know . . .! I've spoken to him . . . I know . . . I'm all right. Rosemary! Stop talking, Rosemary! Listen . . .' She looked at Alice when the sound stopped from the other end of the line. 'Do you mind?'

Alice didn't immediately understand and when she did looked uncertainly around the cramped room. There was a black scurry underfoot when she went into the bathroom and Alice halted just inside the door. It was very thin and although Alice didn't hear everything she heard enough to understand.

Jane was pregnant. What other reason was there for a woman to speak this long with her gynaecologist?

Twenty-Six

'John loved me, very much.'

Alice said nothing. Jane being pregnant didn't change anything. It wasn't something they'd ever talked about – it would have been out of bounds – but of course John had made love to her: it was understood – accepted – without needing to be said.

'And I loved him very much.' She was smiling, as she'd been smiling when she'd called Alice from the bathroom after her conversation with Rosemary Pritchard.

Still Alice said nothing. What would her test show? She was anxious but at the same time reluctant to find out. Surely she had to be! What other reason was there for her being so sick, so often?

'I saw the photograph, the one you tried to hide in the cabin. I saw it by the telephone and found where you'd hidden it, when you were in the bath.' There was no anger in the flat tone.

Alice finally sat on the collapsing, hair-greased chair. 'I know John loved you. Your marriage was never in any danger.'

'That's very generous of you! What did you and he do, just fuck?'

Alice winced. 'Can I try to explain?'

'I want you to. I want very much to have it explained to me. All of it.'

'I loved John, too.'

'And he loved you!' There was a jeer in Jane's voice.

'Yes.'

Jane made a balancing gesture with both hands. 'So that's how it was, he loved us both, fifty-fifty.'

'Yes, I guess. But you were his wife. Would always have been his wife.'

'And you would have always been his mistress.'

'For as long as he wanted me.'

'Or until he didn't want me any more!'

'That would never have happened.'

'Tell me you talked about it!'

'We did! He told me he would never leave you, because he loved you, and I said I didn't want or expect him to.'

'I'm supposed to believe that?'

'It's the truth.'

'How often, once a week, twice a week? All the time when I was out of town?'

She had the right, Alice accepted, although she didn't feel there was anything to defend herself against. 'We were happy.'

'How about the cabin? How often did you sneak away to the cabin?' Jane's face was set, rigid.

Everything she'd told Jane *was* the truth. There was no guilt. 'Just three times. The photograph you saw was the first.' It was back at the cabin, packed in her case, she abruptly realized. Whatever happened she had to go back to the cabin to get it.

Jane jerked her head towards the telephone, upon which she'd made two further calls after that to the gynaecologist. 'Did he tell you why we were seeing Rosemary?'

Alice shook her head. 'I didn't know you were.'

'Something he didn't actually tell you?' It was weak sarcasm.

'No.'

'We were going to have a baby.'

Alice felt a physical lurch at the confirmation but didn't speak.

'How do you feel about that?'

'It will be wonderful . . .' stumbled Alice. 'John would have . . . you will be a wonderful parent . . .'

The rigid face creased slightly, then cleared. 'It wouldn't have made any difference if John was still alive? You'd have gone on sleeping together?'

'Yes,' said Alice at once, holding the other woman's look. 'I'm not ashamed. I know it's difficult for you to believe . . . I guess you never will . . . but I was never a threat to you . . . and I've tried to save you, literally save your life, because you don't know how bad things are.' She knew that Geoffrey Davis, whom Jane had told in another of her calls to block any legal move against John's bank, was the firm's lawyer. Presumably Burt, whose surname Jane had never used and to whom she'd repeated the blocking instructions, was the personal attorney.

'You're right,' said Jane. 'I don't know. So tell me about that, too. All of it, because I can't be hurt or betrayed any more, any worse, than I already have been.'

But she was, her face twisting as if she were in genuine pain when Alice told her everything. Alice held nothing back but conscious of Jane's stricken look said at the end: 'I don't believe . . . John didn't believe . . . that your father did it willingly, in the beginning. John was sure he was tricked . . . cheated . . . and from then on was blackmailed into carrying on . . .'

'And John tried to face them down . . . believing as he did that Dad and Janice had been murdered he still tried to face them down . . . ?'

'Yes,' said Alice, knowing the other woman's need. 'That's how brave John was.'

'But he told you, not me,' remembered Jane, stronger-voiced.

'How *could* he have told you?' pleaded Alice.

'I didn't believe you, not any of it, before. I actually thought you might be mad, although I didn't think you were going to harm me. But I believe you now. All of it . . .' Jane stopped, her voice catching. 'I cried for Dad but I didn't cry for John, not properly. The drugs. And now I don't think I can cry, for either of them . . .'

She did though, so suddenly that Alice jumped at the wail and came forward in her ugly chair, watching helplessly as the sobs racked through Jane as they had racked through her, and finally Alice got up and went to the other woman. At the first touch Jane stiffened and went to pull away but didn't and then she let herself come into Alice's embracing arm and Alice began crying, too, and both women sat on the hard bed, holding each other, both weeping for the same man.

Initially there was an embarrassment at their holding each other, supporting each other, a few moments, once they recovered and stopped crying, of moving awkwardly around the room, neither knowing what to say, how to say it. So neither at first said anything.

Alice broke the impasse. 'They'll say I kidnapped you.'

'You did.'

They both sniggered a laugh, although still awkwardly.

Alice said: 'Don't hate me.'

Jane said: 'I don't know what to feel – how to feel – right now. I don't feel anything, about anyone. I don't think I know how to hate.'

'We both loved John. He loved both of us.'

'I don't know what to say to that, either. I don't understand it. Maybe I never will.'

'That's how it is,' Alice insisted, wishing it hadn't sounded so flip.

'I suppose I know that's how it was. I still don't understand it.'

'Do you understand – accept – that we could both be killed, if we don't get protection?'

'I suppose so.'

'Jane, you can't *suppose* so. You *know* so, surely!'

'I . . .' Jane began, then corrected herself. 'Yes, I know.'

She had to get back to the cabin: get John's picture, remembered Alice. 'Why did you drive away like that?'

'I told you. I didn't believe what you were saying: thought you were mad. These days have been mad. I don't know why I did it, at that moment. I just did. I don't like being manipulated. Everyone was manipulating me, telling me what to do, what pills to take, like I was a child.'

'We've got to go back. Get safe.'

'They can come for us here.'

'There are things I want.' Only one thing, the thing she couldn't do – wouldn't do – without. Her only physical, tangible memory.

'We drove for hours! I don't even know where the hell we are!'

'We'll go back tomorrow.'

'You want to stay here?'

'No one knows we're here. That's what you said.'

'It's filthy! Disgusting!' said Jane.

'No one knows we're here,' repeated Alice. 'No one would expect us to be in a place like this. So no one will look for us in a place like this.'

Jane looked around the stained, night-darkening room. 'No. No one would,' she agreed and sniggered again, this time in head-shaking disbelief.

'Tomorrow?' prompted Alice.

'To what, after that?'

'I don't know,' admitted Alice. 'Some sort of life.'

They were still vaguely red-eyed but they'd washed their faces and combed their hair and touched up their lipstick, which was the only make-up either carried in their bags. They were the instant focus of the truckers in the suddenly hushed adjoining diner and to avoid it they took a booth and shrugged off the two direct, leering approaches to their table. When the waitress with drooping breasts, who clearly regarded them as competition, tried to deliver two unordered whiskies from a third hopeful, Alice said: 'Take them back and say thanks. My friend and I don't need anyone else but each other, OK?'

'They'll want to save you from yourselves,' predicted the waitress, relieved.

'Tell them to go fuck themselves. It's fun,' said Alice.

Jane looked down to cover the smile. As the girl left Jane said: 'You know your way around this sort of place?'

'I go to the movies a lot.'

'You would, I suppose, with time on your hands.'

'Jane, you're allowed any sort of shot you want. I can't think of anything more to say than I've already said. Let's just get through tonight, tomorrow, until we get back to where they're waiting. Then you'll never have to see me, ever again.'

'It'll ruin the firm, won't it?' suddenly demanded Jane. 'Ruin my father's reputation. That's what both of them, Dad and John, were trying to prevent. That's what you said.'

'I know what I said,' acknowledged Alice, concerned at the conversation. 'I also told you John was convinced your father was murdered. And Janice. There's no way other than going to the Bureau.'

'We should call them.'

'We should,' agreed Alice, relaxing.

'Not now, not right away. I want to think.'

'Jane, there really is nothing to think about.'

'Later,' insisted the woman.

The now friendly waitress returned, with iced water and place settings. She said: 'I got nothing against guys like you, OK?'

'Thanks,' said Alice.

The woman said: 'Take the meat loaf. It's fresh. I wouldn't risk anything else.'

'I'll have meat loaf,' said Alice.

As Jane nodded acceptance too, she said: 'John didn't like meat loaf.'

Which was why she'd never made it for him, remembered Alice.

'When?' demanded Gene Hanlan.

'Two or three hours ago,' admitted Geoffrey Davis.

'Two or three hours! What the hell . . . ?'

'Things happened,' said the Northcote lawyer. 'Maybe it wasn't even two or three hours . . .'

'She's under threat,' stopped Hanlan. 'Serious, physical threat. People got to the cabin where she was before us. Wrecked it like they wrecked Litchfield. We don't get her soon, like immediately, she's dead. So where is she?'

'She didn't say.'

'For fuck's sake!'

'Hear me out . . .'

'I don't want to hear you out. I want you to hear me out. You're a lawyer, doesn't matter criminal or civil. You know what I'm saying? We've got a big-time, major investigation here. We lose getting Jane back – lose Jane – I'm going to charge you with wilful obstruction of justice and anything else I can think of and I'm going to recommend the Bureau move for your disbarment. You hear what I'm saying?'

There was a pause from the other end before Davis said, calmly: 'Now you're going to hear what I'm saying?'

'What?'

'She's instructed me to file against any Bureau application for access to John Carver's estate or private affairs.'

'She told me she would do that.'

'She's instructed the family lawyer, Burt Elliott, too.'

'I'm still listening.'

'I had another call,' continued Davis. 'Guy said he was a lawyer, representing clients for whom George Northcote worked exclusively but to whom John had written severance letters. I asked around, among the partners. No one knew anything about it . . .'

'You got names?' interrupted Hanlan, anxiously.

'I finally asked Hilda Bennett, John's PA. She wrote the letters and kept file copies, obviously. We've got the names of all five, all registered in Grand Cayman. It was doing that which took the time.'

'Who's the guy who called?'

'Wouldn't give a name. Told me I'd understand when we met.'

'When?'

'Ten thirty tomorrow morning. I put it back until then because I thought you'd want to know. Be here, waiting.'

Hanlan didn't respond for several moments. 'I think I owe you an apology.'

'Yes,' said Davis. 'I think you do.'

It was late, past nine, before Charlie Petrie got back from Trenton, believing he had made all the arrangements possible with the Cavalcante *consigliere* and anxious to meet those of the other four New York Families within the hour. But Stanley Burcher had to come first. There had been telephone conversations with the other *consiglieri* from Trenton and none of them were happy with what Petrie was going to order but no one had been able to come up with an alternative that was better to get back what was in Citibank.

The slight, self-effacing lawyer was waiting patiently in the familiar Algonquin lounge, the brandy snifter beside the coffee the only thing out of the ordinary for this most ordinary-looking of men.

Petrie ordered brandy for himself, needing it, and said: 'Well?'

'Fixed, for tomorrow morning.' Burcher was frightened, of too many things to know precisely about what. Of the man sitting opposite and what the people he represented could and would do to him. Also, for the first time in his life, of openly putting himself forward as an emissary of such people. The urge to run, to escape from them and from what might happen to him, had grown since he'd spoken to the Northcote lawyer until now it was a knot, something he could feel, deep inside him.

'Why couldn't you go today?' demanded Petrie.

'He couldn't make today. I'm approaching him, remember?'

Petrie hesitated. He didn't want to frighten further the obviously already frightened man but it would be ridiculous sending him in unprepared. He said: 'There's a complication.'

'What?' demanded Burcher, brandy bowl suspended in front of him.

'Alice Belling somehow snatched Jane Carver . . . got the Carver woman to go with her. I don't know how. They're together, somewhere in the Catskills.'

For several moments Burcher's mind refused to assimilate what he was being told and what the consequences were. Then he said: 'But there's no point . . . no purpose in my seeing the Northcote lawyer. Even if he accepted my argument about returning property no longer theirs to keep, Jane Carver is the only person who could legally get it out of her husband's personal deposit box.'

'I want you to make the meeting,' insisted Petrie. 'We've got to be ready.'

'I don't understand.'

'We didn't know there was a relationship between the two women,' said Petrie. 'There obviously is and they obviously know what's in the box. The FBI are looking for them, but for kidnap, according to conversations we've intercepted. We've got some inside tracks. We're going to end this Thelma and Louise shit by tomorrow. Maybe even tonight. We know the car they're driving, the plate number even. We get them, we hold Alice while Jane co-operates, meets the lawyer you're going to meet and gets our stuff back.'

'What about the FBI?'

'Alice Belling is our insurance the FBI don't get told, by anyone, that Jane's back until we've got our stuff. When we've got that, all the Feds have is a kidnap that's nothing to do with us. No proof of anything else.'

'What's Alice Belling going to tell them?'

'Nothing,' said Petrie. 'Alice Belling isn't going to tell anyone anything. She won't be able to. Neither will Jane Carver, after she's done what she's told.'

It was madness, Burcher decided. He didn't want to get involved in madness.

Neither of them undressed nor got beneath the covers, reluctant to have the sheets anywhere around them. Both spread their jackets over their pillows to keep their faces away from the physical contact and there wasn't much talk after the near argument that erupted when they'd got back to the cabin, Alice now demanding that they go at once against Jane's insistence that they were staying.

'I need time to think . . . to think about everything,' was Jane's repeated refusal.

'Please, Jane! We've had this conversation!'

'The morning will be soon enough. I'm the one with the car keys, remember?'

Now, in the darkness, Alice's feelings switchbacked again. There was, she conceded, a peculiar, womb-like comfort in being in a place even as disgusting as this instead of outside in the unknown blackness of the night, hunted by the law and the lawless. The morning would be soon enough. And she was exhausted, not just from this day but from all the days – how many days? – that had gone before. In a surprising self-revelation, Alice admitted to herself that she was content for Jane to make the decisions, for the moment at least.

Maybe, even, that Jane was the stronger, more forceful personality. There was only one thing she wanted to do now, was determined to do now, and tired though she was she was going to do it now, although she was sure she already knew. She wanted to feel the excitement, the euphoria. And to be equal with Jane? The question intruded abruptly, surprising Alice. That was a jealous question. And she wasn't jealous of Jane.

Alice lay for a long time, waiting for Jane to go to sleep before telling herself there was no need for Jane to be asleep. Why shouldn't Jane be awake when she went to the bathroom? Alice didn't put the bedroom light on, though, feeling her way to where she knew the door to be, closing and bolting it behind her. There was more black scurrying when she turned the bathroom light on and she flinched away, shuddering. She'd never imagined such filthy places existed: were allowed to exist by sanitation authorities. Not much longer: just a few hours.

The booklet instructions were very simple – illustrated even – and there was a specimen cup, the need for which was obvious but which she had difficulty filling, so she had thoroughly to wash her contaminated hands afterwards. Alice's fingers were shaking as she immersed the double-windowed, absorbent tester tube, brown for no, blue for yes. The blue was very bright, much brighter than she'd expected, and at once she thought of the symbolism and thought how fitting – how right – it would be if John's baby was a son, the heir he would have wanted.

Alice flushed away what could be dispersed and returned what couldn't to the pharmacy bag and carefully carried it back into the darkened room to put beneath her jacket on the pillow. And then, even more carefully, lay on her back with her arms wrapped around herself, low and protectively around herself because she had so much to protect now. She was going to have John's baby! John's own, real, biological baby! To take with her, to love and to guard and to raise to be the most perfect child there was ever likely to be and whom one day she'd tell all there was to tell about its most perfect father.

Alice became aware of Jane's heavy breathing from the adjoining bed, reminding her of her concern at Jane's delaying insistences. Jane was going to do something stupid: try to protect her father's name and John's name and the Northcote firm's future and risk ending up dead. And not just risk herself. Her baby now.

She couldn't risk ending up dead, Alice told herself. She wasn't simply saving herself any more, either. She had to save – protect forever – the baby she was having by John. She'd done all that she could, all that was humanly possible, to help Jane. Protect Jane. From now on Jane was on her own. Whatever Jane announced tomorrow didn't matter, because she wouldn't be part of it, part of anything. She had to go with the best she had, some criminally incriminating printouts, and bargain as best she could. And she had a satchel full of money, more than sufficient to pay for a cab or a hire car from here – wherever here was – back to Manhattan if Jane insisted upon taking the Volkswagen. To which she was welcome, as she was welcome to whatever else. Alice had more than she'd ever wanted, ever dreamed of. She thought she felt a movement, although she knew it was far too early, but she smiled, enjoying the phantom sensation. What name would John have wanted? That was very important, to get right the name that John might have wanted. Everything was important, getting it right for John.

Since the case began being taken seriously Gene Hanlan had slept in a mess-room cot at Federal Plaza, Barbara Donnelly behind an inadequate separating screen, which was totally unimportant to both, all thoughts of gender discarded. The advantage was that they were both together, able to move at once after Geoffrey Davis made his call.

The now permanently assigned Bureau plane ferried duplicate originals of the documents on the five companies for the financial directorate to investigate and returned to Manhattan with additional agents. Because at last there was a positive development within NYPD jurisdiction Barbara Donnelly and her team shared in every aspect of the planning. Together the two of them personally toured the Northcote building on Wall Street, with Davis their guide, ending totally satisfied that once the mystery emissary crossed the threshold escape would be impossible. Davis provided complete plans of the premises, from which Hanlan and Barbara jointly briefed their combined squads, and by midnight additional CCTV and audio equipment had been installed and tested in Davis's office, where the meeting was to take place.

Barbara said Scotch was fine, which was fortunate because that was all Hanlan had in his office at that time of night. He touched Barbara's glass and said: 'At last, something positive! This time tomorrow, we're going to be properly in charge of the whole damned thing.'

The first edition of the following morning's *New York Daily News* hit the streets around 12.30 a.m. The front page was dominated by a stock photograph of Jane Carver and the headline used the word kidnapped. There were also references to unnamed Mafia Families and organized crime and to a mystery woman, inevitably described as beautiful, who was identified as the intermediary who initiated the kidnap. Just as inevitably she was called the Mafia Madam. There were individual sidebar stories of all three deaths, now under FBI reinvestigation. An anonymous police spokesman predicted the biggest Mafia sensation of the decade.

'Where the fuck . . .?' exploded Hanlan, hurling the newspaper away from him.

'We did well to cover it for so long,' said Barbara Donnelly, philosophically.

'And where did it get us?' demanded Hanlan. 'Nowhere. Which is where we still are, no-fucking-where!'

Twenty-Seven

They were awake early, neither having properly slept. Alice said hi and Jane made a sound and there was the awkwardness of the previous night, after they'd both broken down and cried together. Alice needed to be sick and had to use her toothpaste-smeared finger to clean her teeth and her mouth afterwards. Turning from the basin she trod barefoot on a cockroach, which wasn't crushed but whirled underfoot, and in jerking away Alice hit her stomach without any real force against the sink edge, tensing, motionless, for an internal injury pain that never came. She had to learn, Alice thought, happily: so very much to learn. The awareness stayed. She had to learn how to be a mother! To *be* a mother! It was going to be so marvellous.

As she went back into the room Alice said: 'I left you the toothpaste. You'll have to use your finger. The water's only tepid, even if you're thinking of showering, which I wasn't. And didn't.'

Jane made another sound that Alice didn't make out to be a word. She was ready the moment Jane disappeared into the bathroom, letting herself out of the cabin to hurry to a parking-lot garbage can that had been overturned during the night by a forest scavenger, strewing its contents all around it. She very carefully threw the pharmacy sack holding the bright-blue proof of her pregnancy inside the upturned container.

It was a grey day, relentless rain soaking down from lowering clouds. Everywhere was deserted, unmoving. Alice could hear the wetness hissing against the surrounding trees. She was anxious to get away, now that it was light. Away to a new existence, just her and John jr. The name was instantly adhesive. Absolutely right.

She got back to the cabin before Jane emerged from the bathroom but when she did Jane said at once: 'You're wet. Where have you been?'

'I thought I'd check the car. It's raining.'

'I guess that's why you're wet. And how's the car?' The tone was mocking.

'OK.' Alice hoped the car really was intact. 'We're going to call the FBI.'

'I thought you wanted to go back to the cabin?'

'I want to get us safe.' She had a baby now, thought Alice: something – someone – far more precious and tangible than a photograph. She didn't want to bounce for hours in a hard-sprung car back up a twisting mountain road. She'd ask the Bureau to get her case. Their son should know what his father looked like. She didn't know how to fish. She'd have to learn, if she were going to teach him. So much to learn.

'I'm not sure I want to go in yet,' announced Jane.

'I am!' insisted Alice. 'I'm through running.'

'I want lawyers. Guarantees.'

'We can get lawyers when we're there, where no one can get to us.' Jane was being sensible, objective, Alice acknowledged. But she didn't want to wait any longer: risk anything further.

'I'm not talking about you. I'm talking about my father and my husband and the firm. And me,' listed Jane.

'You've got lawyers: you spoke to them yesterday!'

'Yesterday we hadn't talked completely. I didn't know what I know now.'

'You know now you could be killed. *Will* be killed!'

'I'm going to take proper advice. Go in to the FBI with lawyers, not bare-assed naked.'

'What about the baby?' demanded Alice, openly for the first time. 'You've got the . . .' She only just stopped short of calling it a boy. '. . . baby to think about now!'

Jane matched the hesitation before saying: 'It's the baby I'm properly thinking about.'

'I'm going in now!'

There was another hesitation from Jane. 'I already told you, you're not involved.'

'I understand,' said Alice slowly, who belatedly did. Was there enough in the printouts to get her into a protection programme: to get an amnesty, or whatever the word was, for the deaths of three innocent people in England? Or did she really need Jane and whatever else it was John had hidden? 'I could have gone in a long time ago. I stayed out to save you. For John.'

'I'm grateful. Thanks.' The mocking tone was still there.

Jane had the right, Alice told herself yet again. 'I'm going to call Hanlan to come here and get me.'

'OK.'

'You want a head start, to find somewhere to meet your people, you can have the car. I guess I don't need it any more. Just some things that are in the trunk.' For you, John. Everything's for you and our son.

Jane Carver stood regarding Alice for several moments. 'OK.'

'But I'd rather you stayed with me. That we went in together.'

'I'm looking after myself now. It's about time.'

'Everything I told you was the truth. About John. And you.'

'You keep telling me,' said Jane.

'I want you to understand.'

'I do. Finally I understand it all.'

'You do hate me, don't you?'

'I'm learning.'

'I'm sorry. That you hate me, I mean. And that you're not waiting for them to come and get us.'

'You want to get your stuff out of the car?'

'You don't have any money,' said Alice, going into her satchel. 'You'll need money.' Her hand came out clutching fifties, six of them.

'Three hundred,' accepted Jane. 'It's a loan.'

Alice said: 'You think we're ever likely to meet again?'

'I'll get it to you.'

They walked, unspeaking, through the drizzle to the back of the single-storey building. Jane started the engine and ran the wipers before popping the bonnet trunk for Alice to retrieve the canvas bag in which she'd packed the printouts. Despite the rain Alice didn't move at once, watching the Volkswagen disappear, knowing it would be the last she'd ever see of it. The beginning of her new life, she guessed: everything of the old discarded, abandoned.

Alice went back to the room and shook as much rain off her coat as she could and dialled reception, impatiently waiting what seemed an age for a reply. She thought she recognized the voice of the man who had booked them in the previous day. Before she could speak he said: 'You owe for telephone calls,' and Alice wondered how much he had listened in to the conversations.

She said: 'I'm coming to settle. I need some help. I think we got a little confused on the map yesterday. Where, exactly, are we here?'

The man laughed. 'Just two miles east of Long Valley, New Jersey.'

Alice had never heard of it. 'Where's the nearest town of any size?'

'That would be Morristown.'

'I'll be by in a minute, to settle the charges. Just one more call to make.'

'I'll be in the office.'

'Where the hell are you two?' exploded Hanlan, the moment Alice was connected.

'In a truck-stop motel two miles east of a place called Long Valley, New Jersey. I don't . . .'

'Why'd you run?'

'Come and get me. I'll explain everything when you take me in.'

There was a pause, of half awareness. 'Where's Jane?'

'Gone. She won't come in without her lawyers.'

'Mary Mother of Christ!' moaned Hanlan, who wasn't Catholic.

'What's the matter?'

'Everything's blown. In all the newspapers, on every television channel. Her picture's everywhere!'

'What about mine!'

'Name. The picture's bad.'

'Jane's got my car! It's . . .'

'I know what it is and I know the license. I'm frightened they do, too.'

'They?' There was a déjà vu about the question.

'They got to the cabin before we did, yesterday.'

'How? How'd they know?'

'I don't know. We'll find her, in your car. You just stay . . .'

'Like you wanted me to stay in the cabin yesterday, where I would have been trapped when they got there before you! Go kiss my ass, Gene. I'll make my own way in, so no one knows where I'm coming from.'

'Wait . . .' tried Hanlan, but Alice didn't.

She stayed in the room until the man called from the desk to say the taxi she'd ordered had arrived and managed to remain expressionless looking at the photograph of Jane Carver that filled the TV screen behind the man as she paid the telephone bill. The one of her *was* bad, a blurred thumbnail from a feature she'd written more than a year before. There was a stills photograph of her vintage Volkswagen, too. The sound was mute, preventing her hearing the commentary.

'You guys have a fight?' asked the man, who definitely was the one who had booked them in.

'Kind of.'

'Guess it's difficult?'

'Sometimes.'

'Stop by the next time you're passing, you hear?'

'Bet on it,' promised Alice.

Jane Carver did finally understand and believed she had everything thought out and balanced in her mind, although leaving the filthy motel and Alice Belling like that hadn't been part of her overnight mental preparation. It was a spur-of-the-moment gesture, like hijacking the car the previous day. Irrational, without any positive intention. But she had one now, spur-of-the-moment or not, driving without particular direction back along the still deserted, rain-slicked road that had to be the way they'd come but along which, so far, she hadn't recognized any landmarks.

She had to have Burt Elliott and Geoffrey Davis with her when she met the FBI. Needed them with her *before* meeting the FBI, to talk everything through, maybe discuss it with other more specialized attorneys. Certainly go through in detail whatever it was John had hidden, to assess its importance. No, not its importance. Its potential illegality. That's what had to be examined and assessed, how much and how badly it implicated her father and John and the firm to protect and save them as much as she could.

A logging truck growled by in the opposite direction, spraying water and mud all over the Volkswagen and the splash of it startled Jane, as if waking her up. Why? she suddenly demanded of herself. There was every practical reason for trying to spare the firm, where according to Alice none of the partners had known what was going on. But what did she owe her father or John? They were the two men whom she'd totally loved and totally trusted and whom she'd believed loved and trusted her in return. The two men, these two strangers, whom she now accepted she'd known not at all. So why was she worrying about protecting them and their reputations? she asked herself again. Shouldn't she hate and despise them, like she should hate and despise Alice Belling, for all their total deceits and all their total betrayals? How did you hate? Was it a feeling, a physical sensation, like a pain or an ache? Or a mental determination to hurt back, to cause as much pain and suffering as they caused you, an eye for an eye, a tooth for a tooth? Jane didn't know: didn't think she wanted to know. Or did she? What did she want? The memory, she supposed. As many memories as she could conjure and keep.

Abruptly Jane confronted the hardest, most scourging reality of all. John had loved another woman. Been happy with another woman, shared everything – more than with her – with another woman. Had he done with Alice Belling the special bedroom things he'd done with her? Practised with Alice Belling? Learned from her even? Was it as Alice Belling had tried to convince her, a bizarrely unthreatening ménage à trois of which she was always intended to remain the unwitting third part? Or would . . .? Jane didn't let the question run because she wasn't unwitting any more. A lot of questions she couldn't answer. But a lot more that she could. Most important of all she knew how important she was to Alice's protection, as Alice had been to hers. Into her mind, unprompted, echoed her own voice: *It's the baby I'm properly thinking about*. But she wasn't: not thinking properly at all.

Jane waited for a widening of the still empty, early morning road to swing around into an almost complete U, only needing to reverse once, which she managed easily, without any grating of the gears. Very soon the traffic began picking up against her, although she wasn't held up by slow-moving trucks, like yesterday. Jane hoped she would get back to the motel before the FBI. Persuade Alice to come with her, until she'd got hold of attorneys. That would be the way, convince Alice she needed the help and protection of lawyers more than that of the FBI, because of what had happened in England.

It had been ridiculous, reacting as she had for the second time in less than twenty-four hours without fully thinking everything through. She didn't any longer have the excuse of drugs. No excuse at all. She was on her own, unsupported. She needed the professional advice of lawyers, certainly, but hers had to be the decision how to use that advice, like it was her decision to go back as she was now. Nothing to do with hate for what Alice had done. Or gratitude for what Alice had done. It was simply how it had to be. What was right.

This time Jane didn't bother to conceal the car behind the motel, parking in fact in front of the overturned, garbage-strewn bin in which Alice had thrown her pharmacy bag. She strode directly past, without seeing it.

'Come to make up?' greeted the clerk.

'She should still be here,' insisted Jane, irritated with the man's streetwise pretence. 'She was being collected.' Jane suddenly saw her own face, on a silent television screen behind the man. And then a picture of the sort of Volkswagen parked out in the lot and an unflattering, virtually unrecognizable picture of Alice.

'Don't know about that,' said the man. 'Asked me to call her a cab. Picked her up about fifteen minutes ago.'

Jane felt numb, as she'd remembered feeling when they were pumping all the drugs into her. 'You know where she's going?' she asked, grateful for the steadiness of her own voice.

The clerk shook his head. 'Didn't say. Morristown probably: she asked about the nearest town of any size.'

'How do I get to Morristown?'

'Make a right as you leave here, left at the first junction. Straight run from there.'

'Thanks,' said Jane, already turning away.

'Hey!' stopped the man. 'Don't I know you from somewhere?'

Jane shook her head, without looking back. 'I've got the sort of face people think they've seen before.'

Jane left the truck stop too fast, sounding the tyre on the wet road with her too sharp turn and cutting back at once. Alice's change of mind about waiting for the FBI had to do with whatever the mute newscast had been reporting. What? It didn't matter. Everything was different now. She was identified, her face on television screens. Marked. Most marked of all by the car she was driving. Driving where? Wherever Morristown was, where she could dump the car, hide somewhere – another motel or hotel, she supposed – and call someone to come and get her, like Alice had been so desperate for the FBI to come to get her. Burt Elliott? Or Geoffrey Davis? Whoever she could reach the quicker. She'd be able to watch a newscast in an hotel. Maybe understand better. She needed a restroom. Not desperately but she needed one. She could wait until she'd dumped the identifying Volkswagen. Definitely a restroom would be necessary before she called the lawyers. There'd be mirrors there, too.

Jane saw the Morristown turn at the junction and took it, without screaming the tyres this time. There were a lot more cars on the road and she was glad of the grey, concealing drizzle and hoped it, and the mud from that earlier passing lumber truck, would have hidden the colour of the car – maybe covered the plates, which had been printed alongside the TV picture. A positive description, she decided. Surely the FBI hadn't issued a kidnap alert, after what she'd told Gene Hanlan? But they hadn't waited at the cabin. No reason, then, why he should have believed her: obviously thought she was talking under duress, along with everyone else she'd spoken with.

The town began to build up ahead of her, a place planned

with care, with trees alongside the approach roads and some parks, to her immediate right. The rush-hour traffic was really heavy now, slowing her, and there were people on the sidewalk. She needed a parking lot, filling up with other cars, where she could lose the Volkswagen. She came to a junction and stopped behind a black Buick, a set of lights against them. And looked to her left. There was a Marriott, two blocks down. But before that, a far closer police blue and white, at the side of the road, the driver turned away from her talking to the observer, who was directly facing her. Jane jerked her head around, in the opposite direction, her concentration entirely upon the lights, still at red. Come on! Come on! She was ready to go at amber but the Buick didn't move, even at green. She held back from using the horn, nervous of attracting attention. Come on, for God's sake move! It did, at last, Jane too close behind, swerving out at the first gap to get by, eyes more on the rear-view mirror than the road ahead. Nothing. She let out the pent-up breath, feeling more relief at the mall to her right, the K-Mart and JC Penny and Safeway neons blinking invitingly at her, the car park already more than half full, the build-up greater conveniently close to the stores. Jane found the perfect gap, between a high-sided U-Haul van and a station wagon, a separating wall in front of her concealing the vehicle from three directions.

She went into the complex through the JC Penny entrance, remembering to keep her head down, and found the toilets on the ground floor. She chose the washbasin in the corner, with a wall to her right, and felt more relief at how she looked. She remembered the photograph that had been shown on TV being taken, in a professionally lighted studio, her make-up and hair – longer then than it was now – flawless for a portrait for her father's sixtieth birthday. She was sure she didn't now look anything like she did in the photograph. What was visible in the mirror of her borrowed shirt and jacket really did look as if it had been slept in and her hair was squashed under Alice's woollen cap. Her face was shiny, without even lipstick, and Jane decided that all she needed was a stolen supermarket trolley to be the perfect bag lady. Good for moving around a crowded store. She hoped it wasn't so bag-lady convincing as to get her refused refuge at the Marriott she'd isolated a little more than two blocks away. She had Alice's $300 flash – deposit – if a problem arose.

The telephone bank was open pods but there was no one else in the line. It had to be her own name for the collect call but the operator gave no audible reaction to it, although there was from the switchboard girl who immediately accepted at the Northcote building on Wall Street.

'Is that you, Mrs Carver?'

'Get me Geoff Davis, right away,' said Jane. 'It's me and I'm OK.'

'Where are you?' demanded the Northcote lawyer. 'What's happening? The FBI . . .'

'Be quiet. Just listen,' halted Jane. 'Listen, OK?' There was still no other caller anywhere along the line of telephones.

Jane talked as quickly as she could while remaining comprehensible. She insisted she was physically all right and gave Davis the name of the town and said she was going to book into a Marriott and wait for him: she'd call with the address within fifteen minutes. He and Burt Elliott were to get to her as fast as possible. Hilda Bennett had the name of a helicopter company.

'The FBI are here,' declared Davis, when Jane finally stopped, breathless.

'Why?'

'Someone's coming, about some companies your father handled.'

'Don't co-operate, not yet!'

'Jane. I don't have a choice!'

'We've got to talk first. The firm could be in trouble.'

'All right,' the lawyer placated her, emptily. 'I'll come to get you. Call me, from the Marriott. Where's Alice Belling?'

'Not with me any more. Let's stop talking and get moving. I want you and Burt here, now!'

Jane retraced her steps to leave by the same door through which she'd entered. She was still in the approach corridor when she saw the police car, its lamp bar still flashing, blocking the Volkswagen in its space, the Highway Patrol car doubling the barricade. As she watched, two more police cars, their lights flashing too, swept into the lot.

Jane hurried back inside, but at once cut left for the next exit, guessing the reinforcements were to close the store: search it, certainly. She emerged directly out on to the street, without being stopped, without seeing a policeman even, although she could hear a far-away siren. Jane kept walking, using the crossing further to distance herself from the car park before turning to go back towards the junction where she'd first seen the policemen, who had obviously seen her – or rather the Volkswagen and its plate number – after all. The Marriott could only be 50 yards after she took a right at the junction.

The dark-suited man seemed to come out of the rear of the Mercedes with the same movement of the door opening, completely blocking her path. The blow, low in her stomach, was not hard but professionally expert, winding her, preventing any protesting shout and doubling her up at the same time, so that she was easily thrust into the car with the man tight behind, virtually lifting her. The Mercedes was at the lights before Jane could straighten.

Tony Caputo, the Cavalcante *consigliere*, looked back from the front seat and said: 'If you try to scream now you've got your breath back we'll cut off your tongue, Mrs Carver. Not completely, just about half an inch from its tip. You'll still be able to speak but you'll sound like a retard. You're not going to scream, are you, Mrs Carver?'

'No,' said Jane.

*   *   *

'He won't show,' declared Barbara Donnelly. 'We all know he won't show. He shows, he's pussy-face of this or any other year. And I didn't think we were dealing with pussies.'

Hanlan hadn't heard pussy-face before. He liked it. He said: 'We gotta go with it, everything as planned. It's all we've got.'

They were in the CCTV viewing room of the Northcote building, the FBI installations doubling the number of cameras and monitors. The lobby reception staff were doubled too, the additions all police. The elevators were staffed, which they weren't normally, both with FBI agents. There were FBI and police in every office on the floor on which the nervously waiting Geoffrey Davis had his office.

With philosophical acceptance, Hanlan said: 'OK, what's our recovery going to be?'

'What makes you think there's going to be one?'

'Thanks for that great encouragement!'

'Tell lies, spread lies,' suggested the woman. 'Lure them out of their dark places.'

'My people will never go with it,' rejected Hanlan. 'Their escape is entrapment.'

'My people will,' insisted Barbara, who'd lit a cigarette without protest. 'The prosecution's yours, federal. NYPD isn't federal. You don't entrap anyone. You even say you don't. Your spokesperson says you've no idea what the claim is all about.'

'That puts us not co-operating.'

'We don't, most times. Everyone knows that.'

'So what's *your* entrapment?'

'Defection, from a major New York Family. That's using the *Daily News* invention. The investigation's concentrated on certain specified companies. Which it is. They won't know who the defector is but mentioning companies will convince them there is one. We don't get some playback whispers, life ain't fair.'

'It was your leak, to the *Daily News*,' accused Hanlan.

'I could be offended by a question like that.'

'Are you?'

'It could rattle the cages.'

'We got two women out there, one miscalculation and they're dead.'

'Big-time advantage of the idea,' argued Barbara. 'Our Family – or Families – think there's an internal source, it deflects the attention from Jane and Alice. Diffuses it, too. Maybe even redirects resources, although I think that's being optimistic.'

'You've really thought this through, haven't you?' It was better than anything that had occurred to him since the two women had run.

'Talking as the ideas come to me,' insisted Barbara Donnelly, straight-faced.

They both turned, as the door burst open. Davis said: 'I've just spoken to Jane: I know where she is!'

Before anyone could speak the telephone rang and the lawyer said: 'That'll be her, with the address of her hotel!'

But it wasn't.

When Hanlan took the call from Federal Plaza, Ginette Smallwood said: 'Alice Belling's just walked in. Says she's got things for us.'

Charlie Petrie's first call to the Algonquin was just after nine, directly after hearing from Caputo that their Highway Patrol source had come good with the location of the Volkswagen and that they'd picked up Jane Carver and were on their way into Manhattan. There was no way that Stanley Burcher would have already left for his meeting with the Northcote lawyer that early. Petrie kept calling, every five minutes, right up to ten o'clock, finally slamming the receiver down and saying aloud: 'Where the fuck are you, Stanley?'

At that precise moment, in fact, Stanley Burcher was getting off the early New York shuttle to Washington's

Reagan airport, hurrying directly for a cab for Dulles airport and his already booked flight to Geneva. He believed it to have been an elementary precaution to make his escape with such a dog's-leg detour, just in case Petrie suspected he was running and rushed people out to New York's Kennedy terminals to intercept him. It was, of course, unlikely because another precaution had been to leave the Algonquin without paying his bill, so that callers would be told he was still a resident there.

Burcher had always been a man to take elementary precautions, which was why his recent and direct involvement in the Northcote business had been so unsettling. It had been an elementary precaution years before to obtain a legitimate Caymanian passport in the anonymous name of William Smith, the identity he was now adopting and in which his flight to Switzerland was booked. Another had been, even earlier, to open a numbered bank account in Geneva and regularly transfer his Mafia fees into it, from his equally untraceable Grand Cayman account.

Burcher was sure he was going to enjoy his Swiss retirement. The Swiss understood the attraction – and the benefits – of anonymity.

Twenty-Eight

'Where is she, Alice? Where's Jane?' demanded Hanlan.

'I don't know!'

'Alice, you're in more trouble than you can shake a stick at, working from kidnapping down,' took up Barbara Donnelly. She'd come back to Federal Plaza with Hanlan, leaving their squads in place, after waiting forty-five minutes beyond the given time for Geoffrey Davis's unappearing mystery visitor and for Jane Carver's promised second call, which never came. Throughout that time Hanlan had remained constantly on the telephone from the Northcote building, confirming the finding of the Volkswagen – but not of Jane – at Morristown and moving McKinnon's squad there from West Milford. He sent with them the FBI forensics team, which had completed their examination of the cabin. Despite its trashing, they'd found nothing.

'I told you, we split up this morning at the motel. She said she wasn't seeing the FBI without her lawyers with her and drove off the way we'd come.' Alice was confused by their combined aggression, which started with Hanlan pedantically advising her of her Miranda rights against self-incrimination.

Hanlan acknowledged that fitted with what he'd been told by both Davis and Burt Elliott, to whom he'd also spoken from the Northcote building. 'The way you came from West Milford doesn't go through Morristown, which was where your car was found.'

Alice shook her head. 'I don't know how it got there. I want to tell you what I do know.'

'Finding Jane Carver's the priority,' said Barbara.

'Find her lawyers. It's Geoffrey Davis at the firm. There's another named Burt: I don't know his surname. She spoke to both from the motel.'

'She spoke to Davis from Morristown, too,' said Hanlan.

'I don't know how she got there. What she was doing there?'

'How about you took her there?' challenged Barbara.

'We split up. She took the car.'

'Why'd you run from the cabin?'

'Jane tricked me into running her into town. Persuaded me into letting her drive back but then took off . . .' She hesitated. It was all going to come out so there was no point in avoiding it. 'She wanted me to tell her about John and I. About what I knew about the firm and the Mafia. I'd told her bits but tried to keep some back. It didn't make sense, I guess.' Was she making any better sense now? It didn't seem like it, from the attitude of these two in the cramped interview room with the tape machine with its blinking light, recording everything. 'Please!' she said, urgently. 'Let me tell you what it's about.'

Hanlan looked at Barbara, in whose Manhattan jurisdiction the kidnap had occurred, even though it was ultimately a federal crime. She shrugged. He said to Alice: 'OK, from the beginning.'

Which was how Alice told it, from her first visit to Wall Street to interview George Northcote. She held nothing back about her affair with Carver, even repeating, to Barbara Donnelly's visible scepticism, that she was never a threat to the Carver marriage. Alice expected some interjections when she began talking of John's initial discovery of Northcote's organized-crime connection and of Northcote's insistence that he could extricate himself, but none came.

'And then I got involved,' declared Alice and stopped. No way back, if she continued talking. It was commitment time and she didn't have a lawyer to advise her and she'd been read her Miranda rights, making what she said admissible in court or before a Grand Jury and from this moment on she'd be at the mercy of these unsympathetic investigators if she said anything more, or at the mercy of gangsters who didn't know mercy if she said anything less.

'Go on,' encouraged Hanlan.

'I found out how it worked,' insisted Alice. 'I did it illegally and I know I've committed criminal offences – technically kidnap, even, although it wasn't – but everything I did was to understand and try to sort out what happened to George and Janice and then to John. I want to co-operate in every way and I want to be taken into the Witness Protection Programme because if I'm not I know, as you know, that I'll be killed.'

'Let's hear the story and then we'll talk about witness protection,' said Hanlan. She'd jerked him around, made him look ridiculous, and he didn't intend offering anything until he was as positive as it was possible to be that she wasn't holding out on him, not by so much as a single crumb.

Alice eased the canvas bag up from her lap and tentatively put it on the desk between them. Initially unspeaking she unpacked all the duplicate printouts she'd assembled at the cabin with her hurriedly replaced laptop. As Hanlan and the New York detective frowned down at the jumble, Alice announced: 'IRS records that show how the Mafia laundered their money over a very long time.'

'Obtained how?' pounced Hanlan, determined against any more embarrassing foul-ups.'

'Hacking,' admitted Alice, at once.

'Legally inadmissible,' rejected Hanlan. 'An illegal act, which hacking is, does not provide acceptable evidence of the further illegal act it exposes.'

'I know that! John and I knew that: discussed it! I'm showing you how it was done and how, properly and officially, you or your financial experts – I don't know who, for fuck's sake – can work with the IRS and the company registry authorities and get exactly what I got but in a way that *is* admissible!' She shouldn't have said fuck. She shouldn't have come here like this, to be confronted hostilely like this, without lawyers telling her what to say and what not to say. It irritated her that Jane had been right and she had been wrong. Jane hadn't been right, Alice decided at once. She'd kept the baby – hers and John's baby – safe and Jane was missing. With her own and John's baby.

She wouldn't tell them about England, Alice decided. They weren't impressed by – weren't accepting – what she was offering. Admitting any involvement whatsoever in bomb-outrage murder would get her publicly charged and publicly exposed. A target, even if she were in custody, which was never an obstacle to the Mafia, before she could appear before a court to get any sort of public, protective stage.

'Tell me something I can legally use,' insisted Hanlan.

'The names of the companies through which the laundering worked, worldwide,' snatched Alice, feeling a flicker of relieved hope. 'I didn't *get* them by hacking.'

'Neither did we,' said Hanlan. 'We got them from John's severance letters. The Bureau's finance and fraud division have been working on them for almost two days now.'

'They're offshore, you can't get to them!' insisted Alice. 'The IRS route, through their supply-chain subsidiaries, is the only way. And you wouldn't have known that if I hadn't shown you!'

Hanlan knew she was right. Was aware, too, of Barbara Donnelly's shifts of impatience at what he guessed to be irritation at his persistent obduracy. 'What's in Carver's safe deposit?'

Alice patted the printouts between them. 'A much larger selection of these, showing the worldwide spread of the system: Europe, the Far East. And original stuff that George Northcote kept back. And a tape recording of John talking to a mob lawyer who wanted it all back.'

'Which mob?' came in Barbara. 'Give us names!'

'I don't have any names,' admitted Alice. 'John started to hold back, thinking that the more I knew the greater danger I would be in.'

'But there are names in the safe deposit?' persisted the detective lieutenant.

'Yes,' guessed Alice. She had the right to a lawyer. It didn't matter that she'd waived her Miranda rights by agreeing to talk on the record. She had to have an attorney to negotiate for her, get her the protection she deserved. And without which she – and John's baby – would die. 'I'm not going to say any more. Not without a lawyer.'

'What more have you got *to* say?' asked Hanlan.

'I'm not going to say any more. Not without a lawyer,' doggedly repeated Alice. She hesitated, looking at the recording apparatus. 'Except that I think you're a bastard son of a bitch!'

As Ginette Smallwood led Alice away to another room, to make her lawyer's call in private, Barbara Donnelly said: 'I agree with her. You're a bastard son of a bitch. She's shown you the way, legal or not. And you know damned well the Bureau and the IRS will take it.'

Hanlan said: 'Do you think we got it all?'

'We got enough.'

'I want it *all*.' It was, Hanlan thought, about time.

It was the courtesy that frightened Jane Carver the most. The threat to cut off part of her tongue, which she hadn't the slightest doubt the man had meant, had been made politely and during what little conversation there'd been during the journey the one who did the talking had always addressed her as Mrs Carver. The two men sitting either side of her in the rear of the car did so without crowding her and the one who'd winded her had apologized. Unasked, the man in the front had said she was being taken to meet someone who would tell her what they wanted and that if she co-operated there wouldn't be what he called unpleasantness. No one wanted unpleasantness.

Jane could see the Manhattan skyline and the Hudson river from the top-floor window of the warehouse office in which they'd locked her, thirty minutes before. It was bare, clearly unused – a blank desk without a telephone, three upright chairs and a cabinet – but there was an adjoining toilet, for which she was grateful. Having sat for so long, she was ignoring the chairs, standing at the window gazing down at the car park. There were a lot of lorries bearing the BHYF logo.

What was she going to do? Co-operate, obviously. Tell them whatever they wanted to know, but she didn't know anything more than Alice had told her. Would they hurt her? Do something like maiming her, if they asked something she couldn't answer? Of course they would. It had to be the safe deposit. If they . . .

Jane's thoughts were broken by the sound of the door opening behind her and she turned to face the two men who entered. One was the polite front-seat passenger who'd done the talking in the Mercedes, the other slightly taller, bespectacled, fair hair just beginning to recede. The eyes were unusually – upsettingly – pale, grey more than blue.

'Please sit down, Mrs Carver,' said Charlie Petrie. 'Can we get you anything? Coffee? Water?'

Still the overwhelming courtesy. 'No. Thank you.' Jane sat. So did the two men, on chairs facing her.

Petrie nodded sideways. 'My colleague has spoken to you about co-operation?'

'Yes.' It was a croak, dry-throated. She should have asked for water. Too late now. She shouldn't do anything to upset them.

'Are you going to co-operate, Mrs Carver?'

'Yes.' Better this time. The fear was taking the feeling from her body. She pushed herself very slightly against the chair but could scarcely feel it against her back.

There was a smile, the teeth very even. 'That's good.'

What could she do or say to protect herself, help herself? 'I don't know about Alice Belling! We split up! She's going to the FBI!'

Petrie smiled to Caputo and then at Jane. 'No, she's not,' he improvised, immediately realizing how he could improvise further. 'Alice is quite safe, with us.'

'You found her in Morristown?'

'Yes,' said Petrie.

'She knows more than I do! What's she told you?'

'We're asking the questions, Mrs Carver.'

'I'm sorry.' She mustn't annoy them. They were asking the questions: all the questions. And she had to get the answers right. What had Alice told them? Alice was streetwise, better able to look after herself.

'Do you know what's in your husband's safe deposit?'

'I know you want it.'

'Do you know what's in the deposit?' persisted Petrie.

'Not the details. I know it's something that my father did for you . . . for your people.' They couldn't get it without her! Why hadn't she realized that before! Because she was too frightened to think of anything. But now she had.

'We do want what's in the safe deposit. All of it.'

'I understand.'

'That's what I want you to do, Mrs Carver. Understand. You and I are going to the bank, now. You are going to authorize my coming into the vault with you, along with the bank's securities person with the duplicate key. It'll be just the two of us after it's been unlocked. You don't open the box. I do. And I retrieve the material that belongs to us. Then we leave. It's all got to be done very quickly, no hold-ups. If anyone asks about your being kidnapped you say you are all right. Safe. That it's over and that I am your lawyer. Do you understand all that?'

'What happens then?'

Petrie smiled. 'You go back to East 62nd Street.'

'What about Alice Belling?'

'There's something else you must understand,' said Petrie, his second improvisation perfectly thought out. 'If you don't do exactly what I say – exactly what I've spelled out – Alice Belling will die. Die very badly. You must understand that most of all.'

'I do,' said Jane. She was dry-throated again.

'You're going to do everything you're told, aren't you, Mrs Carver?'

'Yes. Are we going now?'

'Right now,' confirmed Petrie.

'Can I have a glass of water first?'

As it always appeared to be, the Manhattan traffic was close to gridlock when they came out of the tunnel and Petrie told the driver not to turn immediately but to try the next downtown to Wall Street. He was in the passenger seat now, two different men on either side of Jane, both still giving her leg room. Petrie felt better than he had at first, when he'd finally accepted that Stanley Burcher had run and the other *consigliere* had insisted he take Jane Carver to the bank. But not that much better. Petrie had already initiated the search for Burcher, whose proper function this was and for which he'd been paid so much money for so many profitable, untroubled years. Burcher would be found, in whatever rat-hole he was hiding. And made to suffer for this, suffer more than the motherfucker had ever imagined in his wildest nightmares it was possible to suffer. But that was later. Petrie's concern was now. He calculated he had only fifteen minutes to do all that he had to do at the bank. He had the benefit of surprise but someone would raise some sort of alarm after all the publicity about Jane Carver's disappearance. Just fifteen minutes.

They turned on Broadway and Petrie twisted round and said to Jane: 'You got it right?'

'Yes,' Jane said. She was sure she had.

'You worried about your daddy's firm?'

'That's the only thing there's left to worry about, isn't it?' Jane hoped she hadn't sounded too challenging.

'It's over now. The moment I get what I want, it's all over. The firm's safe, your daddy's reputation is safe. Everything's all over.'

'I'd like to think so.'

'Think so.'

She was riding downtown with people who cut out other people's tongues, Jane thought. Did God knows what else. People who held Alice hostage. How much more convoluted – who was hostage to whom or for what – could this kidnap be! 'You – the people you work for – entrapped my father, didn't you? Blackmailed him into doing what he did?'

'I wasn't involved in the beginning,' denied Petrie, who hadn't been.

The traffic was, strangely, easier going downtown. They joined Wall Street and Jane thought how familiar – how safe – it all seemed. How many times had she come this way, past these buildings, with her father? This was her father's place, her father's territory. Everyone on Wall Street knew her father, respected her father: George W. Northcote, the king, the Colossus. Jane saw the Northcote building, the far-away monument, the Citibank closer. Petrie, in the front seat, said something to the driver she didn't hear before turning to her. He said: 'You tell them I'm your lawyer, coming into the vault with you.'

Jane said: 'I know what I've got to say.'

'You know what happens, you get anything wrong.' For the first time, ever, Petrie was frightened. He wanted to be there, watching, when they found Burcher.

The car stopped directly outside Citibank. The unspeaking man to her left got out to open the door to Jane, even offering his hand, which she didn't need. Petrie was already on the sidewalk, coming in close beside her. He said: 'Remember!'

Jane didn't reply.

It was an expansive, crowded lobby, the teller area beyond, the securities area even further back, deep inside the building. Until that moment Jane had forgotten her crumpled, slept-in appearance and the television coverage of her supposed kidnap and actually looked around to be recognized. She wasn't, not until they got to the floor managers' desks and even there, initially, the man at the one they approached frowned up at the way she was dressed, not identifying her.

She said: 'I'm Jane Carver. Get me the securities manager please.' She was aware of Petrie, so close beside her she could feel his tension.

He said: 'Don't forget what will happen to Alice.'

She said: 'No.'

'Or what to say.'

'No.'

The door behind the desk flurried open and a prematurely balding man hurried out. He said: 'Mrs Carver! What . . . ?'

Jane said: 'Don't let this man get out of the building! He's kidnapped me! He's going to kill me.'

For the briefest moment no one moved. Spoke. Petrie appeared frozen. Then, instinctively, he turned to run. The man at whose desk they were standing pressed the attack button. The alarms screamed out, the tellers' shutters slammed down and the metal gates slid closed in front of all the exit doors. Petrie zigzagged in total panic, going first in the direction of the main, already sealed door, then to a side exit, then back towards the way out into Wall Street. It was at that door he was seized by the uniformed security guards. One, unnecessarily, had his weapon out. Petrie didn't struggle.

Jane actually walked from where she was standing, towards

the arresting group. Very quietly she said to Petrie: 'She will die, won't she?'

With only two blocks to cover, the combined FBI and NYPD task force arrived from the Northcote building within minutes. Geoffrey Davis was with them. As soon as he saw Jane he said: 'Thank God you're both safe!'

'Both?'

'Alice Belling gave herself up to the FBI maybe three hours ago.'

Twenty-Nine

It was Jane Carver's adamant insistence that they retrace the two blocks to the Northcote building, where symbolically she took over the office of her dead father over which officially she had no right or authority. There she spent almost an hour – refusing Hanlan's repeated telephone calls and then the FBI man's demand to see him upon his arrival with Detective Lieutenant Barbara Donnelly – while she talked through with Geoffrey Davis and Burt Elliott everything Alice Belling had warned her might be found in her husband's personal security facilities.

'We're into damage limitation, if that's possible,' was Davis's opinion.

Elliott said: 'I agree. But I don't know how. What I do know is that it's out of my league. We need a major, big-time trial lawyer.'

'Find one. The best,' instructed Jane.

'We can explore, though,' suggested Elliott. 'Find out what we might be up against.'

'That's what I want to do,' said Jane. 'What's first?'

'Establishing the awareness, if any, of each and every one of the senior partners,' said Davis, at once. 'God knows – I certainly don't – if it's possible to save the firm. It certainly won't be if even just one other partner was involved. If so, we've got criminal conspiracy. And that's before we know what's in the deposit box. Which we need to find out right now.'

'Nothing's going to happen to it where it is,' calmed Jane. 'I want to work to an order of priority and that's not my first priority.'

Jane much later reflected, as she much later reflected on many things, that there was inherited proof of her father's total autocratic control in how, still without challenge, she was able to summon the senior partners, for which she had even less authority. There was no objection, either, to Burt Elliott accompanying Geoffrey Davis. Her kidnap, Jane insisted, was not the point or focus of her gathering them all together. It was, instead and inadequately – because she could not compromise them – to advise of a situation that could have serious repercussions upon the firm and therefore logically upon their careers.

The concentration upon Jane Carver was absolute and she liked it, totally in control and totally in charge, which she hadn't been for far too long. Her only discomfort was looking like a bag lady without a cart but from her command of the meeting she didn't think that was a disadvantage. She was going to recite the names of five companies, she told them. If any of them, before this moment, had any awareness of the firm's involvement with those companies, they were to tell her. They would be asked again, very soon, the same question she was posing. And more. If any lied – to her questions, not to subsequent ones – they would be abandoned to legal process. Their professional integrity, their very future, depended upon their replies.

Spacing the presentation, allowing silently echoing gaps between each, Jane recounted the names of the incriminating companies – even spelling them out, letter by letter – and then let further space into the demand.

Finally she said: 'I am going around this room, person by person, for your individual answers.'

Which she did, even more adamantly insisting upon a positive, verbal denial, not a head shake. Bewildered denials came from every one of them and when she received the final refusal Jane warned: 'You are, in the coming days, going to be questioned by the FBI. I believe my father failed you. I believe he failed me . . .' She had to stop, to recover from the admission. '. . . and he failed John,' she managed to continue. 'It won't matter a damn to any of you, after what might happen in the next weeks and months, but I personally want to apologize.' Jane looked nostalgically around the heavy room. 'This can't be a time for questions because at this precise moment I don't have any answers. I hope to have, very soon . . .' The emotion surged up again, blocking any more words, and Jane was angry at the breakdown, believing she had steeled herself against it.

'No!' refused a heavy-bodied, heavy-featured man directly in front of her. 'This is ridiculous! Nothing you've said is acceptable. What the hell is this all about?'

She still didn't properly know, Jane accepted. 'A situation I never imagined myself ever being in. All I can ask you to do – hope you will do – is to trust me over the next few days.' No one was culpable if no one had known! So they were personally, individually, safe even if the firm was not. She no longer had any feelings about her father's reputation.

'Where does that leave us?' demanded another accountant, a designer-suited black man whom Jane remembered her father describing as brilliant and wished she could recall his name.

'Uninvolved. Exonerated,' responded Jane, looking invitingly at Geoffrey Davis.

'I know this is bizarre,' came in the firm's lawyer, at once. 'That's exactly what it is, totally and utterly bizarre. You must believe me that all you can do – all any of us can do – is hang in there with Jane.'

Could she remain in charge, for – and of – everything she wanted to do? Had to do? She should feel drained, traumatized, from what she'd already gone through that day, but unaccountably she didn't. Even more unaccountably she felt energized, sure she could go on and resolve everything. At last she was in a position, in a role, in which she knew how to perform. She *was* in charge. In charge of herself and her surroundings and of what was going to happen today. She wished she knew about tomorrow. And the day after that.

The full-featured man said: 'What do we do?'

Jane said: 'Wait! Say nothing, to anybody outside the office. Certainly not the media. But tell the FBI what you've told me. Open all your accounts to them. Co-operate in every way. You've got nothing to hide.'

'Well?' demanded Jane, when the door closed after the last departing partner.

'I know them all,' said Davis. 'I believe them all.'

'They sounded convincingly honest to me,' endorsed Elliott.

'They would, wouldn't they?' said Jane.

'You gave them their chance,' said Davis.

'If one's lying, they all go down,' said Jane.

'You can't do any more than you've already done, on a personal level,' encouraged Elliott.

She could, thought Jane. But not here and not yet with these two men. She said briskly: 'Now let's meet the FBI.'

Gene Hanlan was less able to hide his irritation at being kept waiting than Barbara Donnelly, visibly red-faced. He was cursory with the introductions to the two lawyers and said: 'It's good of you to see us at last!'

'I told your people at the bank I wanted to talk to lawyers before I talked to you.' Jane knew she was treading the slenderest of tightropes, not giving in to any bullying but at the same time not completely alienating the man or his organization. In the opinion of both Davis and Elliott, she was going to need the FBI as much – maybe even more – than they needed her.

There was a slight relaxation from the agent. He said to Jane: 'You OK?'

Jane nodded. 'Who were they, the people who had me?'

'Big-time organized crime,' predicted Barbara. 'The man in the bank is refusing to talk without an attorney. The car that was outside the bank took off in too much of a hurry when the alarm sounded, right into the side of another car. The driver was still unconscious when our traffic guys got to him. The other one snapped an ankle and couldn't run. There are witnesses to one guy running, though. The two we got are muscle: gofers. They'll break.'

'You with them against your will?' asked Hanlan.

'Damned right I was!' Jane said, indignantly. 'They threatened to cut off part of my tongue if I didn't do what they wanted.'

'Kidnap, prima facie,' declared Hanlan, now totally relaxed, all irritation gone. He had a millionaire kidnap and a major Mafia investigation under wraps and life looked sweet, with the sun on his face.

'And what did they want?' asked the other woman.

'I thought you knew,' said Jane. She had to get more than she volunteered. Everything depended on it.

'We need to hear it from you,' said Hanlan.

'This is not a formal deposition,' broke in Burt Elliott. 'Nothing said in this room, about anything, constitutes a basis of evidence. It's all privileged.'

Hanlan sighed. 'We're asking for help, not for a formal deposition, not yet.'

'What happened to Alice Belling?' asked Jane. It was time.

'We're going to need a deposition on that, too,' said Hanlan.

'What happened to her?' insisted Jane. 'What has she told you?'

'That you wouldn't come in, without lawyers, when she decided to. So you took the car and she got a cab into

Morristown from the truck stop and simply caught a train here. Some of it doesn't square, though.'

'Like what?' They were telling her, which she'd feared they wouldn't!

'How you came to be in Morristown, where the Mafia picked you up, when she says you drove off in the opposite direction,' said Barbara.

'What more does she say?' pressed Jane.

It was Hanlan who provided the summary and when he finished Jane said: 'She told you all about the hacking?'

'She acknowledges that it's illegal but said it was the only way to get the proof she and . . .' Barbara hesitated, then plunged on. 'She and your husband needed.'

Jane smiled, humourlessly. 'I know all about that.'

'Yes,' said Barbara, unembarrassed.

'What does she say about me? Getting me from the apartment?'

'She agrees that technically it was kidnap but that it was to save your life.'

'Has she asked for the Witness Protection Programme?'

'Several times,' said Hanlan. He looked at the two attorneys. 'Something else I guess we're going to have to talk about. It's all going to take time.'

'Is Alice going to get it?' demanded Jane.

'She's with her own lawyer now,' said Hanlan. 'It usually takes a while for our people to decide once we've made our recommendation. In your case, Mrs Carver, it's a forgone conclusion . . .' He allowed the gap. 'We're expecting your co-operation, of course.'

'Not a foregone conclusion for Alice?'

'I'm not sure what she's really offering at the moment. What the recommendation will be.'

'Do I definitely need to go into the programme?' demanded Jane.

The two lawyers looked uncomfortably at each other. So did Hanlan and Barbara Donnelly.

Hanlan said: 'Unquestionably, with the evidence you are going to be asked to give before a Grand Jury. And then in an open court.'

'I want to see Alice,' abruptly declared Jane. 'See her alone.'

Everyone looked startled. Hanlan said: 'Depending upon your deposition, you could be a prosecution witness against her!'

'I don't think it's a good idea, Jane,' said Elliott. 'Let's get some trial advice.'

'That's the deal, the only deal,' insisted Jane. 'My co-operation, based on whatever legal advice I get, in return for my seeing Alice Belling.'

'I don't want us to fall out,' warned Hanlan.

'Neither do I,' said Jane. 'So let's not.'

'You're going to be very dependent on the Bureau, in the future,' continued Hanlan.

'The Bureau's going to be very dependent upon me, right now.'

'Why don't we see what Alice's lawyer says?' suggested Elliott, anxious to mediate.

'Now!' said Jane. 'Let's see right now.'

'They'd given your Miranda! Why did you say all that?' The public defence lawyer was a young, dark-featured, eager man named Joshua Dutton who saw his so far impressive success ending as ashes around his feet with this case and was already wondering how he could get out of it. He threw aside in theatrical disappointment the transcript of Alice Belling's earlier recorded interview with Hanlan and Barbara Donnelly.

'I didn't do anything wrong: not with any intent to do wrong! Isn't that a legal principle, committing a felony with intent?' Thank God she hadn't said anything about England.

'Ms Belling! You think any court will accept that, if they offer half the charges available against you?'

'If I am charged with anything, will I still be able to get into a protection programme?' She had to be! She had to safeguard the baby!

Dutton shrugged, shaking his head at the same time. 'At the moment I don't have the slightest idea. It'll depend what I can achieve with plea-bargaining.'

'I'll be killed if I'm not taken in!'

'That's my plea,' said the lawyer. Everything was going to be an uphill battle. He turned at a knock at the door and opened it to Ginette Smallwood.

She said: 'Mrs Carver's lawyer wants to speak with you. Line three.'

Dutton depressed the blinking button, listened and then, to ensure he hadn't misheard, he said: 'Do I have any objection to Mrs Carver meeting Ms Belling?'

'That's what Mrs Carver wants,' confirmed Burt Elliott.

Dutton at once saw the path open up before him. Covering the mouthpiece with his hand he said to Alice: 'She wants to see you.'

'What for?'

'I don't know. But I want you to agree. It's important.'

'Will it help me?' asked Alice.

'It could, a lot,' promised Dutton.

'All right then,' agreed the woman.

Dutton took away his covering hand and said: 'Right now is fine.' The moment they met he had unarguable grounds for a mistrial. His unblemished record wasn't in danger any more.

Thirty

The two women looked at each other, Jane just inside the door, Alice at the interview table, head low although not quite slumped. Alice straightened slightly at Jane's entry. Neither initially spoke. It was Alice who finally did, pushing herself further back in her chair as she did so. 'We do meet again, after all.' Somehow, irrationally, she'd expected Jane to be freshly bathed and groomed, as she'd been in the TV photograph, and was glad that she wasn't but instead as dishevelled and crumpled as she was.

Jane came further into the room, her hand outstretched. 'Here's your three hundred dollars back. I got a ride, so I didn't need it.'

When Alice made no attempt to take the money, Jane put it on the table.

'I heard. I'm glad you're safe.'

'Thanks.'

'Was it bad?'

'It could have been. But it wasn't.' Jane sat on the facing chair, on the other side of the table.

'That's good.' What did she want, wondered Alice.

'Your car's OK. The police or the FBI have got it. I don't know which.'

'It doesn't matter.'

'No, I guess it doesn't.' This was like the strange politeness of the men who'd snatched her.

There was a long silence.

Alice said: 'You wanted to see me?'

'Hanlan isn't impressed: doesn't believe you.'

'He told you?'

'Enough.' Jane hadn't expected Alice to look so beaten.

'It's true! You know it's true! Tell them!'

'That's what I want to talk about. Want to tell them.'

'Thank you!' Alice smiled, the relief moving through her.

'What have they told you about protection?' lured Jane.

'Nothing, not yet. It'll be all right when you tell them.' Alice knew Hanlan hadn't believed her, not completely. Thought maybe that she was holding something back, which of course she was, about England.

'At the moment they're ready to charge you with kidnap,' announced Jane, bluntly. 'They want a statement from me.'

Alice frowned. 'I know. That's why you've got to tell them the truth.'

'You haven't told them the entire truth, have you, Alice?' This was the moment when she had to get it absolutely right, not give Alice the slightest indication she was bluffing.

'Yes!' Alice was tensed now, fully upright in her chair, both hands firmly against the table between them, as if needing its support, even seated.

'What did you tell them about the hacking? Come on! Come on! Give me the guide I want!

'I admitted it was illegal. Why I did it.' Alice was frightened, the uncertainty churning through her.

'That wasn't the question,' said Jane, relentlessly.

'What *is* the question?'

Jane was as sure as she needed to be. She had to take the chance. 'What about *how* you hacked? The self-protective route you took that wasn't so protective for other people?'

'What do you want, Jane?' Why had she told her! Been so honest about everything!

'What I'm due,' declared Jane, flatly.

'What's that?'

'Quite a lot.'

'You would have been dead if it wasn't for me!' tried Alice.

'I saved myself, all *by* myself. The FBI have got three of them and through them they're going to get a lot more. Break Families. I'm very important to the Bureau. I wouldn't be here if I wasn't. And I'm guaranteed the Witness Protection Programme. You're not though, are you?'

'I asked you what you wanted.'

'The baby. John's baby.'

Alice stared across at the other woman, not comprehending. '*What!*'

'I want what you have: what you're carrying. John's baby.'

'But you're . . . ?'

'Not pregnant. I might have been, if John had left a specimen for the tests he'd agreed to have – we were both going to have – but he died before that was possible. You any idea of the noise you made, throwing up all the time? I didn't need the confirmation but I got it in that truck-stop shithole, while you were throwing up again. Found the tester you hid under your coat, showing positive. I was glad then that I'd pretended to be pregnant: convinced you. I couldn't have let you beat me that way, like you beat me in every other way. And then as I drove away I realized how you wouldn't beat me, not at all.''

Alice couldn't think, find the words. Only one. '*NO!*'

'Yes,' said Jane, even-voiced, completely sure of herself. 'If I tell the FBI about Trojan Horses and England – which you haven't done – you'll face murder charges there. Or some indictment, it doesn't matter what. That's as well as the kidnapping when I swear a deposition how you tricked me into leaving the apartment with you. Fed me more drugs to keep me at the cabin . . . threatened to kill me for not giving John a divorce so that he could marry you . . .'

'No!' protested Alice again, although it was a moan, not a shout. 'You can't do this. You can't hate me this much.'

'Yes I can. And I do,' said Jane again. 'I got snatched in Morristown, where your car was found and where you told Gene Hanlan you'd come from, to get here. How'd you imagine the Mafia knew I was there? And here's another question, the real kicker. How high would you put your chances of getting into the Witness Protection Programme with all that coming down on you? I don't think you'd stand a chance in hell, do you?'

'If I get killed the baby dies too.'

'Right,' agreed Jane, easily. 'Think of it as the judgement of Solomon.'

'I won't let you,' said Alice, weakly.

'I know you won't have a termination. You won't destroy John's baby yourself. And let's be realistic. It'll be born, before all the Grand Jury hearings and court appearances are over. And go for adoption. This way the adoption is already properly and legally fixed – we're surrounded by lawyers – and you get to live. I don't tell Hanlan about England but I *do* tell him I came with you willingly from the apartment: that I truly believe you saved my life and that I wouldn't have known about safe-deposit boxes – known about anything – if you hadn't told me. I'll even insist you get into the protection programme. We just got split up in Morristown and I'm as glad as I can be that you didn't get picked up like I did, looking for you . . .'

'You're leaving me with nothing!' said Alice, baldly.

'You *left* me with nothing. Took everything. *You* expect pity from *me*!'

'I won't do it.'

'Of course you will. Your way the baby either dies, with you. Or goes into an orphanage, to an unknown life. My way the baby lives and is loved and wants for nothing. And you live.' Jane smiled. 'It's more than the judgement of Solomon. It's the perfect resolution.' She pushed her chair back. 'I'll deny all of this, of course, if you try and fight me, legally. No one will believe you, against me, the amount of trouble you're in.'

'How do I know you'll love the baby?'

'It's John's. What I inherit from him. Of course I'll love the baby. Treat him as my own. Which he will be.'

'He?' challenged Alice.

'It's going to be a boy,' said Jane, positively.

It was one of the bodyguards, the one who had broken his ankle, who collapsed almost at once under questioning that night, as Barbara Donnelly had predicted, although she hadn't expected it to happen so quickly. Guaranteed entry into the protection programme, a regular pension and paid accommodation ensured he identified the Genovese Family and Charlie Petrie as its *consigliere*. He also named the Cavalcante Family and Tony Caputo as its *consigliere* and the man who'd personally snatched Jane outside the Morristown mall: they'd had inside information, he didn't know from whom. Hanlan thought he knew and said to Barbara: 'That nails Alice.'

By nine o'clock that night Caputo had been seized in a known Mafia-favoured restaurant by a Task Force from the FBI's Trenton field office.

Caputo smirked and said: 'I don't know what the hell you're talking about. *Who* you're talking about.'

The Trenton agent-in-charge said: 'You will, when you see her in court. Like she's going to see and identify you in court, as the kidnapper. Is there the death penalty in New Jersey, for kidnapping? You know, I really can't remember. Maybe your lawyer will remember. You're going to need a lot of legal advice, Tony. All the help you can get.'

Gene Hanlan hadn't expected such an early and certainly not such a sensational breakthrough, any more than Barbara: unlike her, he hadn't expected any confession at all. Although it kept Jane pivotal to the investigation and eventual prosecution, it took the immediate concentration away from her, and took Hanlan on to the conveniently retained FBI plane to Washington and the J. Edgar Hoover building for a conference that included the Director himself. It was Hanlan's assessment of the career potential of what he found himself in charge of that caused him that night to utilize every safe house and apartment available in Manhattan, Brooklyn and Queens to accommodate, under permanent armed guard, not only Alice and Jane but their lawyers, as well. He also installed armed protection upon the Northcote building, Citibank and East 62nd Street.

As he left Federal Plaza he told Barbara Donnelly: 'We got the chance to nuke the New York Mafias.'

'If they don't nuke us first,' cautioned the detective lieutenant.

Alone in the sterile Manhattan apartment assigned to her, tauntingly just two blocks from Princes Street, Alice Belling lay weeping on a cold bed, properly experiencing for the first time what life was going to be like in a protection programme.

Thirty-One

Jane had always been instinctively aware of power and authority: of possessing it through her father. Now it emerged to be no longer subconscious and certainly no longer inherent but hers in her own right. So sure of herself did Jane feel – after Alice's legal surrender of John's unborn child – she refused to let Peter Mitchell, the trial lawyer whose fame had further escalated the overnight media sensation, accompany her into the Citibank vaults.

'Why?' he demanded, although without emotion, because Peter Mitchell never allowed anything he felt to show in how he spoke or looked, no matter how irritated, as he was now. He was a silver-haired, urbane man who calculated representing Jane Carver was worth $1,000,000, for which she'd receive every conceivable legal guidance. For $1,000,000 Jane Carver could be as demanding as she chose.

Jane didn't know why, just that after so much and so long – in drama, not in time – she wanted to be by herself, quite alone, when she finally saw what it had all been about. Careless of the inadequacy, she said: 'Because that's how I want it to be.'

She had obviously agreed, though, to his going with her to Citibank, along with Gene Hanlan and Barbara Donnelly amid the permanent FBI guard which, despite acknowledging their necessity, at this early stage still made her feel more amused than grateful. Part of that protection was to arrange the deposit-box examination at night, after the bank was officially closed, with no one inside apart from vetted officials and bank security and uniformed and plainclothes police inside as well as at every exit and with every kerbside approach cordoned off.

The bank president himself, escorted by his three most senior vice presidents, awaited them. The man, silver-haired like Mitchell, assured the trial lawyer there was an office available for him privately to examine whatever there was in the security vault. There was no surprise from any of the bank officials to Jane's announcement that she was making the initial examination alone. One of the senior vice presidents accompanied her and the securities manager. No one spoke as they descended. After the duplicate-key opening the vice president asked if there was anything else she needed and Jane said no: she'd ring when she wanted the door to be unlocked.

Jane remained for several moments before the numbered box, its narrow rectangular door ajar, looking too small, too insufficient, to have caused so much. She reached out positively with her newly realized command, although aware as she did so that her hands were shaking. The box slid out easily, but was heavy from its contents when she finally lifted it free, and she had to grab it and use two hands to get it to the table. So tightly was it packed that the lid came up by itself when she unclasped it. The printouts she recognized from what Alice had duplicated at the cabin were uppermost, neatly folded in what appeared to be some order, and beneath them were what Jane supposed to be accountancy spreadsheets. There were names she recognized from what Alice had told her, Mulder Inc. and Innsflow, and addresses throughout the United States, but the calculations meant nothing. Nor did the other figures on other spreadsheets, in handwriting she recognized to be John's.

It was beneath them that the other documentation lay, written words she could read and understand, even though they were legal. And photographs, ten in all, of her laughing father with a laughing woman whose name was Anna, from the annotations on the backs in her father's handwriting, with dates and places, Madrid and Capri. There were names, too, on the birth certificate. The mother's name was Anna Simpson. The father's was George Northcote and the child, a girl, was named Jane Northcote. So it was on the adoption papers – the sort of adoption papers to which Alice had that day attested and sworn – and here for the first time appeared the name Muriel Northcote, as well as Jane legally getting the Northcote surname.

Jane wasn't aware she was crying, not until she felt the wetness, but didn't bother to wipe her eyes or her nose, wanting to cry unchecked at the sadness, but most of all – most bitterly – at the matching irony. Nothing left, she thought. Nothing that she'd believed and trusted and loved – *wanted* to believe and trust and love – was left. Everything she had known, everything by which she'd felt secure and safe, was untrue, lies built on lies, deceit upon deceit. She had John's surrogate baby but she wasn't continuing the bloodline she'd cheated and lied to preserve. And it was too late now to undo what she'd turned herself into a monster to achieve.

Jane wiped her face, finally, and repacked the box with the photographs and the legal documents of her birth and formal adoption and put it back into the safe-deposit slot before ringing the bell for the security official and his duplicate key.

As she got back into the elevator, clutching everything referring to the five Mafia companies, Jane wondered how the person she'd believed to be – and loved as – her mother had felt about the laughing, beautiful Anna Simpson. That question inevitably prompted another. How or what did she feel about Alice Belling? Angry at the deception and humiliation, perhaps. Disbelief, at the idea that the woman had never represented a danger to her marriage. But not hatred, which she'd expected – waited – to feel. What then? Sadness, Jane decided. Sadness about too much to examine every reason for it. Too late to undo, she thought again. There was one thing – one further sadness – she could prevent, Jane realized. She wouldn't keep the birth certificate and adoption papers of John's baby where one day his son might find them. Nothing could be left for John's son to discover that his father hadn't been the most perfect man, which was how she planned always to describe him.

When Jane handed what she'd collected to Peter Mitchell the lawyer said: 'I've got your word this is it? All there is?'

'Yes,' said Jane. 'There's nothing left.'

But there was, Jane corrected herself at once. She was going to have John's baby.